THE
GREAT
EQUALIZER

THE GREAT EQUALIZER

by

Rick Borsten

Rick Borsten

The Permanent Press, Sag Harbor, N.Y. 11963

Copyright © 1986 by Rick Borsten

All rights reserved, including the right to reproduce this book, or parts thereof, in any form, except for the inclusion of brief quotations in a review.

Library of Congress Number: 85-63553
International Standard Book Number: 0-932966-69-1

Manufactured in the United States of America

THE PERMANENT PRESS
Noyac Road
Sag Harbor, NY 11963

To Saint Lily, my mother, who taught me sensuality and female strength; Larry, my father, who taught me ethics and male gentleness; and Kim, my wife, who led me to the secret hideout of my soul without ever telling me where we were going.

Author's Note

What follows is a partial listing of those who assisted—directly or indirectly, consciously or unconsciously—in the writing of THE GREAT EQUALIZER:

My thanks to Doris Betts, for teaching me the difference (I hope) between good writing and good fiction; Jo, my sister, who directed my hand into magic soils long before the seed of THE GREAT EQUALIZER was planted; Jim, for helping me to understand that writing well is less important than living right; Dick Clinton, for our wonderful Wednesday breakfasts at The Valley Restaurant, where we despair over the ominous tilt of the world, while delighting over our heavenly coffee and decadently sour-creamed eggs; Coach J.C., for his hospital unionizing story; Amar, wherever he is, for his "3 names" story; Dr. Jake, for embodying the sort of goodness I used to imagine was contained only in fairy tales; Wendy, for her inspiring Florida compost heap; Orin, my uncle, for his timely writer's scolding, which, no doubt, saved me from the indignity of starting my novel over yet another time; Peter, my first writing teacher, who in his command performance lectures raised history to the level of myth, to a higher plateau of truth than facts; Chuck (the machine), for his 8th grade verbal slap across the chops, which permanently turned my head; Pancho, for his Palo Viejo, Latin insanity, and extensive knowledge of South Florida gardens and trees; Joanne, for the many hours she saved me with her swift word-processing of all my query letters (it seemed there were thousands); Will, for assuring me early on that

Nadia might well exist; the Chamberlinians, whose collective spunky spirit dances throughout these pages (if, indeed, these pages ever do manage to dance); David Orr and the Meadowcreekers, for growing their sweet sweet dream right up through the dungheap—yahoo—of the Reagan nightmare; Theodore Roszak, William Irwin Thompson and Wendell Berry, for their lucid vision; Thomas Pynchon, whose fiction I turned to whenever I was in need of writer's inspiration; Martin and Judith Shepard, for their long-distance kindness, and for being the ideal publishers for a naive and trusting neophyte writer; and to the Trees, of course—may they "whoosh" forever.

And in memory of Michael Crane, the laughing poet who "danced beneath the diamond sky with one hand waving free"; and Scott Waugh, who taught me to sniff the Melaleucas.

THE
GREAT
EQUALIZER

PART I

"We are witnessing the erosion, perhaps the final erosion, of the idea of man as something splendid or divine, and its replacement with a view that sees man no less than nature, as simply more raw material for manipulation and homogenization."

THEODORE ROSZAK

"A fool sees not the same tree that a wise man sees."

WILLIAM BLAKE

"Astonishing! Everything is intelligent!"

PYTHAGORAS

Eudora

I've got to admit I'm more than a little concerned about my son, and about this awful new job of his. Of course it comes as no surprise to me that *this* is the sort of work he would choose. After all, Benny is drawn to anything that most normal people find hopelessly depressing. In fact, ever since he got it into his cockamamy head to leave college two weeks before graduation, he's spent 90% of his time holed up in that stuffy bedroom of his, sitting at his desk and reading those horrible books he loves to read. Doomsday books, I call them. End of the world books. Nuclear war, pollution, overpopulation, toxic chemicals, acid rain, dwindling resources, food shortages, water shortages, energy shortages, rising cancer rates, rising climates, *falling* climates, and on and on. Now what sort of person, with the Atlantic Ocean half a block from his bedroom door, would choose to spend his summer days sweating at his desk, his nose buried in those sorts of books; would devour every doomsday book he could get his hands on? For God's sake, even if the problems *are* all real and terrible, what good can it possibly do anyone to drown his brain with floods of information about what a rotten, doomed world we live in? (I sometimes think he occupies himself with these problems simply because they are so big, so overwhelming, that no one in his right mind would ever really expect him to tackle—much less solve—even *one* of them. And so he happily fritters away his time pondering the grimmest, the most formidable, unsolveable problems as a way of avoiding the smaller, more manageable problems of day-to-day living. He claims to

13

want to save the world, yet can't maintain—can't even strike up—a relationship with a girl.)

And if I try to get him to look at the bright side, if I point out to him, for instance, that at least we've got our finest scientists, our most brilliant minds, working round the clock to *solve* those problems, he tells me—looking me straight in the eye with absolute sincerity and conviction—that those fine scientists and brilliant minds are more a part of the problem than the solution. If I explain to him that he's damned lucky to be living in a world where with a flick of the finger he can have light or heat or cool air, he'll tell me the world is running out of oil and that we probably can't afford light or heat or cool air at the flick of a finger; that the price of such convenience is too high. If I suggest to him that he should be grateful to be living in a world where, if he wants, he can fly through the air, crossing an ocean at the speed of sound, he'll say the jet emissions are depleting the ozone layer. Honest to God, if I handed him a glass of sweet lemonade, he would probably find a way to turn it back into a lemon.

But this is really nothing new. Even as a child he dwelled excessively on the negative. I remember, back in Atlanta, when he was only five years old, I heard him crying in the bathroom and rushed in to find him sitting on the pot, punching at his poor little brown thighs, sobbing to me that they were too fat. I tried to explain—oh how I tried to explain!—that when you sit on a toilet seat your thighs naturally spread against the surface and just *look* fat; that his poor little thighs were no fatter than anyone else's. But as patiently as I tried to explain this, he refused to believe me, and wasn't satisfied until *I* finally sat on the toilet seat, hiked up my skirt, and let him see how fat *my* thighs looked. And even then he wasn't completely satisfied; I think he simply suspected that I had fat thighs, too.

And, sixteen years later, he's really no different. He's still that same little boy, sitting on the pot, punching away at his thighs. Which is why it really shouldn't, really doesn't surprise me that when I finally gave him the ultimatum—to find a job until he decided to return to college, or else move out on his own—he found and took this particular job.

The Beginning Point

The radio alarm blasts apart the mist of his dreams like a miniature fog horn, and, turning one ear quickly to the pillow for protection, he lashes out, feeling frantically among the radio-top buttons, fumbling and pressing until he hits the right one. "Oh God," Benny Horowitz groans, then hoists himself to a sitting position and pulls open his eyelids with his thumbs. It's 6:00 Saturday morning. In an hour he'll be starting his new job.

Across the room, piled along the back of his walnut veneer desktop and coming slowly into focus are a haphazard stack of seven books, each delineating in a different way the imminent collapse of modern civilization. Set in front of the seven books are a training manual on the rights of the mentally retarded, a reddish-purple pencil with the eraser chewed to the metal and the metal itself chewed until indented like a driveway trash can smashed by a car, four non-working push-button ball point pens, all sneaked from the teller's window at First Federal Coconut Beach Bank, and thus, he half suspects, instantly karmaed into inklessness (though he's not at all certain he believes in karma, or anything else non-temporal), sixty pages of looseleaf notes scrawled in pencil and nearly illegible (even to him), a wood-framed 8 × 10 wedding photo of his mother and father—the top half of a Sears price tag still stuck, unpeelable, to the glass—taken three years before she became a breadwinner and he a breadmaker, and twelve years before they moved from Atlanta to South Florida, an empty bowl of his father's homemade grapefruit and poppyseed yogurt with a dozen or so unscooped poppyseeds pasted to the veins of dried yogurt running along the inner bowlside, an unfinished letter to the editor of the Coconut Beach Post Intelligencer, outlining the county commission's ignorance on the basic principles of ecology with respect to their land use and development policies, an old "welcome home" poster folded accordian-style into a giant fan and stapled at the handle—"his cockamamy version," according to his mother, "of air conditioning"—and a paperback book on male sexuality, turned face down.

Benny lets go of his eyelids now, which fall slightly, before catching just above the halfway point. Yawning, he swings his legs over the bedside, then stands and slouches over to his chest of drawers, where he dresses in a pair of stiff new jeans, purchased yesterday specifically for this occasion, an olive green t-shirt with a white palm tree on the pocket, and tennis shoes, the rubber soles practically worn through. He yawns again, not bothering to cover his mouth, and with everything unzipped, untucked, unbuckled and uncombed, shambles to the bathroom to splash water on his face, examine his tongue in the mirror—a useless habit he's had ever since he was a small boy—and brush what's left of his prematurely receding dark curls.

Meanwhile, in the kitchen, his father is, as promised, preparing for him a falafel, spinach and sour cream omelette, and as soon as Benny smells the garlicky falafel, he hastily checks himself in the mirror, taking a final peek at his tongue, then hurries to the kitchen.

"The garlic smells like heaven," Benny tells his father. "Thanks for getting up so early."

Winking, Mort Horowitz expertly lifts half the omelette, then folds it over and turns down the gas flame. "I'd be up for my jog by now, anyway," he reminds Benny. He's a slim but vital, balding man with a hawkish, hooking nose, thick black brows—more hair *there* than on the top of his head—and a thin moustache which he grew 35 years earlier as a gift to himself for his 18th birthday after deciding it was simply too much of a struggle for him to effectively maneuver a razor or electric shaver across that narrow strip of flesh between his prodigious nose and beefy upper lip every morning. Physically, Mort is in perfect health. He doesn't smoke, drink coffee or alcohol (except for an occasional glass of champagne), or eat meat. He jogs two miles every morning and evening, moves his bowels regularly, easily, and copiously, uses ivory soap and hot water for all his housecleaning—spurning the chemical cleaners that his wife makes her fortune selling, and distributing to others to sell and distribute, ad infinitum—grows his own organic vegetables and fruits, and plans to buy a small farm so that he can raise his own egg-laying chickens on organically grown grain, and his own cow on organically grown hay. His main goal in life is to be alive and healthy at 100. "So tell me," Mort says now, setting the steaming omelette in front of his son, then pulling out a chair and sitting beside him. "How are you feeling about your first day of work?"

"Well actually," Benny admits, "the more I think about it, the more I wonder if I'm really cut out for this job." He lifts a first forkload of the omelette to his mouth, a chunk of falafel slipping out the side and thunking softly onto the glasstop table. "Who knows? I might be heading back to school sooner than I'd planned." He forces a laugh. "I guess that would make *Mom* happy, anyway."

"Well I'm rooting for you either way," his father assures him, rolling his head to loosen up his neck muscles, a twice daily pre-jog ritual of his. "You've got to do whatever *you* want. Right? Any other way, it doesn't make sense."

"Right. Whatever *I* want." But that, Benny thinks, is precisely his problem (or at least *one* of his problems). He doesn't know *what* he wants, so how can he do it? He envies his parents, who both know exactly what they want. His mother wants to continue making a great deal of money and, as she says, helping build other peoples' futures; and his father wants to postpone death for as long as he possibly can. But to Benny, making money, building futures, and living long are enterprises which seem to be lacking something, though he's not sure exactly what. All he knows is that he has, during the past few years, developed a terrible fear—and this is another of his problems—that if and when he ever does figure out what it is he wants to do, and begins to do it, he will one morning wake up, astonished to find that forty years have somehow slipped past, and that he feels the same as he did forty years earlier (when he fell, unknowingly, into his wakeful sleep), only older. Closer to nothing but death.

The fear started out as a vague uneasiness around the time he was a junior in high school, and intensified throughout college, until one night, three weeks before final exams, when, acutely aware of his impending commencement, he found himself lying awake in bed, stiff and shivering, immobilized with anxiety, and afraid to let his eyes fall shut. The insomnia continued unabated until he made the decision, four nights later, just after 3 AM, to withdraw from college and return home for a semester or two; or for however long it took him to find some strong antidote to, or at least a way of coping with, his terrible forty year fear. Having made his decision, he fell asleep within minutes.

But at home a day and a half later, his mother was livid at his irresponsible decision to drop out two weeks before his graduation, and immediately gave him an ultimatum. As long as he had been a student, she explained, she'd always been happy, honored even, to let him live in her home, rent free. But now that he had dropped out of college she could not, in good conscience, go on supporting him; could not and *would* not sit back and watch while he learned from his permanently jobless father's pathetic example. And so, she told him, he could either find a job until he returned to school, or move out on his own for a taste of the real world.

Benny, who understood, and to an extent even shared, his mother's concerns (he hated housework and gardening, and was surprised his father hadn't died of boredom years ago, in spite of his impeccable physical condition), spent his first month at home shut up in his room, sometimes hunched over his desk, reading books on ecological catastrophe and scribbling notes for some future thesis; and sometimes lying on his back in bed, oblivious to the heat, staring straight up for hours on end (as if waiting for the ceiling to miraculously crack open—though he didn't believe in miracles—while the answer to his fear descended from on high), emerging from his room only to eat, pick up the morning and afternoon newspapers to search the want ads for a suitable temporary job, and ride his ten-speed bicycle to the First Federal Coconut Beach Bank to further deplete his meager savings—in order to pay for his room and board—and cop another non-working push-button ballpoint pen. Occasionally he took a long, solitary walk along the beach, hoping an answer might come to him in a roaring Atlantic vision (though he wasn't sure he believed in visions. But by the time he was hired to work at ARC House, he was no closer to finding an answer or antidote than he'd *ever* been.

Finishing his omelette now, he carries his plate to the sink and reaches for the faucet.

"Never mind with that." Mort, still sitting, waves his son away. "I'll take care of it."

Benny steps back to the table, sets a hand on his father's chairback and squeezes, gently, as if the chairback was his father's shoulder. "Tell Mom good-bye for me. And don't bother to wait up Sunday. I doubt I'll be back before 11:30."

Outside, he bends over to roll up his jeans, wheels his old ten-speed through the pebbled driveway, past his mother's white Mercedes and his father's newly painted bright red '65 Rambler Wagon and onto Gumbo Limbo Lane, then swings a leg over the center bar and pedals off. At the end of the block he squints into the sun, an intense smudge of brightness now just above the horizon, then turns south on Ocean Drive, sniffing Melaleuca Trees and salted air. Along the road, Coconut Palms spaced at regular twenty yard intervals lean over the ocean wall at severe angles, their green fronds rustling in the breeze like the skirts of slow motion hula dancers, while not far above Benny's head a quintet of seagulls, one gray, the rest white, slide with a windcurrent, all hopping at the same instant, as if jumping a gate in the fifty meter hurdles; and higher up, dozens of turkey vultures catch a lift on an Atlantic thermal, spiraling upward, black specks against the blue.

But Benny sees none of this. He's bent over, pumping hard, consoling himself with the notion that he's found the perfect job for himself (though he's admittedly nervous about this first weekend shift); that from Saturday morning to Sunday night he'll be able to please his mother by working and earning enough to pay her a decent rent—proving to her that he's no bum or freeloader—yet still have five free days left every week to devote to figuring out what it is he *really* wants to do, and, even more important, searching for some sort of antidote to, or insurance against, his great fear. Though at the moment he hasn't the slightest idea where to begin looking. (He's already tried the ceiling and the beach, and neither has proven helpful.) But it doesn't matter. Because he is assuming, as he pedals, that from now until he gets off work Sunday night, he'll have to temporarily suspend his search for the beginning point, anyway.

Early Morning Thoughts of The ARC House Wakeful

Elisha

Hot Dog always watching Nadia too close. He stand too close and look at her too close and I hate her. But he say he love me better, and cross his heart that he love me better. I like Nadia, and she not right for him anyway. And I got the ring, anyway. She smart with the trees she make, but I see her how she don't care bout nobody but her trees. She don't care bout Hot Dog. And she leave Friday night and Saturday night and make me wake up when she slam the door. And she don't tell nobody. Cause she strange bout that. She make me nervous bout that and the way he always looking too close. I hate him when he look at her and stand too close. I don't think she would take his ring to wear it, anyway. I don't think she would go with him and let him do it to her anyway. But she might cause she strange and don't care. She make me nervous the way she don't care. And don't care bout what time it is and brushing her hair with all the clay always in it. They get mad *bout it and she don't care. I like that but it make me nervous. I don't think she want him and I hope he stop looking so close. I rub on the ring when he look too close. Sometime it work and sometime it don't.*

Moby

It isn't fair that they do not want me to take no long showers because I cannot do it nowhere else. Not in bed because Lucius Moon is in bed, too, and I can hear the sheets when he does it even when he is quiet and does not make the funny sounds in his throat like sometimes when it is easier to hear him do it. And even if I can get Lythia to do it, it does not matter about that because I would rather be in the shower so no one cannot hear me when I do it. I do it twice in the shower sometimes, but the second time it does not ever feel so good like the first time.

Amar

I'll try to say this: They all try to act like babies around here, and so does Billy Loper. He's okay except when he tries to be able to stab you in the back. But I'd rather know him than Emmy, anyway, because a girl like that should try to be able to be sweet, on account of that's about all she'd be good for. But you try to be able to be nice to her and she's liable to jump off the handle. Last night I tried to tell her Texas was the state closest to the crater—and I know on account of I learned it from my mother because that's where she was born and raised at—and she blew up like a fart in a barnfire. But at least she can hold onto her beer. And *I'll try to say this:* That's more than I can say for Billy Loper. He tries to act like a big baby when he can't get his way. But we been roommates together a long time and I'd like to be able to say I trust him like a brother. He'll be the best man, too, when Elisha and me get ourselves hitched. (And if she don't want to try to stand up for herself and stop trying to agree with everything they say no matter whether it's right or not right, I'll try to be able to switch over to Nadia. She don't love me, but she's got about the darkest eyes I've ever seen.) I'll let him be like an uncle to our children. Because I'd like to be able to settle down and try to have me a family. But you think the staff are gonna help me? No way, when all they try to care about is trying to be able to keep stuff clean. But a man wants to have him a family, and they won't have nothing to do with it. It's better than Palmview, sure. But *I'll try to say this:* You can't keep a man from his dreams any more than you can try to be able to keep light out of a poker sack. And if I hadn't had pneumonia when I was nine months old, I'd never have been here to begin with.

Nadia

How I'm tired now, but like a good tired, cause of the tree, cause of the Banyan, how I was with the Banyan again, climbing the

Banyan how I'm not supposed to climb it, and leaving at night after the dark stuff comes, and the fuzzies with the dark stuff, to climb it how I'm not supposed to. And how the sound was all around, in the Banyan and in my head all around, and whooshing with the Banyan how it whooshes with its arms, and how it stretches and whooshes with its arms how Angela don't know, don't know about no whooshing and rizzing and fuzzies, how she's a smarty britches and thinks she knows, but don't know.

Lucius

Ooooooh-woooooooooo-hyoooooooooo-wowwwwooo! Feel good. Yuh.

Benny . . . The First Day

My first day, my first hour, on the new job and already I'm a nervous wreck; alone in a century old, two-story house with four bedrooms, eight beds, and one mentally retarded adult, asleep—for the moment—in each one.
Ty Callaghan, whose shift ends at 7:00 every Saturday morning—the same time my forty hour weekend shift begins—just left after warning me to keep an eye on Lythia Maywire, who had a seizure last night just before she went to bed. Jesus! A seizure! What the hell am I doing here? What do you do when someone has a seizure? When I asked Ty he shrugged and told me just to make sure she doesn't hit her head on anything when she falls. He also suggested—as an afterthought—that I check to see if she's breathing after a minute or so. But what if she's *not* breathing? What if she swallows her tongue? I've heard the stories. Do I risk losing my fingers between the incisors of a girl—a brainless girl, at that—I hardly know, to fish for her swallowed tongue? Or what if she starts gagging on her own epileptic puke? I've heard that it happens. Or what if she *does* smash her head on a table edge when she falls? What if after a minute she's *not* breathing? Then what?
And to be honest, it's not just Lythia and the seizures I'm worrying about as I sit here drumming my fingers on the desktop, trying to read through this week's daily log entries, and waiting for everyone to wake up. It's everyone and everything! What if all eight of them decide to mutiny when I try to run a "program"—which is what I'll appar-

ently be spending most of my forty hour weekends here doing. What if one of them becomes suddenly violent and heads for the steak knife drawer in the kitchen? God, I'm in over my head here. I know nothing about these people. They're aliens to me.

Last week, as part of my extensive pre-service training, I was taken on a tour of Palmview, the Florida State Hospital for the Mentally Retarded. In one room I was allowed to spend 15 or 20 minutes observing a classful of autistic adolescents, some learning the most rudimentary sort of "give-me-food" sign language, some attempting to distinguish between black discs and white squares—and failing!—and some just spinning like tops out of control, like dervishes gone amok, or sliding back and forth across the floor on hands and knees, grunting, then cuffing themselves across the ear. Christ, how must it feel to have given your own flesh, blood and genes birth to a baby who will never be as smart or as loving (or even, in some cases, as good looking) as a chimpanzee—maybe never even as smart or loving as a pigeon or gerbil—and who will be your responsibility for the next eighteen years or more? How do people cope with that?

In another room—the locked door of which we paused in front of, listening to our tour guide's description of what was happening behind it—was a group of toilet-untrainable, naked men (their naked female counterparts were housed in another locked room) known as "the painters," who, as the name suggests, spend their days wandering aimlessly about, painting everything—the floors and walls, the plastic furniture, themselves and each other—with their own feces. Their own shit! (Which is the reason they remain naked; the reason the institution refuses to clothe them.) Their fingers are their brushes, their assholes their palettes. And this apparently is their singular gift; their one and only God-given talent.

No painters here at ARC House, I'm assured. And I believe it, for I met each of the residents here last week during my training, and they all seemed clean enough. Harmless enough. Friendly enough. In fact from what I hear it seems we've got the cream of the mentally handicapped crop here. The Phi Betta Kappa of the idiot world. A squad of moron all-stars. And still, the thought of spending a full weekend alone here with these people is enough to make me quake in my tennis shoes.

I met all eight of the ARC House residents at dinner last week (ARC stands for the Association for Retarded Citizens, the organization which, with the help of United Way and the State of Florida, funds this group home), after a training session during which I observed Ty Callaghan running what's called a "program" with Elisha Malune. Her bedroom program. (As I've already said, running programs with the residents is going to be a big part of my job here, because the state of Florida requires a minimum of four hours of programming per week, per resident.) Ty sat at the edge of Elisha's bed, the program data clipboard and stopwatch on his lap, and a pen in his hand, and watched (praising her efforts, as prescribed in my training manual, at least once every minute) while she cleaned her mirror and windows, dusted her dresser and stereo, her baseboards and bedframe—things I'd never even *think* about dusting—then vacuumed her carpet. She missed a spot on the carpet, behind the opened bedroom door, and right away Ty started in with the formal "cueing" procedure, correctly beginning (again, as I'd read in the manual) with what's called a "non-directive verbal cue." "What do you need to do, Elisha?" he asked. If I were her I'd have told him that *I* didn't need to do a thing, but that *he* needed to take a good hard flying fuck at the vacuum hose.

But Elisha is 34. People have been running programs with her since she was first institutionalized thirteen years ago. She's apparently accustomed to the constant watching and cueing. Maybe she thinks that's how everyone lives. Or maybe she even likes all the attention. Who the hell knows? After hearing Ty's cue, Elisha stood there clutching the vacuum handle as if paralyzed, knowing she'd done something wrong. Slowly, carefully, she studied the carpet, then looked helplessly back to Ty, at which point he promptly, correctly, dropped to a "directive verbal cue." "You need to vacuum behind the door, Elisha," he said, pointing.

Looking relieved to discover her error, Elisha vacuumed behind the door and Ty marked a "DV" for "directive verbal cue" in the proper square on the program data sheet, along with the time it took her to complete the program, then enthusiastically told her how terrific the carpet looked, especially now that it was clean behind the door, and what a great job she'd done. She beamed at his praise—"positive reinforcement," as it's called in the manual—the purpose of which is to shape desired skills and appropriate behaviors.

Anyway, it was right after watching Ty's program demonstration that I met all the residents, just before they sat down to dinner. Usually I'm terrible with names and faces, but one look at these folks and I knew I'd have no trouble remembering *all* their names and faces.

There's Elisha Malune, the one Ty ran the bedroom program with. She's quiet and small—except for her hips, which are monstrous—and has frizzy blonde hair, a flat, mashed-looking nose, and eyes that are set far apart, like bird eyes, one on either side of her face, so that I'm sure her field of vision covers maybe 270 degrees, unless she's got a blind spot directly in front of her. She proudly announces to the rest of the residents that she already knows me because she was just helping to teach me how to run a program. When I acknowledge this with a nod and a smile she blushes and flutters her eyelids.

Moby Cochrane is built like a snowman. A small round head atop a large round body with no neck in between. He wears a hearing aid in each ear, and has a smile which is somehow very feminine. A Mona Lisa sort of smile—calming and peaceful. But his skin is almost transluscent, the color of surfboard wax or sauteed onions. It looks slightly reptilian, even. I nod at him instead of shaking hands.

Billy Loper is by far the tallest resident, and easily has the worst posture I've ever seen. When I first saw him he was tilted forward at the waist like a stickshift in third gear, while his neck jutted forward at an even more severe angle. From what I've read in Billy's file he often gets terrible neck pains when he walks any kind of distance, because his posture is so awful that he has to tilt his head way back just to see straight ahead. But even with his terrible posture he towers over everyone. If he ever straightened up he could probably dunk a basketball flat-footed. His arms are long and slinky. They dangle as if someone nailed them to his shoulders as an afterthought. He has no eyebrows, a swollen, bumpy nose, and, even though he's thin, a fleshy double chin. His hair is blonde and hangs over his forehead in straight bangs. He calls me "buddy" and familiarly slaps my shoulder when we introduce ourselves.

Nadia Christov has soft-looking, deeply-tanned skin, eyes dark as coffee, and long black hair, which, when I first saw her, was in tangles. She was sent back upstairs to brush it before sitting at the dinner table. (Apparently her tangled hair is a problem they've been working on ever since she began living here eight months ago.) She's tall, thin, and almost fragile-looking from the waist up. Her back is swayed like a young girl's so that her hips and belly bow out slightly, her chest sinks in and her shoulders slump forward. She's 26—5 years older than me—yet I can clearly picture her with a smudge of dirt on her cheek and an ice cream stick poking from her mouth. Her legs are long—like the rest of her body—but, unlike the rest of her body, not thin or fragile-looking at all. She's the youngest of the ARC House residents, and the only one who's never been in an institution. (Until eight months ago she lived with her mother, who, shortly after Nadia moved to ARC House, died of breast cancer.) But the most amazing thing about her is that she builds trees out of clay, and has many of them displayed and sold in the lobby of WCRC—not a radio station, but the sheltered workshop where Nadia and the other residents do assembly line type work every day. One of her trees is the centerpiece for the ARC House dining table. It's an oak tree without leaves, remarkably graceful, and perfectly proportioned. It astonishes me to learn that anyone with an IQ of 74 could artistically fashion trees out of clay.

Lythia Maywire is the one who has seizures. She takes Dilantin three times a day as a preventative, but apparently has a seizure every month or two anyway. But her epilepsy is only a sidelight of her cerebral palsy. She's perpetually bobbing and ducking in slow motion, rocking from her gimpy leg to her strong one. Her movements are so fluid that when I watch her I feel as if I'm seeing her in a dream. Her left hand—same side as her gimp leg—is curled like a hook, and she limps so violently that walking is a real balancing act for her. In fact her walk is more of a semi-controlled fall. She decides where she wants to go, leans in that direction and falls, hoping her legs and feet will follow. She has the highest IQ of any of the residents—in fact on all of her IQ tests she consistently scores in the "borderline intelligent" range—but it takes her nearly a minute and a chinful of drooling to tell me she's glad to meet me.

Emmy Oberst is just 31, yet has a full head of stiff-looking gray hair. She's unusually short, has a pug nose, and breasts that would take a pair of size 7 army helmets to restrain. They swing and bounce every time she makes a move. But she seems not to care or notice. Probably because she's too busy talking. Chattering. Non-stop. In fact when she first shakes my hand she's chattering, but I have no idea what she's saying, or even if she's talking to me. I'm standing there, embarrassed as hell, shaking her hand while trying to avoid having the back of my wrist pummeled by those monster breasts, and at the same time attempting to decipher her chattering. If I could see her lips I might be able to read them, but her face is turned to the side. Cautiously, I interrupt her chatter. "What was that?" I say, cocking my head. And all at once she's facing me and speaking slowly—almost sternly—and without expression, as if reading from a cue card. "My name is Emmy Oberst and I am pleased to meet you."

"Glad to meet you, Emmy," I say.

"Oh *are* you?" she asks, as if she's genuinely surprised, then nods once, almost violently, slaps her hip and is off to the dinner table.

Amar Beldoni has a short black goatee and moustache, and looks as though he stepped out of Greenwich Village in the late fifties. I can picture him with a golden earring, a black beret, and an alto sax strapped around his neck. When he shakes my hand he looks into my eyes and in a sincere, slightly southern sounding voice, says, "Hey. I'm Amar Beldoni and I'd like to be able to personally welcome you here to ARC House if I could be able to."

"Thanks," I say, trying to stare right back into *his* eyes, which are an opaque sort of grayish-blue, and, for some reason hard as hell to focus on. "You sound like a one man official welcoming committee."

"Well I'll try to say this," he says, releasing my hand so that he can gesture with his. "I guess I was trying to be able to put my horses before my carrots."

And finally there's Lucius Moon. He has dirt blonde curly hair, bulging eyes, youthfully rosy cheeks—though he's 56 years old—and a long, thin neck. When I say hi to him he stands in front of me, rocking from side to side, from foot to foot, his fingers interlocked at his chest. "Ooh wow," he says, looking past me, then rubs the back of his long neck, grinning, and heads for the dinner table.

So I've met them all. I've read about them in their personal files and in the daily log. And still they scare me. In fact I'm hoping maybe they'll sleep all day.

No such luck.

Billy Loper is the first one up. I'm sitting at the desk, drumming my fingers and looking over the program schedule, when the bedroom door opens and he steps into the kitchen, bent over like a six and a half foot question mark.

"Hey ya Benny. How are ya, Buddy? How are ya?"

"Fine," I say, surprised by his enthusiasm and pleased that he remembers me.

"Me too, Buddy," he says. "Me too. Me too," then slaps me on the shoulder. Those arms of his are long and thin as whips. "Well I'm the cook this morning, Benny. I'm the cook I am."

"Right," I say, double-checking the schedule on the bulletin board above the desk.

He asks what we're cooking for breakfast and, because an important part of my job is to constantly encourage the residents to do as much for themselves as they are capable of, I tell him I'm not sure what's for breakfast, but that he can find out for himself simply by checking the menu.

"But I can't read, Benny," he says apologetically. "I can't read a word, I can't. Not a word."

"Oh, right," I tell him. "That's fine. We'll read it together."

"Okay Benny. We'll read it together, we will. Read it together. Read the whole menu together."

The menu is held in place on the refrigerator door by two plastic-covered magnets, shaped and colored like miniature strawberries. We check and find out that I'll be helping Billy cook fried eggs this morning. Fried eggs have never been my strong suit—I'm lucky to salvage one yolk out of four when I flip them—but I'm not going to worry about it because Billy's the one who will be doing the cooking. We take a dozen and a half eggs out of the refrigerator, then find a bowl to crack them into. The first egg he *smashes* on the bowl edge so hard that the shell shatters into about a hundred fragments which slide into the bowl with the egg. He tries fishing out the shell with his long, bony fingers, but it's useless and he quickly grows frustrated. I wink at him, glance surreptitiously over one shoulder then the other, and dump the egg and shell down the garbage disposal. I can tell I'm going to be great at this job. Here I'm supposed to be cueing him, getting *him* to figure out what to do, and instead I'm acting like a ten year-old in cahoots with him.

Just to show him it's not going to be *all* fun and games with me, I give him my first non-directive verbal cue. "Okay Billy. What do you need to do now?"

"Break another egg, Benny. I need to break another egg, I do. Break another egg."

"That's right," I say. "But more gently this time."

He whacks the egg on the edge of the bowl, and this time only a few shell fragments slide in with the egg. He fishes for the fragments but they elude him.

I hear the TV switched on in the living room, which is adjacent to the kitchen, so I tell Billy I'll be right back, then hustle through the kitchen doorway and into the living room to find out who just got up. It's Lucius Moon. He's squatting in front of the big color TV, switching channels. When he sees the Roadrunner zipping and beeping across the screen he backs away.

"Good morning Lucius," I say. "Could you do me a favor and let everyone know that breakfast will be ready in about twenty minutes."

He straightens up, interlocks his fingers at his chest, and in an unhappy tone of voice says, "Yuh. I tell." He's by far the oldest resident living at ARC House, and probably isn't too thrilled about climbing the stairs.

"You sure?" I ask. "I can get someone else to spread the word."

"I do," he says, more agreeably this time, then bends forward to switch off the TV.

"Hey. That's great you're switching off the TV," I say, thinking this is the perfect opportunity to try a little positive reinforcement; use my college education to impart some basic ecological knowledge. "You know, switching off the TV the way you did saves energy, Lucius. It saves oil. And we all really need to be aware of conserving oil. Because we're using it all up. And once we use it up it will be gone forever." I pat him on the back, here. "So switching off the TV was good thinking."

Lucius grins slyly at me. Not the proud grin I'm expecting to see. But a sly, shit-eating grin. I feel as though he's grinning at *me*, instead of at my praise; as though maybe he sees a long stalagtite of snot dangling from my nostril. I want to ask him what the hell he's grinning at, but that grin has me unnerved. I turn, brushing the back of my hand across my nose, and head back through the kitchen doorway. So much for ecology lesson #1.

Billy is still fishing through the bowl for the elusive egg shell. Right away he looks to me for help. "This goddamned stupid egg shell won't let me touch it," he rants. "Won't let me touch it. Won't let me touch it."

"Well what can you do about that eggshell?" I cue him, not sure if I should just ignore his profanity or cue him about that, too.

He leans way down to me, setting his forehead on my shoulder, and begins to bawl. I'm standing there, patting his back, waiting for him to stop crying, my shoulder getting wetter by the second, when Amar Beldoni steps through the kitchen doorway, quickly sizes up the situation and says, "Hey. It's no use crying over spoiled milk."

I say good morning to Amar, not bothering to correct him, then pull back from Billy, awkwardly patting his back and explaining that we need to get cracking. Christ, we've been at it for ten minutes already and are still on our first egg. Pretty soon everyone will be up and watching me help Billy destroy eighteen fried eggs. Just the kind of beginning I was hoping to avoid. To hell with the cueing and patience. I want to get breakfast on the table.

While Billy's rubbing his eyes I pin the fragments of eggshell to the side of the bowl and pull them out. "There," I say. "Now how about if you watch me crack a few?"

"Okay Buddy," Billy says, sniffling, bent over as if his head was still on my shoulder. "I'll watch you, I will. I'll watch you."

I crack twelve of the eighteen eggs, but it takes ten minutes for him to crack the other six, and for me to fish out the eggshell. Finally we get eighteen eggs cracked into the bowl with a minimum of shell mixed in. But before putting the pan on the burner and melting the butter, I have to go to the bathroom. I just peed an hour ago, but when I'm this nervous my bladder likes to keep itself empty.

I ask Billy to wait a minute, then I hurry down the hall and push through the bathroom door. Amar is standing there over the toilet, jiggling himself to shake off the excess. Slightly flustered, I nod at him then back out and shut the door. But it bothers me that he didn't think to lock the door, so I push back in and cue him, "Amar, what do you need to do when you're using the toilet?"

"Hey," he says, then spits into the toilet. "Could you be able to try to guess what Amar means?"

"Hmm," I say. "Probably something to do with love." Then I repeat, "What do you need to do when you use the toilet?"

"Amar means *to* love," he says, then spits again and flushes the toilet.

I decide it's time for a directive verbal cue, and so I firmly deliver it. "You need to lock the door when you use the toilet, Amar."

"I'll try to say this," he says. "We couldn't be able to lock the door on account of there's a rule against it. Am I right or am I not right?"

I hesitate, then remember that he is right. The bathroom doors are supposed to remain unlocked at all times. That way if someone has a seizure, or slips and falls in the shower, you don't have to break down the door to get to him.

I'm about to thank him for his reminder and explain to him that this is my first day and I've still got a lot to learn and remember, but before I can he says, "Would you like to be able to hear what my three names are?" He grins like a German Shepherd—a leering, hanging sort of grin—then before I can explain to him that I *do* want to hear what his three names are, but that I don't really have time at the moment because I need to hurry up and pee so that I can get back to Billy and the fried eggs, he says, "Amar, Armour and Hot Dog," then spits again into the now fresh toilet water.

"Great," I say, moving closer to the toilet as he jiggles himself a final time.

He leans close to me now, as if he's about to share something extremely confidential. "Would you like to be able to guess why they call me Hot Dog?" He's just tucked himself in—and there is, I couldn't help noticing, an awful lot for him to tuck in—zipped himself up, and is leaning too close. I'm not *at all* sure I want to hear why they call him Hot Dog. But before I can say no, he's explaining, looking at me intently with those gray-blue eyes of his that are so hard to focus on. "My best friend called me Armour instead of Amar one day and when I asked him why he wanted to be able to call me Armour he told me Armour was his favorite brand of hot dog, and hot dogs was his favorite food, and he wanted to be able to call me Armour instead of Amar because I was his favorite friend and he loved me like he'd try to be able to love a brother. With all his heart and soul. So I kept the name." He spits into the toilet and flushes it again. He's wasting water like a madman, but after a story like that another one of my conservation speeches is only going to be anti-climactic, so I pat him on the back and say, "That's quite a story, Amar. And I appreciate your sharing it with me."

"Hey. You know what kind of car a Honda is?"

"Yeah," I say. "I sure do." Then I move to the toilet and begin to unzip myself, hoping he'll take the hint. He doesn't.

"It's a small car. Right?" He spits into the sink, then turns on the faucet to wash it down. I can't imagine where all his phlegm is coming from. If he wasn't so damned bright-eyed I'd think he had pneumonia.

"Right," I say. "A Honda is a small car. Listen Amar. Could you close the door behind you?"

"My best friend who named me Hot Dog was in a Honda when it ran smack into a phone pole. Head on. And that's how come he was able to be a handicapped person and to be my best friend who named me Hot Dog. On account of how his head got hurt." He turns to spit in the sink, then changes his mind. "Hey. How would *you* like to try to be able to call me Hot Dog?"

"Sure," I say. "That would be fine. Want to close the door there, Hot Dog?"

"All right," he says. "Thank you." Then he steps out and shuts the door.

By the time I've finished peeing, Lucius Moon has rounded everyone up for breakfast, and suddenly over half the residents are milling about the kitchen. My hands have been full dealing with one resident at a time, and here they are forcing me to deal with all of them at once. I feel as if I'm about to be bowled over by the energy coming at me from all directions. It's as though each one, just by the fact of his or her presence, is perpetually screaming. I ask everyone to leave the kitchen so that Billy can finish cooking.

Within twenty-five minutes the eggs and English muffins are ready. I follow Billy out of the kitchen, watching as he delightedly carries his platterful of fried eggs and muffins. If his posture wasn't so horrible he'd have to duck to make it through the doorway.

Only two yolks out of eighteen—the two *I* flipped—are unbroken. But Billy doesn't care. That these eggs can be eaten because *he fixed them so that they can be eaten* is to him a miracle. On the job a little over an hour and already I'm witness to a miracle.

Entering the living room Billy shouts, "They're ready, they are. The fried eggs are ready. I fried 'em myself, I did. Fried 'em myself. Fried 'em all by myself."

I see that Lucius, sitting now on the edge of the couch, is oblivious to the breakfast call because he's so busy rocking back and forth, urgently rubbing the tops of his thighs, heating them up in God knows *what* ways, and grinning as if he's halfway to heaven and still ascending. I stop to stare at him, awed by his simple ecstasy, and when he sees that I'm staring, a shudder of delight ripples through his body and out to his quivering fingertips like an electric charge, while his eyes grow wider, bugging out crazily, like inflating balloons.

And then, remembering that Lucius is on a behavior program to learn to stop rocking and rubbing—for rocking and thigh-rubbing are not "appropriate" community behaviors—I snap out of my dumb stupor and in a voice of omniscient wisdom and authority, calmly deliver my nondirective verbal cue. "What do you need to do, Lucius?"

"Ooh yuh," he grunts, and slowly ceases to rock and rub. The ecstasy drains from his face and body. His eyes deflate. His energy dwindles.

Because he responded appropriately to my cue, I'm now, according to official behavior program procedure, supposed to positively reinforce his response with social praise. I'm supposed to pat him on the back and enthusiastically say something like, "Hey. I see you're sitting still now, Lucius. That's very adult-like." But I can't pat him on the back, or enthusiastically praise him. I can't even look at him. I feel as if I've cut off his nuts. Worse than that; as if I've ripped a hole in his soul and let out all the spirit. (And I don't even know if I believe in a soul or spirit. Christ, if I listened to my father I'd believe we were all soulless as apes. Soulless as mosquitos or dandelions.)

I sit at the table with everyone, squirming and sweating in soul-slaughtering guilt, waiting for the egg platter to come around, and once again thinking that this job is not for me, when I realize that Lucius has already forgotten what happened. (At least he *appears* to have forgotten.) After spotting the two eggs with unbroken yolks he carefully scoops them onto his plate, then grins at them while he slowly cuts away and eats all the white. When the whites are gone he pokes gently at those liquid soft yellow eyes, watching them give and bulge like miniature yellow breasts. "Oooh wow," he says, then grins with magnificent suggestiveness at Nadia, who is sitting beside him, quietly watching and smiling as she chews. Her long black hair is tangled, as usual, and hangs not an inch above her plate. She licks her fingers slowly while Lucius continues to toy with the yolks and grin at her.

The others are all screaming their presences, too.

Amar is bragging to Elisha about some pinball machine he's been beating at the bus station. As he's talking to her, I keep thinking she's looking at *me* instead of at him, and it's only after a minute I realize that with her bird eyes set so far apart she can watch him on one side of her and me on the other at the same time, without moving her head. I wonder if she can work her eyes independently of one another. It's a bit spooky to think about, so I look away.

Lythia Maywire is seated on the other side of Amar. Even when sitting she's in perpetual motion, constantly bobbing, ducking, and swaying, as if she's got a pair of invisible stereo headphones strapped to her ears and is moving to the beat of the music. Her eyes roll as she struggles with her fork, her hooked left hand curled into her shoulder, and trembling. Wisely, she doesn't attempt to drink her milk by lifting the glass to her mouth. Instead she sucks it from the glass with a red and white plastic straw, spiral-striped like a barber's pole. But she can't suck up the *food* through a straw and so for her, getting a decent bit of egg cleanly into her mouth is like pinning the tail on the donkey. Her palsied body slows her down in every way; I get the feeling she knows exactly how and what to do and say, but can't get the message from her brain to her tongue, or to the rest of her body. If it were me I'd have exploded with frustration long ago. But Lythia just bobs in place, almost serenely.

Moby Cochrane is seated next to me. He's the most finnicky, meticulous eater I've ever seen. He carefully spoons a small glob of jam onto the center of each of his muffin slices, spreading it in small circles, the way a lady might spread rouge on her cheeks. He lifts the muffin between his thumb and forefinger, almost daintily, leans his head over his plate, and nibbles. When any jam drips from the muffin he quickly pulls back his head, like a turtle sensing danger, so that the jam won't land on his chin. And if he gets jam on his thumb or forefinger he immediately sets down the muffin and licks his fingers clean before attempting to go on. As he maneuvers his fork—once he finally gets to his eggs—his transluscent arm skin brushes against *my* arm skin and I quickly pull back.

Emmy is seated at the head of the table. She's constantly nodding and chattering unintelligibly. Occasionally she startles me with a distinct sentence which comes out in a perfect monotone. "I am enjoying these eggs," she says, then slaps her hip, violently shakes her head, and starts back in with her chattering. Her prodigious breasts rest on the table edge. I'd ask her to remove them—if elbows on the table are inappropriate I imagine breasts are, too—but I know if I were her *I'd* sure as hell be using all the support *I* could get. Anyway, she seems to be oblivious to her breasts. In fact she seems to be oblivious to everything. It's as though her body is efficiently and briskly going through all the proper motions—eating, drinking, using the napkin—while her mind is a thousand chattering miles away.

Billy is sopping what's left of his egg yolks with his muffin. It's a haphazard process at best. Dip, scoop and shovel. In ten seconds the entire muffin is gone and his mouth has a pasty yellow border. His posture at the table is the worst I've ever seen; worse, even, than when he's standing. *I* have horrible posture myself, but next to him I feel like a marine. He's at least six or seven inches taller than everyone else, and yet his head is closer to his plate than *anyone's* except maybe Emmy's. And Emmy can't be over 4'9".

I cue Billy about his posture, asking him how he needs to sit at the table, and he smiles contritely and says, "Okay Benny. I'll sit up, Buddy. I'll sit up for you, I will. Sit up for you." And up he sits, slowly unfolding until he's a head and a half above us. But he looks exposed and excruciatingly vulnerable up there, and a minute later he's slumped over worse than before.

As I eat I'm actually supposed to be leading a mealtime discussion, while at the same time reinforcing "appropriate" table manners and behavior and pointing out "inappropriate" manners and behavior. But, perhaps because this is my first day—my first morning—all of that seems hopelessly mundane. So I quietly nibble at my eggs, watching and listening. Five miles from home and I'm on a different planet.

From Grodzienska to Willoweep

In 1922 when he was 25 years old, Benny Horowitz's grandfather, Joseph, rode a train from Danzig to Bremen, steamed over 5,000 miles from Bremen to New York, then rode another train from New York to Atlanta, where his Uncle Zeev and Aunt Ruth were happily waiting at the train station to welcome him to his new home.

Six months earlier, Zeev Pifflestein, a small, stout, bowling ball of a man who owned a thriving dry goods business in Atlanta, had sent a letter to Joseph, his nephew in Poland whom he had not seen in seventeen years, explaining that he would soon be expanding his business and needing some dependable and trustworthy help. "I'd of course prefer to work with family," he'd written to Joseph. "So this golden opportunity I offer you is to my advantage as well as yours. In truth I am more of a businessman than an altruist, and it is as a businessman that I assure you, together we would prosper.

"I will tell you my young nephew; this America is a good country—a great country—which offers hope to our people, for here we are free from persecution. Tell me you are interested in this opportunity and I shall straightaway send you your fare."

Growing up in the small Polish village of Grodzienska, Joseph had been learning the skills of carpentry from his father, Isaac, a master craftsman who built everything from violins to rocking chairs, and, in his spare time, painted church steeples and cupolas for the Catholics, whom he regarded as his good friends. In 1909, when he was 12 years old, Joseph had huddled beside his father, his mother, his grandmother, and his two older sisters, watching in terror and outrage from behind the curtains, while his father's workshop was totally destroyed during a pogrom, the first in Grodzienska in nearly twenty-five years. Later that night, as he helped his father salvage what he could from the smouldering rubble, young Joseph vowed that he would one day live in America, where people like his Uncle Zeev and Aunt Ruth could live freely no matter what their beliefs.

"Ah, my Joey," his father had lamented, ponderously shaking his head. "Wherever you go you will find men who behave like apes. I can assure you my son, your America will be no different. You will find many good men there, just as you do here. Jews as well as non-Jews. And yet you will *never* escape the apes."

But whatever his father thought, Joseph knew that in America there were no pogroms. And so, when twelve years later he received the letter of invitation from his Uncle Zeev, he was ebulliently certain that his wildest dream had at last come true.

Joseph knew little English when he arrived. But living with Zeev and Ruth, who did not permit him to speak anything *but* English, he was fluent enough after only four months to converse adequately with the customers in his Uncle's dry goods store. And three years later, by the time he'd moved to Willoweep to open up and run an offshoot of the Atlanta store, he was very nearly as fluent in English as in Polish.

Willoweep was a small town, southeast of Atlanta, populated, for the most part, by hardworking farmers with poor land and little money. Though Joseph was the only Jew in town, he was well-liked by the townspeople. He had, as his uncle had happily discovered, a terrific knack for salesmanship, with his big, crooked smile, bellowing voice, and animated black eyes. (Everyone in Willoweep even tolerated his beard, which his uncle and aunt had begged him to shave off, from the day he arrived.

"In America men do not wear beards," Zeev had tried to explain.

"You are hairy as an ape," his aunt teased.

But Joseph did not believe his beard would offend anyone. And he felt that living in a new country was enough of a strain on his nerves. It would be awhile before he was ready to live with a new face. "I look better this way," he told Zeev and Ruth. "Believe me. The beard brings my nose closer to my face.")

Like a bartender, Joseph listened to and commiserated with his customers. He laughed at their jokes and grew misty-eyed over their misfortunes. He even allowed them to buy, when he could, on credit; without interest.

So much energy did Joseph put into making his dry goods business successful, that he had little time to ponder his loneliness. Except late at night. After he'd swept down the aisles of calico, gingham, tafetta and madras, dusted the shelves of pins, needles, pots, pans, thimbles and scissors, counted the cash and trudged upstairs to fall, exhausted, into bed. It was then that he would stare at the ceiling, fingering his dusty beard, and dream of Grodzienska, where as a boy he'd picked mushrooms in the forest with his older sisters and his grandmother. Every night the ceiling above Joseph's bed came to life with visions of beautiful young Polish girls, who wore long skirts which caught the wind; carried wicker baskets full of magic, and smelled of mushrooms, rain and forests.

Though his business prospered as time went by, Joseph found himself growing lonelier and unhappier. The more he smiled and joked with his customers, the lonelier he felt. He tried to fill every waking moment with busy, purposeful activity, but was unable to keep his dreams and visions from beckoning to him across the nightscape.

One summer weekend Zeev invited Joseph to Atlanta to share dinner and then accompany him and Ruth to a Workman's Circle rally at which Eugene Debs, who five times had run on the Socialist ticket for President of the United States—once, even, from a prison cell—would be the featured speaker. Grateful, as always, for the chance to spend time with family, and eager to hear such a great and famous speaker as Eugene Debs, Joseph happily accepted the invitation.

While they were eating Ruth's fried chicken that night, before leaving for the rally, Zeev lavished Joseph with praise. "You've exceeded my expectations in every way," he told him. "You've already become a master salesman, and are well on your way to becoming a successful businessman. And yet you do not seem happy. I would offer you another raise, but though I know you would smile and thank me, I think it would make you no happier."

Joseph hung his head. His bushy black beard pressed onto his chest. Beneath the dinner table he was ringing his large hands. It touched him that his uncle could so clearly discern the misery behind his smiles.

"You would like to return to Grodzienska, wouldn't you?" his Aunt Ruth said, blotting her lip with a napkin, then pushing the platter of chicken in front of her husband.

"I'm lonely," Joseph admitted. "I miss my family, my friends. I miss the ways of Poland. I miss the people, the countryside."

Zeev was opening an envelope as he listened. With two fingers he pulled something from the envelope, then pushed it across the table to Joseph, who'd already set his half picked-through plate of fried chicken to the side.

Joseph wiped his greasy fingers on his napkin, then carefully picked up what Zeev had pushed across the table. It was a photograph.

"This girl is the granddaughter of my mother's closest friend," Zeev explained, as Joseph stared disbelievingly at the picture. "She's eighteen years old and earning pennies a day working as a seamstress in Warsaw. She would like to come to America. She even studies at night to learn the English language."

Joseph gulped, and found himself unable to look up from the picture.

"But even if she learns the language," Zeev sighed, crossing his pudgy arms, "how is an eighteen year-old girl to come to a foreign country without a man to provide for her, to care for her, and to teach her the ways of the people? I'll tell you something, Joseph. She can't. She needs a husband."

Joseph was not certain he could believe his ears. But he had no doubts about what was before his eyes. He was certain the young woman in the photograph was the most beautiful human being he'd ever seen in his life.

Joseph brought the photograph with him to the Workman's Circle rally, held it carefully in his palm, as if the picture itself was the most precious and priceless thing in the world, and stared at it while Eugene Debs spoke masterfully, and the audience, including Zeev and Ruth, roared and stamped their approval. Every inspiring phrase that urged the continuation of the struggle to achieve the freedom and brotherhood of man, which Joseph had originally come to America to find, passed by Joseph without even distracting him. Brotherhood had simply been wiped from his mind's agenda, and he'd have gladly traded his freedom for an eternity of pogroms if he could be sure it would help him win the hand and heart of his lovely Polish picture girl.

Late that night, sitting wide awake in the guest bed of his Uncle's South Atlanta home, Joseph composed a letter to Rachel Orzech, while frequently glancing at her picture, propped against the brass base of the bedside lamp.

> "I am a lonely man," he wrote. "But I sincerely believe myself to be a good man, and am certain I would make a good husband. I work very hard and save almost all of what I earn. I am by no means rich, but my Uncle Zeev tells me that if I have a son, I will be able to send him to college so that *he* may one day be wealthy. I am honest, although at work I sometimes smile when I do not feel like smiling. I do not drink, though that is not out of religious conviction, as I am not a religious man. There is no synagogue where I live. In fact I am the only Jew in Willoweep. Even so, I am treated with respect, though I am sometimes teased about my beard, because American men do not wear beards. (To me, they look like women with their faces so smooth and shiny.) But since you are from Poland, as I am, I'm sure you will not think my beard is unusual or funny.

"I am a smart man, I think, or at least clever enough to be a successful businessman, though I am not an educated man.

"I hope you will not too harshly judge the photograph I have sent. Many times I have been told that I have a very nice and happy smile, though of course I did not smile when the photograph was taken.

"You look very very beautiful in your photograph, though of course you are not smiling either. I am sure *you* have a nice smile.

"I will send you the steamship and train fare if you tell me you would like to come see what I am like and what America is like. From what I have seen, America is not nearly so beautiful as Poland. But our people are free to live and work here without being persecuted for what we are or for what we believe. This is why I came to America to work for my Uncle Zeev, and this is why I would like to stay here, although often my heart tells me to go home to Poland.

"I hope that I will hear from you soon and that I will then be able to send you the train and steamship fare to help bring you over to see America and also myself. And of course if you are not pleased with one or the other of us after you arrive, I will give you the train and steamship fare to return to Poland, and help you in any other way I am able to.

       Hopefully yours,
       Joseph Horowitz"

While Rachel Orzech found herself wincing slightly at Joseph's photograph (for he looked too old to her; too big and too hairy), she was, at the same time, thrilled by the prospect of such a wondrous adventure and such a rare opportunity, and feared that if she chose not to go *now*, she would likely not go *ever*. And the idea that it would be an open-ended trial visit rather than an intractable, irrevocable acceptance of a new life, made her decision even easier.

Eight months later, in the early winter of 1927, Joseph Horowitz stood under the cover of his black umbrella at the Atlanta train station, waiting anxiously, along with his

Uncle Joseph and Aunt Ruth (who were keeping warm and dry where they waited with everyone else, *inside* the station), for the arrival of the woman whom he hoped would bridge the enormous chasm that so utterly separated his happy dream world from his painfully lonely real world.

A soft chill winter Atlanta drizzle whispered upon Joseph's umbrella like muffled applause. He wore a heavy gray trenchcoat and a new gray wool hat, and bounced on the balls of his feet to keep from feeling so stiff and awkward. He felt stiff and awkward anyway, as if his clothes all fit too tightly. "As soon as she sees me," he thought with a miserable shiver, "she will hop right back onto the train." He combed his fingers through his damp black beard and stared catatonically down the tracks.

By the time the headlight of the train appeared through the haze of drizzle like a twinkling star, Joseph's stomach was performing an upsetting combination of acrobatics and isometrics, fluttering and then clenching, dancing then tightening. He had to pee, but ignored the urge as he hurried back to the train station to babble to his uncle and aunt, "She's here. In a minute. My God. What if from her first glance she doesn't want me?"

Ruth took his free hand and squeezed it. She found it to be startlingly cold, and rubbed it briskly between her palms. "And do you suppose she will not be just as worried about what you are going to think of *her*? It will be a week, maybe a month, before either of you looks at the other and truly sees."

Joseph hardly heard her. "Would it be very improper to smile?" he asked, glancing back over his shoulder as he straightened his trenchcoat collar.

"For God's sake Joseph," Zeev said. "This is America. You are a free man. You want to smile? Smile."

Yes, I think I will smile, Joseph thought, knowing that Rachel had never seen his smile, and that although it might not be quite the proper thing to do, she would likely have a much better first impression of him if he *was* smiling. He shook his arms and bounced, again, on the balls of his feet to loosen up.

The moment Rachel Orzech stepped off the train in her long dark skirt, and dark waistcoat over a white ruffled blouse, Joseph knew it was her and instantly stiffened. Zeev and Ruth helped him along, one at each of his elbows. Ruth had the uncomfortable feeling that she and her husband were leading their nephew to his execution.

As they approached, Joseph quickly forgot about his smile plans. He bowed his head, then did not—*could* not— lift it, even when he stood before her. And though he noticed right away that she carried a black suitcase instead of a wicker basket full of magic, Joseph imagined that she *did* smell of mushrooms, rain and forests. He mumbled an unintelligible greeting as Zeev and Ruth introduced themselves, welcoming Rachel with hugs, which caused Joseph to feel even less confident since he was now the only one who hadn't hugged or received a hug.

When at last he forced himself to lift his heavy head and roll back his eyelids, Joseph saw, in a glance, that Rachel was more beautiful than he could have imagined. Her skin glistened healthfully in the rain. And though there was not one feature of her face that could have been called extraordinary in and of itself, her face taken as a whole was somehow far far greater than the sum of its features. It seemed to Joseph that her face was radiant. Angelic even. She was much too beautiful, he was certain, for a man so plain and simple as himself.

He stared back at his feet, then, like a zombie, spoke, scarcely moving his lips. "You are even more beautiful than in the photograph," he said solemnly. "I did not think that was possible."

Rachel stepped closer, tilting her head and scrutinizing him for a long moment. "You wrote to me that you have a very nice smile," she said. "But it is difficult now for me to tell."

Slowly, stiffly, Joseph raised his head. His smile started at the corner of his mouth with a twitch of his lips, then spread across his bearded face in crooked jerks, like a crack spreading across a dam. And when he saw in Rachel's eyes that she too was smiling, his lips parted and his teeth appeared in all their uneven splendor.

"You too are more beautiful than in the photograph," she said.

Three weeks later the wedding date was set. And two months after that, on the first day of Spring, they were married.

The First Weekend, Continued: A Flood in the ARC and Melaleuca-Scent In The Air

By dinnertime my fears have left me, most likely because I'm staying so insanely busy that I have no time for my fears. After breakfast I have to coordinate, supervise and take program data on the kitchen clean-up; no small accomplishment with Moby meticulously scrubbing every speck off every dish, pan, pot and utensil, before handing them over to Elisha, who quickly rinses them, stacks them in the dishdrain, and waits, hands on her wide hips, her bird eyes rolling with impatience, while Moby scrubs the next dish, pan, pot or utensil, and I cue him to speed it up, then praise him for his efforts. After the dishwashing and kitchen clean-up I run Emmy's dining table clean-up program, watching as she speeds through it so quickly that all she does is *spread* the yolk and toast crumbs so that I constantly have to cue her to slow down and go back over the spot she just missed, while she babbles and slaps furiously at her hip, and I praise her for listening to my instructions.

By the time she's finished with the table and chairs I'm exhausted. But I've only just begun. Every half hour I'm scheduled to run another program with another resident. Following the breakfast cooking and clean-up programs there are the bedroom cleaning programs, personal self-care programs, lawn and plant-care programs, money skills and budgeting programs, and wedged snugly in the midst of that whirlwind schedule, the lunch and dinner cooking and clean-up programs.

On top of all that I'm constantly cueing, counseling and training each of the residents, handing out medications at breakfast and dinner, and writing down any pertinent information in the Daily Log.

Even if everyone performed every task with skillful efficiency and a devoutly cooperative attitude, I'd be going nuts trying to keep pace with the program schedule. But these people *can't* perform with skillful efficiency, and they aren't exactly gung ho about taking time from their weekends to cooperate with me on some boring program. After all, they have paid their dues during the week. From what Ty has told me, Monday through Friday they're up at 5:00 to start their self-care programs (bed-making, face-washing, shaving, hair-brushing, and teeth-brushing) then gobble down breakfast and rush off to catch the 6:30 bus for WCRC, the West Coconut Beach Rehabilitation Center—or, as the residents all call it, "Rehab"—the sheltered workshop where they all stay busy doing tedious but simple assembly line work from 7:00 to 3:00 before returning to ARC House to shower, relax for maybe an hour, eat dinner, then begin their evening chores and programs; laundry, budgeting, vacuuming, dusting, floor scrubbing, bathroom cleaning, trash emptying, and on and on. If college students stayed that busy they'd all be neurotic geniuses by the time they were graduated. But there's no way to make geniuses out of mentally retarded people, so I guess the state is opting for a population of neurotic dimwits.

Anyway, by the time Saturday rolls around they all just want to sleep late, eat a big breakfast, then get the hell out of the house; get the hell away from me and my ubiquitous authority. And indeed, an important part of my job as weekend Skills Counselor is to *encourage* everyone to get away from ARC House and out into the community where they can mingle and integrate with the "normal" people of West Coconut Beach. (Most of the residents head downtown to eat pizza, go to a movie, play pool or pinball, drink beer, or find some other way to use up their meager allotment—usually four or five dollars—of weekly spending money. The rest of their income, which includes their work salaries as well as a combination of government subsidies, is used to pay for their room and board, and personal necessities—with our prompting they budget for and buy more deodorant, mouthwash, soap, toothpaste, Tampax and aftershave than any group of people I've ever seen; it's as if we're giving them the message that if they look and smell good enough, they might fool the normal people into accepting them—or is saved for a rare larger purchase, like a bicycle or stereo, or for a vacation. The few dollars left over becomes their weekly pittance.) Unfortunately, the other part of my job is to see to it that they're all *here* at the house for their scheduled programs, because as I've already mentioned, the State of Florida requires that each resident receive a minimum of four hours per week of formal personal programming; though Angela Geer, the Director of ARC House and my boss, schedules each resident for *five* hours of formal personal programming per week, because she says she doesn't want to be involved in an operation that gets by with minimums. She's a woman who takes her job seriously; a genuine overachiever.

So all day I'm not only running the programs and taking care of all the other things I've mentioned, but trying to coordinate everyone's movements so that they're all at the right place—here for their programs, or downtown for their dose of weekend mingling—at the right time. I feel more like a field general for the army than a counselor for the mentally handicapped.

It's now 7:30. We've just finished dinner clean-up. I've still got five programs left to run tonight, but I'm not even going to *think* about running them. To hell with Angela Geer and her five hours. I've got my sanity to think about. I'm sure Angela—whom I will apparently be seeing only during our Tuesday staff meetings, because Saturdays and Sundays are her days off—will forgive me. After all, it's my first day on the job.

I head out to the front porch, where I slump exhaustedly onto the green, wood-slatted porch swing, pry off my tennis shoes—toe to heel—and kick them away, then slip off my socks, wriggle my sweaty toes and take a deep breath as I sit back to relax for the first time all day. For awhile I'm content to watch the pink sky turn to gray, and the tall Coconut Beach hotels across Manatee Lake turn to silhouettes. But soon I find myself staring intently at Nadia, who's hunched over a small, round work table, finishing up her latest tree of clay, which she's been working on since breakfast. Throughout the day I've been catching hurried glimpses of her tree at different stages. At this point she's painstakingly working on the branches, her nose maybe an inch from her fingers. It amazes me to see her so skillfully and patiently transforming clay hunks into a tree, when I know that she can't keep her hair combed, read, tell time or even make her bed decently. Earlier in the afternoon I spent nearly thirty frustrating minutes trying to teach her to fold her bedspread over the pillow so that it was neatly tucked in underneath. But all I succeeded at was falling farther behind on my program schedule.

After the bedmaking session she told me she was going downtown for awhile, and so, because I'm always supposed to know where everyone is and when he or she will be back, I asked her what time she planned on returning. She couldn't answer.

"Well it's 2:00 now," I said. "How much time do you want to spend downtown?"

"I don't know," she said, then guessed. "A hour?"

"Good," I said. "An hour. So what time does that mean you'll be back?"

She frowned and stared at her shoes: green tennis shoes.

"Well look at your clock," I suggested, and pointed to the clock on her bedside table. "See, it's just after 2:00 now. You said you'd be gone for an hour. Right? So about what time will it be when the big hand goes around once and the little hand moves up to the next number?"

She stared at her green tennis shoes again, and after a

minute muttered, "I don't know, Mr. Smarty Britches Meanhead. I want to see the Banyan is all." She looked up at me and twisted a few strands of her tangled black hair around her fingers. "You know. That big old Banyan by the library."

"If you leave now, at 2:00," I persisted, in no mood to lose another battle after thirty successless minutes of pillow tucking, "and come back in an hour, the little hand will be on the three. So about what time will it be?"

"You mean it will be 3:00?" she said.

"That's right! Great Nadia. That's great that you didn't give up, and figured it out yourself without me having to tell you."

"Thank you," she said, smiling. "Mr. Excitement."

"So, I'll be seeing you at 3:00," I said. "Right?"

"Right."

She returned at 4:15, then, sitting down to go back to work on her tree, ignored me while I tried to explain how important it is—particularly if you're living with eight other people who are all depending on you—to be on time, or at least reasonably close.

But as I watch her now on the front porch, skillfully looping and smoothing tiny coils of clay into branches, I decide I'm going to take a break and step down from my position of authority so that I can talk to her without worrying about training her. I tell her that her tree is looking great, and ask her what kind it's supposed to be.

"I forget," she says, not looking up. "They got those little yellow brushy things and they peel and they smell. You know. How it smells like something cooking. And how it smells good. Or it smells bad. But really how it smells good."

"A Melaleuca Tree," I guess, mostly because of her description of the "little yellow brushy things" and peeling bark.

"Yes," she says. "A Meluca Tree."

She can't remember or even pronounce the name, but she can build a beautiful replica—minus the leaves and "little yellow brushy things"—from a few hunks of clay.

When I ask her where she learned to build clay trees she

tells me that her mother had a potter's wheel in their garage and used to give her a lump of clay to keep her occupied while she, her mother, made bowls and mugs, vases and plates, cannisters and casserole dishes, on her wheel. Even with her first lump of clay Nadia remembers building a tree. She says no one had to teach her. She simply remembers what a tree looks like, and builds it. "Easy as pie," she tells me. The only help her mother ever had to give her was with the glazing and firing of the trees after Nadia finished building them.

She also tells me her mother died of breast cancer last year. I already knew that (it's the reason she left home and moved into ARC House) but I let her tell me anyway because it seems as though she wants to.

"Your mother must have been proud of you," I say, getting up from the swing to switch on the porch light, then sitting in front of Nadia on the wooden railing, so that I can watch her more closely. "Your trees are fantastic. And I mean that!"

She looks up from her leafless clay Melaleuca and smiles at me. She has small, uneven teeth, three or four of which overlap in the front like a fanned-out poker hand. Her eyes are dark—nearly as dark as her tangled hair. Suddenly I'm aware that she's scrutinizing *my* face as closely as I'm scrutinizing hers, and that those dark eyes are focusing at *the center* of my face, just below my eyes. She's still smiling—mostly with her eyes—as she suddenly, happily, pipes out, "Mr. Nose."

My hair (of which there won't be much left in ten years) and my nose are the only two facial features I inherited from my father. His two worst features and he sticks *me* with them. Usually I'm self-conscious as hell about my nose and its size, but she says "Mr. Nose" with such fondness and such delight—drawing out the o and the z sounds far longer than necessary—that for a few moments I feel utterly confused. I'm so accustomed to having negative feelings about my nose—I'd probably cut the damned thing off if its functions weren't so vital—that I'm not sure what to make out of what might be a compliment.

"Mr. Nose? Well I guess that's better than Mr. Meanhead," I finally mumble, realizing as I mumble it that I feel slightly unnerved by her wide dark eyes; the same way I feel when a three year-old looks at me as if she could stare right through to my essence. I quickly turn my head to gaze once again at the silhouetted hotels across the lake, but without seeing them now. This is great. A retarded girl who can't tell time, make a bed, or keep her hair brushed, calls me "Mr. Nose," and I'm suddenly too flustered to look at her. Maybe I should be *living* here instead of working here. Clearing my throat, I stand and nod, very business-like and in control, then head for the door, leaving Nadia with her clay.

Inside, Lucius, Emmy and Lythia are watching TV; a cop program of some kind. Lucius is in a chair, rocking as he watches, though the chair he sits in is not a rocker. I say nothing to him. Training hours are over as far as I'm concerned. Emmy is on the couch, giving an unintelligible running commentary on everything the TV characters say. "Oh really?" she suddenly says very clearly, slapping her hip and leaning forward to stare hard at the TV. "Oh *is* it? Hmmm then. O*kay* then. Ha ha ha ha ha. Oh *did* she? Hmmm then with the rights."

And Lythia is beside Emmy, bobbing and ducking as fluidly as if she were performing an underwater ballet. I pat Lythia's shoulder as I pass, and by the time the pat registers and she looks up, I'm already stepping out of the living room and into the kitchen. Seems as though she's always at least ten or fifteen seconds behind the rest of the world, as if permanently trapped in the wake of the present.

Amar, or Hot Dog, as I've been calling him, is out at a movie with Elisha. They've apparently been going steady for almost three months. He's already given her a ring, which he showed me at dinner by reaching for, then lifting her hand, as if he were passing the biscuits. "We're both engaged to be married," he told me. "To each other. And this here is the proof and the pudding."

It's not a cheap ring as I would have expected, but a tastefully simple silver band with a small diamond which, though I never disputed or even questioned it, he swore up and down—even crossed his heart and hoped to die—was genuine. After dinner he pulled me to the side and whispered, "Hey. You think I'm trying to be able to put all my fish in one basket?"

I keep thinking the law of averages is going to catch up with him and he'll get at least *one* of his old sayings right. But it hasn't happened yet. At least not today.

I decide to visit Billy in his room. He's lying on his bed, staring at the ceiling and listening to an Elvis Presley Christmas album (two weeks before the fourth of July). His legs are so long that his ankles hang over the edge of the footboard.

"Hey ya Buddy," he says, turning to smile when he sees me. "How are ya Benny? How are ya?"

"Not bad," I tell him. "How about you? What are you up to tonight?"

"I'm listening to Elvis, I am. Listening to Elvis." He suddenly scowls. "And I'm still waiting for that goddamned stupid Moby Cochrane to get out of the shower. Out of the shower. Waiting for him to get out of the shower."

I've known people who get stuck on the first letter of a word, or even the first syllable, repeating the sound four or five times before they can go on. I've even heard of people who repeat entire words over again. But Billy repeats entire sentences. It's less of a stutter or stammer than it is a style of speaking.

"He's been in there an hour, he has. Been in there a whole goddamned stupid hour."

I remember reading in the Daily Log that the shower is draining slowly and that for the time being everyone is supposed to be strictly limited to five minutes, *particularly* Moby Cochrane, who apparently has a tendency to take long showers if he isn't cued to get out. (If he scrubs his body as meticulously as he scrubbed the dinner dishes, he'll be in the shower for a week.) I know he hasn't been in there for an hour, as Billy is suggesting, because I was in the bathroom myself maybe half an hour ago and he wasn't in there then. But for all I know he *has* been in there ever since. I ask Billy what he can do about Moby hogging the shower.

"I can't do a thing, Benny," he says, swinging his long legs over the bedside and sitting. "Not a thing. Not a thing. He has the goddamned stupid door locked, he does. Has it locked. Has it locked."

I figure I'd better check this out myself and quickly head from Billy's room, through the kitchen and down the hall to the bathroom. There's a wide tongue of water creeping under the door and steadily spreading. He *has* been in there a long time. Attempting to avoid the spreading puddle, I stand to one side of the door, lean, reach, and try the knob. It doesn't turn, so I pound at the door, shouting Moby's name. No answer. Just the roar of the shower. And it *is* a roar; sounds like Niagra falls in there. He must have it turned up full blast.

I shout for Billy to bring some towels, and he's instantly out of his room and hustling about, looking lost and confused. Emmy has come streaking in from the living room to watch and babble.

"Hey Emmy! Could you give Billy some help looking for towels. We're about to be flooded out of the house."

"Oh *are* we?" she says. "Hmmm then. O*kay* then about those towels." And she's quickly off helping Billy hunt down towels.

No longer worried about keeping my feet dry, I move in front of the door, pound hard, and shout Moby's name again. Still no answer. He might have slipped, hit his head and fallen face down. He could drown in an inch of water that way. I can't believe it. My first night on the job and I'm going to have to kick down a door. The way they do in the movies.

Billy's shouting to me that he can't find any stupid towels because they're all locked in the bathroom with that goddamned stupid Moby Cochrane. But the flood is the last thing I'm worried about now. I take a step back from the door and kick at it with the sole of my tennis shoe. There's a dull sounding thud, but nothing more. The door doesn't give an inch.

Emmy is at the end of the hallway now with an armful of towels she found in the ladies bathroom, upstairs, and Lucius Moon is right behind her, rocking from foot to foot and grinning, his fingers interlocked at his chest. For him this is better than "Adam 12," or whatever the hell cop show he was watching on TV.

I step back again, take a deep breath and kick as hard as I can. I kick *so* hard this time that as soon as my right foot makes contact with the door my left foot slips in the water and I'm instantly flat on my back, my legs in the air, like a dog playing dead. I scramble to my feet, swearing. The tip of my tailbone feels cracked, and my shirt and pants are sopping wet. Lucius has rushed forward to help me, and Emmy is babbling into her stack of towels. Sounds as if she's speaking in tongues.

I'm thinking about going outside and breaking in through the bathroom window—I've got to get in there somehow, and fast—when the shower abruptly shuts off. Silence.

We all freeze and look at one another. Even Lythia is there now, bobbing at the end of the hallway like a buoy in the waves. She probably just noticed that Lucius and Emmy were no longer watching television with her.

"Moby?" I say tentatively. No answer. So I shout his name and pound at the door. Only then do I hear his footsteps slapping through the water toward the door. "Yes?" he says. "Wait a minute. Who's there?" I hear the lock turning and then footsteps are slapping back through the water, receding. When I step in, Moby is standing in front of the sink, looking into the mirror, a yellow towel wrapped around his waist and his hands at his ears. He's fitting both of his hearing aids back in place, and adjusting the volume. Of course he couldn't hear me shouting or pounding. He's practically deaf without his hearing aids, even when the shower *isn't* roaring. He turns calmly to look at me. His head appears to be even rounder now with his hair wet and slicked down. "I know," he says, with an annoyed twang to his voice. "I'll do the mop on it."

"It's not just the water I'm worried about," I say, loudly enough for him to hear me whether his hearing aids are adjusted or not. "I thought you'd drowned in there. I almost broke the door down."

"No," he says. "I not drownded."

I take a deep breath, count to five, and tell myself I should be relieved. "I can see that you didn't drown," I say. "And I'm glad. But I'm wondering what you think we can do to keep this from happening again."

"He has to clean up the water," Billy advises, nudging up to me now in the doorway. "Has to clean it up, he does. Has to clean it all up."

"This is not none of your business, Billy Loper," Moby says.

"Yeah, and you're a goddamned stupid asshole. A stupid asshole. A stupid asshole."

Emmy drops her load of towels, claps her hands over her ears, and shaking her head violently, shrieks, "Make him *stop* it with those *words*. I don't want to *hear* him with those *words*." She shuts her eyes tightly so that her lids turn to wrinkles.

"Ooooh," Lucius says, bending to rub the fronts of his thighs, then straightening up, trying to hide his grin. He bends and straightens again. A shudder ripples through his body and out to his fingertips. I'm glad *someone* is enjoying all this.

I ask everyone to go back to what he was doing. Billy and Lucius respond right away, but Lythia keeps bobbing in place because my request hasn't yet registered with her, and Emmy can't see or hear me because her eyes are shut and her ears are covered. I tap her shoulder and she opens her eyes, then cautiously pulls her hands from her ears.

"What do you need to do, Emmy?" I cue her.

"Well," she snaps shrilly, with a hard shake of her head. "I didn't *like* what he said." When she speaks she puts a strong emphasis on every third or fourth word. It would sound almost musical if her voice wasn't so shrill and grating.

"Why don't you tell him you don't appreciate his swearing. That might work better than covering your ears, shutting your eyes, and screaming. Just be sure to tell him in a nice way. So he'll listen."

"Hmmm then," she says, nodding. "O*kay* then." She slaps her hip as if to signal that she means business, then makes a determined beeline for Billy's bedroom, nearly knocking into Lythia, who's still at the end of the hallway, bobbing and ducking.

I turn back to speak with Moby, reminding him of the five minute limit on showers, then explaining how and why it's against the rules to lock the bathroom door. Throughout my speech, as he dries himself with his big yellow towel, then dresses in his knee length patch-madras shorts and pink golf shirt, he looks me in the eye, listening attentively to all I have to tell him. When I'm through with my lecture he carefully says, "Okay. I understand what you mean. About the showers. And about locking up the door and all that." Then he snatches the mop from the corner and diligently attacks the flood while I pick up the load of towels Emmy dropped on the floor, and set them on the kitchen table.

To show Moby I appreciate his positive, cooperative attitude, I tell him that I know just how he feels about locking the bathroom door; that I like my privacy too, and that maybe we could even rig up a sign system—green on one side and red on the other—and hang it from the bathroom doorknob (the way you can hang a "Do Not Disturb" sign from a hotel room doorknob) so that everyone will know when the bathroom is being used, without even having to knock.

"I would like that," he says, swishing the mop in front of my feet, sending a small ripple of water into the toes of my already soaked tennis shoes. "It would be nicer that way. Thank you, Benny."

Stepping back, out of the way of his mop, I say, "Great. I'll write up the idea in the Log and we'll see what the rest of the staff think about it. I can't see why they'd object."

I head back through the hallway, and am about to sit at my desk and begin writing up the shower incident, along with my idea about the "stop-go" doorknob sign, when I notice Emmy standing frozen in the doorway between the kitchen and living room. Her hands are covering her mouth, the base of her palms pressed together at the center of her lips and her fingers curling across her cheeks so that her middle fingertips are plugging her ears. Each of her arms forms a V around each of her mammoth breasts, framing them tightly, pushing them to the fore. She looks like a wrestler with simultaneous headlocks on twin opponents. Her palms are pressed so tightly to her mouth that her arms tremble slightly from the strain, and her breasts vibrate sympathetically in the cradles of her elbow crooks. Her eyes are shut into wrinkles.

"What's the problem, Emmy?" I ask, dropping my pen, pushing back my desk chair, then standing and cautiously approaching her. She's so wound up it looks as if she might explode at any moment. If she does, I don't want to be in the way. I stop a few feet from her and again ask, "What is it Emmy? What are you doing? You look pretty upset there."

I'm not sure she's hearing me with her fingertips plugging her ears, so I very slowly extend my arm and tap her shoulder as gently as I can. Immediately she shrieks through her palms, "I *am* upset," then pulls one hand away from her mouth to slap her hip and mutter, "Him? Oh *him*!"

"Billy?" I guess.

And she nods—one fiercely emphatic nod—into her remaining hand. "Yes *him*! *He* said those words to *me*. and *I* don't *like* it!"

"Well maybe we'd better go talk to him together," I suggest.

"Oh *should* we?" she says. "Hmmm then. Hmmm. O*kay* then."

We enter Billy's room together. He doesn't see us. He's stretched out on his bed again—on his stomach this time, his face in his pillow—still listening to the same side of the Elvis Presley album. I walk over to the stereo and turn it down. Right away he looks up from his pillow. "Oh hi ya Benny," he says cheerfully. You'd think he hadn't seen me in a month. "How are ya Buddy? How are ya?"

"I'm fine, Billy. But Emmy here isn't doing so well. You got any ideas why?"

"Oh I know, Benny," he says, hanging his head. "I know, Old Buddy. I know." He looks up at her with sad-eyed empathy. "I called her a goddamned stupid asshole, I did. A stupid asshole. A stupid asshole."

Emmy takes off, shrieking, her hands slapped over her ears. I don't bother to follow.

"Jesus Billy," I say. "Why did you do that? You knew it would upset her!"

"I know that, Benny. I know that Old Buddy. But she *is* a goddamned stupid asshole, she is. A stupid asshole. A stupid asshole."

"No. She's not."

"She is too, Benny. Is too." He turns his head back to the pillow and is suddenly sobbing. "They're *all* goddamned stupid assholes, every one of 'em. Every one."

I move to the side of his bed and pat his back. He turns over, lurches toward me with those long gaspump hose arms of his, then grabbing my shoulders, pulls himself to a sitting position and sobs into my chest, soaking the front of my shirt so that I'm wet all over now—shoes, back *and* front. After a minute his sobs have diminished enough for him to speak. "I'm sorry Old Buddy," he says. "I'm sorry, I am. I'm sorry."

"*I* know that Billy. But who's the one who really needs to hear that from you?"

"I know," he says. "I'll go tell her, I will. I'll go tell her right now. Tell her right now." And wiping his dripping nose on his shirt sleeve, he's up on his feet and moving to the door, leaving me wet and alone with Elvis, who's crooning about a "Silent Night."

The rest of the evening I spend writing down information and questions in the daily log, giving out the bedtime medications (Lythia, Lucius, Emmy and Elisha all take medications; Lythia to prevent seizures, Elisha to prevent pregnancy, Lucius to increase his gastro-intestinal absorption, and Emmy to alleviate anxiety), dealing with a few minor crises (a dispute over which television program to watch, and an accident with Lythia falling down the stairs and twisting her ankle) and struggling to keep my eyes open until midnight, which is when I'm required to take an official headcount, lock all the doors, and turn out the lights. The only distasteful part of the evening is going over the self-care checklist with the residents before they go to bed, asking them, one by one, if they've straightened their bedrooms, taken their showers, used deodorant, put on clean nightclothes, combed their hair, and brushed their teeth. I'm actually supposed to ask them to open their mouths wide and smile for me so that I can check to see if their teeth have been adequately cleaned. Looking into their mouths that way I feel like a horse inspector or a slave trader, and have a strong urge to crack a few jokes so that I won't feel like such a villain. But I'm a lousy joke-teller, and can never remember any good ones anyway. Fortunately there's not a peep of protest at my inspecting. Maybe they're all just grateful I don't have to sniff their underarms to check for "inappropriate" body odor.

I get goodnight hugs from Billy and Elisha. Amar shakes my hand, looks me in the eye, and warns me not to let the sandman bite. Lucius Moon grins slyly, rocking from foot to foot, his fingers interlocked and twitching at his chest. Emmy babbles unintelligibly before and after her goodnight. Moby bows, apologizing again for his bathroom flood. And Lythia dances in place, taking half a minute and at least a thimbleful of drool to say, "Sweet dreams, Benny." She smiles, then grimaces mysteriously—possibly because her twisted ankle is bothering her—before finally heading upstairs, pulling herself up by the bannister, teetering precariously at each step. I'm not yet sure if this is going to be the stuff of "sweet dreams," or nightmares. But I'll find out soon enough.

Nadia is the only one I miss saying goodnight to, and the only one I miss going over the checklist with, because she's gone to bed without letting me know. When I last saw her on the front porch she had wet clay streaked all through that long, black hair of hers. It's going to be a real mess in the morning if she forgot to wash and brush it. But when I go upstairs to check on her, the light's already out and she's snoring away, so I leave her to her dreams. I'll just cue her to wash her hair tomorrow morning, which will hopefully take care of the clay and tangles.

With everyone in bed now I lock the doors, turn out the lights, and curl up on the couch. I'd hoped to have a relaxing evening, but even without running those five scheduled programs I managed to stay busy right up until midnight. But I'll make up for it now. I'm so exhausted I'm sure I'll be asleep before I've taken five breaths.

But I'm not.

And I'm not asleep after five *minutes*.

Or ten.

Or forty.

If ever in my life I've been deserving of sleep, it's now. But although my body is relaxed—I've already tried the old routine of relaxing each body part from the toes on up to the head—my brain is still buzzing away.

At last I resort to counting sheep. It's never worked for me before, and after ten minutes I realize it's not going to work for me now. After counting 1100 miserable sheep my head begins to throb, so I quit counting. But the sheep, counted or not, continue to defiantly hop the lingering fence-image in my mind until I open my eyes. I lie there for a minute, my head still throbbing, then push myself up from the couch and stumble my way miserably through the dark and into the kitchen, where I unlock the medicine cabinet, grab a couple of aspirin, pop them in my mouth and chew them up. (My father would be appalled. He's convinced that anyone who relies on aspirin to relieve headaches is a pill junkie, and at high risk for a bloody or cancerous stomach.) I have to chew because I've never been able to swallow a pill whole. Some people never learn to whistle, click their fingers, or blow a bubble-gum bubble. I never learned to swallow a pill. But I don't mind. Chewing isn't half as horrible as most people seem to think.

After washing down all the aspirin grit left on my teeth and tongue, I head back to the couch and sit for a minute, trying to decide whether or not to switch on the television. Usually I hate television. But I'd rather watch an old movie—even a rotten old movie—than sheep leaping, pounding, like woolly white hammers, through my mind.

I switch on the TV and turn the volume way down so that I won't wake anyone. I'm in luck. Late night Championship Wrestling is on. Just what I need. A few laughs.

And I won't have to strain to listen because it's just as absurd without sound as with. I turn the volume down all the way and hurry back to the couch. I've timed it perfectly. It's the beginning of a match. Within half a second I know who the bad guy is and who the good guy is. Which is why this idiotic sport is so popular. It's as black and white as Cowboys v. Indians, Americans vs. the Commies, or Luke Skywalker vs. The Evil Empire. In one corner is a young, handsome, blonde-headed guy with a chin that looks as though it's been chiseled out of stone, and a sleekly muscular body. A flock of his fans are pushing up to the ropes as he signs autographs for them. In the other corner is a great hulk of a man, with black boots, black tights, a shaved head, and a monocle pressed in one eye. The whole bit. He's even goose-stepping back and forth, giving heil Hitler salutes to the crowd, many of whom are actually screaming and shaking their fists with genuine anger. Maybe even hatred. It's unbelievable. One old lady has to be escorted back to her seat by a ringside cop.

The wrestlers have just begun to grapple when I hear a door slamming upstairs. At first I figure it's the ladies bathroom door. But then I hear footfalls on the back stairway. No one's supposed to be out of the house past midnight and I'm sure every resident knows it. But is *is* hot in here—there's a fan in each bedroom, but for most South Floridians, for most Americans, that doesn't seem to be enough—so I figure it's probably just another insomniac stepping out for a breath of fresh air. A reasonable idea, even if it *is* against the house rules. But a minute later I decide to investigate anyway, just so I know who it is. Hell, if she's wide enough awake, and if it's any of the ladies other than Emmy, I'll be tempted to invite her down to watch the wrestling match with me. Maybe pop up a batch of popcorn and douse it with butter. Screw this insomnia. It takes more energy to fight it than to ride with it.

As I hop up from the couch, the Nazi has the hero helplessly tied up in the ring ropes, and is grinning evilly, brandishing his great fist, threatening to use it on the hero's handsome face, while the fans come to their feet, booing. I don't want to miss too much of this, so I hustle out the back door and around to where the fire escape stairway leads down. But nobody's on the stairs now. Must have been a mighty quick breath of fresh air. I skip up the steps to check the door and make sure it's been re-locked. I'm almost to the top when, looking off to the left, I see Nadia heading along the lakefront sidewalk, already two or three blocks away. It's dark out—except for the streetlights—she's nearly a football field away, and I'm only seeing her from the back; but there's something so distinctively unique about each of the residents that it would be impossible to mistake one for the other, or for anyone else, at almost *any* distance. I cup my hands around my mouth and call out her name as loudly as I dare. (It's got to be after 1:00, and I don't want to be causing any trouble with the neighbors my first night on the job.) But of course she can't hear me. I could probably chase her down in a couple of minutes if she kept to the sidewalk, but I'm not supposed to leave the house when there are any residents inside unless another staff person is there to cover for me. If anything happened while I was gone, ARC House—and my ass—would be liable.

I sit on the steps, trying to figure out what to do. I could call my boss, Angela Geer, but I hate to wake her at 1:00 in the morning for something like this. Maybe Nadia always takes late night walks.

Still sitting, I watch until she crosses the street just past Manatee Lake Public Park, and disappears into the darkness; then I stand and head slowly down the fire escape. Back inside I switch off Championship Wrestling. You've got to be in the right frame of mind for that sort of thing. I stretch out on the couch and try to relax, taking some long, deep breaths. Where the hell could she be going? Wherever it is, if she's not back in half an hour I'll call Angela. No use taking any chances. Meanwhile I'll let my body rest. I readjust my head in the crook of the couch arm, take another deep breath and shut my eyes.

When I blink them open again the sun is pouring through the front window. For a few seconds I'm disoriented, then sit bolt upright, and am on my feet and dashing up the stairs, three at a time. I push open Nadia and

Lythia's bedroom door without bothering to knock, and peek in. They're both in bed, asleep. Nadia's black hair is a tangled mess, but a comforting sight. I back out and shut the door so that my winded huffing won't wake them.

After gobbling down in five minutes the Sunday breakfast of french toast and sporadic egg shell bits which took Billy and me a painstaking hour and a half to prepare, Amar, Elisha, Emmy, Moby and Lythia all get ready for a 10:00 church service they've decided to attend. Nadia and Lucius show no interest in church-going, though Lucius looks defensive—as though he's afraid he's going to be yelled at or hit if he says no—when Amar asks him if he'd like to go along with them.

"Hey, well, to each his own," Amar says when he sees that Lucius is looking anxious. He gives him a friendly pat on the back, from which Lucius recoils in apparent fear.

Amar wants to go to St. Paul's, but the other five are determined to go to Lakefront Presbyterian, the church nearest to ARC House. After five minutes of haggling with them, attempting to convince them that St. Paul's is closer to God because "it's got all kinds of monsignors and bishops and candles," Amar finally gives an elaborate sigh, shrugs his narrow shoulders, and turning to me, says, "I'll try to say this: if you can't beat 'em, lick 'em."

I watch from the front porch, shading my eyes from the reflection of the sun off the lake, while Amar, Elisha, Emmy, Lythia and Billy cross the street, then parade down the lakefront sidewalk, with Moby right behind them, leisurely peddling his blue adult-sized tricycle. Lythia leads the way because she can't vary the speed of her semi-controlled fall. She runs for a short distance, all her weight tilted forward, then brakes with great difficulty, and bobs in place until the others have almost caught up with her. Then she leans forward again and is suddenly off and running. It's got to be a maddeningly frustrating way of getting from one place to another, but it's the only way—short of a wheelchair—she's got, and she seems not to mind.

Emmy is next in line, walking alone, her lips constantly moving as she converses with herself in babbles only she can understand. Her prodigious breasts bounce non-synchronously with every step, and occasionally she slaps her hip, as if spurring herself onward, like a jockey slapping the flank of her horse.

Amar and Elisha follow behind Emmy, holding hands, while Billy, apparently unsatisfied being a head taller than everyone else, walks beside them atop the lake wall, the tall, upper half of his body tilted forward like the neck of a giraffe. It makes me nervous to see him walking on the wall. But it is wide and smooth, and even if he *did* fall into the water he'd probably be far too tall to drown. Christ, if he ever stood up ramrod straight I'd bet he could walk right out to the center of Manatee Lake without ever getting his chin wet.

Parading down the street, with Moby riding his tricycle at the rear, they give off such a unique and powerful group energy that it wouldn't surprise me to see the palm fronds swish back, the coconuts rattle and the lake kick up into waves as they pass.

Because all but two of the residents have gone to church, I happily take another break from the program schedule, and relax with Nadia and Lucius on the front porch. Nadia is hunched contentedly over her Melaleuca Tree, which is partially concealed by her curtain of long black hair—while Lucius and I sit together on the green wooden porch swing. I have no more to say to Lucius than he has to say to me, but it's not a big deal. We're soon having a hell of a time, swinging back and forth as far and as high as we can without cracking into the picture window behind us, while listening to the intricately repeated rhythms of the squeaking swing chains, and watching and waving to the churchgoers walking past, and the old Black fishermen heading to and from the Manatee Lake Bridge in their suspender-armed white undershirts, buckets in one hand and poles over their shoulders.

Instead of pushing off with his feet and legs, as most people do, Lucius swings by pulling forward with his head and neck. Every few minutes an excited shiver works its way through his body and out to his fingertips. He has rosier cheeks and brighter eyes, right now, than Santa Claus.

But my stomach is feeling a bit queasy from all the swinging, so I let the soles of my tennis shoes drag across the porch to slow us. Lucius understands what I want and doesn't resist. As we're slowing I look over at Nadia, who's hunched over her round work table, her black hair dangling over and half-veiling her work. She took her shower this morning and combed her hair, but it's already tangled and streaked at the ends with wet clay.

When the swing has slowed to the point where the chains are barely squeaking, I ask Nadia if she slept well last night. When she says yes—not for a moment looking up from her tree—I act surprised and tell her she looks tired. She stiffens slightly at my suggestion, but goes on with her work. It's the first hint I've given that I know she left the house last night.

"I'll tell you what, Nadia," I say. "You look so tired that if I didn't know you better I'd think you were out catting around all night. Are you sure you slept well?"

Lucius delightedly rubs the tops of his thighs, his eyes widening until they're bugging out, then says, "Ooh wow."

Nadia smiles at her Melaleuca Tree. "I slept fine thank you," she says, then turning from the tree to aim her smile at me, adds, "Mr. Curious Beeswax. That Killed The Cat." She suspects something is up now. In fact she's probably guessed that I somehow know she left the house last night. But she can tell by my kidding that I'm not all that upset with her, and am not going to turn her in. And she's right. After all, this isn't a jail for lawbreakers. It's a home where people like Nadia can ostensibly learn to behave in a sensible, or at least normal, fashion. And what more sensible or normal a way of coping with insomnia than a midnight stroll down the street, even if it *is* technically against the rules? It sure as hell beats counting sheep, popping aspirin, or switching on the tube to watch a couple of 280 pound slobs in tank suits and black boots grappling their way around the ring, stomping, slugging, kicking and twisting one another's limbs and bodies to the tune of a thousand screaming spectators, crazy for blood.

And unlike most insomniacs, she does appear to be well-rested, so her method must be effective. No. She's in no trouble with me. However I *would* like to find out if her insomnia might be a recurring problem she needs help with. So I cue her, "Hey Nadia. What do you need to do the next time you're having trouble going to sleep?"

"I don't know," she says. "I never have no trouble with it."

I decide it won't do much good to pursue this any further now. I'll just keep an eye on her next Saturday night. And if she has another bout of insomnia I'll make a note of it in the daily log so we can discuss the problem at our weekly staff meeting.

After another five minute round of swinging in rhythm with the symphony of squeaks, I have Lucius let me off so that I can sit on the wooden rail in front of Nadia and watch while she works on her tree. She's truly an artist. No doubt about it. She's like some kind of tree goddess, creating her baby with the greatest care imaginable, doing everything but breathing life into it.

I remember, however, that I'm supposed to cue Nadia to keep her hair out of the clay by tying it back in a pony tail. That seems reasonable enough to me, but when I *do* cue her, asking her what she needs to do with her hair, she glances up at me with a dark-eyed scowl, then hunches back over her tree.

So I drop to a "directive verbal" cue. "Okay Nadia. You need to tie your hair back in a pony tail."

But she doesn't look up, or in any other way even acknowledge my suggestion. I'm about to cue her again, when it suddenly hits me; of course she doesn't want to tie back her hair! It's a part of her creation. She needs that clay streaked through her hair the way a painter needs paint splattered on his smock and pants; the way a writer needs ink on his fingers. And, maybe even more important, she needs that veil of darkness surrounding her work. Maybe it helps her focus and concentrate. Maybe it helps her feel more a part of her creation. I'm not exactly sure because I'm no artist myself. (All through school the only C's I *ever got* were in art.) But I *am* sure I'm not going to bother her about it again.

I continue to watch in silence as she smooths and shapes her clay. At one point she looks up, shakes back her hair and smiles at me. "Mr. Watcher," she says, then adds, "Mr. Nose." And finally, a few seconds later, "Mr. Kind Eyes."

I hide my face in my hands so she can't pick out any other facial features to call me by, and when I finally crack my fingers to see if she's still looking, she says, "Mr. Silly Billy. Mr. Peek-A-Boo-I-See-You."

I've always been nervous around kids. Maybe that's why I get so nervous around her. She's too much like a kid. I stand up, nod to her, then head for the front door.

"Mr. Nervous Purvis," she calls after me.

Lucius rubs the tops of his thighs, then pulls forward with his head and neck to start up the swing.

After everyone returns from church I immediately start in with the programs, one after another, from lunchtime to dinner; bang bang bang. Dinner is neither fun nor relaxing because everyone's mad and barking at everyone else because *I've* been mad and barking at everyone in a frustrated effort to keep pace with the program schedule. So far I'm managing to keep my head above water. But just barely. And at the expense of everyone's good humor, mine included.

After dinner it's more of the same. Moby is upset with me because I watch to make sure he doesn't lock the bathroom door, then cue him to get out of the shower after five minutes even though he complains that he hasn't had time to wash his hair. Emmy's mad at me because I have to cue her to wash the rice pot three times—until *all* the stuck bits of rice are gone. And Elisha, who's drying the dishes, is mad at Emmy because she's taking such a long time to wash the rice pot that it's keeping her from starting her last load of laundry, which she's understandably anxious to finish before bedtime.

Amar, who's been in the bathroom ever since I chased Moby out fifteen minutes ago, emerges now, grinning proudly, stroking his chin. He's shaved off his goatee and moustache. "Cleaner than a baby's bottom," he boasts to Elisha.

But Elisha looks sharply away.

"Hey," Amar says, stepping toward her, reaching for her shoulder. "What's a matter?"

Elisha jerks her shoulder back from his hand. "Could've told me, Hot Dog," she says. With one of her bird eyes she glances at me—a cornered-looking, frightened glance. I wonder what's going on with her other eye.

"Well hey, lady," Amar says. "It's my face ain't it?"

Elisha throws down her dishtowel, brushes past Amar, out of the kitchen, and stomps up the stairway to her bedroom.

"Well hell," Amar says, and leans over to spit into the side of the sink that's empty.

"Stop it! "Emmy shrieks, her hands in the soap suds. "I don't *like* that spitting!"

Amar ignores her, then calmly folds his arms across his chest and turns to me. "A man's got to be able to try to stand up for himself," he says. "It's my face and she had no right to try to be able to go and get all upset about it." He turns in the direction of the stairway, apparently hoping she'll hear, and adds loudly, "It ain't nothing but dumb!"

"I'm not so sure about that, Hot Dog. What if she shaved her head without telling *you*?"

"I'll try to say this," he says. "That'd be different. That'd be *really* dumb!"

"All right. Then how about if she got a new hairstyle you didn't like without checking it out with you first?"

"That'd be her business," he says, then spits in the sink and turns on the faucet to rinse it down.

"Make him *stop* that *spit*ting!" Emmy shrieks.

"Hey. *You* stop it, Lady!" Amar shrieks right back.

And she's instantly streaking off to her bedroom, her sudsy hands clapped over her ears.

"Well there goes the rest of my kitchen crew," I tell Amar. "You're making life rough for me."

"I'm trying to be able to stand up for myself is all," he says, his arms floundering in a helpless gesture. Then he picks up the soapy sponge and mutters, "*I'll* try to be able to clean up the rest of this mess. Too many hands in the pie spoils the broth, anyway."

"Hey Amar," I say. "Hot Dog. Don't you care about what just happened? Don't you want to do something about it? Maybe try to straighten things out?"

"Yes I'd like to be able to do something about it. I'd like to be able to find me another girl."

"Oh. So you think ending a relationship is *that* easy?" I ask him. "Like throwing away a pair of good pants as soon as they get a little rip?"

"Hey," he says, then spits. "When you got a pair of pants all full of rips there ain't nothing to do *but* to be able to try to get a new pair."

"The point I was making," I say, astonished that he not only understood my lousy analogy, but extended it and used it to his advantage, "is that a relationship is *not* like a pair of pants. You can't just throw out the old one and buy a new pair."

He sponges off a coffee pot, then says, "There's plenty of fish in the ocean."

"Come on, Hot Dog. People aren't like pants. And they aren't like fish either. There's love involved. Isn't there? And pain. And anyway you're just upset. In an hour you'll feel differently. I shouldn't even be wasting my breath on you."

"I've been wanting to be able to find a new girl for a long time anyway." He turns to me now, his hands dripping soapy water, and whispers, "I want Nadia." Then he giggles slyly. One eyebrow—his right eyebrow—lifts and falls, lifts and falls, punctuating each laugh. I almost expect him to rub his hands together, like the lecherous old movie villains in black capes and moustaches who captured pretty girls and tied them to the railroad tracks.

"What about the diamond ring you gave Elisha?"

"I'll try to be able to get it back from her," he says, turning back to rinse off the pot. "She won't want to be able to wear it anymore, anyhow."

"Hot Dog! By tomorrow she'll like you *better* without the goatee."

"Hey. It wasn't no goat nothing. It was a beard."

"Okay. Without the beard. I mean, you've even got a dimple on your chin. She won't be able to resist for long. Come on Hot Dog. Think about all the effort you've put into this relationship. Isn't it worth salvaging? Don't you even want to try?"

He shrugs. "No use crying over spoilt milk."

And it's no use trying to convince Amar that he's being immature. In fact I have no idea why I'm trying so fanatically to convince him at all. What the hell. If he wants to drop her he should drop her. He'll learn more from experience than from my lecturing. I've always sworn that if I were ever a parent I'd avoid shoveling the benefit of my experience down my kids' throats. And here I am now, not yet a parent, but already trying to shovel my experience down someone else's throat. And Amar probably has more experience with women than I do, anyway. The bastard. I leave him to his dishes and his villainous fantasies.

When Lena Coltrane comes in to relieve me two hours later (Lena works the Sunday, Monday and Tuesday night shifts), the program clipboards are all hanging on their hooks, the medication cupboard is locked, and the residents are in bed. I've run all the scheduled Sunday programs except two—the two evening self-care programs with Elisha and Emmy, who, after leaving the kitchen, never came out of their rooms.

I'm more exhausted than I used to be after final exams. Three nights of sleepless cramming is child's play compared to *this* work.

"God, I'm glad to see you," I gratefully tell Lena as I hand over the house keys.

"They wore you out, did they?" She smiles as she cups the keys in her palm. "No doubt about it. The weekend shift's the roughest."

"So I hear," I say.

She jingles the keys like loose change, then shoves them

in her blue jeans pocket and sits at the desk to read through the daily log and catch up on all that's happened since her last shift.

Though I'm eager to leave—to crawl into my bed at home, curl up, and sleep my brains out for a few dozen hours—there's a part of me that wants to be here in the morning when everyone wakes up. This is some job I've got. Forty crazy hours, and at least part of me is craving more.

Outside I unlock my ten-speed, walk it across the street to the lakefront sidewalk, and take off. The warm night air smells like Melaleucas—the wind must be blowing out of the west—and feels soothing on my face and arms. The lake water laps against the wall, while a gusty breeze rustles through the palm trees so that the fronds shimmer and whisper, and all the way home I listen closely, as if I might hear something important.

The Birth of The Great Equalizer

Joseph and Rachel spent their honeymoon building a modest A-frame house on a cheap acre of land, a mile and a half from the Willoweep Village square and the dry goods store, where they lived—until the A-frame was completed—in a small room above the shopping area; the room which, for over a year, had been Joseph's lonely home.

Their new house was perched atop a knoll, set back nearly forty yards from the main road into town. At the bottom of the knoll, behind the house, was a forest, and just beyond the first few trees of the forest, where plenty of sunlight still beamed through the treetops and spread across the forest floor, ran Willoweep Creek. And there, on the pine-needled banks of the creek, Joseph and Rachel picnicked on hard-boiled eggs, bread, and dried nuts nearly every afternoon while Joseph (along with the handful of workers he'd hired) was building their home.

By the time they had moved into the house and settled into a daily routine, Joseph and Rachel were deeply in love, and thoroughly satisfied with their simple, happy life together. Monday through Saturday Rachel arose at 5:30 to prepare three fresh eggs and fried potatoes or a batch of oatmeal and goat cream for Joseph, who left by 6:15 to walk the mile and a half to his dry goods store, which he opened for business every morning no later than 6:55. He actually looked forward—now that he was no longer so lonely—to going in to work and dealing with his customers.

With Rachel as his wife Joseph grew even more popular with the townspeople. If she'd been only beautiful they might have resented her, and him because of her. But she was as generous with her smile as Joseph was with his, and never acted in any way aloof or superior. Business, already good, picked up. The Willoweepians seemed proud to be customers of Joseph's. Most of them took it as a propitious omen that such a lovely Jewish couple had, like a part of history leaping from the pages of the Bible, come to live in their small town.

During the day, while Joseph was at work, Rachel expertly sewed clothes for herself and for him, grew fresh vegetables, herbs and spices, milked her two goats, churned the milk into butter, fed their egg-laying chickens, hiked into town to buy food and supplies, and to visit with Joseph, kept the house clean and neat, and cooked up a hearty dinner for Joseph, who was always ravenous by the time he walked the mile and a half home at the end of each long day.

Though Joseph never went to synagogue on Sunday (and probably wouldn't have gone even if there *had* been a synagogue in Willoweep and *if* it had services on Sunday instead of Saturday) he did consider it a holy day of sorts, for every Sunday he and Rachel slept late, lounging leisurely in bed, peacefully drifting in and out of sleep and dreams until he quietly slipped from under the sheets to prepare a splendidly decadent brunch of pancakes, rolled and stuffed with Rachel's homemade jam, fresh butter and sour cream, and topped with hot maple syrup. (During the three years he lived with Zeev and Ruth, he'd enjoyed his aunt's thin, crisp pancakes so much that he'd insisted she teach him how to cook them.) Not only did Joseph prepare the Sunday breakfast; he brought it to Rachel in bed. "For my queen," he would tell her, bowing dramatically as he served the plateful of steaming, rolled-up pancakes.

After their Sunday brunch they played together, walking through the woods behind their house, holding hands as they sprawled on the ground in the slatted sunlight by Willoweep Creek, sniffing the pine-scented air, watching the birds, the frogs, or even the ants, and exchanging stories of their former lives in Poland. (Joseph even shared the embarrassing story of his trainride from New York to Atlanta, and how, when confronted at his first breakfast with a banana, the likes of which he'd never seen in Poland, he'd hungrily bitten right into the skin so that the fruit itself had exploded through the seams, like toothpaste through a broken tube, and oozed into his beard, while the people sitting across from him snorted through their noses to keep from laughing—a universal gesture, which Joseph understood—before calming themselves enough to demonstrate the proper way to peel and eat a banana. "I have not had one since," he admitted to her. "I've learned they are food for the monkeys.") Sunday was their day of togetherness and love.

Nighttime was different. Very nearly *every* night was a time of togetherness and love. Before they went to bed they would often sit hugging on their small couch, she curled in his lap, her cheek pressed warmly to his cheek, her temple to his temple, neither of them moving except to sigh and tighten their mutual squeeze, nuzzle a bit closer, or shake some life back into a sleeping limb. It might have seemed a sedentary and boring way to spend an evening to most people. But to them it was bliss.

In bed they made love with a startling amount of passion. Joseph loved Rachel completely, from head to toe, and she wallowed in his thorough and gentle attentiveness. Occasionally at first, and then more and more frequently, Rachel was able to struggle past the fear and confusion of her newly uncloseted sexuality, letting herself go, feeling euphorically wild and free, as if her ecstasy were so humanly natural she might have experienced it in precisely the same way at any other time or place in history. (Their nighttime passion was their secret. In public—even in front of Zeev and Ruth—they acted like teenagers out on their second date together. They held hands and smiled bashfully at each other, but nothing more.)

Even before she became pregnant there was something, for Joseph, ineffably intriguing about Rachel's stomach. Often he fawned and dawdled over her stomach for such long stretches of time—feeling, pressing, probing, and petting; losing himself in its fleshy-soft mystery—that she would grow impatient, take his hand in hers, and slowly push it farther down to where she was *really* wanting to feel his lovingly gentle caresses.

And when, toward the end of July, after they'd been married for four months, Rachel announced that she was pregnant, Joseph became even more entranced with her stomach, expanding now like a fleshy dome. Daily he watched it grow, degree by degree, hardly able to conceive of the new life being nurtured by Rachel within it.

Her stomach became a kind of holy fixation to him. He kissed it. He nuzzled it and licked it, laughing out loud for joy when he felt the baby kicking from the other side; kicks like tiny heartbeats. He stroked her stomach even while he slept, for hours on end, until Rachel was certain he would rub it raw. "I am afraid you will rub right through to the baby," she complained one night as they sat on their small couch, she on his lap, his chin resting on her shoulder, both of his arms around her six month waist, and his hands, naturally, upon her belly.

"The sooner I see him," Joseph said, rubbing his bearded chin upon her shoulder, "the better."

"Him?" Rachel pretended to challenge him.

"Or her. It does not matter to me," he quickly assured her, though in truth he believed it would be a sign of good fortune if their first-born were a son. "As long as he *or* she is healthy, I will feel blessed."

Just after they'd gone to bed one night, five and a half weeks before the baby was due, after an easy and seemingly perfect pregnancy, Rachel began to experience stomach cramps, then suddenly went into labor.

"It's all right," she told Joseph, as he stumbled from the sheets in a panic. "There is still plenty of time for you to get the doctor."

"But am I to leave you alone?" he asked, pulling his trousers over his long underwear, and his stiff work boots over his bare feet. "While you are in pain?"

"Unless you want to deliver the baby yourself," Rachel said, then jerked back and winced, holding onto her rounded belly as if it had just fallen upon her from the sky.

"No." Joseph bent over to kiss first her stomach, then her mouth. "It is early. The baby will be small. I must run for the doctor."

In his boots with no socks, Joseph did run for the doctor. Over a mile he ran, stumbling down the road in the darkness and the spring-night cold, his lungs burning, his face shrouded in the swirling fog of his breath as he puffed and gasped, sweating while his bare toes froze at the tips of his boots.

Meanwhile, on her back, her knees raised, Rachel tried to convince her body to relax. "It is not yet time," she repeated over and over, each time feeling more outraged that her body should be behaving so imprudently, against her wishes, against her sweetest coaxings and sternest commands. "There is over a month, still, to go. Please! It cannot yet be time."

When Joseph returned he gave Rachel's stomach a final soft rub, then squeezed her hand and backed out of the room as Dr. Ainsley Doakes, a somber, slow-moving man with immense hands and bulging eyes, shut the door behind him.

It was a surprisingly short labor. Joseph could tell when the baby was starting to come, for the quality of Rachel's groaning changed dramatically. In fact it seemed to him that she'd begun to sound inhuman; to sound like a wild, wounded animal. He stood stiffly at the door, listening with such aggressive attentiveness that though his eyes were opened wide, his ears did all the seeing.

So worried was Joseph, that he did not think to listen for the agonized cry of new being. Even so, the silence following the doctor's slaps, pierced his ears and left them momentarily ringing, the way no cry or scream could have. Pushing open the door, he stepped in and saw Rachel sprawled back, naked, her legs spread and bloodied, her arms limp and twisted. For half a moment he thought she was dead. But then her eyes flickered open and she turned her head to stare blankly—too exhausted to even cry—at the tiny creature in the doctor's arms, a boy, whose lungs were not yet developed enough to suck life from the air.

There was nothing the doctor could do other than keep

Rachel and Joseph calm, assuring them that she would have many perfectly normal births in the future. "It is not uncommon with the first," he said knowingly. "You are lucky you carried him long as you did."

But in bed that night, Joseph and Rachel wept together; Rachel, not only because she felt so saddened by the loss of her baby boy, whom she'd carried so lovingly and worrilessly for nearly eight months, but because she felt so humiliated and betrayed by her body, which now seemed to her a strange and alien hulk of flesh completely detached from her; and Joseph, not only because he too was heartbroken by the loss of his son, whose tiny kicks had already made him seem like a being of the world, with a will and even a personality, but because he was so relieved that Rachel was still alive and warm beside him.

After she'd lost her baby, Rachel remained shaken by her body's dictatorial decision to eject the fetus too early. She felt a deepening resentment toward and distrust of her body, and began to think of it as a thing utterly apart from her. Whenever Joseph lovingly touched her now, she felt a nauseating discomfort, for it seemed to her almost as if he were attempting to seduce a stranger before her eyes. And three weeks after the death-birth, when Joseph began to sensually caress her newly flattened stomach as they lay in bed, Rachel immediately caught his hand, then rolled onto her side, her back to him, and whispered, "Not yet, Joseph. Please. It is too soon." She slid her knees up toward her breasts and hugged herself to keep from shivering. "I'm sorry. You must be patient with me."

"As long as you are so warm beside me," Joseph answered, "I can be patient." He shimmied up close to her, softly kissed the back of her shoulder, then wiggling away, wished her happy dreams.

The next few months, any time Rachel sensed the slightest hint of impending sexual affection coming from Joseph, she quickly squelched it, retreating to her side of the bed, her back to him, her knees to her chest. And always when she retreated, Joseph was sympathetic, for he knew she'd been through a terrible ordeal—had in fact borne the brunt of their mutual tragedy herself—and he was content now to be carrying the load himself, to be enduring *his* fair share of suffering.

As the months slipped past, Rachel was so filled with and lifted by her husband's loving patience and understanding that she at last felt compelled to let him love her completely in spite of the continued enmity between her and her body. However their first amorous moments together quickly turned into a disaster; Rachel found Joseph's lovemaking to be more urgent and desperate than it had ever been. His use of her body—the way she saw it—as a receptacle for all his pent up animal energy only confirmed the loathing she'd been feeling for her own body, and left her repulsed by *his* body as well, for though she understood the difficulty of his position and the valiancy of his silent self-abnegation, her understanding could not change the way she felt, and so once again she sadly turned her back to him at night.

And when, after almost two *more* months of Joseph's enduring patience and gentle understanding, she allowed him to make love to her once again, she found that his lovemaking was not only urgent and desperate, but clumsy and inept. In his eagerness he exploded before he could enter her, and the cold spurts of jism that puddled onto her stomach as he heaved and groaned atop her, seemed to her indecent and disgusting.

As time went by, Joseph began to feel less and less adequate. He started to wonder if his sexual incompetence was all that was preventing their return to normalcy, and soon became very nearly as apprehensive of bedtime as Rachel. Slowly, their sexual difficulties began to intrude upon and finally engulf their relationship, and though they still loved each other deeply, they could no longer hug, hold hands, or even look into each other's eyes without feeling a profound and frustrating unease. And yet they never directly discussed their problem, because they both were certain they understood its origin and dynamics, and believed no discussion was necessary.

"It's up to me," Joseph unswervingly told himself. "My

God, she's been through hell. She needs time, and she needs my love. I must prove to her *that* is all I care about. Not my own selfish needs."

"It is up to me," Rachel constantly thought. "I must be stronger and put the past behind me once and for all. Then I shall be able to give him the love and attention he deserves."

Thus they dealt with their problem, each taking full responsibility, each feeling like a failure as their relationship slowly but ineluctably spiraled downward.

Joseph's appetite steadily diminished until he was eating even less than Rachel, whose appetite had begun to increase, perhaps because she was burning up so much energy worrying about Joseph.

"You must eat, Joseph," she constantly tried to persuade him.

But he would only smile, answering with a question, "And why must a man eat when he is not hungry?"

Eventually their sex life ceased to be an apparent problem—the way crumbs swept under a rug cease to be an apparent problem—for when Rachel was ready for bed at night, Joseph began to wave her on. "I will be in in a few minutes," he would tell her. "I'm not yet tired enough to sleep."

One night early that autumn, several hours after she'd fallen asleep, Rachel awoke to find Joseph's side of the bed still empty. Pushing back her covers she stumbled into the living room. The oil lamp was still burning dimly, and Joseph was slumped in his chair, his eyes shut, and his mouth gaping open. While he slept she draped a white wool blanket over him, and smiling sympathetically, whispered, "You are not so beautiful with your mouth open, my husband. And you will catch a cold falling asleep in your chair that way without cover. Especially when you have been eating so little. You really must start eating more. That is no little bird's stomach you have to fill." Gently, she brushed his black curls to the side, then, as he shifted and murmured, bent close to him, touched her lips to his forehead, and left them there for a few moments before pulling back. "Things will soon be better," she continued to whisper. "I am beginning to feel stronger." It was the easiest it had been for her to talk to him since the death-birth. Slowly she backed away, keeping her eyes trained upon his face so that before she sat she had to find the couch with her hands. Sitting, she leaned back, her head cocked to one side like a parakeet's, and studied every feature of his face—every bump and angle, every tooth that peeked from between his lips, every hair and wrinkle—until she fell asleep, uncovered, the oil lamp flickering shadows and gold over them both.

The next morning Joseph jerked awake and was, for a moment, so disoriented that he was not sure if it were night or morning; if he'd slept for ten minutes or ten hours. Grumbling, he shook his head, then rubbed his eyes with his fingertips and blinked them until the fogginess cleared. He glanced down at the blanket draped over him, raised his arms beneath it as if to make sure it were real, then stood and gratefully wrapped it around himself, Indian style, for the morning was chilly and he had not fed the pot-bellied stove since the fire had begun to die after dinner. (It was still mid-October and he hated the thought of squandering wood when summer had officially ended only three weeks earlier.)

It was only after Joseph had stood and wrapped himself in the wool blanket that he saw Rachel curled on her side on the couch, the top of her head flush against the side of the couch arm. Except for her nightgown she was uncovered. Feeling warmed by the sight of her—it was apparent to Joseph that she'd covered him with the blanket, then fallen asleep watching over him—Joseph quickly unwrapped himself and covered *her* with the blanket. He knelt to lift her, thinking he would carry her to bed, then suddenly not wanting to risk waking her—which in truth he'd already done—changed his mind. Quietly as he could, Joseph put out the flame in the oil lamp, dressed in the dark, and tiptoed out the front door in his workboots to gather some pine kindling and an armful of oak from the woodpile beside the porch, then, with Rachel watching through a squinted eye which shut every time he turned toward her, built a fire in the woodstove. When the wood was popping and snapping steadily, the flames leaping up the mouth of the flu, Joseph knelt over Rachel again, setting a hand on her shoulder as he gazed at her, sadly wondering if their relationship would ever again be as easy and loving as it once had been.

As he was stepping out the door, Rachel's eye blinked all the way open. She listened through the crackling of the fire as he tried to tiptoe across the porch and down the steps in his workboots. Then smiling, she pulled the blanket over her ear, wriggled until she found a more comfortable position, and drifted into a peaceful sleep.

Joseph was walking briskly along the road, breathing the cool, clean pine air and admiring the day as he warmed to it, when, rounding the last bend leading to town, he heard, then saw, the crowd—at least sixty or seventy Willoweep men and women, and even a few children—gathered near the center of the grove of old oaks at the edge of the village square. He was practically to the rear of the mob before he could locate the object of everyone's slightly upturned gaze. Gasping, he hurried forward, pushing past the people in his way, many of whom happily called his name or patted his back in greeting as he struggled to the front, then stood and stared.

Like a lamb carcass strung up for show behind the butcher counter, a young Black man was hanging by his neck from the thick bottom arm of a Willoweep Oak. (Though Joseph did not know him by name, he clearly remembered this young man's offer to help with the building of his home. Contritely, for the young man seemed eager, Joseph had turned him down, not only because he'd already assembled an adequate crew, but because he'd heard from his friends that the young man was unreliable; that as soon as he'd earned even a small amount of money he would spend it on corn whiskey, and then disappear until he was ready for more.) The man's pink-bottomed bare feet were tied together at the ankles, and his hands were secured tightly behind his back so that his chest was distended, like the chest of a giant crow. The noose knot had been drawn tight, directly under his chin—instead of to one side or the other—and when he dropped, his head had snapped straight back, his face aimed to the sky, his eyes still open.

A freckled teenager, knife in his mouth, was shimmying out along the oak limb from which the body was hanging. As he neared the dip in the limb, around which the rope had been tied, he reached to his mouth for the knife and lost his balance. Joseph felt the entire crowd, himself included, start forward, arms extended, as if preparing to rush ahead en masse and catch the boy before he hit the ground. But the boy deftly recovered, grinning as if he'd planned to slip all along—just part of the show folks; everyone back to his seat now—and went to work cutting at the rope with a short, quick, expert sawing motion. It almost seemed to Joseph as if the boy had been cutting lynched men from tree limbs all his life. While he hacked away at the rope, the body, with the chin pointed up, began to slowly spin, a quarter turn one way, then a half turn back the other. And as the young man cut deeper, the threads of hemp began to snap back from the blade more rapidly, like the thin rubber bands of an unravelling golf ball, until finally the rope gave out and the body fell to the ground in a crumpled heap. The crowd cheered the boy, who grinned and bowed, then tossed his knife down beside the body, and skillfully lowered himself from the limb, showing off with a few pull-ups, before finally letting go and dropping to the ground.

Many in the crowd were already turning to leave when Grady Hunsucker, the village butcher, an obese and quiet man with flaccid jowls and puffy, somnolent eyelids, who'd always treated Joseph with a laconic sort of civility, charged the dead body, moving with surprising quickness. He swore, spat, then kicked viciously at the lifeless shoulder with his workboot. For a few seconds he stood there, slightly bent over as he growled, his arms poised as if he were challenging the body to stand up and fight. Then, with everyone watching, or turning back to watch, he pulled back his thick leg and kicked at the cheek, crushing it in, then pulling back to kick again, his chunky arms flailing at his sides for balance.

It was then that something inside Joseph's head snapped, and the world suddenly sharpened into focus about him, so that he could now clearly discern that this man with a wife and two young daughters, this fat but courteous village butcher whom he and everyone else had always called Grady Hunsucker, had a face that was bestial and without intelligence; the face, and even the body now, of some viciously wild, ape-like animal.

Joseph turned to see if anyone else had yet noticed this frightening transformation and was startled to discover that he was surrounded by a mob of these noisy, ape-like creatures. It was as if they'd all suddenly shed their disguises and stepped from the cover of their collective closet to proudly reveal themselves for what they were. He gawked at them all, disbelieving, then turned back in time to see Judge Howell Watson grab the butcher by the elbow and gently but firmly pull him back as he continued swearing and kicking, at the dirt now. But even the judge's tidy black suit, blue eyes, and impressive head of thick white hair could not hide his own apish essence. And the crumpled black body with the rope leading from its neck like a tangled umbilical death cord, was also the body of an ape-like animal. The only real difference Joseph could see, was that this animal was dead. Shuddering, he glanced down at his own hands, his own fingers. He turned them over, scrutinizing them carefully; the hair and wrinkles, the pores and veins, and the nails, bitten just past the rounded ends of flesh. He squeezed his fingers into his palms. Slowly, he opened them. And then, looking up from his hands, he bolted through the crowd, hearing himself grunt involuntarily as he pushed and shoved, and finally broke into the clear, running, running, running; running as much from himself as from the others.

Rachel was still half asleep on the couch, snuggled under the wool blanket, her eyes shut, when Joseph's boot clomped loudly onto the first porch step. She heard him push open the door and step in, out of breath, and opened her eyes as he lifted the blanket and slid beside her, pushing her roughly against the back of the couch.

"Joseph?" she whispered, startled by his peculiar demeanor and wild, glazed eyes. "Why have you come home? Are you all right?"

Without answering, he purposefully placed his hand upon her stomach, atop her nightgown. Hesitantly, Rachel set her hand upon his and patted it. "Joseph?" she whispered again, as his hand—with hers riding on top—slid across her belly to her hip, and from there, slowly down the outside of her thigh. Just before his hand reached her knee, it changed direction, moving across the top of her leg, from outside to inside, then back up her thigh, pulling the nightgown up with it.

Rachel pressed upon his hand, ineffectively attempting to pin it in place. "God, what's the matter with you?" she said loudly, then swallowed, frightened, pressing even harder upon his hand and squeezing her thighs together as tightly as she could, while his hand continued, undeterred, more roughly now, to wriggle and dig its way higher. With both her hands now, she clung to his wrist and barked, "Stop it Joseph! This is *me!* You are hurting *me!*"

And still he did not respond. But he thought, "No. You are only an animal, an ape. The same as the rest of us." He drew his face nearer to hers, then suddenly, violently, covered her mouth with his mouth. His knee wedged between her thighs, forcing them apart while she screamed into his mouth and let go of his wrist to strike at his head with both her fists. Calmly, he ducked into her blows and rolled onto her, pinning both her arms to the couch cushion, his knees keeping her thighs propped apart as she twisted beneath him. He waited, expressionless, implacable, while she struggled, until she was too exhausted to struggle any longer. And then in two quick motions he ripped open the front of her nightgown, for he wanted her naked. Undisguised. He tried to go slowly, and though he started out that way it was over quickly, in seconds, a copulation as quick as a dog's.

Afterward, Rachel lay limply beneath him, responding

to neither his desperate hugging nor his weeping. And when he choked out the words, "I'm so sorry, Rachel. I love you so much," she pulled away, now the stronger of the two, and hurried into the bathroom to take a long bath, leaving him to sob himself to sleep on the couch.

For a week after the rape Rachel would not speak to Joseph; would not listen to him, or allow him anywhere near her. She even, at one point, contemplated demanding the money to pay for a steamship ticket back to Poland. But Rachel found it impossible to maintain such an intense level of hatred; she knew, after all, that Joseph had been deeply depressed (because of their relationship; because, she still believed, of *her* weakness), and soon became convinced that the rape had nothing to do with Joseph finally tiring of his state of sexual deprivation; but rather, that when he'd witnessed the terrible lynching, something in his head had, as he'd described it to her, finally snapped. Which made a great deal of sense to her. Too much pressure had built up and there had been an inevitable explosion. Horrible (particularly for her, since she was the one who felt the full effects of the explosion), but understandable. In fact it was really not so different, she decided, from what she herself had gone through after the death of her baby. For she too had succumbed to a distorted, hallucinogenic reality when she contemplated her body. And if Joseph had been unfortunate enough to set his hand upon her stomach that first night after the death-birth, she might well have tried to twist it off at the wrist, or perhaps bite it in two.

By the time they learned—a month and a half after the rape—that she was pregnant, Rachel and Joseph were once again speaking easily, and Joseph's appetite had returned, along with his toothy, beard-breaking smile. And though he was still at times, overly cautious and solicitous with her—which nearly always distressed her, for there was no longer any real need for such meticulously careful behavior in her presence, and she wanted him to *know* that; to give her credit for her newfound strength, and treat her accordingly—their relationship began to spiral upward now, as they each grew stronger, and more confident and comfortable with each other. And Rachel grew more confident and comfortable with herself; the pregnancy seemed to somehow re-connect her with her body, so that she felt settled back into it, with no sense of separateness. It wasn't long before she was—at first tentatively, then more and more easily—touching and hugging Joseph, even sitting in his lap again at night on the couch, feeling warm and safe as a kitten in his huge arms; and at last loving him, as completely and thoroughly as she ever had, until the only remaining source of tension was in the ambivalence they shared toward the changing shape of her belly.

Rachel tried not to think about the remote possibility of prematurely giving birth to another dead baby, but the fear was there, like a tiny lump under the flesh that can't be ignored because there is such a dreadful potential packed into the otherwise insignificant smallness. Most of the time she *knew* it would be different this time around. The doctor, and everyone else, had assured her that it was not at all uncommon to have problems with a first pregnancy, and that the chances of the same thing happening again were demonstrably small. But *there* was the catch. That smallness was what she could almost, but not quite, ignore.

Joseph's fear was different. Instead of mouldering and gnawing, ever present, his fear came in great dark waves, then vanished completely. It was not the process of the impending birth that frightened him, but the product. For though he was neither a religious or superstitious man—he believed in neither devilment, nor Providential punishment—the memory of the rape caused him, in his occasional sleepless bed-night darknesses, to wonder what evil might transpire out of such a violent-loveless conception. (Several times he even dreamed that *he* was pregnant and giving birth to a snake, which, as soon as it was born, slithered up his leg in coils, squeezing slowly about his waist and chest and neck.) But always with daylight came rationality. The dark fog of fear and dreams was burned off by the sunshine of solid day reality.

And Rachel grew bigger. And they could feel the tiny kicks. And eight months passed, then eight and a half, and she did not have to command or argue with her body. Steadily, their fears began to ebb, diminishing beneath their mounting expectations and hopes, beneath their re-burgeoning love.

She went into labor almost precisely on schedule. Joseph fetched and returned with Dr. Doakes, then waited, pacing in front of the woodstove, grimacing with each of Rachel's groans, until he heard the slap, and sudden cry of new life.

He was so ecstatic when the doctor handed him his healthy, wailing baby boy, that he never even had a chance to take Rachel's hand as her eyes blinked open, then rolled upward in confusion, and her chest heaved with a final breath.

At first Joseph blamed himself, believing he had actually killed Rachel nine months earlier with his loveless act of violence. But later he found it more sensible—more comforting, in any case—to blame the world, which he came to see as a cold, hard, heartless, soulless, and capricious place, where the good are as subject to terrible misfortune as the bad, and where, in the end, no matter what we aspire to or pretend at in life, we are all precisely the same. All dead apes. "Death," he would later explain to his motherless son, Mort, "is The Great Equalizer."

Benny's First Dream

The Friday morning before my second weekend shift I wake from a wild dream. I'm a passenger aboard some huge modern jet; like a 747 only bigger. There's a pool table at the rear, and even a fat guy running a small hot dog stand. We're flying smoothly along when without warning we start diving from the sky and, while everyone's screaming, are forced to attempt an impossible landing on a snow-covered mountainside. The wheel mountings snap like toothpicks as the jet touches down and plows through a snowy field on its belly, right up to the edge of a cliff, before at last screeching and shuddering to a halt. After everyone peeks tentatively up and about at each other, we begin to pat ourselves and our seatmates, to prove to each other that we really are alive. There's laughter and cheering, and when the pilot steps out of the cockpit the cheers grow louder. He bows gallantly, acknowledging the cheers, then explains that we were forced to land because we ran out of fuel in mid-flight. He checks his watch, scratches his chin as he does some silent calculations, then calmly announces that we'll be taking off again in about five minutes. He nods and ducks back into the cockpit.

I'm stunned. I'm flabbergasted. I can't believe my ears. Our madman pilot said nothing about our snapped-off wheels or our position at the cliff-edge of the mountain. And even crazier, he neglected to explain how we're going to take off without gas. I look around, waiting for the others to protest or make some sort of decisive move, but they're all just chattering away, going about their business as if nothing was wrong. The hot dog man has resumed his sales barking, and someone's already racking up the pool balls for a new game. I quietly unbuckle my seat belt, then stand and wander down the aisle, toward the front door, which is swinging freely on its hinges like a windblown shutter. Taking a final sweeping glance over my shoulder at the insane passengers—lambs, they are; all on their way to the slaughter—I leap through the doorway and land softly in the snow on my hands and knees. It's icy cold and blindingly white. I hug myself and dance in place to try keeping warm. But my nose and hands and eyebrows have gone instantly numb. The jet door swings and bangs while I watch and wait for the others to come to their senses and hop out after me. But only one other passenger, a dark-haired girl, hops out. She pinches her nose as she jumps—like a little girl jumping into a swimming pool—and as I reach out to help pull her to her feet, I see that the girl is Nadia.

"God, it's good to see you," I happily tell her. "I'm glad you were smart enough to get off."

"They made me," she says, but not sadly. "They told me I couldn't stay on account of I didn't do my hair right."

The jet door suddenly bangs shut and the engines rev up while Nadia and I back away, covering our ears to muffle the sky-ripping scream. The jet begins to slide slowly forward on its belly, its nose—black-tipped like a dog's—going over the edge of the cliff, followed by the fuselage and finally the tail. I keep waiting for it to tilt downward and begin its dive to doom, but instead, it slowly angles upward and into the sky, picking up speed and altitude, *flying without fuel!* I rub my eyes and shake my head, but it's no illusion. The jet's really flying and we're left alone on the mountainside, shivering in the cold, the snow to our knees. I wonder what the hell was wrong with me to get off, and I angrily tell Nadia she should have brushed the clay and tangles out of her hair.

"I'm cold," she says, then smiles, and staring at me with her dark eyes, adds, "Mr. Shiver Lips."

Her face moves toward mine. Our cheeks press together. We hug, and a thrilling warmth passes between us. But it's hard to enjoy the warmth for more than a moment, because I keep wondering what the hell was wrong with me to get off.

An Unexpected Visit

Saturday morning it's beautiful out—hot, as always, but noticeably less humid than usual. More like early May than late June. During our pancake breakfast (it's Elisha's turn to cook breakfast this week, and she does a great job, needing my help only with the measurements of the ingredients, and the temperature setting of the burner) Amar suggests that everyone walk up to the beach together, and spend the morning swimming and sunning. "I got to try to be able to get some sunshine on my chin so it'll be the same color as the rest of my face," he says.

Everyone seems excited about the beach idea except Elisha, Nadia and Billy. Elisha is still furious with Amar, who, since their little spat Sunday night, has apparently been flirting around. She immediately turns her nose up at the idea. "Some of us got programs to do this morning," she says huffily.

"Hey," he says. "We can try to be able to do our programs when we get back."

Billy is slumped over his pancake dish, forking up the extra syrup and licking it from between the prongs. "Who wants to go to the beach anyway?" he says. "It's too damn hot, it is. Too hot. Too hot."

"Hey," Amar says. "You're just afraid of the water is all."

"Yeah, and you're just a goddamned stupid asshole," Billy says. "A stupid asshole. A stupid asshole."

"Stop it," Emmy shrieks, from her usual place at the head of the table.

Lythia suddenly grunts and moans and everyone shuts

up respectfully—even Emmy—and turns to watch her as she bobs and ducks in her chair, sputtering, straining, and drooling for three or four agonizing minutes, her arm with the hooked hand moving in aimless jerks as she struggles heroically, and in the end successfully, to remind us that she can't make it all the way to the beach; that it's too far for her to walk. When she's finally through telling us, and we've all acknowledged that we understand what she was saying and are sorry she can't go, she sits back, exhausted, and smiles gleefully, triumphantly, even though what she had to tell us was, for her, not anything to be particularly gleeful about. That she was simply able to communicate her thoughts to everyone is victory enough for her.

"What about programs?" I ask everyone, hoping someone other than Amar will answer. "Elisha's got a good point."

"Hey," Amar says. "Like I was trying to be able to say. We can try to do them when we get back."

"That's not a bad idea, Hot Dog," I say. "The problem is that I can't run everyone's program at the same time. That's why we have a schedule worked out. Right? So I can run a program every half hour."

"Yeah," Elisha says. "That's why we got a schedule worked out."

Amar immediately throws up his hands in that helpless gesture of his. "The problem of the matter is that we're too tied up with these dumb idiotic programs to be able to have any time left over to be able to try to have fun for ourselves, or together, or whatever." A little work on his delivery and he'd make a great rabble rouser. He's gotten right to the heart of the problem. The dumb idiotic programs.

"I think you're right, Hot Dog," I admit to him. "You do have too many programs; and maybe some of them *are* idiotic. But one thing you should keep in mind is that the program time is the idea of the state government. And you know where we get the funds to run ARC House?"

"The state governments?" Amar guesses.

"You got it."

"Well hey," Amar says. "The state governments are full of baloney."

I'm about to ask him if he's ever heard the expression, "Don't bite the hand that feeds you," but I don't, because I'm sure he has. (I'm sure he's heard every hackneyed expression in the book.) And that's really not at all the point I want to make anyway. I guess I'm just trying to let him—and the rest of them—know that I'm running the programs only because I have to—if I plan to keep my job—not because I want to or because I think the constant programming is a good idea; that if I had my druthers things would be different. But the more I think about that, the more it seems an easy way out. I'd be giving them the old "I'm just a pawn . . ." speech. I've heard it myself at least fifty times from fifty different bureaucrats (and I'm only 21) and it's never made me feel the slightest bit better.

"All right. I'll tell you guys what," I say. "You can all go to the beach this morning if you promise me you'll get your programs done *some* time today."

Amar bangs his fist on the table in triumph, and laughs through his teeth, his right eyebrow lifting and falling, lifting and falling, while Lucius Moon pushes back his chair and stands so that he can bend forward, rubbing the fronts of his thighs and grinning.

Not wanting Amar to think I'm relinquishing my authority, I quickly add, "Even if it means you stay home *tonight* to do them."

Amar, Lucius, Emmy and Moby all agree they'll do their programs at my convenience, when they return from the beach, even if it interferes with their Saturday night plans. At the last minute Elisha decides to go, too. Maybe she just wants to keep an eye on Amar. She's still wearing that diamond ring, so she apparently hasn't lost hope.

Billy tells me he's going downtown for the morning, and when I ask him what he plans on doing there, he says, "I'm gonna drink beer all morning, I am. Drink beer all morning until I'm drunk on my ass. Drunk on my ass."

Technically our house policy regarding alcohol is fairly lax. If a resident drinks to the point of intoxication, but is not behaving "inappropriately," there is no problem. But if, while under the influence, he or she crosses that gray line separating appropriate behavior from inappropriate behavior, or if, as a result of his drunkenness he is unable to adequately participate in a scheduled program, we are supposed to slap him with an official warning. Three warnings and he's automatically kicked out of ARC House. From what I've read in the daily log and the residents' files, Billy, Amar, and Moby are drinkers; and each has been given one warning for inappropriate drunkenness. Emmy is a heavy drinker, but has never been given a warning because alcohol apparently quiets and subdues her, and no one in his right mind is going to complain about that. Lythia can't drink because she's an epileptic, and Lucius Moon isn't allowed to drink—unless under direct staff supervision—because alcohol was officially interfering with his successful habilitation at ARC House. (It's all there to read in his file and in his Individual Habilitation Plan.) At least it interfered with his habilitation one night five months ago when he peed in the sink of the ladies' bathroom in Capital T's Saloon, then, ten minutes later peed again in the back seat of the police car he was picked up and brought home in. A little earlier that night the police had received an angry complaint from a Coconut Beach yachtsman whose boat deck and girlfriend had been peed upon while he was cruising under the Manatee Lake Bridge. But the yachtsman's girlfriend could not see the offender clearly through the bridge railing, and when the police asked Lucius about the incident, he apparently flashed a great drunken grin, gave them one of his usual "Oooh wows," then denied that he'd done it. (I imagine all the old Black bridge fishermen had themselves a hell of a satisfying chuckle, watching a 56 year-old rosy-cheeked White man happily whipping it out to whiz off the bridge, onto the deck of a 40,000 dollar yacht.) Subsequently Lucius was given the option of being kicked out of ARC House or signing a behavior contract that prohibited him from drinking alcoholic beverages of any kind without a staff member being present. (Christ, maybe we are growing slowly more civilized. I'm not at all sure how I feel about behavior contracts, but I'll gladly admit they're an improvement over early twentieth century American justice for minority citizens. I'll always remember the awful story my father tells about my grandfather witnessing the lynching of a young Black guy, who was hung from a tree for peeing—like Lucius, in a drunken stupor—in the presence of a curious young White girl, who immediately and excitedly reported the incident to her outraged father, the village butcher.)

Anyway, when Billy tells me he's going to get drunk on his ass, I ask him if he thinks that's a wise thing to do, considering that there are two programs he needs to be sober enough to do this afternoon, and that he has one official "alcohol warning" already.

"I don't care if it's a smart thing, Benny. I don't care a-tall. Not a-tall."

"You mean you don't care if you get a second warning?"

"Why should I, Benny? Why should I?"

"Because if you get three warnings you'll be kicked out."

"Who wants to live here anyway?" Billy says, teary-voiced. "It's a goddamned stupid place to live anyway. A stupid place to live." And with that said, he storms through the kitchen and living room, shoves the front screen door open, steps out, and slams it behind him. You'd think that when a thirty year-old man who's over six and a half feet tall loses his temper he would be fairly intimidating. But when Billy loses his temper he only seems more helpless and vulnerable than usual. Even the slamming screen door sounds sadly feeble. Following after him I push open the screen door and call out, "I *know* you'd rather live here than back at Palmview! Come on Billy. You're upset about something. Let's talk about it. You're supposed to be an adult, not a kid."

Without turning back Billy lifts his long arm to the sky, his middle finger extended, then hops up onto the lake wall and hurries along, determined not to stop for anybody or anything. I just hope he doesn't get so drunk that he misses his programs. I'd hate to be the one to have to give him his second warning. (But I'm really not too worried. Even if he *is* too drunk to participate in his programs today, I can always squeeze him in tomorrow.)

So I'm left here with Nadia and Lythia. This should be a nice, quiet, uneventful morning, and I'm grateful for it, even though I know it will make the afternoon and evening that much more panicked. The times I seem to enjoy this job the most are the times I'm relaxing with one or two residents, getting to know them without feeling the need to come across as the authority figure, the schedule keeper, who has all the right answers and knows precisely what is appropriate behavior and what is inappropriate behavior.

Lythia has decided that although she can't get to the beach with the others, there's no reason she can't get a suntan, so she spreads out a huge Rebel flag beach towel, and lies on her back. She wears a pink bikini which is about four sizes too large for her, and a white tennis hat with a dark green plastic sun visor built into the brim. Even lying down she is in constant aimless motion, like some giant, squirming infant, still struggling to get used to the fit and feel of her new body. Nadia is in her favorite spot on the front porch—probably her favorite spot in the world—hunched over her worktable. She finished her Melaleuca (though it still needs to be fired in the kiln at West Coconut Beach Junior College) and has started building a new tree. When I ask her what kind of tree *this* one is, she says, "The big Banyan."

"*The* big Banyan?" I say, sitting on the porch railing in front of her, the sun beating on my neck and shoulders.

She nods.

"Which big Banyan?"

"You know. The one by the library."

"Oh right," I say. "So that's why you went to see it last week. You wanted to get it pictured in your mind so you could build it."

"No," she says, stopping her work to look up at me. "It's my favorite is all. How it does the whooshing. You know. Does all the whooshing and stretching with its long arms strong arms." There's a gleam of excitement in her dark eyes. They're as dark as they were in the airplane dream.

"It's not exactly accurate to say trees stretch with their

arms, Nadia," I kid her. "But I think I know what you mean."

"Mr. Smarty Britches," she says, blinking then looking down at her clay. "Who *don't* know."

"What do you mean, 'Who doesn't know'?" I ask her.

But she's bent over her Banyan Tree and won't answer. She's working on the trunk and root system, which is already quite complicated and intricate; like one of those huge, convoluted stalagmite formations you might see in Carlsbad Caverns.

"I'll bet this one is going to take you quite awhile to finish," I say.

"Yes. It might take quite a while."

"And that doesn't really matter to you. Does it?"

She looks up at me, rubs some clay off her cheek with the back of her wrist, then smiles and says, "Mr. Admire Eyes."

She's right. I not only admire what she can do with her hands. I admire her. To her it's no big deal that it doesn't matter how much time it takes.

"You think I could buy this tree from you when you're finished?" I ask.

She looks up, not surprised, and shakes back her tangled black hair. I wonder if that black hair makes her eyes look darker than they really are.

"Okay," she says. "You can buy it. Mr. Strong Nose."

"Great," I say. "About how much do you think you'll want for it?"

She shrugs.

"Well it's going to be a lot bigger than your other trees," I say. "How much do you usually get for one of them?"

"They do the money at Rehab. I think most of 'em are like fifteen."

"Then this one should probably sell for thirty or forty dollars."

"*You* pay *me*?"

"That's the idea. Unless you want to *give* it to me."

"Okay," she says. "I'll give it to you. You know. Give it how if it was a present."

"I was kidding, Nadia," I quickly explain, trying to figure out how Angela Geer would want me to handle this. "I want to pay you. It's better that way. I mean, you'll be spending so much time on the tree you ought to get something in return. Right?" As soon as I finish speaking I want to kick myself. Here she's doing something because she loves to do it, because she wants and has to do it, and I'm trying to teach her that that's not good enough; that she should rightfully seek something more than that in return, as if it were the exchange value of her creation that legitimized it. I think about telling her I *will* accept the tree as a present, but then I realize it wouldn't look right; it would look as if I were taking advantage of her.

I'm trying to figure out a way to explain all this to Nadia in a way that's understandable to her, when out of nowhere I hear Angela Geer's voice. It's a distinctive voice which always sounds smooth as honey; no edges. "Lythia," I hear that voice say behind me. "Is that an appropriate towel for the front lawn? How would a Black person feel if he saw you lying on that towel?"

I turn, shade my eyes, and see her standing over Lythia in tight, waist-high white jeans, a brown danskin tank top, and thick, wooden-heeled shoes. She's got a medium to thin build, yet her clothes fit so tightly that they seem to be choking her, especially around her crotch, where those white jeans are all bunched up and straining. She waits for Lythia to respond to her cue, but when, after five or ten seconds, Lythia *hasn't* responded, she says, "A Black person might feel angry. Or sad. They don't like what the Rebel flag stands for." She waits for all that to sink in, then asks, "So what do you need to do about that towel?"

A moment later Lythia smiles, then struggles to her feet, a pink shoulder strap dropping loosely to her elbow, and takes a good half minute to tell Angela she'll go get another towel. Listening patiently, nodding encouragement, Angela praises her decision, then tells her she can use the towel in the back yard if she wants. Just so long as it's in a private spot, where it won't offend anyone.

Lythia leans forward, then begins her semi-controlled fall toward the back yard. Almost immediately she trips over her towel, falls hard to her knees and hands, then picks herself up with surprising quickness and lurches forward again.

Angela turns toward the porch now and greets me with a friendly, honey-smooth, "Hey Benny," as she approaches. Already I feel as though I've been indirectly—and rightfully—rebuked for allowing Lythia to bare her Rebel flag towel in public, but Angela's not halfway up the porch steps when she puts her hands on her hips, tilts her head, and with an exaggerated look of surprise and dismay, says, "What do you need to do with your hair, Nadia?"

Nadia doesn't look up.

"You need to pull your hair back in a ponytail, Nadia. Can you tell me why?"

"The clay," Nadia says.

"Good, Nadia. That's exactly right. And what will people think if they see your hair full of knots and clay, the way it is now?"

Nadia doesn't answer.

"They'll think you don't know how to take care of yourself, and that you don't belong in their community."

She waits for Nadia to look at her, but Nadia is watching herself play with the clay.

"What do you need to do when someone is talking to you," Angela says, and right away Nadia looks up at her. "Thank you, Nadia. Now you're looking at me so I know you're listening, and that makes me feel good."

Nadia nods.

"So what are you going to do with your hair now?"

"Tie it," Nadia says.

"Good," Angela says. "That's a very good idea, Nadia."

I'm standing there with my fists shoved deep as they'll go in my blue jean pockets—wishing I could fit my head in one of my pockets, too—when Angela smiles and asks me how it's going.

"Oh, pretty well," I say, and pull one of my hands from my pocket to scratch behind my ear, which is what I often do when I'm nervous. "Quiet right now."

"Well I just thought I'd stop by to see how you were doing."

"Great," I say. "Thanks. I could always use some feedback." I feel like an obsequious little mouse standing here in front of her, scratching my ear, practically begging her to crush me with one of her thick-heeled shoes, and put me out of my misery. Feedback my ass. I feel as though I've had enough of her feedback the last thirty seconds to last me through the year. She's too damned good at this job.

"Is anyone else here?" she says, looking past me.

"Billy's downtown," I say. "And the rest of them are at the beach."

"Ah. Did Moby and Elisha remember their suntan lotion?"

"Oh gee," I say. It's an expression I haven't used since I stopped reading the "Happy Hollisters" in fourth grade. "I think they might have forgotten about suntan lotion."

"And Emmy went too?"

"She was leading the pack."

Angela looks concerned for a moment, then takes a seat on the wooden railing. Her white pants bunch up even more, forming strained ripples around her hips and across her thighs. "What do you need to do, Nadia?" she suddenly says.

"I don't have no thingy," Nadia says.

"What's that 'thingy' called, Nadia?"

Nadia thinks for a moment then says, "A lastic?"

"Right Nadia. An elastic. You've got a good memory. Now what do you need to do if you don't have an elastic with you?"

And Nadia wipes her hands on her clay-spattered white painter's overalls, then stands and turns to go inside, presumably in search of an elastic. As soon as the screen door slams shut behind her, Angela tells me, "The problem is that when Emmy goes to the beach there's a good chance she'll take off looking for shells, and walk for miles without thinking about where she is. It's happened a few times already, so it's in the behavior problem section of her file, I'm sure, but you really just have to be here for awhile to know those kinds of things about everyone."

"You're true," I say, nodding. Actually, I meant to say

either "you're right," or "that's true." But it comes out clearly, "You're true." I scratch behind my ear again. She probably thinks I'm not only mindless and incompetent, but infested with fleas or lice.

"How have the programs been going?" she asks. "Did you get a chance to get most of them out of the way before everyone left?"

"Well, no," I admit. "But they all agreed to do them when they get back." I proudly add, "Even if it means staying in tonight!"

"Ah. That's good you had them agree to that. But they know better. They're really supposed to finish their programs *before* they go anywhere; or else be back to do them at the scheduled time."

"Right," I say. "They just seemed so excited about all going *together*. I thought it would be all right. As long as they *did* agree to do their programs."

"Well, certainly we're not so rigid here that we can't make exceptions," she says. Her white pants are stretched so tight you could probably bounce a quarter off the top of her thigh, the way you always hear they do in the army to test the tightness of bed sheets.

"Right," I say. "I'll make sure when they come back that they understand this was a special occasion."

"Fine," she says. "That's a good way of handling it."

She's thirsty, so we go inside for a drink. The house isn't looking so hot because they all left right after breakfast. The dining room table is a mess, and the kitchen is strewn with syrupy dishes. Mercifully, she says nothing, though I can tell by the way she's looking all around that she's concerned; maybe even appalled. She pours herself some grape juice and sips it, while I ask her as many questions as I can think of, trying to sound eager and bright.

I'm starting to impress her, I'm sure, with my questions and my attentive way of listening (or at at least *looking* as though I'm listening) to her answers, when the screen door crashes open and a drunken voice shouts out, "I told you I was gonna get drunk on my ass, Benny. I told you, I did. I told you. I told you."

I cringe harder with each "I told you," until Billy stumbles, howling, through the kitchen doorway, and seeing who's in there with me, rears back and says, "Uh oh."

Angela leaves after giving Billy his second alcohol warning and helping me put him to bed. She also tells me to give her a call if Emmy doesn't return with everyone else.

I'd guess that my chances of being fired are fifty-fifty. I'm sure she thinks I'm not firm enough or serious enough. But it's only my second week on the job and she must believe, after all my eager questions, that I'm sincerely interested in learning and improving. At least that's what I keep telling myself.

The rest of the day—the rest of the weekend—I'm a tyrant. Elisha and Moby complain loudly about their sunburns, which *are* nasty-looking, and Billy gripes about his hangover symptoms, but none of them gets any sympathy from me. Sunday morning I even cue Nadia to tie back her hair, and, though she ignores me I keep after her until she finally calls me "Mr. Meanhead," tells me she won't sell me her tree, and runs upstairs, crying.

By the time Lena Coltrane relieves me at eleven, I'm feeling as though it might be best for everyone involved if Angela *does* fire me. I'm not cut out for this kind of work.

Boy Into Ape

The first time Mort Horowitz clearly understood what his father, Joseph, meant when he said that all men are apes, it was late spring of 1943, a time when men almost everywhere were (or soon would be), with their guns, bombs, and other devices of death, torture, and mass destruction, behaving far worse than *any* ape had *ever* behaved. Mort, who was not yet twelve years old, had just returned from baseball practice to find the house empty, and a note from his father tacked to the cork bulletin board on his closed bedroom door. Quickly skimming the note (in which his father explained that he had stepped out to pick up a load of groceries, and would be back shortly), Mort hustled to the kitchen, where he threw his baseball glove and cap on the table and poured himself a tall glass of apple cider. After downing the cider in eight or nine quick gulps, and setting the empty glass in the sink, he spotted the latest issue of Life Magazine on the kitchen counter, picked it up and headed to the bathroom.

He'd already finished wiping himself, but was still sitting, leafing through the magazine, when he flipped a page and froze, staring wide-eyed at a picture of Rita Hayworth, who he secretly believed was the most beautiful woman in the world. In the photograph she was kneeling on a silk-sheeted bed, her body in lovely profile, her face turned toward the camera. With her eyelashes flipped coyly up, her eyes were dark and alluring, and her lips full and turned down slightly at the corners. She wore a silky chemise, wrinkled at her hip and across the lower part of her belly and, over the chemise, a lacy black top, cut extraordinarily low, revealing the soft upper flesh of her breasts. Her neck was taut, in marked contrast to her shoulders and arms, which appeared relaxed and smooth as caramel, right down to her hands and long fingers, which rested sensually upon her thigh.

Hearing himself swallow loudly, young Mort carefully lifted the magazine from the floor, and set it on his lap so that he could study the photograph from close range. As he stared, trance-like, he noticed that his stomach felt weak and tingly. And when he finally lifted the magazine to find out what the sweet aching between his legs was all about, he was startled to behold an arching erection, throbbing upward in tiny ascending jerks. He'd been aware of his erections before, of course, though until this moment he'd considered the hardness nothing more than an annoying obstacle to pissing on target every morning when he awoke. Now, however, in a single illuminating flash of conceptual lightning, he understood that the hardness was somehow much more than that. He pressed down upon it until it angled well below seat level of the toilet, then letting go, watched with curious fascination as it sprang back up, resilient as a diving board. Once again he pressed down, let go and watched while it sprang back into place, a bit sturdier, if anything, than before.

Utterly astounded, Mort wondered just how strong and sturdy his erection was. Underpants at his ankles, he stood now and shuffled his way to the towel rack, pulled off a green towel, and tentatively draped it over his penis, which sagged two or three inches under the weight, then held steady. Afraid he might be straining himself—perhaps even giving himself a hernia, which was something he'd heard a great many grizzly locker room stories about—Mort quickly whisked off the towel, like a matadore lifting his cape to reveal his hidden sword, and watched incredulously as his erection sprang potently back into place, looking ready to take on the weight of the world.

He waited for a moment before slowly, ever-so-cautiously, replacing the towel, his entire face contorting into a studious knot of concentration, and his tongue sneaking out the corner of his mouth. With the towel back in place, secure, it seemed to him, as a saddle on the back of a sturdy horse, Mort pulled a second green towel from the rack, and was preparing to drape *it* over the first towel, when the telephone rang.

He jerked up, startled by the unexpected noise, then scowled, his heart pounding at his ribs. Reluctant to interrupt his experiment before it was finished, and not wanting to have to start over again from scratch, Mort slung the second towel over his shoulder, then stepped deftly out of his underwear and pants, and with the first green towel still hanging before him, marched naked out of the bathroom and through his bedroom like a flagman leading a parade.

He was already through the kitchen, halfway through the living room, and ten steps from the ringing phone, when the front door burst open and his father stepped in, carrying two loaded bags of groceries.

Over the tops of the grocery bags, Joseph Horowitz saw the green towel hanging before his naked son. He sucked in his breath, then stared, frozen in place, his arms straining and quivering under the weight of the loaded bags, while Mort turned and scampered back through the living room and kitchen, his test towel falling to the floor as he slammed his bedroom door behind him, the cork bulletin board flying from it's nail and crashing to the floor.

Joseph stood where he was for another moment, then dropped the grocery bags onto the kitchen counter and followed after his son, snatching up the green towel and carrying it with him to the bedroom door. He knocked. There was no answer. The telephone rang one last time.

After bending to pick up the bulletin board, Joseph knocked again, then opened the door and stepped into the room, dropping the towel and bulletin board onto Mort's bed. He heard his son crying in the bathroom. Stepping to the bathroom door, he knocked, then softly called out his son's name. "Morty," he said. "It's okay son. Listen to me." He paused, and resting his hands and forehead against the door, wrinkled his nose, shook his head, and waited for Mort's crying to let up.

"Listen to me, Morty," Joseph finally began again. "Don't worry. We are *all* apes! All of us." He drew back his head and let his hands slide down the doorfront and fall to his sides. "You've just had the misfortune to be caught at it. That's all."

No Fire, But Hard Love

At the weekly staff meeting on Tuesday, I'm half expecting Angela to fire me, or worse, shame me in front of the rest of the staff by describing to them the many horrors she found on her suprise weekend inspection. But she spends most of the meeting time discussing the importance of something she calls "hard love;" a concept she describes as the ability to love the residents enough to help them, train them, and shape their behavior, even when the helping, training or shaping seems to be the hardest—and perhaps even, at the time, the cruelest—of all courses to take. The only thing she says directly to or about *me* (though I've no doubt that the "hard love" pep talk was mostly for my benefit), is that the upcoming Saturday is the 4th of July, one of two occasions during the year—the other being New Year's Eve—that the residents are allowed to drink beer on the front porch.

"Of course you should use your discretion," she says to me with her honey-smooth voice and tight, thin-lipped smile. "I think we'd all agree that drinking a few beers here at the house is perfectly appropriate on the 4th of July—even for on-duty staff; that's you, Benny—as long as it's kept under control."

After the meeting she pulls me to the side and tells me she's already spoken to Billy about Saturday night. "He knows he can handle two beers," she says. "But any more than that and I've made it clear to him that he'll be flirting with his third warning, and a trip back to Palmview. So I think he'll be no trouble. Same with Lucius. Two beers. And as I said, with the others you can use your discretion." She folds her arms in front of her. "And if they do give you trouble, just remember. Sometimes it takes a lot of hard loving to do this job well."

"Right," I say. "And did I hear you say it's even okay for *me* to drink a beer or two?"

"Well technically, of course, it's against the State Mental Health law. But as long as you are discrete, and can keep things reasonably quiet, then yes, I'm willing to look the other way. A few beers is fine. In fact I think it's a healthy way of giving the residents the message that normal people often *do* drink on such occasions, but in a responsible and appropriate manner."

I tell her that sounds good, and assure her I'll get all the programs run Saturday morning and afternoon before any beer cans are popped open.

"That's a super idea," she says, and I smile, but uneasily, for her encouragement always sounds a bit too much like positive reinforcement; more calculated than spontaneous and sincere.

I'm backing away, wishing her a happy 4th of July, when she says, "Yes, well I might just see you on the 4th. Our porch here is one of the best spots in town for watching the fireworks on the lake."

"Oh great!" I say, trying not to sound too surprised or dismayed.

"And if I don't make it for the fireworks I might drop in Sunday to see how everything is going."

"Okay," I say. "Then I guess I'll be seeing you *sometime* this weekend."

"There's a good chance," she says. "Whenever I'm in the area I try to stop by."

What she means, of course, is that whenever I'm working I shouldn't be surprised if at any moment she pops unexpectedly out of the woodwork. But I really can't complain. At least she didn't embarrass me in front of everyone at the meeting. And if I was in her position I'd probably be concerned about me, too, after last weekend; Billy drunk at noon, Nadia's hair in clay and tangles, Lythia lying on her Rebel flag towel on the front lawn, Emmy possibly lost on the beach, Moby and Elisha getting broiled in the sun, programs not run, the house a wreck. Hell, she'd be crazy if she wasn't worried.

The Not So Great Equalizer

At the time Mort Horowitz became a senior at Loblolly Hill College in 1954, he was an idealistic pre-med student, peculiarly—and yet, healthfully—ambivalent about death. On the one hand, because he was not inclined toward the religious or mystical, he thought of death as the enemy of life, and believed that the noble, Sisyphean mission of physicians was to do battle with this most formidable, and in the end, unconquerable foe, keeping it at bay for as long as humanly, medically possible. On the other hand, he had learned from his pessimistic father (who had died nine years earlier of a massive coronary, leaving Mort parentless at fifteen) that the lives of men were no more important or significant than the lives of apes; that in the end we all die, and so in the end—no matter what we've aspired to, pretended at, or actually managed to achieve in life—are all the same. "Death," Mort had learned from his laconically morbid father, "is The Great Equalizer."
But being an almost fanatical idealist (perhaps in reaction to his father's dour cynicism, or perhaps as a natural consequence of having grown up during two decades of evil—the depression and the Nazis—fought and conquered), he held his father's death truth to be a self-evident blessing in disguise. For if all humans really were, as his father suggested, equal in death, equal in the end, then they must also be equal in life. (Like a ballgame, Mort thought, the score *at the end* was what counted, was what went into the record books and became synonymous with the game itself.) So while death was his avowed enemy, to

be steadfastly and unremittingly battled every step of the way, it was at the same time his humanist-idealist egalitarian inspiration, for he knew that even if he *could*, as a doctor, somehow help his patients live forever—if he *could* somehow tilt them toward that Frankensteinian, Ponce de Leonian dream of immortality—then the inequalities between those people would, instead of diminishing to zero at the end, at death (and so, throughout), widen steadily and irrevocably into a non-egalitarian, albeit deathless future.

Thus he'd carefully, rationally, and idealistically chosen his profession, intending to become a doctor, or, in his view, a midwife of egalitarianism, ushering people through as healthful a life as possible on their way to The Great Equalizer.

When he entered Loblolly Hill College as a freshman in 1951, Mort took a job as an orderly at Loblolly Hill General Hospital in order to earn enough to pay for his tuition, room and board—and, at least once every two or three weeks, a new classical record—and save whatever he could for medical school. And so every semester he worked six days and forty-eight hours a week, from 3 PM to 11 PM, while carrying a minimum course load of fifteen hours. He studied late at night, after work, slept for three or four hours, then studied again early in the morning, before classes. He had no free time except Saturday mornings (and on Saturday mornings he almost always studied) and Sundays. But by Sunday he was inevitably too cumulatively exhausted from his frenzied work schedule to do anything more than sleep late—sometimes until two or three in the afternoon—then putter about his apartment, fixing chicken liver or egg salad sandwiches and listening to Beethoven, Mozart or Bach.

Following such a tight schedule, Mort had few opportunities to go out with, or even meet, any young Loblolly Hill women. But what made this inherently difficult situation nearly intolerable for him, were the dual facts that

Loblolly Hill College was not yet coeducational, and that Loblolly Hill General Hospital seemed to employ women only if they were over thirty, and married. (And in fact this *was* the tacit policy of the hospital administrators, who assumed they would lose any younger female employees they hired, to marriage and/or children.) And so he would never have had the time or chance to meet and get to know Eudora Bacon, a young piano teacher who lived just west of Loblolly Hill with her parents, had she not fallen asleep at the wheel of her father's Plymouth late one night, on the way home from a concert given by the Atlanta Symphony Orchestra during the fall term of Mort's junior year, and ended up at Loblolly Hill General Hospital.

Years later he often kidded her that even before their first official date together, she spent all her time with him on her back, in bed, and furthermore, that before they ever even spoke their first words to one another, he'd come to know her intimately (literally, for he'd emptied her bedpan the first afternoon of her hospital stay).

Eudora, a pouty-mouthed girl who thought her cinnamon-colored hair was too thick, her hips were too wide, and her chin was too angular, remained in traction for seven weeks. And it would have seemed far longer than seven weeks if, in passing, she hadn't mentioned to Mort that she'd been on her way home from the symphony when she'd had her accident.

Surprised and delighted to find a girl his own age (a year and a half older, actually, but to Mort, given his circumstances, a year and a half was close enough) who shared his zeal for Beethoven symphonies and Mozart operas, he happily brought in for her his portable hi-fi, along with his entire record collection, and from 3:00 to 11:00 managed to get up to her room at least once or twice an hour to flip over the records so that she wouldn't have to constantly buzz for the nurses.

Mort was thrilled the first time she stood and awkwardly walked with crutches, and during the next two weeks he came in half an hour before his shift every day to help her out of bed and slowly walk with her through the hospital corridors, coaching and encouraging her; praising her efforts and delighting in her progress.

Eudora fell in love with his energy and enthusiasm, and with his ineptitude at hiding his feelings for her. It was the Sunday before she was to be discharged from Loblolly Hill General that Mort appeared, blushing, at the doorway to her room with seven long-stemmed red roses (he'd sniffed through every red rose at the florist's and selected only the most fragrant of them), and stayed with her all afternoon and evening. They talked, drank apple juice, listened to Rachmaninoff, Grieg, and Tchaikovsky, held hands, and smiled at one another, as if cautiously trying on the relationship for size. And less than six months later, the summer after Mort's junior year at Loblolly Hill College, they decided they were indeed a perfect fit, and were married a week later by a justice of the peace.

It was during the autumn of Mort's senior year that two of his closest friends from Loblolly Hill General—Clyde Spurrier and Hack Pennock, both of whom had been working at the hospital for years—met him, at the end of a Thursday night shift, just outside the emergency room entranceway, and told him they wanted to talk.

"Of course," Mort said, buttoning his knee-length tweed coat, alarmed by their unusually business-like and purposeful manner. "Let's talk."

"Not here," Clyde Spurrier looked over his shoulder at the hospital. "Let's go on to my house. Nancy ought to be heating us up some coffee about now."

The Spurriers lived in a small clapboard house with faded and peeling blue paint, just three blocks downhill from the hospital. As soon as the three men arrived, Spurrier's wife served coffee, and saltines with margarine and peach jam, while Mort called Eudora to let her know he'd be home late. When they were all sitting in a circle, Spurrier, a middle-aged white-haired man who'd been working in maintenance at the hospital since he was a teenager, said, "Listen Morty. You been a good friend to all of us ever since you started to working here. And you are the only one we know that's got enough education to help us out."

Hack Pennock, who'd been hired to work in the Loblolly Hill General laundry room after losing an arm in Germany toward the end of World War I, nodded. "And when Clyde says 'we,' he is not just talking about him and me. He is talking about everyone works over to the hospital. All the ones that's not been educated."

"Listen here Morty." It was Spurrier again. He curled his fingers around the coffee mug and let the steam rise into his face. "You working at the hospital to pay your way through college. In a year you will be gone, and in five years you will be making more money in a day than any of us make in a month."

Money had little to do with Mort's idealistic vision of doctoring, yet he knew Spurrier was right. There were over 200 unskilled laborers working at Loblolly Hill General, who, like Mort, put in a *minimum* of forty hours every week, and earned no more than forty cents an hour; $3.20 a day (for hospitals were not covered by minimum wage laws). Unlike Mort, however, as Spurrier now pointed out, many of them had worked here for a long time already, most of their adult lives, and virtually all of them would still be working here long after Mort had moved on and up. Working until they were forced to retire. By illness, infirmity, or death.

"What can I do to help?" Mort, the idealist, wanted to know.

Spurrier set his mug on the coffee table, stood, then pulled a sheet of yellow paper from his pocket, unfolded it, and handed it to his young friend, explaining, so that Mort was simultaneously listening to and reading the same information, "We want 75¢ a hour; minimum wage. We want sick pay, and overtime. And maybe retirement pay. Now we know that all sounds like a lot—"

Mort held up his hand. "It is *not* a lot. It's no more than you deserve. But how can *I* help?"

"You are educated," Pennock said, gesturing with his stub of an arm.

"*Getting* educated," Mort corrected him.

"You speak their language." Spurrier took the yellow sheet of paper from Mort and flipped it toward the coffee table, missing, so that he had to bend over with a quiet groan, holding the small of his back as he snatched up the paper and carefully *set* it on the table this time. "I don't expect you heard, because we did not want to make a big fuss, but last year Hack and me, and Marge and Furry Eckler from the kitchen, tried talking to some of the department heads. But all they said was that they had nothing to do with what we was complaining about, and how we ought to take our complaining somewhere else. And not on hospital time. So we took it somewhere else. We went to see Muckley, and near about got ourselves fired. He don't even want to listen."

"You are educated," Pennock said again. "He might listen to you. You can explain it better."

Mort agreed. He believed himself to be a hard and competent worker, and was confident that he was highly respected and well-liked by the hospital administrators. He'd spoken with Chet Muckley, the chief administrator, perhaps a dozen or more times. Always short, friendly conversations. To Mort, Muckley seemed a reasonable, but driven man; the sort you might have to slap in the face with some attention-getting words, if you wanted him to stand and listen for more than a few seconds.

Thus, Mort thought it was quite possible, quite likely even, that his friends were absolutely right. All they needed was a spokesman who was eloquent enough to command this busy administrator's attention and verbally paint for him a clear picture of the despair these good people were suffering at the hands of his administration.

Before Mort left, having promised to speak with Muckley in the morning, Spurrier added, "If he does not listen to *you*, you can tell him we are prepared to go further."

"Don't worry," Mort assured him. "He'll listen."

The next morning, during the hour break between his zoology and anatomy classes, Mort walked to the hospital, which was at the top of the same hill that the college was at the bottom of. He climbed the stairs to the fourth floor, knocked on Muckley's door and was invited in. As soon as Muckley saw that it was Mort, he stood and extended a heavy arm across the desk. "Morty. How's my school boy?"

"Fine thank you, Mr. Muckley. And you?"

"Well, you know, I can't complain," Muckley said, hitching up his belt, then walking around to the front of his desk to half sit on its edge, one foot on the floor, the other dangling just above it. "Working too hard, my wife keeps telling me." He winked at Mort. "But she is a woman, and will not understand that it's hard work what keeps a man going."

Muckley was a big, thickish man, and though at first glance one might have thought him to be more flaccid than muscular, there was about him an inscrutable hardness, as if maybe half an inch below his fleshly exterior he was heavily and dangerously armoured. He had a disproportionately small head, the smallness of which was accentuated by a close-cropped hair style; the same hair style he'd worn in the navy, a decade earlier. His hair might have been brown, blonde, or even gray; it was so short that it was impossible to tell.

When Muckley, all the amenities scrupulously out of the way now, asked Mort what he could do for him, Mort clasped his hands behind his back. "I think you might have a problem here at the hospital, Mr. Muckley."

"A problem?" Muckley's dangling leg went rigid.

"Yes sir. A situation which needs to be straightened out." Now that he had Muckley's attention, Mort was determined to get right to the point. "Your non-skilled employees—and I've checked and found there are nearly 230 of them—are unhappy with the working conditions here. They are working forty-eight, and, in some cases, fifty-six hours a week, yet barely making ends meet. And the worst part is that they feel they are not given the courtesy and respect by the administration that is due them. They are a good, loyal, hardworking group of people, and yet when they bring a legitimate grievance to one of their department heads, and ask them to sit down and talk about it, they are simply told to get back to work; and so they feel they have nowhere to turn."

Muckley slid off his desk edge. "Well I'll tell you what, son," he said. "I'm not the one's got the problem. *You* are."

Mort, the implacable idealist, was stunned. He unclasped his hands and backed up a step. "Okay Mr. Muckley. But I don't think this will be the end of it."

Muckley re-hitched his pants. "You threatening me?"

"No sir." Mort held up both hands, as if to show Muckley that he was unarmed. "I'm only telling you that these people are unhappy. And sincerely determined. And I really don't know what they have in mind, but I do know that asking me to speak to you was just their way of taking a first step. So I don't think this is a problem that's going to simply go away if you close your eyes long enough."

"You're the only thing's going to 'simply' go away," Muckley said, his cheek muscles beginning to quiver. "Now get on out of here. Vamoose!"

"Yes sir," Mort said.

After work that night, Mort met again at Spurrier's house, with Spurrier and Pennock. It was the chilliest night yet that autumn, and the three of them huddled about Spurrier's portable heater, Spurrier and Pennock, listening carefully, but reacting without surprise or emotion, while Mort described for them his meeting with Muckley.

"We are prepared to go further," Spurrier said, when Mort had finished speaking.

"You damn straight we are!" Pennock bent toward the heater, rubbing his one hand across his thigh to keep it warm.

"Well, I was sure you were," Mort said. "And that's what I told Mr. Muckley."

"We are going to bring in a union," Spurrier said.

"Ah," Mort smiled, feeling proud to be friends of these older, uneducated men, who seemed as determined and idealistic as any of his younger college classmates. "I half suspected so. And I think that's exactly what you *should* do."

"We want *you* to bring it in, Morty," Spurrier said.

"Me?! Jesus, Clyde!" Mort shook his head. "There's no way in the world. I can't. I'm already working forty-eight hours a week, and carrying eighteen hours at school. And I have a wife who, if I'm lucky, I see, awake, two or three times a week."

"We all know that," Spurrier said. "But you going to be leaving here next summer."

"If I don't flunk out, trying to do too much."

"We all will still be here," Spurrier went on. "Still earning the same. We got no place to go."

"And we believe you can pull it off," Pennock said.

"You think *I* know how to bring in a union?"

"You are educated," Spurrier reminded him. "You got the know-how."

"I'm studying to be a doctor," Mort pointed out. "I'm taking courses in anatomy, zoology and chemistry. Not unionizing."

"We believe you can do it," Pennock said again.

Mort crossed his arms, let his head tilt back, and looked at the ceiling. The paint was peeling in half a dozen places. He shut his eyes, unable to imagine that while working full time, carrying a heavy course load, and trying to be a loving and attentive husband, he would have time to learn how to organize, and then bring in a union. And yet these were his friends. Their cause was just. And while his own lot was about to dramatically improve, they were stuck here, trapped, as it were, by fate and circumstance. Helping, he knew, had to be the right thing to do. For if he simply turned his back on them now, he would be letting them down for good; letting down nearly 230 of these decent, hardworking people. How would he ever live with himself? What did all his noble ideals matter if he was not willing to sacrifice and struggle for those ideals. "I'll tell you what," he finally said, his eyes blinking open, his chin dropping back toward his chest. "Let me talk to Dorie and sleep on it. I'll get back to you tomorrow night."

And although when Mort spoke with Eudora she was appalled by the idea of his spearheading a union at the same time he was working and studying to get into a fine medical school, the next night he told Spurrier and Pennock he would try to help them out.

The only problem was that he didn't know how or where to begin.

The first person he sought help from was George Lieberman, his political science professor, an energetic, reform-minded young man who, in the 1952 presidential election had campaigned vigorously for Adlai Stevenson. Lieberman happily put Mort in touch with Wilson Foy, the union representative of the Georgia Pencil Company in Atlanta. Arrangements were quickly made, and the next Saturday morning Mort rode the bus to Atlanta to meet with Foy, a tall, wiry man who spoke with a Boston accent, but chewed toothpicks with the ease and grace of a lifelong southerner. Foy explained to Mort that he simply needed the signatures of half the non-skilled hospital employees on a petition requesting that an election be held to determine whether or not those non-skilled employees wished to unionize. If he could get those signatures, the hospital administration would, by law, be forced to allow them to hold that election.

Back in Loblolly Hill, Mort jubilantly explained to Eudora how easy it would be to force an election. Respected as he was among the employees, he believed he could quickly and easily solicit all the signatures he needed without even missing a class.

Monday afternoon, as soon as he came on shift, Mort began explaining to his friends and fellow employees that he was helping them bring a union into the hospital, and that all he needed from them were their signatures on the petition (which Foy had quickly drawn up Saturday, in Atlanta).

Within five minutes, Hugh Warner, one of Muckley's assistants, had Mort by the elbow, and was pulling him to Muckley's office.

"I have heard," Muckley began, as soon as Warner pushed Mort through the office door, "that you are passing around a petition for a union election."

"Yes sir," Mort said. "That's right. I tried to tell you the last—"

"Well let me try to tell *you!*" Muckley cut him off. "We will not have a union here, and if I *ever* catch you even *talking* about a union on hospital time, I'm going to fire you. You understand me?"

"Yes sir."

"Good. Then got on out. Vamoose. You got a job to do."

"Yes sir."

Shaken by Muckley's threat, yet more determined now than ever to overhaul the terrible injustices of Loblolly Hill General, Mort, instead of openly soliciting signatures, began to surreptitiously organize petition-signing meetings after work, at Spurrier's house.

Within a week he had all but three signatures of the 78 non-skilled employees who worked on his shift. But because there were 226 non-skilled hospital employees, he needed at least 113 signatures. And Foy had told Mort that 125 signatures would be safer. So Mort figured he would need about fifty signatures from those employees who worked the 7 AM to 3 PM shift before him, and the 11 PM to 7 AM shift after him. And to get those signatures he began to sneak into the hospital before and after his own shift, hide in the utility rooms and linen closets, and hijack the workers as they walked past, pulling them into the closet with him and trying to persuade them to sign the petition. It was more difficult to convince the people on these shifts to sign, because even though they would have all heartily supported an improvement in their working conditions, most of them didn't know Mort as well as the employees on his own shift did, and were more reluctant to sign; more frightened that their signatures might gain them nothing, but cost them their jobs.

With his sedulous efforts to solicit signatures, Mort began to miss some classes now, and had to study harder and later to catch up on what he missed. He slept less, ate less, and appeared increasingly gaunt and red-eyed. But he assured Eudora it would only be a matter of weeks before he had all the signatures he needed to force an election.

And while she worried about his health and his grades, she was, at the same time, proud of him, believing in her heart that although what he was doing was inconvenient and worrisome for her, while difficult and risky for him, it was nevertheless the right thing, the honorable and ethical thing, to be doing.

Early on a Monday morning in the middle of November, Mort knocked on Muckley's office door, petition in hand.

"I thought I told you," Muckley said, "I didn't want to talk to you about any of this again."

"Yes sir. You did tell me. But you're going to *have* to talk about it now." Mort didn't bat an eye. "By law."

"Huh?"

Mort showed him the carbon copy of the petition. Briefly, Muckley looked it over, then crumpled the four pages of signatures into a tight ball with both hands, dropped it into the wastebasket by his desk and calmly told Mort to get out.

"Okay, I'll get out. But you've got to let us have an election now."

"We will *not* have an election."

"Look, Mr. Muckley. The law says we *will* have an election. Now up to this moment we've tried to contain this disagreement; tried to keep it in the hospital family. We haven't taken our case to the community. But we are prepared to do that. And we believe the community will be supportive."

Muckley slammed his hands down on his desktop. "*You are fired,*" he screamed. "Now get the hell out of here. And if I see you set *foot* in this hospital I will have you arrested."

"Yes sir," Mort said.

Now Mort met with his ex-fellow employees on the sidewalk in front of the hospital as they were coming to and leaving from work, and organized additional meetings at Spurrier's house. Mort planned it so that the strike would take place on December 13th, the day after his last final exam of the semester. (Not having to work at the hospital, he was able to spend more time studying than he ever had, and after each exam felt confident that he'd done his best.)

At 3:00, the afternoon of December 13th, the employees who worked the 7 AM to 3 PM shift walked out of the hospital to join with Mort, Spurrier, Pennock, and the rest of the 3 PM to 11 PM employees, who'd arrived in front of the hospital with protest signs, mittens and thermoses filled with hot coffee. From 3:00 that afternoon until 7:00 that evening, over 100 employees marched around the hospital in a quiet, resolute circle, their placards hoisted high. The next morning there were nearly 150 employees on the picket line by 7:00. During the next few hours less than twenty non-skilled workers crossed the picket line; and those that crossed it, crossed apologetically and without incident. The Administrators also crossed the line without incident, glowering carefully at the strikers' faces, as if storing the memory for future reference. The doctors, nurses and lab technicians crossed the line, many of them patting the backs of the strikers, or voicing their support. And dozens of students and professors from the Loblolly Hill campus—in fact George Lieberman's entire freshman political science class, along with Lieberman himself—came up the hill to watch and talk with the strikers, and cheer them on.

By noon all the hospital patients who weren't in critical or serious condition were sent home. And at 3:00 that afternoon, Eudora found Mort on the picket line and told him that Warner, the assistant administrator, had just called and asked her to find her husband and send him up to the office so that they could have a talk.

Certain that this was the breakthrough they'd been hoping for, Mort lifted Eudora off the ground, then hugged Spurrier and Pennock, who were directly behind him in the picket line. Holding up crossed fingers, he turned, marched into the hospital and up the stairs to Warner's office, thinking, "Muckley is so outraged he won't even concede honorably, face to face. Instead he deals with me through his crony."

He knocked on Warner's door, and Warner immediately called for him to come in.

"Sit down, Morty." Warner spoke pleasantly and with a smile. He was an average-sized man with huge hands; the sort of hands Eudora would have envied, for they could have easily spanned an octave and a half of a piano keyboard. Fortunately or unfortunately, Warner had never attempted to play the piano. However, he occasionally wore a sweater with the numerals "66" stitched to one pocket, because nineteen years earlier, when Mort was only four, Warner had set a Loblolly Hill single season Division III College football record, catching 66 passes with those monster hands, 14 of them—another record—in one game. He opened his record-setting hands now, turned them palms up, and still smiling, said, "Morty, we have all had an eye on you for nearly four years now. And I mean to tell you, we really think you are going to be something."

"Thank you," Mort said cautiously, shifting in his chair and beginning to wonder exactly what Warner had called him upstairs to talk about.

"We all deeply, sincerely regret that you were fired, because, well, I'll be frank with you, Morty. You have been our all star. You have been our fair-haired boy."

Mort didn't even *have* fair hair, nevertheless he nodded, and again politely thanked Warner.

"Now I'll tell you what, Morty." Warner leaned forward, closing his palms and folding them together into an impressive mound of flesh at the center of his desk. "You get those people out there back to work today, and *the day you graduate from college* we will give you an administrative position on this staff." Warner's smile was gone now. "We'll guarantee you free medical and hospital care. You and your family. Long as you are alive. We can write it into your contract." He leaned back, his huge hands sliding from the desk, then lifting to link behind his head, pushing forward his ears. "We have also been thinking you would make a fine city councilman for Loblolly Hill, and are prepared to do everything in our power to see to it you are elected. And certainly if your wife, if Eudora, wants to work here, why we can arrange for that, too. And your children too, when you have children." He laughed. "That's some deal. Seeing as how all you got to do is get those people back in here today. You do that for us and we will draw up the contract. Now of course we *could* put you back to work today if you like, but we thought you might want to wait, on account of how that might appear to your friends."

Mort was surprised how instantly, easily and painlessly his answer came. (He was also surprised at the extraordinary powers of influence everyone seemed to be attributing to him.) "Even if I *wanted* to," he told Warner, "I couldn't do it. They are not going to go back to work without an election."

"Well," Warner said, bringing his hands from behind his head and letting them fall, out of sight, onto his lap. "I hope you will consider changing your mind. I hope you will decide you can talk them into coming back. Just the same way you talked them into walking out. Because we believe you *can* do it if you try. And if we have not, with our very generous offer, convinced you to try, why we have other ways of convincing you."

"Other ways?" Mort shifted again in his chair, the springs squeaking.

"You think about it, Morty. And maybe you will decide that free family medical care, lifetime family job security, and a paid seat on the city council—plus the many privileges that go along with that—are not the sorts of things a young man in your position would want to refuse."

"But," Mort said. "What makes—"

"Listen to me," Warner interrupted. "How long you think those people can stay out there, anyway? How long you think they can go without a paycheck? Without food in their stomachs, and their children's stomachs? Without heat to keep them warm through the winter? How long?! You just ask them that, and I guarantee you they will come back to work."

"*We* are prepared to stay out there as long as *we* have to," Mort said.

"Well, we'll just see about that."

"We'll see," Mort agreed, then returned to the picket line, explaining to Spurrier and Pennock only that there had been no breakthrough. He was grateful that neither of them seemed surprised or overly disappointed. (At least not as vociferously disappointed as Eudora, whom he was unable to appease when he unhappily called to let her know that their victory hug had perhaps been a bit premature, and that he would once again be late for dinner.)

That night, on his way home from the picket line, Mort found out what Warner meant when he said that they had "other ways" of convincing him. He was two and a half blocks from home when someone jumped from behind a hedge and pressed something firmly to his back before he could turn around.

"What do you want?" Mort asked cautiously, raising his arms above his head, imagining he was about to be robbed. "Do you want my money? I don't have much, but I would be glad to—"

"Keep it," the man growled. "And shut your mouth. Another word and it will be your last."

A hand dropped roughly onto Mort's shoulder and turned him, shoved him, to the left. "This way," a second voice said. "Move it!"

With the gun—or what he assumed was a gun—still pressed to his spine, Mort was directed by the two men through some bushes, up and over an embankment. Just beyond the top of the embankment he was struck on the back of his head. It was a hard blow, but it did not hurt him so much as it stunned him. He spun about and, in the moonlight saw the two men, both dressed in dark pants, navy pea coats and ski masks, so that all he could see of their faces were their eyes and mouths. Neither seemed to be carrying a gun. They came after him now, one of them, the smaller but thicker man, grabbing Mort's forearm and trying to move quickly behind him. Mort, who'd never in his life been in a fist fight, lunged into the smaller man, lowering a shoulder, and driving him to the ground. The tall man jumped on Mort's back, pulled him up roughly by his coat, and held back his arms while the man who'd been tackled scrambled to his feet, and grunting, punched Mort twice in the stomach, then five or six times in the chest and shoulders, and finally in the stomach again, knocking the wind out of him. The taller man now let go of Mort's arms, and stepped back, allowing Mort to slump to his knees, his lungs struggling to work. By the time he'd caught his wind and looked up, the two men were gone. In the distance he could see the hospital, lit by the glow of the parking lot lights.

He hoped, as he hobbled home, that he would be able to hide from Eudora what had happened. And indeed, were it not for the two rips in the knees of Mort's pants she might never have suspected, for there was no fleshly evidence of the attack; not one visible bruise.

But Eudora, who was sitting, waiting, on the couch, reading the Loblolly Hill Gazette Times, her legs tucked beneath her and to one side, noticed the rips immediately. And then she noticed that her husband was pale, and somehow not quite solid, but instead, peculiarly blurred, because he was trembling like a hypothermiac. When she asked, frightened, what the matter was, he sat beside her, and, while she hugged and calmed him, recounted the events of the past few hours.

Eudora was outraged, yet at the same time relieved, for she was certain Mort was too shaken now—too wisened up—to continue with his union crusading. "You've done everything you can," she said soothingly but firmly. "You've done the hardest part, and now your friends can do the rest. Without you."

But Mort shook his head, even as he shivered in her arms. "They're only trying to scare me," he said. "Not hurt me. I have them backed into a corner, and they are *that* desperate.

Astonished, Eudora hissed, "My God. Already you've lost your job. You've been threatened and beat up. How much more are you willing to risk losing?" She pulled away from him to let him shiver on his own. "And if you will not worry about yourself, what about me? What if they come after *your wife* as their next method of persuading you?"

"They won't, Dorie," he assured her, extending to her a trembling hand. "They can't. You see they already know they can't hurt me. That's why they hit me in the chest and shoulders, and the back of my head; why they left no marks. They can't hurt me and they know it." Eudora stood, the newspaper falling from her lap as she moved away from Mort, toward the kitchen. "If they'd wanted to hurt me," he went on, "Or even *kill* me, they could have done it easily. But these were not professional thugs, Dorie. They weren't even very good." He slumped against the couch back, shut his eyes, and laughed. "My God, I'm no fighter, but if they hadn't taken me by surprise I think I could have given them all they wanted."

The next morning at 7:00, Mort was back on the picket line with his friends. And at home that afternoon, while eating a late lunch of leftover cornbread and Brunswick stew with Eudora (who, though resigned by now to the intransigence of her husband, was nevertheless sullenly reticent, picking at the stew in silence, her head tilted languidly to one side, her cheek propped up by her fist), he received a telephone call from a woman who warned him, "They are going to flunk you out of school."

"Who is this?" Mort demanded. But he was speaking to the dial tone, for she'd already hung up.

Leaving his Brunswick stew half eaten, and explaining to Eudora that he had some school business to attend to, he ran the six blocks to the Loblolly Hill College Administration Building, and quickly found his advisor, Marshal Kendall. He sat down with Kendall, a bushy-browed man with sunken eyes and cheeks, and an oddly flexible mouth which appeared to be unusually small when he was silent, and unusually large when he spoke, and told him the entire story of his union involvement, beginning with the day he was approached for help by his unhappy and uneducated co-workers, and ending with the anonymous caller, who'd warned him that he was going to be flunked out of college.

"How are you doing this semester?" Kendall wanted to know.

"You mean, how are my grades?"

Kendall nodded.

"The same as they've always been," Mort said, more defensively than he'd intended, hurt that Kendall, who'd been his advisor for three and a half years, would even have to ask. "As I told you, I've been busy with the hospital, so I've missed more classes than usual, but I'm sure I did well on my finals."

"Then you've got nothing to worry about," Kendall assured him.

"They can't flunk me out?"

"There is no way they can flunk you out."

Relieved, Mort returned to the picket line, and was almost immediately approached by a nurse, who told him that Warner wanted to meet with him.

"I was checking to see," Warner began, as soon as Mort pushed open his office door, "if you had given any thought to that offer we made you?"

"No sir," Mort told him, having decided beforehand to say nothing of the assault two nights ago. "There is really nothing for me to think about."

"Well that's too bad," Warner said. "Yes sir, that surely is too bad. Because we still believe it is the sort of offer most smart young men would *jump* at." Warner thrust his chin forward in such a way that the tendons in his neck somehow jumped, as if to add credence to his claim. "Now I know I am not telling you anything you don't already know." His eyes opened wide here, along with his huge hands. "But it is not everyone wants to be a doctor gets to *become* a doctor."

"Of course not," Mort admitted.

"Well then, supposing you couldn't be a doctor. Supposing you did not have the grades for medical school. What would you want to do *then*?"

"I guess I would teach," Mort said. "But I *do* have the grades, so that's an academic question."

"Teach?" Warner smiled disparagingly. "You going to be a school teacher?" He said the word "school" as if it were spelled with half a dozen o's. "Too bad. A boy with your education, your intelligence, ought to be able to do better for himself."

"As I said, I'm going to be a doctor," Mort told him. "And that is as well as I *want* to do."

"Ain't everyone wants to be a doctor *gets* to be a doctor."

"What is this?" Mort demanded. "What are you trying to tell me?"

"Not anything you don't already know."

Abruptly, Mort turned and reached for the door.

"Hey!" Warner shouted. "Ain't no way in the world they can stay out there much longer."

"No?" Mort said. "You just watch us."

Two days later grades came out, and Mort found that he had been given a "D" in his anatomy class.

The first place he went was to the office of his anatomy professor, Dr. Adrian Hocott. But Hocott's office door was locked, and the lights were turned out, so he looked up his professor's address in the Loblolly Hill phone directory, walked half a mile to his house, and knocked at the front door.

Hocott's wife, a middle-aged, red-headed woman, with curls wide enough to fit a drainpipe through, opened the door. Her shoulders were slumped, her chest sunken, and she wore green wool pants and a loose gray sweater.

"Is Professor Hocott in?" Mort politely asked, his hands in his coat pockets.

Hocott's wife narrowed her eyes. "Who are you?"

"A student of his."

"He's away on vacation." She started to shut the door, but before she could, Mort caught the door with the toe of his boot.

"I don't believe you," he said evenly. "Please. I'd like to come in and talk to him." He pulled his hands from his pockets and made a helpless gesture with them, turning up his palms, his shoulders hunching. "This is important."

"Get your foot out of my doorway." She spoke in a stern, no-nonsense tone. "Or I will call the police."

Mort pulled back his foot and Hocott's wife slammed, then locked the door.

"When will he be coming back?" Mort shouted through the door.

"Go away," she answered, her voice more abject now than stern. "Or I swear I will have you arrested for trespassing."

Next Mort hurried back to the campus administration building to show Marshal Kendall his anatomy grade.

"I'm sorry, Morty," Kendall said. "But there is nothing I can do about that."

"Nothing you can do? What do you mean?" Mort pointed again to the "D" on the grade sheet. "Two days ago you guaranteed me—"

"Two days ago I told you there was no way they could flunk you out of college. This is just one class you're talking about, here. And I have no way of knowing how Dr. Hocott determined your grade. It's his viewpoint against yours, and I've got nothing to do with that."

"*Just* one class?" Mort rolled his eyes. "You think I will be accepted into *any* medical school with a 'D' in anatomy?"

"Take the course again," Kendall suggested. "You show you can get an "A" the second time around and I am sure they *will* accept you."

"Jesus," Mort said. "If I want to take the course again I'll have to stay in school another year. Hocott only teaches it during the fall semester. And even then, how do I know he won't give me another 'D'?"

"I'm sorry about that," Kendall said. "Maybe you shouldn't have missed so many classes."

Before he left campus, Mort, with relief, thought of a person who would not let him down, a person who could not ever, he was certain, be bought by anyone; George Lieberman, his political science professor, the man who'd put him in touch with Wilson Foy (the Georgia Pencil Company Union Representative), and who, on the first day of the hospital strike, had led his entire freshman political science class up the hill to talk with and cheer on the strikers. Lieberman, a Swarthmore graduate born in Braintree, Massachussetts, had come south in hopes of turning around the heads of as many southern, small town college freshmen as he could. It was Lieberman who'd fanned the already glowing fires of Mort's idealistic passions, back when *he* was an impressionable Loblolly Hill freshman. And it was Lieberman whom, only three months ago, Mort and Eudora had heard give an impassioned speech in the Loblolly Hill auditorium, hailing the

Supreme Court "Brown vs. the Board of Education of Topeka, Kansas" decision as a triumph for the cause of justice, progress, enlightenment, and the future well-being of all humanity. Nearly a quarter of the outraged Loblollians—students, faculty and townspeople—attending the talk had simply stood up, as if on cue, and walked out in silent protest. But their collective attitude had done nothing to stem the conviction in Lieberman's voice, which thundered on that afternoon, unwavering, unhesitant, until he'd said all that he'd come to say. Never one to hold back or pull punches, Lieberman, Mort was easily able to convince himself now, was the sort of man who, if your cause was good and just, would fight with you to the end.

So before returning to the picket line for the remainder of the afternoon, Mort phoned Eudora to let her know what had happened, and to explain to her that although he was aware his resolute stand was making life difficult for them both, he was nevertheless steadfastly committed to behaving as ethically as he knew how, and needed her support and encouragement now, more than ever. After the phone call he visited Lieberman in his office, invited him to dinner, and that night, over Eudora's chicken and dumplings, steamed squash and onions, and black-eyed peas, told him the entire story, including his firing by Muckley, Warner's attempted bribery and threat, the subsequent attack—which Mort could only construe as the carrying out of that threat—the anonymous phone call regarding Mort's flunking out of school, and the incredible "D" Hocott had given him in the course he was certain he deserved an "A" in, a "B" at the very worst.

As Mort had suspected and hoped, Lieberman, a tall, gaunt man with misleadingly sleepy eyes and small, delicate hands, was moved and outraged by the story, and anxious to help out.

"I always thought Hocott was a decent guy," he told Mort, shaking his head as he stirred cream into his coffee.

"That's what I thought," Mort agreed.

"Muckley obviously has something on him. But it's hard for me to believe that there's any sort of deeper connection, any complicity between the hospital and college. And most likely, there *is* no complicity. After all, Kendall's attitude isn't at all suspicious or surprising. Because Kendall is a stooge and a philistine, who wouldn't stick his neck out for anyone, for any reason. So at this point I think it's safe to assume it's only Hocott they've blackmailed."

"Blackmail." Eudora shuddered at the word. "So what can we do?"

"Try not to worry," Lieberman said. "Your husband is right. The chances are remote that they would be stupid enough to hurt either of you." He turned to Mort. "Tomorrow morning I'll speak with Chancellor Creasey. We should be able to arrange to see a copy of your final exam, which I'm sure will be all we'll need to have that "D" removed from your transcript."

Beneath the table Eudora found and squeezed Mort's hand, and he smiled at her gratefully.

"And if we can somehow get Hocott to talk," Lieberman went on, "to admit that Muckley and Warner blackmailed him, we may be able to convince Muckley to hold your union election whenever we *want* him to hold it."

The next afternoon, while Mort was walking the picket line, Lieberman drove up in his blue Oldsmobile and waved Mort over. Handing to Hack Pennock the placard he was carrying, Mort hurried to the curb, and squatting, looked at Lieberman through the rolled-up passenger window.

Lieberman shook his head, then patted the car seat. "Get in," he said grimly. "I've got some information you'll be interested in."

Mort pulled open the door, slid in, and Lieberman immediately drove off, heading down the hill, then turning left on Campus Way, which cut through the heart of Loblolly Hill College, dividing it into North Campus and South Campus.

"What's going on?" Mort asked Lieberman. "What happened?"

"What happened is that this thing is a hell of a lot bigger than I thought," Lieberman said. "Hocott is only the tip of the Goddamned iceberg."

"What do you mean?" Mort swiveled to his left, his back against the car door, his left knee lifted onto the seat so that he could face Lieberman without having to turn his head. "What did you find out?"

"Only that the chancellor of Loblolly College is in on this, too," Lieberman said.

"Creasey? He won't help with my grade?"

"I never even got that far," Lieberman said, his fingers opening and closing, gripping and re-gripping the steering wheel. "Soon as I mentioned that I thought he had a problem with one of his teachers being blackmailed by the hospital, he told me I'd do better to not go poking my nose where it didn't belong." Lieberman circled through the gymnasium parking lot and back onto Campus Way, his tires squealing as the car lurched back in the direction it had just come from. "I told Creasey I was sorry, but that my nose had never been able to resist poking into places that smelled fishy, and that it had only recently found a place that smelled *particularly* fishy, and was, in fact, smelling fishier all the time."

Lieberman started to turn toward town, then changing his mind, wrenched the steering wheel to the right and headed back up the hill toward the hospital. "Don't mind my driving," he said, switching off the heat, then cracking open his window. "I don't know where the hell I'm going." He laughed. "And I mean that literally. The bastard fired me."

Mort sank into his seat, his stomach going weak. "God, but how could he do that? On what grounds?"

"Same question *I* asked him." Lieberman unbuttoned his coat with one hand, and loosened his tie. "Is it just me? I'm sweating like a dog in here." He rolled his window down another inch. "I told him there was no way; that he had no reason for firing me. So he asked me if I would be willing to sign an affidavit stating I was not now and had never been a member of the Communist Party. Christ! And I've always admired the bloody bastard because he never went in for that McCarthy garbage."

"You wouldn't sign?"

Lieberman didn't even answer. It was as if he'd assumed Mort's question was rhetorical. "They're up to their asses in *something* here," he said, pulling to the same spot in front of the line of protestors where, five minutes earlier, Mort had ducked into his car. "I don't know. Creasey's a bigwig on the City Council, and you mentioned that Warner offered to help get you elected. Maybe there's some kind of embezzling going on at the hospital, and Muckley is cutting Creasey in. Maybe the hospital, the college, and the City Council are all in on it together. Listen. You think you could get into the hospital books? Are you friends with any of the accountants?"

"No!" Mort said immediately, unable to picture himself doing battle against the impossible odds of this evidently monolithic evil, as if he was some heroic dragonslayer. "I mean, I *am* friends with an accountant there, and I might be able to get into the books. But it's not worth it." He slid his hands under his thigh bottoms and stared at the rubber floor mat. "I already feel terribly responsible."

"For what?" Lieberman asked sharply.

Mort shrugged. "It's on my account that you've lost your job."

"Wait just a minute there," Lieberman snapped. "Don't flatter yourself. I'm the only one responsible for my actions."

Mort frowned, shivering. "Of course," he said. "I'm sorry." A minute later he added, "I'm just using you as an excuse, to cover up my own cowardice."

"Achhh!" Lieberman dismissed Mort's confession with an insouciant wave of his hand. "You're right. Muckley and Creasey aren't worth it. Even if you get them, there's a hundred more just like them, lined up, waiting to step in and take their places."

Mort looked up at Lieberman, sadly. It was hard for him to believe that this was a conversation between two idealists.

"I'll tell you what," Lieberman went on, patting Mort on the shoulder and smiling. "If you can bring this union in here, and still get into medical school with a "D" on your transcript, *that* will be plenty!"

"And what about you?" Mort wanted to know.

"Don't worry about me." Lieberman opened the glove compartment and pulled out a pen. "I originally came to Loblolly Hill with the intention of staying for five years. So you see, I should have left two years ago, anyway." He turned around to tear a small blank corner from a newspaper on the back seat, then, using the center of the steering wheel for backing, jotted down his parents' Massachussetts address. "Write and let me know how you fared with all this,"

Mort assured Lieberman he would write as soon as there was any news, but while he shook hands with his professor friend, thanked him and wished him luck, he felt as though something sadly irrevocable were slipping through his fingers and forever beyond his reach.

Three days later, Wilson Foy and two of his union attorneys met briefly with Muckley and Warner. After Foy's attorneys explained the federal law on union elections, Foy informed them that he'd contacted three major Atlanta newspapers and a radio and television station, and was ready to bring them to Loblolly Hill if the election was not held within a week.

That afternoon, Muckley called Mort up to his office and asked him what it was that the workers wanted.

"That's simple," Mort said, "They want a chance to negotiate."

"Negotiate? Negotiate what?"

"A contract," Mort said. "They want to be guaranteed minimum wage. They want a forty-hour work week, and overtime pay for anything beyond forty hours. They want sick pay. They want paid vacation. And they want some kind of retirement program."

"Retirement program?" Muckley ran his hand slowly over his bristly head, from front to back. "What the hell they think I'm running here? A bank?" He gestured toward the wall. "They think I got me a vault in here with a million dollars?"

"No sir," Mort said. "They just think they deserve a chance to negotiate."

"There's that word again," Muckley complained. "Ne*go*tiate. Sounds like a word that maybe come from Africa. Ne*go*tiate." His jaw dropped two inches as he said it. "So I don't suppose they would be able to work and negotiate at the same time?"

"Yes sir. If you just let us have the union election, they will all go back to work. And they'll elect someone as their representative to negotiate for them."

"And they will work all the while we busy negotiating?"

"Yes sir."

"And what if they don't like what comes out of the negotiating?"

"I don't think you'll find them to be unreasonable."

"Well hell, go on and have your damn election then, and as soon as they go back to work you and me will negotiate."

"Well, it will be up to the union to elect a representative to negotiate," Mort explained. "And Mr. Foy will probably help out, since he's had experience at this."

"Oh boy," Muckley said. "An experienced negotiator. Ain't we lucky?"

Four days later the election was held. The union of nonskilled hospital laborers was approved with over 90% of the vote, and Mort was unanimously elected to carry out the contract negotiations along with Foy. The following morning the striking hospital employees went happily back to work.

For the next two months, while Mort negotiated and studied, Eudora, who'd been earning thirty dollars a week with her piano lessons, now, in order to support herself and her unemployed husband, had to take a job ladling out mashed potatoes, green beans, salisbury steak, and the like, at the Loblolly Hill College Cafeteria, five afternoons and evenings every week. She hated her work, hated sweating and ladling, and wearing a hairnet, but consoled herself with the notion that the job was only temporary; was only for the duration of the contract negotiations.

Meanwhile, Mort and Foy had little problem persuading Muckley to agree to pay minimum wage, and to cut the work week to forty hours, with time and a half for any employee who worked more than forty hours. But the ideas of sick pay, paid vacation, and a modest retirement program did not sit well with Muckley. "There is no way I'm going to pay anyone to not work!" he insisted. "They can take two weeks off every year if that's what they want. And I have never stopped anyone from being sick or retiring. But I'll be hanged if I'm going to *pay* anyone to do it."

After a month and a half of incessant haggling, meeting and re-meeting with Muckley, then with the union members, even threatening, at one point, to go back on strike, Mort and Foy at last convinced Muckley to agree to pay half-time sick wages—eight hours every month—which, if accumulated by healthy workers over the course of the year, could be used as paid vacation time. But Muckley insisted he would shut down the hospital before he agreed to any paid vacation above and beyond the un-utilized sick time, or to *any* sort of retirement program. And he would only sign the contract if it were good for ten years. In the end, reluctantly, he agreed to a six-year contract.

A meeting of all union members was called, and Muckley's final offer was explained. Mort assured everyone that he and Foy had wrenched as many concessions out of Muckley as they thought possible, and that in any case, they could re-negotiate the contract again in six years. A vote was taken, and the next day the contract was drawn up and signed, and Muckley was so relieved to have everything behind him for another six years that he even re-hired Mort, whom he knew to be one of the hospital's most dependable and competent employees.

It was two weeks later that Clyde Spurrier ran into Mort, who was washing his hands in the emergency room lavatory, and told him there was talk going around the union that he, Mort, had sold them out with that six-year contract in order to get his job back. "See, it wouldn't have been so bad," Spurrier said, leaning against the paper towel dispenser beside the sink. "But there's quite a few that's due to retire the next six years. Only they don't want to retire because there is not any retirement program at all. And they are afraid that before Muckley signs a new contract in six years *with* a retirement program, he will *force* them to retire so he can save himself some money."

"Sold them out?" Mort thought, too astonished, too outraged, to speak. Without bothering to dry his hands he turned away from Spurrier, walked out of the lavatory—*"Sold them fucking out?!"* his voice screaming inside his head now—out of the emergency room, and out of Loblolly Hill General Hospital. Forever.

Of course he could no longer justify his once-impassioned desire to attend medical school and eventually become a doctor, for his carefully constructed rationale—his wish to Hippocratically escort people through as long and healthful a life as humanly, medically possible, on their way to The Great Equalizer—had simply cracked apart at the foundation. Because although he remained convinced that death was life's indisputable equalizer—its miraculous instrument of egalitarianism—the equality ensured by death no longer seemed to him necessarily "great," or even good. (What good, after all, was equality, when it simply meant equally selfish, equally avaricious, equally petty and small-minded, and, as his father would surely have argued, equally ape-like?) And so, his healthfully ambivalent view of death now plunged out of balance as if it had been suddenly abandoned on a see-saw by some deviously prankish playmate. All at once death became the enemy, pure and simple, no two ways—nothing good—about it. And of course, with his nobly humanistic vision of doctoring wiped clean, and his idealistic spirit crushed, the only people he had any interest in protecting from death, from the enemy, from the not-so-great equalizer, were his wife and himself.

It was at this point that his singular goal of living to be

old and healthy began to impinge upon, and later dominate, his life agenda; and, concomitantly, at this point that he began to dream of moving to Coconut Beach, where, when he was thirteen, Mort had spent two memorable weeks with his father—the winter before he died—at the famous Sand and Surf Hotel on the shore of the Atlantic Ocean, and where his most vivid memory—aside from the lush winter greenery, the wide, white beaches, the startling abundance of January sunshine and tree-plucked citrus, and the unseasonably warm ocean water—was of the healthy aura that seemed to surround the people living there, particularly the old men playing the Sand and Surf Golf Course. He'd spent one entire day sitting tranquilly on a hill behind the 18th green, sniffing the grass-scented air, listening to the roar of the ocean and rustling of the palm fronds, and watching old men—far older, he was sure, than his pale, already weak-hearted father—with healthy winter suntans on their arms and faces, striding briskly up to their golf balls on the green, putters in hands, looking as if they didn't have a care or worry in the world, even though beyond the white beaches across the Atlantic, a world war was raging. (Even the Negro caddies in their green work uniforms seemed well-satisfied with their lot, walking behind their foppishly-attired employers with long, bouncy strides in spite of the heavy golf bags strapped like oxen yoke across their shoulders.)

With these blazing adolescent memories of Coconut Beach rekindled, Mort decided that immediately following his graduation, he and Eudora would move to the big city, to Atlanta, where there was a far greater likelihood that he could find a lucrative job; could save up and stash away as much money as possible, to be used, *as soon* as possible, to put a downpayment on a home in Coconut Beach, where he and Eudora would be free to live long and healthy lives in a peaceful and quiet, clean and serene, balmy and easy, blissful and splendorous, tropical island setting.

Independence Day Weekend At The ARC

Saturday morning, the 4th of July, I lock my bike to the front step railing and walk into ARC House, apprehensive as hell. I'm afraid that after my day-and-a-half dictatorship last weekend, the residents will all be dreading my appearance.

I confess my fears to Ty Callaghan, but he just waves his hand and says, "Don't sweat it. You've got to be a real asshole for these people to stay mad at you."

That's all I need to hear. Now when they scowl and hoot at the sight of me I'll know it's only because I'm a real asshole.

Five minutes after Ty leaves I'm sitting at the desk, reading through last week's Daily Log entries and wondering if I'll soon be proven a real asshole, when the bedroom door swings open, and out walks Billy, grinning as though he's never in his life been so happy to see someone. He enthusiastically slaps my back and says, "Hey ya Benny. How are ya Buddy? How are ya?"

And I can't keep from smiling and feeling grateful to be working here.

Lythia is the breakfast cook this week, and though she's eager to do well, it terrifies me to see her ducking and bobbing in front of the stove, waving her spatula in the air like a magic fire-wand. When she tries to stir the panful of scrambled eggs, they slosh over the side, sizzling, then turning black and smoking on the burner. I keep her away from the bacon pan because I'm afraid bacon grease sloshed onto the burner won't be as innocuous as scrambled egg. I assure her that the eggs and toast are the most important part of the meal, anyway; that lots of people, like my father, won't even eat bacon.

At the breakfast table I'm enjoying being with everyone so much that I apologize for my authoritarian demeanor the last weekend, and try to explain why I was feeling so much pressure. When they appear anxious to forgive me, I warn them that I'm feeling the same type of pressure *this* weekend. "It's mostly the programs," I tell them. "I think I already hate them as much as you all do."

"Hey," Amar says. "Now you're knocking on all ten cylinders."

I'm not sure I've ever heard *that* expression, and I don't know exactly what he means by it—or even if he said it correctly—but I take it as encouragement, and go on. "I figure if we all get the programs done early today we won't have anything to worry about later on, and we can all have a good time together. Maybe even drink a little beer tonight while we watch the fireworks."

Everyone cheers. Lucius Moon begins to rub his thighs, but I call out his name to stop him before he really gets going. "Okay everyone," I say, so stupidly enthusiastic that I sound like a church camp counselor or a bright-eyed mouseketeer. "Let's get those programs out of the way!"

The first few programs go smoothly, but halfway through Nadia's bedroom program I hit a snag. She's done a fair job of dusting, window washing, and vacuuming, but she refuses to re-fold the pants and shirts in her chest of drawers, which are obviously—even to me—in need of refolding. When I ask her what she needs to do about the wrinkled clothes in her drawers she says, "I know," but continues to sit on her bed, showing no inclination to move.

"What's wrong?" I say. "You tired?"

She nods.

"Okay. I am too. Why don't you take a rest. I'll go run

another program then come back and finish this one up with you. All right?"

"All right," she says. "Mr. Busy Bee."

I go across the hall to tell Elisha it's time to start her stove cleaning program, but find her sitting on the bed like a statue. Her bird eyes are frozen wide open, her fists clenched, and as I move closer I notice that she's trembling at a high frequency, like a tuning fork.

"What's wrong, Elisha?" I say, and when she doesn't respond I sit beside her and drop my arm across the back of her neck and shoulders. "Is it Amar?"

That does it. A sob bursts out of her and she nods.

"Go ahead," I tell her. "I've got a good crying shoulder, so you might as well take advantage."

But she chokes back a sob and begins trembling again. "Hey Elisha," I say. "It really doesn't do much good to hold it in." But she just goes on shivering as if it's thirty degrees. Christ, after seeing how easy it was for Billy to sob I figured one problem these people *didn't* have was holding in their emotions. So much for *that* generalization. "All right, Elisha. If you don't want to cry, how about if we talk?"

She nods, her teeth practically chattering, and says, "I think him and Nadia is . . . you know." And now the tears fill her eyes, overflow, and stream down her cheeks. But it's eerie. There's no sound with her crying. Just the tears. I tighten my shoulder squeeze and rock her from side to side while she moans, sounding like the tin man in *The Wizard of Oz* when his mouth was rusted shut and he was trying to tell Dorothy to use the oil can on him. She coughs out a single sob, then the moaning starts up again. I continue to rock her, until after three or four minutes she takes a deep breath, and the moaning stops.

"Now what about Nadia and Hot Dog?"

"He wants a go with her," she says, then takes another deep breath and adds, "Instead a me."

"How do you know?"

"Last night. They went agether. Downtown. With each other."

Old Don Juan Amar Casanova. I'd like to box his ears.

"Have you talked to him about it?" I ask.

She blinks her glistening bird eyes, then shakes her head.

"Well, do you think that might be a good idea? To talk to him?"

She gives a one-sided shrug, her tiny right shoulder practically lifting to her ear.

"Give it a try," I urge her, giving her shoulder a final squeeze before dropping my arm. "It's better than just sitting here and not knowing, isn't it?"

She doesn't look so sure, but takes another deep breath, pushes herself up from the bed and moves tentatively toward the door.

"Good lady," I say, then call after her, "We'll catch your program later. Okay?"

I head back to Nadia's room, but she's gone, so I hurry downstairs and find her hunched over her Banyan Tree on the front porch, her hair hanging freely, the ends dabbing at the clay. I squat directly in front of her, my knees popping, my back sliding down the porch railing. She knows I'm there but doesn't look up.

"It's looking great!" I tell her. "You still interested in selling it to me?"

"When I finish," she says, her eyes still focused on her work. "*If* you're not no meanhead to me."

"Does that mean you *won't* sell it to me if I remind you that you need to finish your bedroom program?"

"Maybe," she says, at last smiling up at me. I admire her overlapped teeth and decide I'm glad she never had them straightened with braces.

"Well under the circumstances I'll give you half an hour to work on your tree," I say. "But no more. After that you do your program." I can picture myself as a father. I'd be terrible. My kids would walk all over me, flashing sweet smiles to con me whenever they wanted a new toy or a piece of candy.

I watch while she carefully joins a branch to a thick limb, then I say, "So you and the Hot Dog are going together, huh?"

"He's a silly Billy," she says. "We're friends."

"Regular old buddy-type friends?"

She nods, smoothing out the joint where the new section of branch was attached.

"Does Hot Dog know that? That you're just friends?"

"Course," she says, then shakes back her tangled curtain of hair to squint at me with her dark eyes and add, "Mr. Curiosity Beeswax."

I watch for another minute as she continues smoothing the connecting points of the new branch, then walk back inside to see how Elisha is faring in her confrontation with Amar. Now that I know the truth I can find out if Amar is being straight with her.

On the way to Amar's room I pass Lucius, Emmy, and Lythia, who are sitting on the living room couch, watching Saturday morning cartoons. Lucius is rocking, but slows, then stops, as soon as he sees me.

"Do adults watch cartoons?" I ask them, then wait for an answer, hands on my hips.

Lythia bobs in place, smiling, probably because she saw my lips move and knows the sound will be registering in a few seconds. Emmy slaps at her hip and jerks her head to the side, whining. Lucius grins, then begins to rock again. It's as much of an answer as I'll get from them unless I wait around a few minutes for Lythia to slowly formulate then grunt out *her* answer. But I don't have time to wait around, so I shrug and say, "Well, it's up to you guys what you watch." What am I supposed to do? Force them to watch the Saturday baseball game? I'd suggest that they switch off the TV and take a walk along the lake, but I've already asked everyone to hang around all morning so we can get programs out of the way. And though I'm quickly falling behind in that regard, I haven't yet given up hope, so I leave them to watch their cartoons.

Amar is in his room, sitting on the floor with Billy. They're both sorting out change, putting each denomination into a separate pile. Elisha is nowhere to be seen.

"Hey ya Benny," Billy says. "Come on in, Buddy. Come in. Come in."

"You guys look like a couple of misers," I tell them.

"What are you doing?"

"We're putting our money together, Benny. Putting our money together, we are. Putting our money all together."

"What for?"

"Hey," Amar says, rubbing his hands together and grinning. "We're just trying to be able to figure out how many sixpacks we can buy with what we got."

"Hey you guys. I said a couple of *beers* each. Not a couple of six-packs each."

"Oh come on, Benny." Billy reaches up with a long arm to grab my hand and squeeze it. "It's the 4th of July, it is. The 4th of July. The 4th of July."

"Listen Billy," I say sternly. "I like you too much to stand by and watch you drink your way back to Palmview. I'll tie you up like a calf and sit on you if I have to, to keep you from getting kicked out."

Billy uses my hand to pull himself up and hug me, his blonde bangs tickling my ear as he nuzzles my cheek. "You know I wouldn't do that to you, Buddy. Wouldn't do that to you. Wouldn't ever do that to you. I love him, I do," he says to me, meaning that he loves *me*. "You know I do, Benny. You know I do." And I hug Billy back, surprised at how much love I *do* feel—from him and *for* him.

"So how many beers are you going to drink tonight?" I ask.

"Oh," he says casually. "Just four or five, Benny. Just four or five or six. Five or six. Five or six."

"Let's make it two or three," I say. "You and me both."

He puts his hands on his hips as if I've offended him—challenged his masculinity with a two or three beer limit—then laughs and says, "Okay Buddy. I'll do it for you, I will. Do it just for you. Just for you."

"Thanks Billy. You're great."

"Hey," Amar says, looking up from his stack of dimes. "What about me?"

"You, I'm not so sure about. Did you just talk with Elisha a few minutes ago?"

"Hey," he says. "I can't help it if she's upset with me. It's her own damned fault."

"What did you tell her?"

"I'll try to say this," he says. "That's my business."

He's right, of course. So I admit to him that it *is* his business, but that I'd like to help him out, if he'll let me. "That's what I'm here for," I tell him.

"Well," he says. "I tried to be able to explain to her the way things were. I tried to be able to tell her that me and Nadia was going together and that I wanted to be able to have back my ring. But you think she tried to listen? No sir. I'm gonna have to be able to sue her in the city courts in order for her to be able to give me back my ring."

"Is it true that you and Nadia are going together?"

He hesitates, then sullenly mutters, "I'm trying to be able to work on it."

Billy is counting his pile of quarters for the third time. "How many quarters you got there, Billy?"

"I don't know, Benny. I counted 'em all, I did. Counted 'em all. But I don't know how many I got. I just don't know. I don't know."

I count them quickly. "There's eleven of them," I tell him. "How much money is that?"

"I don't know, Benny. I got eleven quarters, I do. Eleven quarters. Eleven quarters. Counted 'em all myself, I did. Counted 'em all myself."

"Ten quarters would be $2.50," I say, wondering why I'm even bothering. "So one more would give you how much?"

"Hmmm. I don't know, Buddy. I don't know. I just don't know,."

"It would give you $2.75," I say, then turn back to Amar. "Well from what Nadia tells me, she and you *aren't* going together. You're her friend. Like a buddy-type friend." I feel like a bastard, because I'm getting such pleasure out of forcing him to admit the truth.

He glares at me, but those gray-blue eyes are still too opaque for me to focus on. "I'm trying to be able to work on it, I told you. You know it ain't as easy as picking up on a new pair of pants."

"Well do you think you've been honest with Elisha?" I say, trying to avoid another duel of pants metaphors.

"I think I been plenty honest," he says. " I *know* I been. At least I'm not trying to be able to lie to her about how I still love her. Because I don't. And she knows it. So there.

The stew is in the pudding. Am I right or am I not right?"

"You're right, Hot Dog" I admit. "I guess you *have* been honest. But I still don't think you've been very considerate of her feelings."

"Hey," he says. "What about *my* feelings?"

"What about them?" I say. "How many nickels you got there, Billy?"

"I don't know, Benny. I don't know. I just don't know."

He's counted them at least ten times. "How many did you count?"

"Well Benny, I counted 'em, I did. I counted every one. Every one." And he begins to count again.

"What *are* you feeling, Amar?"

He shifts uncomfortably, then swallows and looks away, picking at the side of his tennis shoe, where the rubber is peeling away. "I give her my ring," he says. "I go with her a year—"

"A year?" I say. "It hasn't been anywhere near a year, has it?"

"Well whatever. I give her my ring and try to be able to go with her, and she don't want me to do what I want to be able to do with my own private face."

"That's all?" I say. "You're still sore at her because she liked you better with a goatee?"

"Hey," he says. "It was a beard. And she don't like me without it." His eyes are glassy.

"Have you talked to her about it?"

"The hell with that", he says. "I ain't doing no begging on my knees, I'll tell you that much. And I'll try to say this: If *that's* what she wants, she's got another thing coming." He slaps angrily at the torn side of his tennis shoe. I want to tell him that I wasn't suggesting that he go begging on his knees, but I can see he's not exactly eager for any more of my wise counsel, so I help Billy count the rest of his change.

When I leave Billy and Amar it's almost lunch time and I've only run four and a half of the fifteen scheduled programs. I feel the pressure beginning to knot my stomach.

After lunch clean-up it takes me nearly an hour to finish Nadia's bedroom program. I feel intrusive as hell squatting beside her, checking through each of her dresser drawers. Almost the same way I feel when I have to check her teeth to make sure she's brushed them thoroughly. I can see the reasoning behind it—her drawers *are* often messy, and her teeth sometimes *do* need to be rebrushed. But I'm sure if I checked the beds, the dresser drawers, or even the teeth of a group of college students on any given night, I'd find that half of them—maybe more—were in worse shape than the beds and drawers and teeth of the people here at ARC House. And that's not even the point. I'm not sure what the point is. I just know I'm invading everyone's privacy here in a way that I would not want *my* privacy invaded. And it's more than that. It's worse than that. It doesn't feel right. Though I'm sure Angela would tell me it's just a matter of "hard love;" that it's difficult enough for the mentally handicapped to be accepted into the community when they're acting perfectly normally; that even the slightest hint of inappropriateness can only compound their difficult struggle to fit in, and that's why we sometimes must invade their privacy or re-shape their behavior until it *is* appropriate. Until they've been normalized.

"Mr. Sad Eyes," Nadia suddenly says, startling me out of my gloom. She pats my head, then gently ruffles my hair. She smells good. Like clay and kitten fur and sweat. I should probably cue her to take a shower and use deodorant, but I'm not going to.

Her hand is still ruffling my hair. I slowly turn up my face so that my forehead, and then my nose, slide under her hand.

"Mr. Strong Nose," she says, then pinches and shakes it between her thumb and forefinger while we both laugh, and her black, clay-tangled hair brushes my cheeks. "I've been wanting to do that," she says. "You know. To touch your strong nose."

"Thanks Nadia," I say, then stand to leave. "You've made me feel better. And your bedroom looks great!"

After dinner I sit on the front porch steps to relax for a few minutes. Moby sits beside me smoking a cigarette. Although he smokes quite a bit—maybe two packs or more per day, at least on weekends—he truly seems to savor each puff. He doesn't even like to talk while he's smoking. He just sucks in the smoke, then tilts back his head and lets it out slowly, watching it billow into the air. He's so pale, and has such a round head and body that if he smoked a corncob pipe instead of his cigarettes he'd look like Frosty the Snowman.

Billy and Amar tell me they're ready to head downtown to pick up a load of beer. "I've still got six programs left to run," I let them know.

"Well we're through with *our* programs," Amar says. "Both me and Billy."

"I can see that," I say. "But how about if you hold off drinking until *everyone* is through with programs?"

"I'll try to say this," he says. "We'll try to burn *that* bridge when we come to it." Then he elbows Billy in the ribs, and spits over the railing of the porch steps. "Let's go Billy Boy."

"Okay," Billy says. "Let's go. Let's go. Let's go."

"You'll hold off on drinking until everyone's ready, Billy?"

"I'll hold off, Benny. I'll hold off for you, Buddy. Hold off for you, I will. Hold off for you."

And off they go, snickering. I wouldn't really mind if they started drinking *now*— I know *I* could sure use a cold beer—but I already assured Angela I'd finish all the programs before I allowed any front porch drinking, so I'm not taking any chances. She could show up any time now, and I don't want her finding anything going on that she'd consider inappropriate.

I leave Moby on the front porch steps to take his last few loving sucks of smoke alone. I swear, when he's smoking it's the same as being around someone who's deep in meditation. In college I paid forty dollars to learn Transcendental Meditation. After attending three compulsory TM lectures I learned my personal secret mantra—during a mysterious private ceremony with my instructor in an incense reeking room of a small old house, while kneeling before a large color photograph of the Maharishi. For the next three months I was a happy, avid, twenty minutes, twice a day, meditator; until the TM promoters started plastering ads all over campus claiming that scientific studies had proven TM could bring you—in addition to inner peace—higher grades in the classroom, and success in the business world. After learning that *those* were the goals of Transcendental Meditation—A's in school and high profits in your daily business transactions—I couldn't bring myself to meditate anymore, even though I'd been enjoying it so much, because every time I sat down to shut my eyes, fold my hands in my lap, and silently chant my personal secret mantra, I felt like a genuine P. T. Barnum, once-every-minute, sucker. It was almost the same way I felt as a six year old, when my mother bought me a pair of T.C. Wingers, a new tennis shoe I'd seen advertised on Saturday morning TV as "the shoes so fast, you'll think you're wearing wings on your feet." In the commercial, a cartoon, a young boy is shown to be running so fast that white wings sprout from his heels, and he leaves the ground, running into the sky, over the clouds, above a rainbow, past the moon and sun and stars, before returning to earth. For a month I'd begged my mother to buy me a pair of Wingers, and when she finally did I ripped them out of the box, hardly able to sit still as she helped me lace them up and tie them tightly. I dashed into our backyard and raced around, trying and expecting to take off and soar into the sky, or at least hop our clothesline or fence. After a miserable and exhausting two hours I tore off my T.C. Wingers and buried them in a corner of our back yard. Practically the same thing I did with TM. Too bad, because before all those ads I was meditating every day and enjoying it. I'm sure I'd have enjoyed my T.C. Wingers if I'd never seen that Saturday morning commercial. And I'm sure I'd still be meditating today if I'd never seen those lousy ads.

I could use some T.C. Wingers now, as I hustle back and forth between the kitchen and bathroom, trying to save time by running two programs at once—Emmy's dinner dishwashing, and Lucius Moon's bathroom clean-up. Lucius has finished his bathroom and Emmy is maybe halfway through the dinner dishes, when Amar and Billy, the rest of the residents crowding behind them, come tromping into the kitchen to set a case and a half of beer on the table. A case and a half is thirty-six beers—four for each of us. It's going to be a real zoo here tonight if everyone drinks his share.

"Here's the beer, Benny. Here it is, Buddy. Here it is." The beer is some kind of generic brand. Must have been the cheapest beer they could find. But I'm not complaining. In fact I congratulate them on their smart shopping. The cheap beer—however bad it might be—probably means that Amar was using his powers of reason. (From what I've seen, Billy *has* no powers of mathematical reason, so I doubt he had much to do with the cheap beer selection.) He didn't just pick out a brand arbitrarily, but did some real shopping and comparing.

The generic cans aren't so thrilling to look at—they're white with a black "BEER" printed across the side—but they're good and cold, and I'm as anxious to pop one open as everyone else. "All right," I announce dramatically. "Programs are suspended while everyone has a beer. But just one! Then we hold off until we're finished with all the programs. Deal?"

Everyone cheers, except Emmy, who is already grimly ripping one of the cans from its plastic six-pack collar. Within seconds everyone is heading for the front porch, beer can in hand. Lythia trips and falls over Amar's heels while she's running for the front door. As I'm helping her to her feet I tell her she must have gotten drunk just looking at her can. It's not much of a joke to begin with, and after she stares at me for ten or fifteen seconds without responding, I begin to wish I'd kept my mouth shut. But when my joke finally registers she tilts back her head like a robin swallowing a worm, and gurgles out a laugh, her eyeballs rolling upward as she bobs in place and shakes a warning finger at me. Then her smile suddenly disappears, and she leans, then runs, toward the bedroom stairway.

"Where are you going, Lythia?" I say, chasing after her, catching up after she grabs the stairway bannister to stop herself. "You can't drink beer upstairs, or *anywhere* inside."

I wait for half a minute before she begins her answer,

which comes out so slowly I feel as if I'm listening to a record played at 16½ RPM's. "I'm going to get my straw," she tells me.

"Oh, right," I say. "Good idea, Lythia. Here. I'll hold that beer for you so you can hang onto the bannister. If you trust me."

A few seconds later she smiles, then turns to face the stairway and pull herself up, a step at a time.

Outside, the last pink tinges of sunset have faded from the cloud bottoms, and a full moon is rising, huge and yellow, pulling behind it a cloak of darkness. It will probably be an hour and a half before the fireworks begin. Not much time to finish Emmy's dishwashing as well as the four other programs I'm scheduled to run. And the more I suck on my beer can, the more it appeals to me to pop open the next can and forget about the programs. When Emmy quietly reaches for her second can I force myself to cue her, "What do you need to do, Emmy?" She whines something undecipherable, so I tell her she needs to finish the dinner dishes before she has another beer. "But I'll tell you what, Emmy. I'll help you out with the dishes. Don't worry about drying, Elisha. Emmy and I will take care of everything. And fast." I wink at Emmy, adding, "so we don't miss the fireworks."

"Oh *won't* we?" Emmy says, then slaps her hip, jerks her head sharply to the side, and in a business-like tone of voice, grunts, "All *right* then. Let's *go* then."

With me washing and Emmy drying we knock out the rest of the dishes in ten minutes flat. It's not exactly the officially prescribed method of running the dishwashing program, but it's a hell of a lot faster this way, and besides, I'm sick of standing over the residents like a taskmaster, watching *them* do all the dirty work. Maybe it's the beer, but right now I'm not overly concerned about following *any* officially prescribed methods. In fact, by the time we've finished the dishes I've decided to skip the other four programs I'm scheduled to run tonight. I'll squeeze them in sometime; maybe early tomorrow morning, before breakfast.

I've also decided not to worry about Angela showing up.

Hell, she may take her job seriously. But not *that* seriously. There's no way she's going to spend her 4th of July cueing and directing a porchful of half-drunk dimwits to behave appropriately. More likely her concept of appropriateness is, at this very moment, being broadened and sweetened by her third margarita at some fancy 4th of July party on the other side of the lake. Bottom's up, Angela. Here's to an evening of *easy* love and *in*appropriateness, which we *all* need, at least occasionally.

After cleaning around the sink, squeezing out the sponge and re-hanging the dishtowel, Emmy and I hurry back out to the porch and grab for our second beers. Amar and Elisha are at one end of the porch, drinking, and talking seriously, staring into each other's faces from two inches away. Hopefully, now that they're talking they'll resolve their differences and he'll give up trying to seduce Nadia.

Nadia, Lucius, and Billy are crammed shoulder to shoulder on the porch swing, laughing wildly and spilling beer as they swing higher. Lythia and Moby are on the front steps, Moby smoking another cigarette between sips of beer, and Lythia sucking on her spiral-striped straw, her head tilted as she dreamily watches Moby's smoke swirl upward. Emmy sits cross-legged on the porch floor beside the case of beer, to the right of the screen door, her incredible breasts drooping onto her thighs as she strikes up a mumbled conversation with herself.

With the porch light shining brightly upon us, I feel as though we're all on stage, so I switch off the light, offering the explanations that we'll attract too many moths, and that the darker it is, the brighter the fireworks will appear to us. The living room light, shining through the front windows, will give us all the light we need, even later on, when it's darker.

I'm standing beside Emmy, in front of the screen door, slowly sipping my second beer and having a fine time watching and listening to everyone, when the porch swing slows, and Lucius hops off. He crushes his empty beer can, drops it into the brown grocery bag where we're collecting all the empties, then heads toward Emmy and the beer.

"Hey Lucius," I say. "How many beers have you had?"

He grins proudly, holds up two fingers and says, "Two beers."

"And how many are you supposed to have?"

"Three beers." He stares at his hand and, when a third finger pops up, looks up at me as if that third finger is some sort of unchallengeable, conclusive proof.

"Two beers, Lucius," I counter, holding up my two fingers as evidence against his three. "Two is your limit."

"One more," he says, his eyes growing wider, his grin spreading.

"Lucius! You know what Angela told you."

"One more," he says again, a shiver of excitement tremoring through his body and out to his fingertips, the way the tremors of a dog shaking off water work their way through his body and out to the tip of his tail.

"All right," I say, giving in. "But you need to stay right here on the porch where I can keep an eye on you."

"I stay," he promises, and kneels eagerly, grabbing for his third beer.

"What about me, Benny?" Billy now asks, pushing himself from the porch swing to stand and stare at me accusingly, hands on his hips. "What about me, Old Buddy? What about me?" He looks huge in the dim light.

"Yeah, go on Billy. But you need to stay on the porch too. Quietly. And this is your last one."

"Okay Benny. Okay Buddy. Okay. I'll stay on the porch for you, I will. Stay right here on the porch."

Meanwhile, Lucius is taking his time selecting his third beer, and it's only after watching him for a minute that I see he's taking his sweet time fiddling with the beer cans, because he's busy staring down the front of Emmy's blouse, grinning like a wild man. Emmy is chattering to herself, non-stop, studying her black and white beer can, tilting it at different angles to the light, then touching it to her nose, her lips, and her chin. She has no idea Lucius, or anyone else, is even in the vicinity.

Loudly, I clear my throat, hoping Lucius will respond to my non-verbal cue. Instead, he looks up at me from where he's kneeling beside Emmy, says, "ooh wow," then taps her shoulder to get her attention and asks, "I touch you tit?"

I freeze, expecting Emmy to shriek and lunge at Lucius

like a mongoose at a snake. But after saying nothing for a few seconds she whispers, "Okay then," and standing, takes Lucius's hand to lead him inside.

"Hold it!" I lean back against the screen door, blocking their way. "You need to stay on the porch, Lucius. Remember? And anyway the fireworks will be starting soon."

"Ooh yuh," Lucius says. "I stay." And he shakes free of Emmy's hand, leaving her to stand there as he bends to grab a beer can.

Emmy slaps her hip, sits back down and buries her face in one hand, her fingertips at her forehead, the base of her palm at her chin. I feel like an intrusive parent, but I really want to keep an eye on Lucius. (I'd do some counseling with him about more appropriate ways of, and places for, verbally expressing his sexual feelings and desires, but I'm not worrying about appropriate behavior tonight; and even if I was, I'd *never* be able to convince Lucius that his method was in any way unsound or inappropriate and should be changed. Not after he just clearly demonstrated his method to be 100% effective.) After popping open his can he sits beside Emmy, grinning at her, while Billy, who's already taken a long chug from *his* new can, stands beside me, then taps his beer against mine, and says, "Cheers, Benny. Cheers, Old Buddy. Cheers."

I'm halfway through my third beer and feeling that initial rush of mild intoxication when the first of the fireworks lights up the sky. Angela was right. We really *do* have ringside seats here. And the light of the full moon doesn't seem to detract at all. Oohing and aahing, nearly everyone moves out to take a seat on the front steps. Amar and Elisha keep to themselves in their corner, and Nadia swings gently on the porch swing. The steps are too crowded already, so I sit beside Nadia. Even in the open night air I notice that same distinctive odor of clay, sweat and kitten fur. I'm glad I didn't cue her to use deodorant.

Fireworks light up the sky again, gold and red streaking outward from the center.

"Like trees," Nadia says to me.

"Trees?" I say. Everything is trees to her.

"Yup. Watch." She points to the small silver dot of light

zooming skyward. "See? The trunk." And when the dot explodes into green and yellow she says, "Poof. The branches. Magic."

"You're right," I say. "Sky trees." I'm feeling just happy-drunk enough to agree to almost *anything anyone* says. "You sure are crazy about your trees."

She nods. "I miss 'em like in the north. How they change colors. You know. How the leaves change colors and fall off, and you can see the trees underneath the leaves, and how underneath the leaves, when they don't got no leaves, how they do the whooshing. And you can see 'em do the whooshing and reaching. Like a bunch of whooshing, reaching arms, how they're all real happy and whooshing. And when it's spring how the leaves whoosh up out of the ground with the tree, and whoosh up through the tree, and poof! There's the leaves."

"You know you ought to meet my father," I tell her. "He's nuts about his Avocado Tree and his three Grapefruit Trees. I mean, he even talks to them. And he's got this incredible flower and vegetable garden. I know you'd get along great."

"Okay. I'll meet him," she says.

And somehow I really *can* picture her and my father hitting it off. She loves making trees and he loves growing them. They'd have to admire each other's fanaticism.

After a few more fireworks I hop off the porch swing to grab another beer, my fourth, and find Billy already standing there with a guilty grin, his hands behind his back. "You're not drinking another beer, are you Billy?"

He cackles gleefully and brings the can out from behind his back. "This is my last one, Benny. My last one, Old Buddy. My last one." It's not easy to be mad at someone who laughs the way Billy does. His mouth turns into a devilish V, while his forehead, his eyes and the upper half of his nose are practically lost in wrinkles.

"Billy!" I say, sternly as I can, happy-drunk as I am, then whisper, as if the front porch was bugged, "If Angela comes walking up now, you know what will happen to you? And to me? You promised me!"

His long right arm loops around my shoulders, the

crook of his elbow catching behind my back. He pulls me to him and says, "I know I promised you, Benny. I know, Buddy. I know." And down comes his great head to rest on my shoulder. "I love him, I do. You know I do, Benny. You know I do."

And, as I did earlier, I hug him back as hard as he's hugging me. Maybe harder, now that I have thirty-six ounces of beer bubbling through my veins. "Billy," I whisper. "If I let you drink the rest of the beer in that can, will you go straight to bed?"

"I will, Benny. I will for you, Old Buddy. I will for you."

I give Billy a final hard squeeze, pat his back a few times, then gently, but firmly, push him away. He'd hug you all night long if you let him. "Okay. Drink your beer and enjoy the fireworks. Then as soon as you're through, right to bed."

Opening *my* beer can, I move toward the front steps, where Lythia is still facing Moby, sucking on her plastic straw. Her eyelids flutter as she sucks—a strange sort of flutter—and it's while I'm staring at her fluttering eyelids that I remember she's an epileptic and should not be drinking beer. Quietly, afraid a sudden or panicked move might set her off like one of the fireworks, I edge closer to her, then slowly lower myself onto the step beside her, and say, "You know you're not supposed to drink beer, Lythia. What can happen to you if you drink beer?"

Two long minutes later she's explained to me that one beer won't hurt her, and that she's still on her first can, not quite halfway through. She must be blowing on the straw more than she's sucking. But I confiscate her can anyway, leaving her the red and white-striped straw to suck air with. She's probably right—one beer won't hurt her—but I'm not willing to chance it. Because the last thing I'm ready to deal with right now is my first grand mal.

After confiscating Lythia's beer I'm nervous as hell, so I take a few long swigs from my white and black can, then sit beside Nadia again on the porch swing, and watch the fireworks with her. I haven't really enjoyed fireworks in years, probably because to me they mostly represent the thrill of "bombs bursting in air," a thrill I can happily live without. But thinking of the fireworks as instant, sky-painted trees, the way Nadia does, I'm more easily able to enjoy them for their spectacular beauty, and before long I'm oohing, aahing, and wowing, and, between each explosion, having a great time watching everyone.

Lythia is standing on the steps now, bobbing and weaving like a shadow boxer, and sucking on her straw as if it were a cigarette. Maybe she's trying to imitate Moby, who's chain smoking like a fanatic. He doesn't even use matches; just lights up a new cigarette with the burning tip of his old one, then crushes the old one in the ash tray on the step behind him as he slowly exhales the first puff from the new one.

To our right, Lucius Moon now has his arm around Emmy, and she's doing nothing to resist. Every few minutes I hear Lucius say, "Ooh wow," or "Ooh, I like ut." But they're sitting with their backs to the wall, where the light is dimmest and the shadows darkest, so it's hard to tell exactly what they're up to. The front porch may not be the most "appropriate" place in the world for them to express their affection, but I need to keep a close eye on Lucius—he's already finished his third beer—so it's the *only* place they've got. No matter. They don't seem to be upsetting anyone else, and they're obviously happy with each other.

Billy is wandering from twosome to twosome (which is how we all, except for him, happen to be grouped), slapping backs, getting drunker and louder by the minute, bragging between gulps, "I'm drunk on my goddamned ass, I am. Drunk on my ass. Drunk on my ass." When he drinks, instead of lifting the beer can to his mouth, he lowers his mouth, along with his head and neck, to the beer can. It's got to be ten times more difficult to drink that way, but Billy could care less. The closer he can get to the ground, the better. He staggers over to Nadia and me, steadies himself, then plops between us so that we have to quickly make way to avoid having our laps crunched. "Hey ya Nadia," he says. "Hey ya Benny. How are ya Buddy? How are ya?" One long arm drops across my shoulders and the other across Nadia's. "They're the two best friends I ever had, they are. The best friends I ever had." He's probably said the same thing to each twosome already, but he sounds so convincingly sincere that I'm helpless to do anything but sit there, feeling touched that he considers me one of the two best friends he's ever had.

Lucius has stood up and is bending at the waist, rubbing the fronts of his thighs, from the tops down to his knees and back up again. Down and up, and down and up, faster and faster, until the time is right for him to spread his arms like wings and let the tremors of delight shoot through his fingertips. He must have discovered something about Emmy that excited him. She's sitting cross-legged, at his feet, her face in a shadow.

Billy lassoes me with his ropey arm and pulls me close to nuzzle at my shoulder. He'd make a terrific house pet. I tilt my head slightly to look past him. It awes me as I stare around at everyone, how astonishingly unique each of them is. Their distinguishing characteristic is supposed to be their feeble-mindedness, not their uniqueness. Maybe they're unique *because* of their lack of intelligence; they're not smart enough to understand or imitate or be molded to fit someone else's idea of normality, not smart enough to be anything other than utterly original, utterly deviant, utterly and helplessly themselves. I may know how to *act* normal, but they genuinely know how to *be* exactly who they are.

Billy's face is still pressed to my shoulder. When I tap the back of his head he jerks back. Apparently he was already half asleep. "Looks like you're pretty tired, there, Billy."

"I am a little bit, Benny. I am just a little bit."

"Well you've finished your beer, so I guess it's time for you to hit the hay, anyway."

He yawns and stretches, retracting his head like a turtle, while slowly extending his arms until, way above us, they finally reach their limit and become taut, so that for a few seconds he looks as though he's hanging from the porch ceiling by two thick ropes. After straining for another moment, the tautness goes out of his arms, and they begin their slow, crumpling descent.

By the time I've helped Billy into bed, and peed out a few ounces of beer, the fireworks display is over. Moby and Lythia are settled on the couch, watching TV, and Amar has announced that he, Nadia, and Elisha are going for a walk, or, "a little walk," as he puts it, with some sort of emphatic significance placed upon the word "little." He loves to be at the center of dramatic events; the star of his own soap opera.

Nadia's hair is clay-streaked and tangled, as usual, so I cue her, "Hey Nadia. Before you leave what do you need to do about your hair?"

She folds her arms across her chest and glares at me with those coffee-colored eyes. Amar and Elisha have started down the front steps. Amar carries the grocery sack full of empty beer cans. "I wouldn't mention it," I tell her, feeling too happily intoxicated for this kind of encounter. "I *haven't* mentioned it. But you're going out now. Right? Out into the world. And if you want to look normal—"

She turns to the door with an angry swishing of black hair, but before she can pull it open I say, "Wait a second, Nadia."

She turns back, but only with the upper half of her body. The toes of her green basketball shoes still point toward the screen door. Her fingers curl through the handle.

"Forget what I said," I tell her. With four beers under my belt I know that my judgment isn't what it should be, but I go on anyway. "Go ahead. You look fine the way you are. I mean, your hair looks just the way it *should* look." Like an idiot, I hoist my empty beer can to toast her tangled hair.

Her fingers slip from the door handle and her hand falls to her side as she turns to face me, smiling with those overlapping teeth. Overlapped perfectly. "Mr. Funny Bunny," she says, then slowly moves closer to me. Her eyes are fantastically dark. And I can smell her again. That ineffable smell. "Mr. Kind Eyes," she says. "Strong Nose Kind Eyes." And then she's skipping down the steps—her arms stretched to her sides for balance, like wings—to join Amar and Elisha, leaving me with a weak stomach. It must be all the alcohol. I'm even feeling dizzy now. Spinning slightly. And though I sit on the porch swing, and tightly cling to the chain, I continue to spin. A few minutes later I slowly, carefully, stand and leave the porch. Inside, Lythia and Moby are still watching TV, but sitting much closer to each other than before. Their knees are touching. Could be a new romance. God, those touching knees must feel good. I say hello and stagger as steadily as I can to the other end of the couch, where I sit, then snuggle into the corner. I feel much better curled up here. More warm than drunk. And then it hits me that I've lost track of Lucius. Last time I saw him, he was on the front porch with Emmy. But he's not out there anymore. And he's not in here watching TV. Hopefully he's *somewhere* in the house with Emmy. If so, then I at least know he's not peeing in the ladys' bathroom of some redneck tavern, or entertaining the old bridge fishermen, happily casting his golden line into the lake, fishing for millionaires' yachts.

Moby suddenly stands, then waddles around the back of the couch and bends down to tell me he's going to take a shower. "A short one," he says. "Five minutes."

"Take your time," I tell him. What the hell. It's a special night, so if he wants a long shower he can have it. Long as he doesn't lock the door or neglect to mop up the flood. When he's gone from the living room, Lythia looks to her left, finally noticing that Moby is no longer sitting beside her; that their knees are no longer touching. What a world it must be for her! People disappearing without warning or explanation; minute-old voices suddenly flashing into her mind with no apparent source. I wonder if she's even certain which of our faces belongs to which of our voices. "You're great, Lythia," I say to the back of her head, then snuggle deeper into my soft corner and shut my eyes. My head spins and spins, and I don't resist.

Emmy and I are slouched on the porch steps, talking to and smiling at each other, when suddenly I'm aware that she's changed. Her speech, gestures, and appearance no longer seem so ridiculous. In fact she's quite personable and attractive. She's normal. I'm smiling and listening to her, trying to figure out the cause of this dramatic change, when all at once I realize the difference is that I'm seeing Emmy through her own eyes, from inside out; that I *am* Emmy. And I'm looking at and speaking to him—to

Benny—who is aware now that I'm a normal person; a bonafide human being. In fact he sees that I'm an attractive, even sexy, woman. Our knees touch and the heat from his stare and his knees feels good. Feels right. As if this is how it should be. He's interested in me, and other men are interested in me, and we both know and accept this. But then I notice that even though he's interested, he's afraid. Not afraid of my handicap, but of something else. And he's shrinking as he sits there. Literally. Diminishing in size like a balloon with a pinhole leak. A door slams shut between us, and I jump back.

My eyes pop open. The television is off, the lights are off, and I'm alone. All is quiet, though I can hear my heart pounding. Slowly I uncurl, drop my legs over the couch edge, and sit for a minute trying to clear my head, which is still confused with dream fragments, and spinning slightly from all the beer I drank earlier. I have no idea what time it is, so I push myself to my feet, walk carefully through the darkness, into the kitchen, where I switch on the light over the stovetop so that I can see the oven clock. It's nearly 1:45. I slept right through the official midnight door-locking and head count. For all I know anyone or everyone could still be out . . . Lucius Moon could be pressed against the Manatee Lake Bridge railing, unzipped and waiting for a yacht; Emmy could be wandering the beaches, looking for shells, slapping sparks from her hip to light the way; Moby could be just now drying himself, having used up half the city's water supply before deciding he was sufficiently clean; and Amar could be out on the town with Nadia and Elisha, evilly sweet-talking them into drinking more and more beer, attempting to seduce them both at the same time.

First I check the doors. Front, back and basement. All are locked. At least *someone* around here has a sense of responsibility. Now if he or she just took a head count before locking up I can breathe easy again. Snuggle back into my favorite couch corner and attend to my dreams.

I push open the door that connects the kitchen to Amar and Billy's bedroom. They're both snoring away. Billy's feet have pried loose his sheet bottom, and his toes jut toward the ceiling, exposed to the night. He'd never survive a winter anywhere north of South Florida.

In the front bedroom I find Lucius and Moby asleep. Since Lucius is home and in bed then I'm sure Emmy's in bed, too. And because Amar is home, I know Nadia and Elisha must also be home. That leaves only Lythia. And, since I can't imagine how half a beer's worth of alcohol sucked slowly through a straw could be lethal to *anyone*, I have no worries about her. Until I realize that I neglected to give her her bedtime dose of Dilantin.

I switch on the kitchen light, unlock the medicine cabinet, grab for and pop open the brown plastic pill bottle, half filled with small white Dilantin tablets, then quickly fill a glass with water and rush upstairs, the water splashing over the rim. When I push open Lythia's door the glow of the hallway nightlight spreads across the floor like an expanding wedge of pie, and settles over the lower left corner of Lythia's bed. Stepping in, I kneel beside her, surprised to see her lying so still—not bobbing, ducking, dipping, or swaying—and jiggle her shoulder. When she doesn't respond I whisper her name in her ear, then, beginning to worry, shake harder. Her head jerks up so suddenly that I jump back, spilling more water over the glass rim. "Here's your pill," I whisper, wiping my wet wrist on the side of my pants leg. "We forgot."

A few seconds later she's struggled to a sitting position and her head and shoulders have begun their familiar bobbing. Carefully, she pinches at the pill and pulls it away, as if removing a splinter from my palm. When I hand her the glass of water she slowly, droolingly, grunts, "You were asleep. I didn't want to wake you." She grunts so loudly that I put a finger to my lips and point to Nadia's bed.

"Shhh. You'll wake Nadia." It's then that I notice something is wrong. Blinking, I stare hard through the dim glow of the nightlight. Nadia's sheets and covers are thrown back. Her bed is empty.

Almost instantly my mind flashes back to the door-slam that popped the bubble of my dream, and it occurs to me that Nadia has probably stepped out for another of her late night strolls. Jesus, even if she can't sleep she shouldn't be out alone on the streets of West Coconut Beach at 1:45 in the morning. Where the hell does she go, anyway? And what does she do? I ought to wait up to nab her as soon as she returns. Demand some answers. But I'm too tired to stay awake for long. And if I wait until tomorrow morning to question her she'll be as evasive as she was the first time I caught her. My only chance is to go after her. Catch her in the act and put her on the spot. I'd be breaking the rules, leaving the house unattended, but now that I've spent a few Saturday nights here, I know the odds are low that anything would go wrong in the ten or fifteen minutes I'd be gone.

"My straw," Lythia grunts, pointing to her dresser top. I grab the straw, hand it to her, and leave her to suck down her water and pill in solitude.

Across the hallway I push through Emmy and Elisha's bedroom door, and walk quietly past their beds to the fire escape door, hoping to spot Nadia from the landing. I'm turning the knob when I hear a rustle of sheets and glance to the side to see Elisha propping herself on her elbows, her frizzy curls of hair catching the glow of the nightlight. "Nadia gone out," she whispers. "A few minutes ago. She always make me wake up."

"So she *did* just leave. You got any idea where she went?"

"Don't know, Benny. Every time she go out, she wake me 'cause the door don't fit good so she got to do it hard, make it shut tight. And I always been a light sleeper, wake up easy."

I turn the knob, push open the door, and step onto the landing. The streets are empty except for a few cars and an old Black man trudging home with his fishing pole and bucket. I lean through the doorway and whisper to Elisha, "I doubt anyone is going to call at this hour. But since you're a light sleeper would you be my secretary and answer the phone if it rings? If anyone wants to talk to me, tell her I can't come to the phone, but that I'll call back in a few minutes. Okay? You don't need to tell anyone that I went out looking for Nadia."

"Okay. I be your secretary. Tell 'em call back."

"Thanks Elisha. You're great. And don't worry about it.

I'm sure no one's going to call. And even if they do, it's no big deal if you don't answer the phone."

"You're welcome, Benny." She lies back, then, as I'm shutting the door, props herself up again. "Hey Benny. Tonight me and Hot Dog, we back agether again. We gonna get married at the church with the candles, move out our own."

"Great Elisha. Congratulations. I want to hear all about it in the morning." I push the door shut, trying to muffle the slam by keeping my shoulder pressed snugly to the wood. Then I skip down the steps and cut through the yard and across the street so that I can hustle along the lake front at a half jog. The full moon, already more than halfway across the sky, reflects brightly off the craggy-rippled surface of Manatee Lake, while the fronds of all the Palm Trees catch the breeze, converting it into a symphony of whispers. I sniff for Melaleuca Trees but the wind is from the east so I smell only the ocean.

I'm following the path Nadia took when I watched her from the fire escape two weeks ago, though for all I know she walked in the opposite direction tonight. When I'm near the point where I remember seeing *her* crossing the street, *I* cross the street, then cut caddy-corner through Manatee Lake Park, coming out beneath a Cabbage Palmetto at Jasmine Street. I turn up Jasmine, jogging past a streetlight, toward the State Movie Theater and the downtown area of West Coconut Beach, which has been slowly dying ever since the huge shopping mall, west of town, was opened eight years ago.

The city has since tried to renovate downtown West Coconut Beach; they've planted trees and flower gardens, and opened up free parking lots. But it's a terminal case. The slow death continues. All that's left, aside from the office buildings and banks, are half a dozen bars and pawn shops, the public library, the State Movie Theater—which now shows only X-rated features—the Trailways Bus Station, a few junky five-and-tens, and a large department store which will be moving to the mall next year. Spreading north, south, and west from the center of town is a burgeoning glut of fast food and family restaurants, gas stations, lounges and discos, used car lots and condominiums. To the east, Manatee Lake is now nearly lined with newly built high rise apartments and condominiums (populated almost exclusively by old people who are constantly dying and being replaced by more old people), and the lake itself has become so polluted that only an occasional skier is brave enough, or foolish enough, to challenge the murky waters. I'm amazed there's anything alive left in the lake for the old bridge fishermen to catch. But, incredibly, the population of West Coconut Beach continues to swell, the town boundaries moving ever outward and upward. Aside from the luxury of year round warmth (which, April through October is a "luxury" almost everybody staves off with air conditioning), I can't imagine why anyone would choose to move here, though I guess West Coconut Beach is really not so different from any other South Florida town. In fact from what I've seen of it, the entire country seems to be rapidly turning into an unbroken, coast to coast strip of hamburger joints, gas stations, condominiums, and traffic-crammed highways, all of it spilling over, spreading across and consuming the continent like a hungry cancer. My father moved to Coconut Beach thirteen years ago to escape the madness, but if he, and the rest of the Coconut Beachers across the lake, hope to preserve even a semblance of their tropical island solitude, they'll soon have to burn the bridges connecting them to the mainland.

I'm moving along the deserted main drag of downtown now, but have no clearer idea than before where I might find or even look for Nadia. She's not much of a drinker, so I can't imagine that she'd be hanging out in any of these seedy downtown bars; Capital T's or Garibaldi's. More likely she's already back at ARC House, in bed and asleep, as I should be; instead of risking my life tiptoeing past the mouth of this shadowy alleyway behind the bus station. Or maybe, just maybe, it suddenly occurs to me, she's *inside* The Trailways Station, playing pinball. I remember now that Amar and Billy have both been known to feed their entire allotment of weekly spending money into the bus station pinball machines; they get hooked, like gamblers.

Of course it's really not too likely that Nadia is a closet pinball freak, but it's the only half-plausible idea I've come up with, so I might as well check it out.

I push through the swinging glass door and stand at the station entrance, looking around.

A fat, middle-aged Black woman wearing a gray dress, stockings with three or four runs, and a hairnet over her unnatural looping curls, sits in an orange, hard-plastic chair, staring at a small TV bolted to the end of her chair arm. It's one of those pay TVs. You push two quarters through the slot for thirty minutes of viewing time. She glances up at me, then shifts in her seat and looks back to her fifty cent program.

Beside her, uninterested in the TV, is a little girl dangling her bare feet above the scummy floor. She holds a one-armed plastic doll by the leg so that it hangs upside down, while she stares at me, wide-eyed, chewing and sucking two fingers up to her knuckles.

An old Cuban man with a flat ass, a beer gut like a beach ball and dust-colored gloves, is bent over as he sweeps up the litter, his faded lime shirt half-tucked and half-buttoned, the cuffs of his checkered double-knits dragging the floor, pulling along the cigarette butts and gum wrappers, the dust and the grit.

A young Black man slinks against the wall by the silent pinball machines, hands in his pockets. He rolls a toothpick between his lips. His hat brim shadows his eyes and nose.

I hurry back into the night, shivering in spite of the warmth and high humidity, ready to give up the search, when, after half a dozen steps, another idea pops into my head. Believing I might be onto something, I leg it almost full speed back toward the movie theater, slowing to a jog beneath the marquee, then a half jog, and finally a walk, catching my breath, wishing that I'd had enough sense to ride my ten-speed. Two blocks beyond the movie theater I turn left on Hibiscus Street. The library is at the end of the block, almost to the lake. As I approach it, the Banyan Tree looms, huge, before me, silhouetted in the moonlight like a giant black mushroom, its intricately twisting root system spread across the ground in long, humpbacked tentacles.

Just seeing this fabulous tree makes me certain I've guessed right; that she's come to study it, to fix its image in her mind before she begins working on her clay replica in the morning. As I move closer I look all about, trying to calculate the most likely vantage point for tree gazing. But there's no sign of her.

It's while I'm still on the sidewalk—which has been split open in a dozen places under the steady pressure of the Banyan roots—and quietly moving under the outer canopy of leaves, that I glance up and see her through the branches. Or rather, I see the movement. If it weren't for the movement my eyes might have swept over her, mistaking her for another of the silhouetted limbs or branches. She's at least thirty feet up, sitting with her back to me, straddling a thick limb as if riding the neck of a brontosaurus. Her arms are stretched to the sky, but dropping as slowly and gracefully as the arms of a ballet dancer or Tai Chi master. All I see of her is the upper half of her body. Her legs are invisible, probably locked together at the ankles beneath the limb she straddles. The full moon filters through the branches and windblown leaves above her so that her arms and hands appear to be pulling back from dancing slivers of light. In slow motion her arms continue to drop until they are still, at her sides. For a moment I'm sure she was doing nothing more mysterious than yawning and stretching; like any little girl who's been sitting in a tree too long. But then her shoulders heave slightly—as if she's taking a deep breath—and all at once she lifts her arms, thrusting them upward, her face tilting to the sky, her long hair sliding down her back. At the peak of her thrust, she freezes, and for a moment is part of the tree, frozen, yet stretching with it. And then she's contracting, slowly pulling down her arms, her head bowing. And for a few moments she's still, before beginning the cycle again.

For another ten, maybe fifteen or twenty minutes, or maybe five—it's difficult for me to fit her tree dance into a framework of ticking, progressing time—I watch her, imagining that she is at the hub of the universe, conducting the rustling of the Banyan leaves, the creaking and swaying of its branches, the ebb and flow of the winds, the movements of the moon and the stars; the entire cosmos inhaling and exhaling, expanding and contracting with her. Until at last she drops her arms and remains still. Then shaking back her hair, she turns and grabs the branch behind her, slowly pulls herself to her feet, staring about at all the branches, and begins her descent.

As she's climbing down, I consider sneaking away and hurrying back to the house. I feel a bit like a peeping tom who has just spied on someone doing the most intimately personal thing imaginable. And yet for some reason I *want* her to know I'm here, and that I saw her. "Nadia," I call up to her as she works her way down a limb. "It's me. Benny."

She stops and turns to look over her shoulder. I wave both arms so that she can pick me out on the shadowed sidewalk. She says nothing, but continues her shimmying descent, seemingly familiar with each limb and branch along the way. When she reaches ground she brushes first the seat, then the fronts, of her jeans, then turns to me, smiling with those overlapped teeth, and says, "Mr. Surprise Package." Seeing and hearing her close up, it's hard for me to believe it was *her* up there, mesmerizing me with her tree limb ballet. She looks like such an overgrown little girl standing here with her green tennis shoes, tangled hair, and wide eyes. Her little girl tits push at her pink t-shirt like a pair of Hershey's kisses. And her little girl back is so swayed that if you tied a string from the base of her neck to her tailbone you could use her for shooting arrows.

"How'd you know where to find me?" she says, curious, but not at all upset. "You know. With it so late and all."

"I don't know," I say. "I figured it out. You know you could get kicked out for breaking the house rules!"

She turns and begins walking.

"Nadia!" I catch up and walk alongside her. "Nadia, I'm not really mad. I was just worried. To hell with the rules; it's not safe to go out alone at night in a city."

"Mr. Worry Head," she says, still walking. "Nothing bad

never happens to me. You know. Not 'cause of the Banyan." Her legs aren't quite as long as mine, but she's really got them moving in high gear. I walk sideways alongside her, at times even backward, trying to get her to slow down and look at me, and every fourth of fifth step I have to take two running hops forward to keep up with her.

"Bad things *do* happen Nadia. Especially in a city in the middle of the night. Christ, if you could read the papers you'd know."

"Mr. Smarty Britches Paper Reader. Who don't know."

"I *do* know, Nadia. And I'm just trying to tell you that if you maybe climb your tree during the day instead of in the middle of the night, you won't have to worry about getting caught breaking the rules and getting kicked out. And *I* won't have to worry about where you are and what's happening to you."

She shakes her head. "I used to go in the day. You know. Used to go to climb the Banyan. But how the library lady saw me and told me to come down so I wouldn't fall down and break my neck. And Angela, when she found out from the library lady, she told me how adults didn't do it. You know. Didn't climb no trees. And she asked me if I ever seen a adult person climbing a tree, and I told her how no, I never. 'Cause I never have. You know. How I never have seen no adult climbing no tree. Unless they got one of them motor saw thingys to buzz off the branches."

"Nadia! Will you slow down!"

But she doesn't slow down, so I grab her elbow to stop her, then turn her around to face me, my hands resting on her shoulders. "Okay. Forget everything I've said. Just tell me. I want to know. What was it you were doing up in the tree?"

But instead of answering she tilts back her head and stares at the huge Australian Pine beside us.

I hear the sound. The rizzing I have to hear to see the trees be alive and reach with their arms how they whoosh from under the ground to the sky. The sound I fall back into, in the back of my head. The sound I hear in bed at night when the dark stuff comes, and it's all dark with the dark stuff and fuzzies, and with everything dark and quiet except the sound. How it sounds like crickets in my head and all around. A million thousand crickets, everywhere in my head and all around. And he don't hear it, so he don't know nothing about it. Don't know about the sound, how I have to hear it to do my trees how they whoosh with their arms. And he can't hear it. Can't hear how it does the rizzing and whooshing, and can't see no whooshing, how it whooshes, and with the sound at the back of my head, how when I fall back everything is quiet and fills with the sound, and the trees are alive and loud with the sound, how I am with them in the sound, and with him, in it, but how he can't hear and don't know he's there with me, with everything in the sound.

"Nadia," I say, gently jiggling her shoulders to get her attention. She looks down from the tree. "That's okay, Nadia. You don't have to tell me if you don't want to. I was just—"

But she's already pulling away and walking off, and I'm hustling to catch up with her.

"What's wrong, Nadia? Why are you so mad at me?"

"'Cause you don't know about it, so how you'll say it to Angela. You know. Say it to her how I left against the rule and you caught me in the tree. How you said it. About I was gonna get caught and kicked out."

"I've been trying to tell you, Nadia. I just don't want to see you get hurt because you went out alone in the middle of the night. And I'm hoping you and I can talk and figure out what to do, so I won't *need* to tell Angela."

But Nadia's in no mood for talking. She stares straight ahead as she hurries along, her corduroys swishing and her green tennis shoes slapping the sidewalk.

"You know, my job isn't to make you obey the rules and turn you in to Angela if you don't. My job is to do whatever I can to help you and teach you. Right?"

No answer.

"And to hell with the job. Even if I wasn't working here we'd be friends. Wouldn't we? And friends try to help each other. Right? And trust each other."

We're approaching ARC House already. At this pace it's

no more than a five minute walk from the Banyan Tree. (Christ, at this pace it wouldn't be much more than a five minute walk to Miami!) We cut through the yard and around back to the fire escape. The grass, already moist with dew, dampens my tennis shoes and jean cuffs. Elisha must have switched on the spotlight over the back door, thinking it would help. But the moonlight would have been better because that spotlight is aimed right at us so that we have to shield our eyes to see. Nadia starts up the stairway ahead of me, blocking out the bright beam, her tennis shoes leaving a wet print on each stair step. At the top of the fire escape she moves across the landing to the door, and stands directly under the spotlight so that I have to use my hand as a visor and squint to see her.

"So you promise you won't say it to her? Say it about me? How you said it before?"

Ducking under the spotlight beam I step toward her, shouting in a whisper, "Jesus no, Nadia! I'm not going to tell Angela. I swear to God. I just want you to trust me. Talk to me." Her back is against the door, her fingers gripping the doorknob. Over her head kamikaze moths dive and crash softly into the spotlight. "This isn't a jail, Nadia. I'm not a jailer who's here to force you to follow every rule. Of course I'd hate to see you get hurt because you *didn't* follow the rules. But that's up to you. I mean, I even remember reading in my training manual that you have *the right* to take risks, and make bad decisions. And that makes sense to me." She stares at me blankly. She has no idea what I'm talking about. "I guess all I'm saying, Nadia, is that I don't care if you break the rules. As long as you have a good reason. And *whatever* it was you were doing up in the tree seems to me to be a good reason." She smiles. Maybe she understands. Or maybe she's just smiling because she recognized the word, "tree." "You were beautiful up there, Nadia. I swear. I couldn't take my eyes off you." Her lips peel apart and she beams up at me, baring all her overlapped teeth, and her gums. "Way the hell up in a tree in the middle of the night. A block from downtown. Moving your arms that way. Like a dancer or something. I don't know, Nadia. There's something very special about you. And I really mean that."

As if she's heard all she needs to hear, she suddenly blurts out, "Mr. Niceness And Everything Nice!" And then the whole of her upturned face is smiling. Every part of it, and all at once. A radiantly unself conscious smile which makes me smile back helplessly, the same way. And her face somehow *looks* the way I feel now; as though it's no longer completely solid, but made up of a thousand radiant points of light, blending into each other like a fuzzy picture on the TV screen.

And then we are in each other's arms and hugging so hard that the rest of the world is gone. I smell her and feel her everywhere; kitten fur and clay, hair and flesh. And there's a texture where our flesh and warmth meet; a smoothness, familiar somehow. And an intense silence. The same as when a gentle snow is falling and you can *hear* its silence. She squeezes harder and I squeeze harder. I rub my hands up and down her swayed, arching back, admiring the way it curves into a valley, then slopes up into the soft hill of her ass. I pull away to look at her face again. Her chin quivers and wrinkles; a shy, surprised quiver. Her eyes are glassy and dark. She blinks and I notice that her black lashes curve upward and crisscross like broken comb teeth. *Even her eyelash hair* is tangled and stiff from dried clay. Her eyebrows are arched like twin frowns, like painted clown eyebrows, and her forehead slopes back to the spot where her tangled black hair is parted—except for a few frizzy strands—at the center.

"Mr. Hugger," she coos, shaking her head, almost laughing. "Mr. Softness And Warmth." Rising up on her toes, she hangs onto my shoulders, rubs her nose against mine and gleefully adds, "Mr. Strong Nose."

When she sinks down from her toes, her eyes are wide and dark, and moving back and forth across my face as if it's a page out of a book, and she's reading the same line over and over again, enjoying the hell out of it. Then once again we're in each other's arms, squeezing, pressing; and nothing else matters except the magic of all this flesh warmth and tingling energy we're creating as we hug and squeeze.

And then the door opens and a headful of frizzy hair pops out. "Didn't get no phone calls, Benny," Elisha says, then looks us over before frowning and pulling shut the door. Jesus, how did she know we were out here. She must have heard us talking. She *is* a light sleeper.

In half a second I've come to my senses and am out of Nadia's arms and jerking open the door in a panic. "Thanks Elisha. You're great. We were just coming in. I mean, I found Nadia and she's all right. We were just getting things straightened out."

"Oh *were* you?" Emmy alertly says from her bed. "Well then, with *that. Hmmm* then."

That's all I need! Emmy blabbering to everyone about Nadia and me getting things straightened out on the fire escape landing at 2:30 in the morning.

"Hey, I'm talking to Elisha, Emmy. Why don't you go back to sleep?"

"Well *I* don't like you being *in* here. I can't *sleep* with you *in* here. *You!*"

"I don't blame you, Emmy. And normally I wouldn't be in here. But this was an emergency."

"Yeah," Elisha says from where she's sitting at the foot of her bed. "This was a mergency."

"Oh *was* it?"

"Yes it was," I say. "And we'll be out of your room in about two seconds so you can go right back to sleep."

"Oh *will* you? Well *hmmm* then. *Okay* then."

I'm in the room now and Nadia is pushing up behind me, pulling shut the door. But it doesn't shut all the way, so she re-opens it and *slams* it shut.

"Tell her to *stop* it with that," Emmy shrieks. "I don't *like* that slamming."

"Hey Emmy," I say. "You know when you act this way you're a real pain-in-the-butt!"

"Oh *am* I?"

"Yeah," Elisha says. "A real pain-the-butt."

"Make her *stop* it with those *words!*" Emmy shrieks again. "*Her!*"

"If I can't make *you* stop it with *your* words, what makes you think I can make *her* stop it?"

"*Oh* then. *Nothing* then." And under the sheets I hear her slapping her hip.

"You know, Emmy, there are lots of things you can do

when you're upset aside from shrieking like a lunatic. But instead of *telling* you what you can do I'm going to let you figure it out for yourself, because I honestly think you're smart enough."

"Oh *am* I? *Hmmm* then. O*kay* then."

"Okay Emmy. Good night. Good night Elisha. Thanks for being my secretary." I reach over to switch off the fire escape light. "And that was thoughtful of you to turn on the light for us. You're great."

"You're welcome, Benny. G'night Benny. G'night Nadia."

"Good night," Nadia says.

I think I pulled it off. Elisha doesn't seem to be at all suspicious of Nadia and me. I just hope that image of us hugging out there doesn't stick, then begin to fester, in her mind. We're almost to the bedroom door when Emmy suddenly shrieks, "*I* did the downstairs *lights* out and the TV. And locked the doors *too*, because nobody *else* did. *You* were asleep on the couch. *You!*"

"Well thanks, Emmy. I told you you were smart."

"O*kay* then. You're *wel*come then."

I pull open the bedroom door for Nadia and she steps into the hallway ahead of me. When she turns around I hold up a finger, signaling her not to say anything until I close the door. As soon as I've pulled it securely shut, and pushed on it to *make sure* it's shut, I turn back to her. She's waiting for me with her shoulders slumped forward and her fingers interlocked in front of her crotch, like a little girl shyly come to tell me she has to pee. The hallway nightlight shines up from the baseboard outlet, softly illuminating half her face, half her gummy, toothy smile, half her tangled head of black hair, and one dark eye.

"Good night," she whispers. "Mr. Prince Charming." Lifting a hand, she touches the top of my lit-up cheek, and when I smile—helpless to do otherwise—the cheek puffs out and she quickly lifts her other hand to feel my other puffing cheek. "Mr. Smiley Cheeks. Mr. Lovehead Lovebunny. That I love."

She has the intelligence of a child. And a personality to match. (She *is* refreshingly impulsive and spontaneous, but that's not unlike any other healthy seven year-old.) And though she has beautiful eyes, and a nice ass and legs, the rest of her body and facial features range from ordinary to peculiar. And yet, if it's not her mind, her personality, or her physical beauty that I'm so helplessly attracted to, what is it? What's left? I set my hands on her shoulders, the same way I did when I stopped her on our way back from the Banyan Tree. "Listen Nadia," I whisper. "All those things I said out there on the fire escape . . . I meant them."

She has no idea what I'm getting at. As I speak she's beaming up at me with that smile. If someone handed me a photograph of that smile I might not even be impressed. It's just that there's so much behind it. So much going into it. It's like some vortex of energy sucking up and reflecting out all of her. Every bit of her. I can't, even for a moment, look at that smile without losing my train of thought; without being hopelessly distracted. I focus my attention on one of my hands at her shoulder and go on. "And that hug, Nadia. I swear to you I've never been hugged that way." She joyfully starts forward, her arms lifting, but I hold her back, the heels of my palms at her shoulders. I loathe the part of me that has taken command. "Listen Nadia. I want you to listen now, and be serious."

Her arms slowly fall. Her gums and teeth disappear behind her lips.

"We can't hug like that anymore. We can't even smile at each other like that. Not the way we did out on the porch."

She takes a step back so that I'm no longer pushing at her shoulders. I allow my arms to fall to my sides. My hands seek my jean pockets. "How come?" she says. I motion for her to lower her voice, and she obliges, whispering, "You know. How come we can't hug or smile?"

How am I going to even begin to explain the impossibility, the absurdity, of a serious relationship between us, without crushing her? Without devastating her? Without making it sound as though she were my inferior? "We *can* hug and smile, Nadia. But just not the way we were hugging and smiling on the fire escape. Not if I want to keep my job." That's it. I'll blame it on the job, which *is* at least part of the problem.

"How come?" she whispers. Like a little girl, she's going to keep asking "How come?" no matter what I say.

"It might be hard to explain," I begin. "It's just that when someone has a job like this he's supposed to be helping the people he works with. Right? But if he's involved with any of those people in other ways, it would be harder for him to be helping them."

Her forehead wrinkles as she squints her eyes. If I can't get her to understand how to tuck in a pillow, how can I possibly get her to understand *this*? It's not that she's my inferior. It's just that being with her requires a lot of patience and understanding. More than I can spare, except in short spurts. "What I'm trying to say, Nadia, is just that it wouldn't look right to other people if they saw us hugging. Angela would fire me. She'd have to."

"Well how about if they didn't see us?" she whispers. At least she's following *some* of what I'm saying. "You know. How if they didn't see us when we hug and smile?"

I shake my head. "It's too dangerous. Like when Elisha saw us on the fire escape just now. I mean, you don't want me to get fired, do you?"

"No."

"Okay. So you understand. If we hug that way, and someone happens to see us, I'll get fired. It's as simple as that."

"Okay," she says, not whispering. Her shoulders slump farther forward. She turns to her bedroom door. The nightlight illuminates only her back now.

"Maybe when you leave ARC House," I whisper, knowing that I'm lying. "Or when I leave. It would be different then."

No response.

"And until then we'll still be good friends."

She steps toward her door, her veil of black hair hiding her profile, except for the tip of her nose.

"Won't we?"

She turns the knob, pushes open the door, and steps in without looking back.

"Good night Nadia," I whisper. I stare at the door for a few seconds, then head downstairs.

By the time I'm curled up on the couch I'm in a sort of shock state. My palms are sweating and I keep wiping them on my jeans, unable to get them dry. I can't believe that the last hour was not some wild dream I just awoke from. Could it possibly have happened? Could I have actually felt love—and love as I've never felt or even imagined I could feel—however fleeting, for a girl because she was sitting thirty feet above the city sidewalk in a Banyan Tree, stretching with her arms? Because she smiled at me with a quiver-wrinkled chin, wide eyes, and a mouthful of overlapped teeth? Because she hugged me and rubbed her nose against mine? Because she called me Mr. Surprise Package, Mr. Lovebunny, and Mr. Strong Nose?

How could it possibly be? How could I have felt such love, such passion, for a girl who cannot read, write, add, subtract, tell time, keep her hair brushed, or make her bed so that the pillow is decently tucked in? How could I have allowed myself to feel love for a 26 year-old with the mind of a 12 year-old, a 10 year-old, a 7 year-old? For a mental retard who, like a monkey, climbs from tree limb to tree limb, and whose IQ, before the energy crisis, would have barely surpassed the national speed limit? For an illiterate know-nothing who's never even read the comic book version of *Moby Dick*, who's never heard of *Anna Karenina*, and who might have difficulty with the spelling of Joseph K.'s last name.

How could it be that out of all the arms I've ever seen, it is *her* arms I choose to fall into, as if I belong there, forever frozen in a gushing of love-energy, pressed so close that I don't even notice the indecent brain-chasm of difference between us.

And worst of all, how could I have ever put myself in the incredible position of having to convince her that we can't be lovers? That we are not now, and never will be, Romeo and Juliet (whom she's likely never heard of). I couldn't have! I must have dreamed it. Imagined it.

Yet even as I lie here, rubbing my sweating palms on my jeans and wondering how I could possibly have gotten myself into such a ludicrous mess, in my mind I continue to picture Nadia's moonlight ballet—her Tai Chi in the tree—her arms and fingers thrusting upward, reaching toward the moonslivers, toward the sky. And I picture, I feel, those hugs, warm and silent and familiar. And I picture that wondrous view over her shoulders; the view of her swayed, arching back, curving so smoothly, so softly, so perfectly, from her neck to her ass. And most of all I picture her radiant, whole-faced smile, with those overlapped teeth, those wide, dark, gleeful eyes, darting back and forth across my face, those criss-crossing eyelashes, and those few black threads of hair, frizzing up where her forehead meets her center part—frizzing up as if lost and lonely and searching for the rest of the pack.

I picture that smiling face turned up to me like a sunflower, radiating her essence, and I have to smile. I have no choice. Here I am curled on the couch, feeling hopelessly, miserably, confused; and still, all I have to do is think of that upturned smiling face, and my lips start stretching toward my ears, and my cheeks puffing toward my eyes. I take a deep breath, wipe my palms over my jeans a final time, then relax, shut my eyes, and picture the tree dance, the smile, and the hugs, over and over, until the pictures all turn to dreams.

Billy shakes me from my sleep. "Good morning Benny. How are ya Old Buddy? How are ya?"

His face is a blur until I blink a few times. "I don't know. I'm too tired."

"Me too, Old Buddy. Me too. I've got a hangover, I do. A goddamned stupid hangover. A stupid hangover." He cackles proudly about his hangover while I stare at him, wondering why the hell he's so damned happy and bright-eyed this early in the morning, why he's even *awake* this early in the morning, if he's got a hangover. I'm about to ask him when Lythia suddenly bobs into view and hovers over the couch-back, bidding me a painfully dragged out good morning.

"Lythia's the cook this morning," Billy says, patting her shoulder. "She's the breakfast cook, she is. The breakfast cook."

"Great," I say, without much enthusiasm. "But it seems that you two are the only ones up, so I guess we'd better not start cooking yet." I turn over and shut my eyes, hoping they'll both take the hint and leave me to sleep for another few hours.

But Billy moves around to the front of the couch—his knees at my face—and grabbing my left elbow with both hands, tries to pull me to a sitting position. "Come on Buddy. I'll help you get up, I will. Help you get up. Help you get right up."

In spite of their extraordinary length, his arms are not strong; certainly not strong enough to pull me up if I don't want to be pulled up. But his hands are pesky and persistent, like hyperactive puppies pulling at socks or blanket corners. I try to ignore the tugging at my elbow, but it's impossible, so I jerk my elbow free of his hands, and bark, "Okay already, Billy. Enough! You win. I'll get up."

He pats my shoulder, and in a sympathetic tone of voice says, "I know you will Buddy. I know it. I know it."

"What time is it anyway?" I push myself, without the help of Billy's hands and arms, to a sitting position.

Billy has no idea what time it is—he's as bad with clocks as he is with counting change; worse even than Nadia—so he repeats my question to Lythia, and a few seconds later she looks at her watch, smiles, and grunts to him that it's 9:30.

"It's 9:30, Benny," he proudly announces. "It's 9:30 in the morning, it is. 9:30 in the morning."

I look at Lythia skeptically—it can't be *that* late—then lean over the couch and take her left wrist. She's right. 9:32. It's a good thing Billy was so insistent upon waking me. As it is now we'll be lucky to have breakfast on the table by 10:30 or 11, and to have the breakfast clean-up finished by noon. Then come the rest of the Sunday programs, in addition to the four I decided to forego last night.

"Okay you guys. Thanks for waking me. Just give me a few seconds to clear my head here. I'll meet you in the kitchen in a minute."

"Okay Benny. Okay Buddy. Okay."

Lythia bobs in place—peering after Billy to see where he's going—then leans and falls after him, her legs catching up just in time.

I push myself to my feet, yawn and stretch, then head out to the front porch for a breath of fresh air. The sky is dark with thunderheads—no wonder everyone is sleeping so late—rolling along like some evil, invading army. There are low, long rumblings in the distance. Two cardinals squawk angrily in pursuit of a blackbird twice their size, the three of them zig-zagging crazily in the wind gusts, while the long-necked coconut palms lining the lake front sway and creak, their fronds rustling loudly, like the blended whisperings of a huge congregation.

I'm not at all ready to face Nadia this morning. And I'm sure as hell not yet ready to face that long list of Sunday—as well as those four Saturday night-programs. Of course, on top of that I've got my other responsibilities; meals to cook, medications to give out, information to record in the Daily Log, behaviors to shape, conflicts to mediate, and the movements of eight people to coordinate and keep track of. If I had a choice I'd curl back up on the couch, and try to dream the rest of the day away. But I don't have a choice; not if I want to remain employed. So after a final deep breath I turn from the invading thunderheads and hurry to the kitchen, trying to assure myself that there is no need to panic.

Cooking breakfast with Lythia takes twice as long as it would with anyone else. Every time she tries, without my help, to flip a pancake, she either flips it out of the pan and onto the stovetop or floor, or onto another pancake so that the two instantly fuse together with an oozing, uncookable center. (I shouldn't be surprised. Not even my father would be able to flip pancakes while bobbing and ducking the way she does.) Before we're halfway through we've ruined so many pancakes that we have to shut off the burner while we mix up another bowlful of batter.

We're falling farther and farther behind schedule, so *I* cook the second batch while Lythia watches at my shoulder. But I can't seem to get the heat adjusted the way I want it—I'm still used to the instant response of our gas range at home—and either burn or undercook all but a few pancakes, while Lythia bobs beside me, making me seasick with her constant motion. If I hung around her all day I'd probably start craving Dramamine.

By the time we've finished cooking it's nearly 11:30. Amar, Billy, Elisha, and Emmy are all milling hungrily about the kitchen and dining areas. Lucius and Moby are watching the thunderstorm from the front porch; Moby calmly puffing his cigarettes and Lucius excitedly rubbing the tops of his thighs with each crack of thunder. Nadia has yet to make an appearance.

Emmy volunteers to run upstairs to call Nadia for breakfast. But when, a minute later, she comes skipping down the stairs, her breasts flopping up and down from her shouldertops to her ribs, she slaps at her hip and barks, "She don't *want* no breakfast, *her*. She's not *hungry* for no breakfast."

Fortunately no one seems overly concerned or suspicious. They're all in a happy, lively mood this morning; all eager to boast about their drunken 4th of July escapades and their severe 5th of July hangovers. In fact they're probably unconcerned about Nadia because they figure she's in bed with a hangover.

"I was drunker than a skunk!" Billy says as he reaches for the pancake platter with a long arm. "Drunker than a skunk, I was. Drunker than a goddamned stupid skunk."

Emmy doesn't even protest Billy's language; just slaps her hip under the table, nods once, almost savagely, as if jerking her head free from some invisible grip, and says, "Oh *were* you? *Hmmm* then. Hmmmmmmmmmmm."

Lucius grins across the table at her, then sets down his fork so that he can rub his thigh tops. "Ooh wow," he whispers.

Hoping to change the subject to something a bit more educational, I say, "Does anybody know why the 4th of July is also called Independence Day?"

"It's called Independence Day, it is," Billy answers proudly. "Independence Day."

"Great Billy. But why? Anybody know?"

"Hey," Amar says. "I got something I'd like to be able to announce if I could be able to."

"Oh *do* you?" Emmy says. "O*kay* then. Go *on* then."

"Well you know Elisha and Nadia and me was *all* drunker than skunks last night. And by the time we come back from our little walk, Elisha and me—" He turns to look at her and laugh through his teeth, while his shoulders hunch to his ears and his right eyebrow lifts and falls, lifts and falls. "We was back together again. Just like two peas in a pot."

So much for my American History lecture. Everyone at the table—with the exception of Lythia, who's busy concentrating on maneuvering a forkload of pancake and dripping syrup into her mouth without stabbing the prongs into her lips or cheeks—cheers the good news. Elisha, who's sitting beside me, blushes and wipes her mouth with a napkin, behind which she smiles, one of her bird eyes blinking at me. "See Benny," she whispers. "I told you Benny."

Amar, still grinning, rubs his jaw and says, "Hey, y'all see what I'm trying to be able to grow back onto my chin?"

Elisha squeezes shut her bird eyes—I can only see one, but assume she has shut them both—and nods. Billy's mouth is full, so he bangs his fork on the table to show his approval. Lucius rubs his thigh tops and Emmy laughs as if she was reading from a cue card, "Ha-ha-ha-ha-ha-ha-ha." Everyone else contributes some sort of cheer, again with the exception of Lythia, who gazes blankly around the table from face to face, perhaps still lost in the echoes of our *first* round of cheers. Suddenly her mouth falls open, she grunts a few times, then begins to tell us, with her straining constipated voice and syrupy drools, that she drank beer last night and got drunk too. More cheers. They're all having as much fun *talking* about being drunk as they had when they *were*—or in some cases, weren't—drunk.

But the fun ends as soon as we finish breakfast and start in with the programs. After a tedious breakfast clean-up with Moby and Elisha it's 12:30 and I'm already more than two hours behind schedule. But hopefully I'll have a chance to catch up, not only because the thunderstorm should keep everyone at home for a few hours, but because we all ate such a late breakfast there will be no need for lunch.

After running Emmy's budgeting program and Lythia's living room vacuuming program, and helping Lucius get started with his laundry program, I check the schedule and find that it's time for Nadia's bedroom program. I consider postponing it until later, then decide to at least find out how she's doing (though I know she can't be doing too well, because it's 1:30 and she hasn't yet come down to start working on her clay tree), and, snatching her program clipboard from its hook, hurry upstairs and knock on her door.

"Just a minute, Benny," I hear her say. I have no idea how she knew it was me. Maybe she's been waiting for me all morning, eager to suck me into some melodramatic lovers' quarrel, hoping everyone will hear. It's really just what you'd expect from a girl with the social mentality of a twelve year-old.

After a few seconds I hear her creaking footfalls. The bedroom door swings open and she's standing there in a white terrycloth bathrobe and her green tennis shoes. Her hair is wet and combed. Small beads of water have collected on her upper lip. I step in and push the door shut behind me.

She's obviously been busy the past few hours. Her room has been straightened. Her bed is made and the pillow is tucked in, corectly, except for a nearly inconspicuous sliver of white pillow case peeking from under the top edge of the bedspread. She's up to something here.

"How did you know it was me who was knocking?" I demand.

"Mr. Stair Runner," she says. "Who runs up the stairs, boom boom boom, faster than anyone."

She's right. I'm always running up the stairs. Somehow it's easier for me that way. One at a time is more of a strain. I'd rather take them two or three at a time, and fast. "You washed your hair," I say cautiously. "It looks nice."

"Thank you." She grabs a handful and pulls it in front of her face so that she can inspect it. "It was dirty. You know. How it was dirty with the clay."

"Well that's good you washed it and combed it."

"Brushed it," she corrects me. "With a brush."

"Great Nadia." I shake my head to show her I'm impressed. And more than impressed, I'm relieved. Maybe I'll escape without a scene, after all. Maybe she thinks that what happened with us last night was a dream. Hell, maybe it *was* a dream. "And your room," I go on. "It looks better than I've ever seen it. You even made your bed and tucked in your pillow."

"Yes," she says. "Thank you."

"That's super, Nadia."

"Thank you."

"It looks to me like maybe we don't even need to run your program. You already did everything. And independently!" I've yet to cheat on the recording of program data, but this seems to be as good a time as any to start. I lift her program clipboard and pull out the section for taking data on her bedroom program. "I'll just check off these steps here. Let's see. How long did it take you to make your bed? Ten minutes?"

She shrugs.

"Okay, we'll say ten minutes. And your vacuuming and dusting? Ten minutes each?" I mark them off; July 5th, "I" for "Independent," and ten minutes each. "Window washing? That's a quicky. Let's say five minutes. Straightening your closet and dresser? Ten minutes each? Or let's say fifteen for your dresser. There." I mark it down, go back and total the times—fifty minutes—then mark the total in on the cover sheet, which Angela will check on Monday.

Nadia looks up at me and smiles for the first time. And I have to smile back. And when I smile back her smile grows bigger. Her eyes grow wider. Her lips pull back like a drill chuck from a bit, so that all her overlapped teeth and her gums are exposed. Last night was no dream. And we both know it.

"That's all?" she asks. "You know. That's all I gotta do of the program?"

"That's right," I assure her. "You did a great job."

"Mr. Smiley Puss," she says.

"You're the Smiley Puss."

She denies it with a shake of her wet head, still happily displaying all her teeth and gums.

"Okay Nadia. I've got to get going on the rest of the programs. You really helped me out with the great job you did, but I'm still over an hour behind."

"Mr. Busy Bee," she says.

"Just one thing before I go," I say, staring at her tennis shoes, having decided to cue her; to ask her if most people she knows normally wear tennis shoes with their bathrobes. But I can't. I don't want to. Who else in all the world would unselfconsciously wear green tennis shoes with a white bathrobe?

"What?" she demands, waiting to hear what that "one thing before I go" is.

I stutter for a moment, looking up from her shoes, then say, "I was wondering if you were hungry. You missed breakfast."

"Oh," she says. "I was sleeping. I can make some peanut butter. You know. How I can make it when I come down."

I hardly hear what she's saying because I'm busy agreeing with the voice in my head that reminds me I'm not cut out for this kind of work; that I'm a failure at teaching these people to follow rules and to behave appropriately. To fit in rather than stand out. And yet somehow, the idea that I'm *not* cut out for this kind of work no longer seems so terrible to me. In fact it hardly even bothers me. I skip down the stairs, two at a time, smiling at the thought that ten years from now, when today's latest fashions have long since been trashed, mothballed, or recycled through half a dozen second hand clothing stores, Nadia will still be happy and comfortable in her white terrycloth bathrobe and green tennis shoes.

The next few hours all goes surprisingly smoothly, perhaps because of the heavy rain, which drums steadily and soothingly on the roof and windows, keeping all the residents here at the house so that it's no strain for me to keep track of their whereabouts, and I can quickly nab whomever I'm scheduled to run a program with. Nearly everyone is sprawled around the television, watching cartoons, talking, or napping. Lucius and Nadia are on the front porch—undaunted by the rain, wind, lightning and thunder—Nadia working on her tree, and Lucius swinging on the porch swing. Just as I step out to cue Lucius to check his laundry, a forked bolt of lightning rips open the sky above the lake and I instinctively recoil from the thundercrash that instantly follows, my arms thrown above my head for protection. When I look up, Lucius is rubbing his thightops and grinning wildly as he swings, his eyes bugging out, and Nadia is smiling at me. "Mr. Nervous Purvis," she says.

Still crouched and staring distrustfully at the sky, I explain to them that it's not safe to be outside in a lightning storm; that while the porch cover might keep them relatively dry, it *won't* keep them from being instantly zap-fried by a bolt of lightning. But to Lucius the lightning and thunder are better than last night's fireworks. He continues to grin, and says, "Ooh, I like ut. I be okay. Stay on porch. Yuh."

And though Nadia takes my advice, moving her clay and worktable from the front porch to the basement, I get the feeling she does it only to humor me, for as she carries her bag of clay past me on her way through the living room, she smiles and says, "Mr. Worry Head Worry Wart. Who worries all the time about the bad things will happen."

At least I'm not the only one in the house who doesn't like the thunder and lightning. Every time the thunder crashes, Emmy shuts her eyes and covers her ears so tightly that her face and arms tremble from the strain, sometimes for as long as a minute. And when—while I'm watching Billy vacuum his bedroom floor—the lights flicker, the vacuum hesitates, and thunder booms loudly, he drops the vacuum handle as if it were a hot wire, falls to his knees, and crawls quickly over to me, latching onto my waist with those long arms and assuring me, "It's okay Benny. It's okay Buddy. It's okay."

But in spite of the lightning and thunder (which seems

to come only in short, violent spurts, with long, quiet interludes in between) the first three hours after breakfast go as smoothly as *any* three hours have gone since I've begun to work here. Everyone is happy. Everyone is cooperating. (Maybe we should all get drunk *every* Saturday night.) The programs are being run right on schedule. In fact by 3:00 I'm only a half a program behind—not counting the four Saturday programs I still need to run—after that ridiculously late start.

I finish up Amar's refrigerator cleaning and defrosting program, then announce to everyone that they've all done such a great job with their programs I've got time to take a much needed break. I thank them for their efforts, then tell them that if they need me I'll be in the basement for ten or fifteen minutes.

Nadia is hunched over her worktable, near the corner of the basement farthest from the heat of the washer and dryer, which churn and rumble almost non-stop during the weekends. I still can't believe she took my rejection so calmly, and want to make sure she's not hiding all her hurt and anger inside, waiting for Angela to come before she lets it out.

Moving toward her corner, I pull a blue ladder-back chair in front of her, and sit, straddling it the wrong way, its back at my chest. Nadia's hair, which was clean and brushed three hours ago, is already clay-streaked and tangled. Her face and arms, her shirtfront, and the tops of her white painter's pants legs are all spattered with the red-brown clay. But the Banyan Tree is going to be better—more complicated, intricate, and difficult—than anything of hers I've seen. She's completed the trunk and root system and has already built and attached several of the major limbs. I'd like to build a tiny clay replica of Nadia and set her in the tree straddling a limb, her arms stretched like branches. As I watch her working, it hits me once again that she's truly an artist, which, oddly, is something I never seem to remember until I see her hunched intently over her clay. "God, it's fantastic," I tell her, as enthusiastically as I can without making it sound as if I'm just giving her the usual positive reinforcement.

She leans back, wipes her sweaty forehead with the back

of her hand, then smiles at me, rubs her clay-covered palms on her pants, and stretches, arching her back.

"Looks like you need a break, too," I say.

"Yes. My neck is sore. You know. How it's sore from the bending."

"Then you stay right where you are," I say, standing and moving behind her. "Now just relax." I pull her hair back in a pony tail, then set it all in front of her left shoulder, out of the way, and begin to massage the base of her neck. Her tight muscles and soft skin feel familiar.

"Mr. Gentle Hands," she says. "Mr. Gentlepuss. Who makes me feel gentle all over." She suddenly twists around to stare at me, still in her chair. "And all gentle and soft inside . . . and all squishy with the flooding." Her dark eyes move back and forth across my face and I swallow loudly and with difficulty, my throat tightening.

I can feel the flooding how it's all stirred up in his tummy and he wants to do his flooding to me, and I want him to do it, to do me his flooding and whoosh with his flooding, and how I can whoosh back to him with my flooding, and it will be our whooshing and flooding. And we both want to do with the flooding, how it feels good to both whoosh with the flooding, but he don't know, how it's all stuck in his back with the flooding, and don't know which way to go with it, with the flooding, and I keep looking at him, at his brown eyes scared eyes, and then he knows but it's still stuck, and he don't smile, but how he touches my hair, and soft, and we kiss, and soft with our lips, then hard, how we do it hard with our tongues, and then he looks around nervous, and takes my hand and leads me to the office, Angela's office, where it's cold how she is, in the office, and cold like glue-paper and scissors, but it's okay about the cold, how the rizzing and fuzzies are thick and warm, and he shuts the door and pushes the button and looks at my eyes like he wants them to hold still so how he can climb right through with his eyes, and how he smiles and his cheeks puff, and I smile and touch his cheeks that I love and his strong nose, and how it's all how it was before, how it was last night with us, but how the flooding is there with the sound, and we want to give it, and we know how we are going to give it, how we have to give it, and we hug and kiss, and kissing, press together where our flooding is and how he feels it and shivers and rubs his hands over my bottom and rubs and pulls me into his flooding, how I press back with my flooding, and I'm on the floor and he's there on top, and how we're kissing and with our tongues pushing, and our legs pushing at the chairs in the way, and we are flooding and breathing and moving with the sound. An then he pulls back to ask about the babies and I tell him how before I came to here, to ARC House, and Dana Jones was my boyfriend, they told me I was a adult woman and would have babies like a adult woman 'cause of Dana Jones, how if I let him do me with the flooding, and whoosh with me with the flooding, and how if I didn't want to have no babies there was stuff I had to do not to have 'em and they told me the different things and how if I was sure I didn't ever want to have no babies they could get me a operation to not have no babies, and when they asked me if I ever wanted to have some babies I told them no I never, 'cause I never do want no babies. And how they gave me the operation to make me not have no babies, and now I don't have to worry about having no babies. And when I say it to him, say it to Benny, he's upset in his eyes about it, and says how he thinks he remembers about it now in my file, how it's in there in my file, and I tell him he's a sad eyes and how it's okay about the operation 'cause I never do want to have no babies, how I'm not no smarty britches to have no babies and would not know what to do how to have one and make it grow up good like a smarty britches but not like a smarty britches who don't know. And after I tell him, we hug, and I press back with my flooding, how it's still flooding, and strong again with the flooding, and I do off with my shirt, and he does off with his shirt, and I help him, and how he helps me with the bra they make me wear how I'm a adult girl, and he looks at me where my bra was, and looks serious, and I stop smiling how he looks so serious, not-smiling and not-whooshing with the flooding, and how it's stuck there in his back with the flooding, how it was before, and not-flooding how it was before, and not-flooding he zips down my pants in the front with his hands that are cold-colored and shiver-hands, and how his eyes are big and scared and looking scared where my pants are zipped down, and he rolls off me onto the floor and onto his tummy, and how he turns his head away and don't say nothing with his mouth, but I can feel how he is not-whooshing and not-flooding, how it's all stuck in his back with the flooding, and how he don't know how to get it from his back and which way to do it to whoosh with it with the flooding, and whoosh with it with my flooding, and don't want to do it, and can't do it, how it's so stuck and not-flooding, and not-knowing which way to go with it with the flooding.

Three times in a row is enough. I don't have to go all the way through with this a fourth time to know it will turn out just the same. I've got a dick that chokes when the pressure is on, like a ballplayer who bats zero with the bases loaded; with the "ducks on the pond," as they say. Well the ducks are all on the pond and I can't even hold up my bat. And I don't even want to try. It's just the same. I'm excited all over except the one place that counts. For a minute there I thought it might be different with a girl I at last had strong feelings for. (Although three years from now, when I've maybe filled up with enough crazy hope and frustration to risk another try, I'll probably use her—her retardedness, of course, and my understandable reluctance—as the justification, the rationale, the excuse, for my last failure. Always an excuse. This time I found it before trying. Hell, maybe I knew it would end with this all along.)

Lying on her side, staring at me, Nadia touches my cheek now and whispers, "You do *me*. You know. Do me down here. How you can do me to help let out the flooding. How I'm still flooding, and whooshing with all the flooding."

I don't know exactly what she means, but I get the general idea. It's okay with me if she wants me to "do" her. As long as she doesn't expect me to use anything more fallible than my fingers. I roll onto my side so that we're face to face, front to front, and she takes my hand in hers, sets it on the inside of her thigh, and moves it up along the soft inseam of her painter's pants.

He watches me with his brown eyes wide eyes and I help him do me with my hand, and his hand on my flooding, where it wants to whoosh out with the flooding, and when he feels me there how I'm pushing hard with the flooding, and hard against his hand with the flooding, he smiles like a smileypuss, and does me good with his hand, and how still there on his side he comes up closer, like a wiggle-waggle, wiggling right up close, so the back of my hand is feeling his flooding how it's not-stuck no more with the flooding, and how he feels it's not-stuck no more, and looks at me with his wide eyes surprise eyes, looking to see how if I know about it, how he's flooding, and I do know about it, and do him with my hand, the back of my hand, cause of how he wiggled so close I don't need to turn it to feel his flooding, and how I'm doing his hand with my hand against my flooding, and against his flooding with the back of my hand, and doing harder, and how he's making the "mmmm" sounds and pushing hard with his flooding, and I pull away with my hand so his flooding is doing against my flooding, but with the pants, and I reach down to do off the pants, but how he's already flooding hard, how the flooding is whooshing, and he's doing so hard with the whooshing, how he's a Mr. Excited and a giggle-gut with his giggling, and whooshing hard against me, happy with the giggling and flooding, and then done with the flooding. And how he hugs me warm with his warm arms, and does the hugging and giggling how he's a silly Billy giggle-gut, and hugging and nuzzling like an old nuzzle-nut.

I pull back slightly from our hug to peek at the front of my pants.

"Uh oh," she says happily. "Mr. Excitement. Who shows his excitement."

"It's okay," I tell her, then start in laughing again like some idiot madman. Here I've just creamed my pants, and you'd think I discovered a cure for growing old. "Listen. We'll rub some wet clay on the spot and I'll pretend I got wet from your clay. And maybe Lucius can lend me a pair of gym shorts or something while my pants are getting washed and dried. I think he's about my size."

"Mr. Smarty Britches," she says, beaming at me with little girl excitement. "Mr. Wet Britches."

And I laugh and rub noses with her, too deliriously happy to wonder or care if I've gone completely bonkers.

The sound is everywhere now, and rizzing everywhere, at the back of my head and all around my ears and everywhere all around, and how everything smells good now, how mushrooms taste when they are alive and dirty, and broccoli how when it's alive and dirty, and he looks at me everywhere like he wants to find a place to come inside somewhere how he likes everything so much with me, and he knows me now and don't care about no wet spot, and hugs me so warm we both feel the warm, and his eyes are warm and brown like a big brown cow, and his nose is strong and good, and how he's a gentle head and a silly Billy nuzzle-nut, and don't care how I'm not no smarty britches. And he's a smarty britches how the rest are, but not too much of a smarty britches how the rest are to know stuff they don't want to know how they know it all already. And I know now I have him and he has me and we can do together with the flooding and whooshing, and whoosh with the sound how it rizzes everywhere and all around, and he won't say we can't because he knows.

After borrowing and slipping into Lucius Moon's white gym shorts—which are too tight and keep creeping up my thighs so that I'm constantly having to slide a finger under the leg hems and pull them back down—I sit on the porch swing with him. Lucius has been swinging this way (with an occasional break) since before breakfast. By now the slatted wood has probably pressed permanent stripes onto his ass and the backs of his thighs. But he couldn't care less. The swing is still squeaking and the clouds are still looking mean enough to excite him.

Every time I have to pull at the creeping leg hems of my—of his—tight white gym shorts, he grins and rubs his thightops, while his eyes bug out crazily. I smile back at him now, rubbing my thighs in unison with him—a thigh rubbing duet—our eyes connecting. "Ooh wow," he says, and looks down to his thightops to rub harder.

Five minutes later we're still swinging away, feeling high on the storm ozone, my thightops tingling from all the rubbing, when a yellow Datsun with a black racing stripe pulls up and Angela Geer swings her legs out of the passenger's side. The guy in the driver's seat has a beard and wire-rimmed sunglasses (though the sun is nowhere to be seen), and as soon as Angela steps out he spreads a newpaper across the steering wheel. Looks as though he came prepared. I, on the other hand, am anything but prepared. She's finally arrived for her promised weekend inspection, and here I am lazing the afternoon away on a porch swing, wearing gym shorts which are on the obscene side of inappropriate. But I shouldn't complain. At least she didn't drive up five minutes ago, when Lucius and I were rubbing our thightops, egging each other on. Or thirty minutes ago, while Nadia and I were borrowing her office floor. Or last night, when Lucius and Billy were happily chugging their fourth beers, and Lythia was sucking up what for her was a twelve ounce can of seizure sauce.

"Hi Morty," she calls out in her honied voice, halfway to the porch steps. "Hi Lucius."

Her black jeans are tight around the crotch and thighs. She must like the way they look because they couldn't *feel* very good. Not when they fit *that* tightly. Her thick wooden heels clop loudly and solidly along the walkway. She probably flattens three or four ants with each step. Lucius and I both say hi, and by the time she's halfway up the stairs I'm on my feet, tugging at the hems of my—of Lucius's—gym shorts.

Angela is always nice, friendly and reasonable. I don't know why she intimidates me so much. She's my boss, of course, and I'm sure that has something to do with it. And she's so good at what she does, so sharp, that whenever she's around I'm from moment to moment trying to figure out the most appropriate things to say and do; not only for the residents, but for me. And it's more than that. Somehow I think it has something to do with all the tightness that surrounds her. And I'm not just talking about her pants. *Everything* about her is fit too tightly together.

"How's it going?" she says.

"Great," I say, trying to sound confident. But my gym shorts have no pockets for me to hide my hands in, so I scratch behind my ear. "Everyone is hanging around because of the rain, so I've been able to get a lot done. I'm just taking a break before we start dinner."

Lucius senses that I'm talking and acting peculiarly, and reacts by grinning and rubbing his thightops.

"What do you need to do, Lucius?" I immediately cue him. Nothing like giving him mixed messages. Five minutes earlier I'm rubbing along with him, trying to outdo him, and now I'm cueing him to knock it off. He stops rubbing and squeezes his hands into tight fists. Everything goes tight when she's around. "Good Lucius," I say. "Now you look like an adult." The cue and reinforcement are for *her* benefit, not his, and I'm sure he somehow realizes that. But if *I* hadn't said anything to him, *she* would have. At least this way she doesn't get the upper hand on him *or* me.

"So everyone's staying dry?" she says, glancing down at my tight gym shorts, apparently noticing them for the first time.

"Everyone except me," I say, itching at my other ear. "I was helping Nadia move her worktable into the basement and got wet clay on my pants. That's why I'm stuck with these shorts." I look down at them as I tug again at the hems. "Lucius was nice enough to lend them to me."

Soon as he hears his name, Lucius starts to open his fists and rub his thighs, so I look hard at him until he stops. "My pants are in the dryer."

"How about programs?"

"No problem," I say. "With everyone home it's been a lot easier to keep up."

"Sounds as though you've been busy." Her eyes keep turning down to my gym shorts. I'm half afraid that she's searching for some clue; that she already senses exactly what was going on with me and Nadia.

"You sit down and finish up with your break," she says. "I'll step on in for a short visit."

When the screen door bangs shut behind her I sit back on the swing, beside Lucius, and tug at the hems of my gym shorts, hoping he'll grin at me and start rubbing his thightops. But he just sits there with his fists on his lap, so I push off and get us swinging again. I can breathe easy knowing, thanks to the rain, that the house is relatively clean and the residents aren't doing anything Angela might consider inappropriate. Emmy's the only one I worry about. It wouldn't surprise me if she went into a blabbering monologue about everyone getting drunk last night, or about her having to lock the doors and turn off the TV herself, or even about me and Nadia straightening things out on the fire escape at 2:30 in the morning, keeping her awake.

But when Angela steps back out she nods at me and appears to be satisfied. "I can see you've been busy," she says. "Everything's looking good."

"Thanks," I say. "It's been that kind of day. No problems."

"Well that's great," she says. "Keep up the good work." She gives me a nod of encouragement. "I'll see you on Tuesday. At the meeting."

"Okay," I say. "Thanks for dropping by."

When the yellow Datsun pulls off I take a deep breath and realize I feel vaguely pleased with myself. I wish her positive reinforcement wasn't so damned effective with me. "Hey Lucius," I say, gazing after the Datsun. "I think it's okay for you to rub your thighs and rock back and forth the way you do. But you've got to learn *when* it's okay. You know what I mean?"

"Yuh," he says. "I do."

I push off and we start swinging slowly. Behind us the screen door slams and I turn to see Nadia standing in front of it, her tangled black hair hanging over the front of her shoulders. "Mr. Nose," she says with delight, dragging out the o and z sounds. "Mr. Smiley Swinghead." Her lips pull back from her overlapped teeth and her gums as she beams at me.

"You're the smiler," I tell her. "You with your green tennis shoes." As soon as I say "you with your green tennis shoes," it hits me that I sound as delighted and loving as Nadia sounds when she says, "Mr. Nose." I even drag out the oo and z sounds at the end of "shoes."

Letting my feet drag across the porch floor, I turn to ask Lucius to slow down so that Nadia can hop on with us. But he's already pulling hard with his head and shoulders, his eyeballs bugging out as he grins wildly and rubs his thightops. When he looks at my dragging feet I quickly lift them and begin to rub *my* thightops. If he's headed to heaven, I might as well head there with him. "Right Lucius," I say. "*This* is a good time to rock and rub."

"Ooh wow," he says.

Behind me I hear Nadia laughing, and I rub my thightops harder and faster, wondering if my eyeballs are beginning to bug out.

PART II

"The force that through the green fuse drives the flower . . . drives my red blood."

DYLAN THOMAS

"You'd think we would never stop dancing."

LEWIS THOMAS

"Urge and urge and urge
Always the procreant urge of the world."

WALT WHITMAN

Humming For Home

The air is thick with the scents of citrus, gardenia and ocean, and the sounds of palm fronds, crickets, and humming bicycle tires; and he has the Sunday night streets all to himself as he wheels smoothly through the darkness, breathing hard, hunched over, his sweat blown almost cool by the wind he's creating as he pedals for home after his wild weekend shift.

The real wind, which has shifted 180 degrees since the afternoon, is blowing from the East now, and steadily instead of in sudden, violent gusts. The thunderheads have been pushed west with the mosquitoes, so that the sky, except for the moon and stars, is wiped clean as a blackboard. Along the roadside there are still puddles from the morning and afternoon thundershowers, and Benny races, splashing, through the widest and deepest of them, yahooing like a 7 year-old.

Mort

We're seated at the dining table, resisting sleep while awaiting Benny's return. I've managed to arouse Dorie's curiosity, but it's well past 11 and she's already yawning two or three times every minute. The champagne bottle shifts in its bucket as the ice cubes melt and settle, and Dorie begins nodding toward sleep by increment, the way she always falls asleep. Reluctantly. As if struggling against it every inch of the way.

I've dozed off myself when, out of nowhere, his voice startles me. "Hey, what are you guys doing?"

Dorie jerks up, then quickly orienting herself, holds a hand to her heart and says, "What are *you* doing? Sneaking up on us like that!"

"Surprise!" I finally manage to blurt out.

"It's a little late for that, Dear. He's the one who surprised *you*."

"Geez. Piper Heidsick!" Benny stares from us to the champagne bottle in the ice bucket, and back. "What's going on here?"

"It's your father's big surprise for us," Dorie tells him. "Who knows? Maybe after twenty-five years he's finally found himself a job."

Ignoring her, I call for a drum roll, hoping to build the suspense. "Ready? Okay then." I slide the folded letter from under my thigh, set it on the table dramatically as I can (though I've never really had much of a flair for the dramatic), then remind them that I've been wanting to buy a small farm for five or six years now; a place to raise my own chickens, cows, and goats, so I'll know that our eggs and milk, our cheese and butter (and I do intend to become an expert at cheese and butter making; in fact I already make my own paneer by adding lemon juice to boiled milk, then hanging it in a cheese cloth to drip overnight, and already clarify my own butter to use for stir-frying in place of vegetable oils, which either contain artificial preservatives or else go quickly rancid) don't come from animals fattened on chemicals and rapid growth hormones.

Excited, but nervous—for Dorie is eyeing me with a look more of dubious suspicion than eager anticipation—I tell them I finally found what I was looking for; a beautiful ranch house—Dorie will love it, I'm certain—on three and a half acres, just west of West Coconut Beach. Nearly half the property has been used for growing oranges, and in addition to the grove, there's already a nice garden space; maybe 1500 square feet, all of it worked into fertile raised beds, French Intensive style. All we'll need are some chickens, goats, and a cow. And I tell her I figure we'll be able to afford those animals with the profits I make from the oranges. I'll grow them organically and sell them to all the local Co-ops, health food stores, and vegetarian or natural foods restaurants. There's got to be a growing market for that sort of thing.

All the while I'm explaining this, Dorie is staring at me as if I was speaking in tongues. Slowly, she pulls the letter across the table, unfolds it and glances at maybe a sentence or two before pushing it away, as if she's taken one bite too many of some vile-tasting stew.

Benny picks up the letter now and looks it over, grinning. "Wow," he says. "You're going to try it again?"

I nod. "If I have to. I'm working on a list of *five* hundred names *this* time."

Dorie is **still** staring at me wide-eyed, her face flushed. "My God, **Mor**t. It's an illegal pyramid scheme. They'll throw you in jail." She looks at Benny. "You know it's a miracle they didn't catch him the last time. And the only reason they didn't is that he used phony names. Not to mention the fact that we picked up and left the state without telling anyone."

She's right of course. But instead of admitting it, I tell her I'm not actually sure I understand how my letter is, in principle, so different from the money-making scheme of her soap company. "You've got a lot of people at the bottom of your pyramid, too," I point out. "At least in my letter I admit it's a gamble. The people who participate know exactly how much they stand to lose."

"How could you even attempt to make a comparison?" she snaps, leaning closer to me across the table, nearly knocking over her empty champagne glass with an elbow. "We operate a legitimate business. Not a scheme. Goods and services are exchanged. We earn our money, pay our taxes, and have acquired an international reputation for the quality of our products. And, even more important than our products, we help build people's futures. We *give* them futures where before they *had* no futures."

"Well, that's exactly what I'm trying to do," I point out. "Only faster."

I'm half counting on Benny to remind us, at this point, that two wrongs don't make a right. But he's not even listening; just studying the label of the champagne bottle, which he pulled from the bucket as soon as we started arguing. He's always hated arguments, I know, but I've never seen him withdraw from one so quickly and completely. He seems to be in another world.

Dorie, meanwhile, is telling me that even if I'm not nabbed by the FBI I'll never make enough money with the chain letter to buy the farm outright, because people are smarter—or at least more wary—today than they were fifteen years ago. And since I'll never make enough to buy the farm outright, she wants to know how I intend to make monthly payments without a personal income.

Actually I *don't* intend to make the monthly payments, or even the *downpayment*. And I certainly have no intention of sending out my chain letter. (I *was* lucky last time, and *don't* want to spend the rest of my life behind bars, frittering away my good health with an 8 × 10 jogging area, and a diet of white bread, nutrient-free canned vegetables, and carcinogenic meats.) I've simply typed it up as a simple way of convincing her that I'm serious. "Of course, there's a good alternative to my letter scheme," I tell her now. "A much simpler alternative. You know this house is legally mine, Dorie; the title is in my name." I wait for her to nod, but she just keeps staring. "So if I sell this house, my house, I'll have all the money I need. *Without* the chain letter."

She pulls back, once again nearly knocking over her empty champagne glass, and smiles at me in a way I haven't seen her smile in years; with an intimidatingly psychotic smile, her eyes incredibly wide, and her mouth turned up only at the corners. It's the same smile she used to flash at customers who made blatantly unreasonable demands or obnoxious comments or complaints to her when she was waitressing at the Cracker Jack in Atlanta. "You would never do that to me," she says, her eyebrows lifting.

"Listen to me, Dorie. You have all your savings and investments. You're a wealthy woman. But the equity of this house is really all *I* have. So I should be able to do whatever I want with it. And I'm sure the courts would agree." (Actually they won't agree, for though I'm certain they technically *would* agree, I don't ever intend to give them the opportunity to agree, because they would probably be curious about how I earned the money to pay for the house in the first place. And *that's* a Pandora's Box I have no intention of allowing *any* lawyer to pry open.)

"You're blackmailing me," Dorie hisses through her psychotic smile.

"Bartering with you," I correct her. "And I'm sure we can work out an arrangement we'll both be happy with. If worse comes to worst, I can always sell the house to *you.* Then we'll both have what we want." I reach awkwardly across the table for her hand, which she quickly pulls away. "Come on, Dorie. Don't be such a party pooper. At least try to keep an open mind. For God's sake, you haven't even *seen* the place yet."

But she's already shaking her head, her smile finally

gone. "And I *won't* see it. If you want to live on a farm you'll have to do it without me."

There's a sudden, explosive thwock, causing Dorie and me to reflexively duck, hunching our shoulders for quick protection. The cork from the champagne bottle ricochettes off the ceiling, then drops through the lampshade at the far side of the couch. Across the table Benny smiles and says, "Ooh wow! Two points," then laughing, reaches for and fills our glasses, while the bottle steams at the mouth like a smoking gun.

Monday: The Plan

I lock my ten-speed to the chain link fence behind ARC House. Not yet twenty-four hours apart from Nadia, and already I'm beginning to doubt my feelings for her; doubt them at least enough to know I'm not yet ready to admit to myself, much less to Angela or the rest of the world, that I might be falling in love with—might already have *fallen* in love with—a woman who is five years my senior, chronologically, but five *light* years my junior, mentally. And before I *do* admit *anything* to *anyone*, I want to be sure. And I figure the only way for me to *get* sure is to spend more time with Nadia. Alone. Away from ARC House. And without arousing suspicions. It took me just three glasses of champagne last night (after my parents retired, champagneless, to their bedroom to continue their battle) to figure that out. But it took me all this morning and part of this afternoon to come up with a workable plan.

I circle 'round to the front, surprised that no one is on the porch, and skip up the wooden steps to pull open the screen door. Inside, most of the residents are sitting in front of the TV, watching an afternoon re-run of Star Trek. Soon as the screen door slams behind me they look up—except for Lythia—see that it's me, and are instantly—except for Lythia—mobbing me, as if I just crossed home plate with the winning run. Amar, Billy, and Elisha pound my back and shoulders, laughing as they greet me. Lucius Moon stands in front of the couch, watching and grinning, eyes bugged out as he bends to rub his thightops, whispering, "Oooh-wooo-wow." Emmy, a pink towel wrapped around her dripping hair, is already racing down the stairway to see what the commotion is about. She stops on the bottom step to slap her hip and happily shake her head. "Come on now, *you!* Come *on* there." And finally Lythia looks up and grins from her chair, then pushing herself to her feet, leans, and falls toward the crowd.

Surrounded by my entourage I step into the kitchen, feeling like a conquering hero, like a guru among his devoted, adoring disciples. I'm so overwhelmed by my reception, in fact, that for a minute I don't even realize Nadia is missing. Moby too. Then I remember that this is the usual time for daily showers; Nadia must have gone in as soon as Emmy came out. And down the hall I can hear the shower running in the men's bathroom, so I *know* where Moby is.

"My God, Benny." Angela is sitting at the kitchen desk, shaking her head. I'm not sure if she's impressed or disgusted. "What on earth could you have done to rate such a greeting?"

"Gee," I shrug, wondering what she's *imagining* I've done, then deciding to give her as honest an answer as I dare. "I guess we just all had a fun weekend together. You know. It being the Fourth of July and all."

Everyone cheers. Three or four hands slap my back.

"Oh, that's right. You had the Fourth of July shift."

"He's our buddy, he is." Billy's long arm has looped around my shoulder and halfway back across my chest, so that his fingers are stretched in front of my neck. "He's our buddy, he is. Our buddy. Our best buddy."

"Fireworks and beer," I say to Angela. "I guess that's the secret."

"Two beers," Billy says. "That's all I had. All I had. Just two beers. Isn't that right, Benny? Isn't that right, Old Buddy? Isn't that right?"

"I'd like to be able to try to say this," Amar not only tries to say, but says, before I can answer Billy. "We all tried to be able to have two beers." He nods toward Angela. "Just like Angela told us we could be able to have."

"Yeah!" Elisha says, hooking her arm through Amar's

and tilting her head so that while one eye blinks up to him the other aims toward the floor. "Just like Angela told we could."

"Oh *did* she?" Emmy slaps her own cheek. Loudly. "*Hmmm* then with the *two*. All *right* then about the *two*."

Beside me, Lucius bends to rub his thightops, and Angela immediately cues him. "What do you need to do, Lucius?" She waits until he's stopped rubbing, praises him for being able to so quickly correct his inappropriate behavior, then looks back to me, sucking on the tip of her pen, waiting for me to go on.

"Have you got a few minutes?" I ask, wishing I was brave enough to cue *her* to curb her inappropriate pen-sucking.

She nods, then politely asks the residents to excuse us. When they've all left the kitchen—Lythia, ten seconds after everyone else—I pull a stool to Angela's deskside and sit. Setting her pen on her desk calendar, she wheels backward in her chair, swivels until she's facing me, and crosses her leg. She's wearing tight red pants, and those ant-flattening sandals with the thick, wooden heels.

"I wanted to talk with you about this idea I had," I begin, scratching behind my ear, too nervous to look her in the eye. "While I was still in training I remember you telling me how hard it was to find and keep good volunteers. Right? To take the residents shopping and bowling and stuff; two or three of them at a time, I think you told me."

"That *has* been a real problem for us," she admits, bouncing her crossed leg so that the wooden heel of her sandal yo-yo's down and up from the bare heel of her foot. "Most people who've expressed an interest in volunteering either don't want to take the time to go through the training, or are reluctant to commit themselves to any sort of regular schedule, which we've found is absolutely necessary."

"Well *I've* already *been* through the training," I tell her. "And after thinking about it last night I've decided I'd be willing to volunteer my weeknights. You draw up any schedule and I'll follow it. There's no problem with that. Not for me."

"You want to volunteer your weeknights?"

I nod, and she smiles. Not the excited smile I was hoping for, but a wry, "You've got to be kidding me" sort of smile.

"I'm impressed by your willingness to give up such a large chunk of your free time," she says. "But you have to remember, Benny, that it takes time to mentally distance yourself from this job. And for that reason I've taken great pains to set up the support staff schedule with decent interludes between shifts. Because nine times out of ten, staff burnout and staff turnover are the most persistent and difficult problems a director faces in running a group home." She uncrosses her legs and leans back in her chair. Those red pants are straining so tightly around her crotch and hips that I'm half afraid her flesh might at any moment come bursting through the seams, like foam through the cover of an overstuffed cushion. "I'm sure," she continues, "that ARC House has the lowest staff turnover rate of any state-funded group home in Florida. And you can bet that's due almost entirely to our scheduling; to the fact that each support worker here has a minimum of four days to recover from his shift."

I can't believe it! I was sure my plan was infallible, because I never dreamed she'd refuse to allow me to volunteer. "But if I come in as a volunteer I'll be doing mostly fun things, and with just a few residents at a time. Right? Movies and picnics and those kinds of things. And just a couple of hours a night. I'd still have five full *days* free every week, so I can't imagine I'd get burned out."

"You'd be surprised," she says. "I've seen it happen more times than you'd ever believe."

"Really?" I say. "But you know the thing is, if I thought I was getting burned out I could just cut back my volunteering hours. Or even cut them out altogether. I mean, if I'm getting burned out I'll quit my volunteering, not my job." I turn my hands palms up, and shrug, hoping to appear more casual than desperate. "We could at least give it a try and see how it goes."

"Well," she hesitates. "Experience prevents me from even *considering* five nights a week. But maybe, since you work the weekend shift, you could handle a night or two every week. How about if I think it over and let you know."

"That would be great!" I say, eager as a poodle, practically licking her toes because she's so generously agreed to *think* about *allowing* me to volunteer *my* free time. "Thanks Angela." It's absurd. Who should be thanking whom, here? "Oh yeah," I go on, almost forgetting "part two" of my plan. "There's one more thing. My mom and dad are really anxious to meet the residents, so they've asked me to invite them all over for a cookout on Thursday."

"Terrific!" Angela says, catching me off guard with her instant enthusiasm. "Sounds like fun." For a second or two I'm afraid she's going to invite herself along—I never considered *that* possibility—so I quickly explain to her that I'll be driving my father's station wagon and shouldn't need any help with transportation.

"Fine," she says, rolling her chair back to the desk, her strangled red legs disappearing from view.

"I figured I'd come by around 4 or 4:30."

"Sounds good."

"And I was wondering when I should have them back . . . for their programs and all."

"Uh, let me think." She picks up her pen and doodles—mostly hard angles and corners; no soft curves or circles—at the bottom of the desk calendar. "Since they'll be eating out, there won't be any dinner cooking or clean-up programs for Ty to run. And long as you're with everyone and cueing them appropriately, we can actually count a supervised group outing as official program time, because the learning of appropriate interacting on supervised group outings is written into each of their training plans. Just remember to mark it down on their cover sheets." She pauses to examine her doodlings, then looks up at me. "So if you can get them back by 9 or 9:30, that should give Ty plenty of time to get everyone settled down and ready for bed."

"And it should," I tell her, "give my parents plenty of time to get to know everyone."

"Probably a lot more time than they bargained for," Angela jokes.

"Nah," I say. But she may be right. Especially since my parents aren't expecting *anyone* for a cookout on Thursday night.

Attempted Bribery

I'm back again on Tuesday for our weekly staff meeting, the last twenty minutes of which is devoted to Lucius Moon's thigh-rubbing. Angela says that in spite of all our informal cueing, she's noticed, during the past few weeks, a significant increase in this undesirable and inappropriate behavior of his. Ty and Lena immediately and emphatically concur. And when Angela asks me if I've also noticed the increase, I hesitate, then reluctantly nod, feeling like Judas nodding the soldiers toward Gethsemene.

Angela suggests that we start Lucius on a formal behavior extinguishing program, using token reinforcement; explaining to him that we're going to give him a token, a poker chip, every night at bedtime, *if* he can make it through the day without any of us having to cue him to stop rubbing his thighs. At the end of the week he can turn in his accumulated poker chips for a reward. (A beer, she thinks, is the perfect reward for Lucius. The house can easily afford it, and it's something he'd undoubtedly be willing to work hard for.) The first week he would only have to collect a small number of poker chips to earn his reward; maybe two or three. But after whetting his appetite we'd boost the chip requirement to four per week, then five, six, and finally seven. By the time he's earning seven chips a week she says his behavior will have been extinguished. Ty and Lena seem to think it's a great idea. But to me, "extinguishing" a behavior sounds ominous; not so different, in principle, from exterminating a race or a species. Of course I know Angela would never buy *that* argument, so I keep quiet while she goes on to say that she'll draw up the contract tomorrow, explain it to Lucius, and have him sign it so that we can put it into effect next Monday.

At the end of the meeting, before I can stand up, Angela says she'd like to have a quick word with me. I'm hoping she's made a decision about my volunteering, however after Ty and Lena have started up the basement stairs, she just smiles and says she wanted me to know that I've been doing a terrific job. I'm delighted, naturally, to hear the praise, but something subtle in her tone makes me think there's more to come; that her praise was only a primer. A bracer. And sure enough, just as I'm smiling back, getting ready to thank her, she adds, "There is just one thing, Benny. And I realize your last shift was during a special holiday weekend, so I'm not at all overly concerned. I simply thought I should bring to your attention that your program time for Saturday was low—quite low, in fact—and the upstairs bathroom was a bit of a mess when I checked it Monday morning." *One* thing wrong, but she's managed to squeeze in two things. "And I wanted you to know," she goes on, leaning closer to me, as if she's about to share some confidential information, "I'm still mulling over your proposal to volunteer. Of course at this point I'm leaning toward one night a week. But," she gestures here, a thumbs-up signal, "*If* you can get that program time up a bit, to where it should be, I think I'd be more inclined to let you try two nights. Maybe even three."

"Great," I say. "No problem." But I can't believe it. She's actually going to use my desire to volunteer as a reinforcer; as an incentive to increase a desired behavior. It's as if she believes she can change the world for the better by bribing people. (To her, this must be a world full of Pavlov's dogs, all of us salivating at the prospects of our steak dinners.) Promise Lucius a cold beer, and me an extra night or two of volunteering, and she'll move behavioral mountains. And maybe she really will. Lucius *would* do almost anything for a beer, and *I'd* do almost anything for an extra night or two of volunteering; for a greater number of opportunities to spend time alone with Nadia.

Revenge of the Househusband

It was in early May of 1957, three months after Mort Horowitz had been hired as one of the eight assistant managers of the Golden Peach Hotel, and nearly two years after he and Eudora had moved from Loblolly Hill to Atlanta, that, with what was perhaps a final flicker of his nearly extinguished idealism (but more likely a stubborn clinging to his principles), he quit his job before his boss could fire him for refusing to kick out of a fourth floor room a Black Boston doctor, whom Mort had knowingly and willingly registered as a guest—against explicit hotel policy—three hours earlier.

"But he's a doctor, Mr. Shoffleberger," pleaded Mort, who, even in his increasingly frequent moments of non-idealism, of *anti*-idealism, continued to believe that all human beings were equal (equally bad, perhaps—equally greedy and shiftless—but nevertheless equal), and therefore entitled to equal rights and equal treatment. "Every day, as a matter of course, he uses forty or fifty words *you* could never pronounce. He is intimate with parts of *your* anatomy that you've never even heard of."

"But he is a *colored* doctor, in case you hadn't noticed," said Morris Shoffleberger, the avuncular general manager of the Golden Peach (who'd hired Mort, in spite of his lack of hotel experience, as a special favor to his, Shoffleberger's, old, decrepit friend, Ruth Pifflestein, Mort's great aunt, whose husband, Zeev, had died nine years earlier). "And it does not matter *what* all he knows about my anatomy," he continued, with an easy smile, "if half of our guests walk out of here, and tell me they are never coming back."

Mort was about to answer when, at that moment, little Eddie Hemmingway—the assistant Bell Captain, who, three hours earlier, had, on Mort's direct orders, reluctantly carried the Black doctor's suitcases up to his fourth floor room—shuffled past the front check-in counter (behind which, Mort and Shoffleberger stood) huffing and panting, his forehead beaded with sweat, a suitcase clamped under each arm, two suitcases in each hand, the tops gripped together at the handles so that the bottoms angled outward like sawhorse legs, and a trenchcoat tucked under his chin. The gawking, incredulous family, whose luggage he was carrying, followed closely behind him.

Hemmingway was a tiny, but remarkably strong and nimble, middle-aged man with jet black hair, who could carry more suitcases (and earn more tip money) in one trip than any of the taller, longer-armed Bellmen, all of whom preferred to use the hotel luggage carts so that they could *wheel* to the proper destination any luggage they were responsible for, in spite of the smaller tips they invariably earned with this far less spectacular method.

A notorious liar, Hemmingway had, for a brief period, claimed to be the nephew of Ernest Hemingway, and insisted that *The Old Man And The Sea* was actually based upon a story—a personal experience, in fact—he had once related to his "Uncle Ernie." Many workers and guests half believed these lies until a part-time dinner waitress who was working her way through Emory College, pointed out that Eddie spelled his last name with two M's, while the famous Hemingway spelled *his* name with one M. And though the Uncle Ernie anecdotes slowly faded, and eventually disappeared, from Hemmingway's repertoire of lies, they were scarcely missed among the abundance of equally dubious tales Hemmingway continued to share with his friends.

For instance, he insisted that he was one of the six men—the fifth from the front—who'd been immortalized by photograph and statue in the famous flag-planting at Iwo

Jima. To his men friends he boasted that he'd twice slept with Marilyn Monroe when she spent a week in the penthouse suite of the famous Waldorf Astoria Hotel in New York, where he'd worked, so he claimed, for three years as the Head Bellman. And he was always telling everyone that he was one of three triplets; that one of his brothers was a world renowned brain surgeon who'd once performed a top secret emergency operation on Vice President Richard Nixon, inserting a metal plate in his skull after he'd tripped over his infamous dog, Checkers, and fallen backward down the stairway of his California home; while his other triplet brother was a scientist who had almost won the Nobel Peace Prize in 1951 for his astonishing discovery of the cure to a rare, but deadly, Asian blood disease, and who was now on the verge of successfully concocting a vaccine for the prevention of Leukemia.

One day Hemmingway had pulled his wallet from his pocket, flipped it open, and showed Mort what appeared to be a photograph of Eddie himself in an army uniform. "These are my brothers," he proudly told Mort.

"Brothers?" Mort said, perplexed. "But that's just a picture of one man."

"We're triplets," Eddie explained, as if bemused by Mort's dimwittedness. "Why should I overload my wallet with pictures when we all look exactly alike?"

But in spite of—or perhaps because of—his wild fabrications, Hemmingway was a favorite of the hotel guests, and popular among most of the hotel staff, who were always goading and cajoling him into telling more and more outrageously monstrous lies, egging him on with raised eyebrows, cocked heads, and general—though never quite outright—expressions of skepticism.

And yet the kidding and teasing were never carried too far, for it was rumored that little Eddie was as notorious a gambler as he was a liar; that he even had numerous and "high up" connections with the Atlanta Syndicate—whatever *that* was—and that for slightly above-average interest rates, he could, and would, in an emergency, loan a friend *any* amount of money. These rumors were easy enough for everyone to believe, not only because Hemmingway never talked about (and so, never boasted or lied about) his gambling or his connections with the Atlanta underworld, but because one month he might be seen driving to work in a brand new Lincoln Continental, and the next month in an eight year-old Studebaker. One week he would show up wearing three gold rings on each hand and eighty dollar 'talian shoes on his feet, and the next week with only his high school class ring and a pair of scuffed-up Buster Brown loafers.

But as Eddie Hemmingway huffed and grunted his way past the front desk now, Mort didn't care or notice *which* pair of shoes, or which ring or rings, he was or wasn't wearing. He hardly even noticed Hemmingway's impressive load of luggage, for, aside from the trench coat tucked under his chin; it was not, for Eddie Hemmingway, an unusual load (although as it turned out, this particular load would play a critical role in the unfolding of events both five minutes and thirteen years later).

Mort paused, waiting with a forced, impatient smile for Hemmingway and his wide-eyed, breathless entourage to pass out of earshot on their way to the hotel elevators. And when they finally *did* pass out of earshot, Mort, still a man of principles—if not ideals—announced to Shoffleberger that he could not continue to work for any establishment which upheld and supported the absurd and obscene dictum that one group of human beings was superior to any other group of human beings. ("My God, we're not even superior to the apes," he thought, though he kept this information to himself.) And so saying, he walked directly out of the hotel—the same way he'd walked out of Loblolly General Hospital two years earlier; never once looking back—and drove home, where, in a frustrated rage, he grabbed an old shovel (which Eudora had purchased for a quarter at a yard sale three weeks earlier, and *with* which she'd been begging her husband to prepare a small patch of soil, so that she could plant some onions, carrots, greenbeans, and two or three tomato plants) and proceeded to till by hand a forty by fifty foot garden plot; the entire back yard, fence to fence, of their small, rented South Atlanta home.

That night, Shoffleberger called Mort and asked him to consider returning to his job. He even surprised Mort with the news that he'd had a sudden change of heart and allowed the Black doctor to stay at the Golden Peach.

"Why?" Mort demanded, skeptical. "Have you really decided to change your policy?"

"Well not exactly," Shoffleberger reluctantly admitted. "You might say we made an exception this time." He then went on to explain that minutes after Mort left the hotel, and minutes *before* Shoffleberger had had a chance to send one of his other assistant managers up the the fourth floor to inform the doctor that the Golden Peach rooms and facilities were for the use of white guests only, Eddie Hemmingway had collapsed with a massive coronary in the fourth floor hallway at the feet of the horrified family whose heavy load of luggage he'd been straining with. The Black doctor, hearing screams down the hallway, had rushed from his room and literally brought Hemmingway back to life with ten minutes of vigorous heart massage and Cardio-Pulmonary Resuscitation. By the time the ambulance and paramedics arrived, Hemmingway was conscious, and breathing on his own.

It was a fantastic story—the sort of story that even Hemmingway might have had trouble dreaming up—but of course it did nothing to woo Mort back to the Golden Peach, and when he said good-bye to Shoffleberger it was for the last time.

A week later Mort received a short note from Eddie Hemmingway which read, "Mr. Horowitz. IOU. You name it, you got it. Call me anytime." Apparently Hemmingway had figured out that he owed his life not only to the Black doctor, but to Mort, who had, fortunately for Hemmingway, registered the doctor against explicit hotel policy. Mort, who wondered why it seemed so much easier for people to speak in terms of debt rather than thanks, never responded to and soon forgot about the IOU, and about the life he'd indirectly saved.

During the next month Mort spent his mornings half (or less) heartedly searching the want ads in the newspaper, and whole heartedly sweating and digging out his tensions and frustrations while attempting to break up the heavy red clods of Georgia clay in the garden, where Eudora planned to plant her starts and seeds. Then one day, Eudora returned home after a busy lunch shift at the Cracker Jack Cafe (the slightly seedy, but always bustling diner, where, two weeks after Mort quit his hotel job, she'd applied for a waitressing job, and, to her surprise and chagrin, been hired on the spot, even though she admitted to being interested in the job only as a temporary source of income) and found her husband lying on his back in the middle of her still-seedless garden, staring at the sky, hands pillowed behind his head, and the clay-smeared shovel at his side. Concerned, she hurried over to find out what he was doing, and if he was all right.

"I'm resting," he said, smiling up at her almost serenely. "Everything looks different from down here."

Relieved that he was only resting; that he, in fact, at least *appeared* to be happier and calmer than he had in the month since he'd left the Golden Peach, she knelt beside him, kissed him lightly on the lips, then asked hopefully, "How did the job hunting go this morning?"

"It didn't," he said.

"It didn't?"

"That's right. It didn't."

She laughed uneasily, perplexed by his oddly insouciant tone of voice. "What do you mean?"

"I mean it didn't go, Dorie. I didn't look."

"Oh." She considered his explanation for a moment. "You mean you took the day off?"

He shook his head. "I mean I'm not looking. Period. I've retired."

She laughed. He laughed. He sat up, and they hugged and laughed. Then she went inside.

From the window she watched while he slowly stood, picked up the shovel, and began pile-driving it into the clods of clay. Something about the purposefulness of his movements and stiff-browed concentration sent a tingle scrambling up the ladder of her backbone, for she suddenly understood that he was not joking. He'd retired.

She walked slowly back out, stopping at his side. "You're serious then?"

He looked up, huffing, and nodded.

"I don't understand," she said.

He shrugged. "It's simple, Dorie. I'm tired of the rat race out there. It's insane, and so I've decided I don't want to be a part of it anymore."

As he started in again with the pile driving, Eudora raised her voice, "The rat race?! It sounds to me like maybe you've been watching too much television."

"I never watch television," Mort reminded her. "I hate television. It's just that I've been doing a lot of thinking about it the last few weeks, and it makes sense to me now that in the forty years or so I have left, I should be learning to appreciate life. I should be doing exactly what I *want* to do."

"I see," Eudora said, kicking at one of the heavy red clods while her husband went on with his tilling and pile driving. "And *this*," she gestured toward his shovel with her head, "is what you've decided you want to do?"

He nodded.

"And what will we eat while you are doing what you want to do? From a small garden you plan to feed two people year round?"

"That's not likely," he admitted, pushing a lump of clay from the shovel-edge with the toe of his boot.

"Then what?"

"Goddamnit, *you* tell *me!*" he snapped, ramming the shovel straight into the ground so that it stood, perfectly vertical, by itself, the handle vibrating for a few seconds like a long, wooden tuning fork. He stepped back, staring at the shovel, and took a deep breath. "I'm sorry, Dorie." Shaking his head. "But you know, just because I am a man it does not mean I should have all the answers. That isn't fair. To either of us."

"And what about a family?" she said, hardly hearing him. "How do you plan to support a family, doing what you want to do?"

He set a hand atop the shovel handle, looked toward the

fence, watching the leaves of the Catalpa Tree rustling in the spring wind, then frowned and nudged sweat from his cheek with his shoulder. "I don't know."

"Oh, well, terrific!" Eudora practically sneered at him before whirling on her heels and heading for the back door, stopping half way to turn back and hiss, "I really can't believe you're serious about this. I can't believe you would be *that* irresponsible."

Inside she shut herself in their bedroom, crawled under the covers, still wearing her black and white waitressing uniform, and tried to console herself with the thought that her frustrated husband would soon come to his senses.

It was twelve years later, in early October of 1969, the day after their son, Benny, turned eight, and nearly a year after Richard Nixon was elected President (Nixon's election didn't phase Mort, who, since voting for Stevenson in 1952—since his union organizing experience in 1954—had given up on politics in general, and on elections in particular. "Tweedle-Dum and Tweedle-Dee," he liked to say of the differences between *any* two politicians running for *any* office), that Mort and Eudora Horowitz received the letter which was to dramatically alter the course of their lives.

Mort had been a househusband for thirteen years now, and an expert gardener—becoming more expert all the time—for at least the last five years, while Eudora was giving a dozen piano lessons a week on her old Gulbransen piano, and working long hours at the Cracker Jack Cafe to support herself, as well as her husband and son. She hated living in Atlanta, but believed that with a husband who refused to work, a young son whose appetite increased, it seemed, daily, and the combined meager salaries of her piano teaching and waitressing, she would be stuck there forever. She'd begun, more and more frequently, to have fantasies of running away, perhaps to New York, where she could find a piano-playing job in some classy restaurant or nightclub whose patrons were all sophisticated and urbane. Yet, in spite of her vivid and increasingly prolific fantasizing, deep down she knew she would never be able to abandon her son, even temporarily, with a father who was too irresponsible to support him; *so* irresponsible that his only interest was in doing what *he* wanted, what *he* enjoyed.

There was nothing out of the ordinary about the envelope the letter arrived in—though the return address was unfamiliar—and after Eudora ripped it open, then pulled out and read the letter, she nearly tossed it in the waste basket, for not only was it an impersonal form letter, signed by three women she'd never even heard of; it was a *chain letter,* with an aggressively sales-pitchy tone about it, concerning recipe-collecting, a topic without interest for Eudora, who, thirteen years earlier, had stopped cooking meals altogether.

As she moved to drop the letter in the waste basket beside her old piano, she hesitated, then decided to pass it on to the *real* "homemaker" of the family. And although Mort was no more interested in recipe-collecting than his wife was (he preferred to improvise, and seldom cracked a cook book or glanced at a recipe), he *was* intrigued by the letter itself:

Dear Mrs. Horowitz, (The name, Mrs. Horowitz, was typed in, while the rest of the letter was obviously zeroxed.)

As a homemaker, interested in providing my family with the widest variety of delicious meals, I am sending this letter to you, and nine other homemakers like you, and, for reasons that will presently be explained, requesting that you simply 1) send to me—and to the two women whose names appear directly below my name at the end of this letter—your very favorite, most often and highly complimented recipe, and 2) copy the body of this letter, word for word, and send it on to ten of your own homemaking friends or acquaintances. Please take just a few minutes to do this now! Today.

If no one breaks this chain, you will, within weeks, receive exactly 1,110 (10 plus 10 × 10, plus 10 × 10 × 10) guaranteed-to-be-great recipes, a collection vastly superior to any ordinary cookbook. And all for only a few cents postage, and a few minutes of your time.

But please act today. Do not break or delay this magic chain. Thousands of homemakers and their families are counting on you, and I sincerely trust that you will not let us down.

When you re-type this letter—word for word, please!—simply sign your name directly beneath the word "sincerely," and move the other names down one place, omitting the name at the bottom, for she will have already received her 1,110 guaranteed-to-be-great recipes. (Of course, after re-typing the letter, and the names and addresses at the end, you may, to save time, simply xerox the other nine copies.)

Sincerely,

Mrs. Betty Sampson
2780 SW Lee Street
Atlanta, Georgia

Mrs. Belinda Dykstra
PO Box 471
Atlanta, Georgia

Mrs. Susie Kemp
117 Rt. 3
Marietta, Georgia

P.S. Remember. We are all placing our faith in you.

Mort chuckled at the ingeniousness of the letter, marvelled at the extraordinary, almost magical, powers of geometric, or exponential, progression, which he'd first contemplated while studying Malthus's *On Population* in a college biology course, and which the success of this clever chain letter depended upon; then on his way to the kitchen, deposited the letter in the waste basket.

Five minutes later, feeling miserably guilty and (Eudora would have been astonished to learn) responsible; not wanting to be the party pooper to break the magic chain, to spoil the event of the year for thousands of hopeful homemakers, he retrieved the letter, grudgingly hauled his old gray Royal typewriter from the back of the closet, and sat down at the kitchen table to type out the ten short letters along with the three requested copies of his favorite recipe: fresh chicken thighs (he was not yet a vegetarian) smothered in paprika and freshly pressed garlic, then baked in half an inch of teriyaki, dark beer, and lime juice.

Six days after he'd sent off his chicken recipe to Betty, Belinda, and Susie, and his xeroxed letter to the ten women whose names he'd chosen at random out of the Atlanta Phone Directory, recipes began to arrive in the mail. And when, just two weeks later, the postman knocked on the door to deliver three rubber-banded packs of envelopes, with over 110 recipe-stuffed envelopes in each pack (which brought the total number of recipes he'd received to nearly 480), Mort was suddenly struck, as if by a lightning bolt, with a thought, an idea, a scheme, which was so appealingly simple, so potentially, staggeringly, lucrative, and perhaps best of all, so deliciously poetic with its perfect irony (for *this* time he would be *using* human greed—that same ubiquitous commodity which had, fourteen years earlier, shattered his ideals, while radically changing, very nearly ruining, his life—to *rebuild* his life; to reclaim what he could of his lost plethora of opportunity, not only for himself, but for his devastatingly affected family) that he knew right away he must pursue it at once; pursue it to its possibly astonishing, and wondrously tropical, end.

And so, as soon as he'd cooked breakfast for his wife and son, and kissed them both good-bye (Eudora dropped Benny off at school every morning on her unhappy way to the Cracker Jack Cafe), Mort once again hauled out his typewriter, along with the original recipe letter, and, grinning with a luscious sense of anticipation and self-satisfaction, began to type:

Dear _____

As a breadwinner, trying my best to provide for the needs of my family, I am sending this letter to you, and 19 others like you, and, for reasons that will presently be explained, requesting that you simply 1) send to me—and to the three men whose names appear below mine—a one dollar bill; and 2) copy the body of this letter word for word, and send it on to twenty of your own breadwinning friends or acquaintances whom you trust, and who you feel deserve to prosper.

If no one breaks this chain, you will, within weeks, receive in the mail exactly 168,420 dollars (20 plus 20 × 20, plus 20 × 20 × 20, plus 20 × 20 × 20 × 20—work it out for yourself if you're afraid it sounds too good to be true); not by gambling, but by participating in this simple chain of faith. And all for an incredibly inexpensive, low-risk investment of four 1 dollar bills, plus two dollars postage, and a few minutes of your time.

But please do not break this magic chain. Your own bright future, and the futures of thousands of men like you (and, of course, their deserving families) rests in your hands, so I sincerely trust that you will not let us down.

When you re-type this letter today—word for word, please!—simply type in your own name directly below the word "sincerely," and move the other names down one place, omitting the name at the bottom, for, if no one has broken the chain, he will have already received his 168,420 dollars. (Of course after re-typing the letter, and the names and addresses at the end, you may, to save time, xerox the other 19 copies. Just be sure to type in a different name at the beginning of each letter.)

Now if all this still sounds confusing, or too impossibly good to be true, I invite you—I urge you!—to simply re-read the letter carefully, get out a pencil and a piece of paper, and add up the numbers for yourself. No matter how you look at it you will find that the risks are painlessly low, while the potential profits are stunningly high. So please, do not break this chain. You have everything—168,420 dollars; a new life—to gain, and almost nothing—a few hamburgers' worth of your money, and a few TV commercials' worth of your time—to lose. We are all placing our deepest faith and trust in you. And ultimately, that is what this letter is all about. Faith in the power of ordinary humans.

"Faith," Mort thought, when he'd finished re-reading the letter, and typing in his name and address, "in the power of *extra*ordinary human greed." And then it occurred to him that his was the only name and address at the end of the letter; and that, in fact, there would be fewer than the four described names and addresses at the ends of each of the letters sent out by the first three groups of twenty. So in order to avoid confusion, he added the following post script:

P.S. If the letter you received has four signatures below the word "sincerely," omit this post script from your letter, and ignore the explanation that follows. If there are fewer than four signatures beneath the word "sincerely," send your dollar to the one, two, or three men who have signed the letter, then copy this letter—including the post script—and send it on to your twenty friends, signing your name below the word "sincerely," and moving the rest of the names down one place, exactly as explained in the main body of the letter. If you do happen to be among the first three groups of twenty, your investment will be slightly smaller (one, two, or three dollars, as opposed to four dollars) but your return will be precisely the same.

When he re-read the post script, Mort groaned aloud, for he feared the instructions had become so complicated—so equivocal and suspicious-sounding—that some, or even many, of the letter recipients might be dissuaded from participating. He spent the rest of his morning attempting, without success, to clarify and simplify the instructions. And then he came up with another idea; an idea which, in addition to eliminating the need for a complicated post script, would prove to be many times more lucrative.

Below his own signature, Mort now signed three invented names; then, suddenly worried about the legality of his scheme, added a fourth invented name in place of his own.

Early the next morning, he told Eudora he needed the car for grocery shopping, and, after dropping her off at the Cracker Jack Cafe, and his son off at South Atlanta Elementary School, drove to the nearest post office to rent a post office box under the first of his four invented names and addresses. Behind the counter, a man with blonde hair and a reddish-brown moustache handed Mort an application card to fill out, then asked to see some identification.

"Uh, identification?" Mort stammered, momentarily panicking. Then he smacked himself in the forehead, laughed, and backing away from the counter, patting his coat pockets as if to frisk himself, explained to the man with the moustache that he'd left his wallet back at the office.

Outside, he sat in his parked car, sweating—though his coat was unbuttoned and the air was so cool that he could see his breath, which was already fogging up the windows—and thinking that this was going to be a bit more complicated than he'd figured. Somehow, it was clear, he was going to have to come up with four phony, but official-looking, identification cards.

The first idea Mort had was to drive straight to the seediest section of downtown Atlanta, park his car, and walk among the pimps and prostitutes, pushers and peddlers, wheelers and dealers, who were always slinking about in front of the adult bookstores, topless and bottomless taverns and dancehalls, S and M apparel stores, massage parlours, and Palaces of Love Wrestling ("three falls for a dollar"). Surely if he offered any of these nefarious characters a few dollars, he or she, if unable to offer direct assistance, would at least be able to point him toward the person who *could* offer direct assistance.

But by the time he'd started his car, wiped his fogged-over windows with his coat sleeve, and pulled into the street, he had already decided that this plan was far too dangerous; for as soon as he pulled a few bills out of his wallet—and he would be needing to pull bills out of his wallet at every risky step along the way—the vultures would descend. Inevitably, he would be mugged. Maybe even knifed or gunned down. And not even the luminous prospect of a healthfully blissful future in Coconut Beach (which had been, of course, his plan, his goal, from the beginning of his chain letter scheme) was worth *that* risk.

Obviously he would be better off dealing with someone he knew personally. But when he tried to think of friends of his who were particularly unsavory, who might have even the thinnest *thread* of a connection with the criminal world, he drew a blank. "Christ," he thought, feeling helpless. "I don't have *any* friends anymore. Savory *or* unsavory." And then he remembered Eddie Hemmingway. Who owed him.

Though Hemmingway had apparently left the Golden Peach years ago—for not one of the first half dozen bellmen with whom Mort now spoke at the hotel entrance, had ever worked with or even heard of him—there *was* a young black bellman who, overhearing Mort discussing the matter with one of the older bellman, interrupted to say that *he* knew Eddie Hemmingway.

"*You* used to work here with Eddie Hemmingway?" Mort asked, astonished, because the young bellman appeared to be no older than 18.

"Hell naw, Man. He got him a pawn shop over to 13th Street."

"Eddie Hemmingway? Are you sure?"

"Yo! Eddie Hemmingway. He old, he white, and he stand about that high." The young bellman held his hand level with his chest. "But old as he look, he still built solid."

"God, that sounds like Eddie," Mort admitted.

"Little Eddie, he awright, Man. His brother be one of them scientists looking to cure Sickle Cell."

"He told you that?"

"Yo. That's why all the brothers buy from him. Eddie say for every dollar he make, he gave a nickel to his brother. The scientist. And that nickel go to research for Sickle Cell."

"That's Eddie all right!" Mort said, elated. "You say his shop's on 13th?"

"Yo. 13th and Llewelyn. On the corner. You ain't gonna miss it."

Hemmingway, whose pawn shop, "Hemmingway's To Have and Have Not," was, so he claimed, the largest and busiest in Atlanta, appeared genuinely delighted to see Mort, and happily delivered on his thirteen year-old IOU, no charge, no questions asked, no eyebrows raised. He simply took Mort's driver's license, then jotted on a yellow piece of paper the four phony names and addresses that Mort wanted him to put on the phony identification cards.

"I got a friend who'll take care of this for me, no problem. My brother operated on one of his kids—took out a tumor the size of a fist—so he owes me."

A week later Mort received in the mail a large golden envelope containing his driver's license, along with four perfect replicas (each with a different one of his phony names and addresses), and four matching U.S. Merchant Mariner's identification cards, with photographs on the front (these, unlike the driver's license photographs, printed in black and white) and phony thumbprints on the back. "Consider the Mariner's cards an insurance policy, compliments of me," Hemmingway wrote. "Just in case they ask to see a second piece of ID. Good luck."

The next morning, after dropping his wife at work and his son at school, Mort drove to four Atlanta post offices, using, with each post office box application he filled out, a different one of his phony driver's licenses. (He was never asked for a second piece of identification, so never had to use his complimentary insurance policy.) After renting his fourth and final post office box, he bought all the stamps and envelopes he would need, and drove to a printing shop to have 200—instead of 20—copies of his letter run off. (That way, he figured, he would be way ahead of the game, even if only 50 out of the first 200 letter recipients responded.) He spent the following day at home, selecting 200 names from the city phone directory, then addressing, stamping, and stuffing 200 envelopes, and dropping them all in a mail box.

It was one month, two weeks, and three days after he'd sent off his 200 letters that Mort picked up Eudora at The Cracker Jack Cafe, and found her in a miserable mood. She was tired, she told her husband, of men pinching or oogling at her, then leaving insultingly small tips when she refused to flirt back. She was tired of the cooks complaining whenever she took special orders from the customers, and the customers complaining whenever she *refused* to take their special orders. She was tired of dealing with the daily lunch rush; tired of having three tables full of people finish their meals and leave the restaurant at the same time, to be replaced by three *new* tables full of people, all of them in a rush, all of them wanting, expecting, and demanding immediate service, while the customers at her remaining tables were wanting, expecting, and demanding re-fills, extras, desserts, or their checks; and the cooks were wanting, expecting, and demanding her to pick up and take out her orders before the food grew cold. She was tired of waitressing. And tired, she made it clear now to Mort, of living. It was only her son, she tearfully told him, who was keeping her going.

On another day Mort might have taken her comments personally. (And bitter as she felt, she was *intending* that he take her comments personally.) But on this day Mort simply nodded, poker-faced, and watched the road closely, driving even more cautiously that he usually did. And as soon as they were safely home, he found and showed to Eudora a copy of the letter he'd sent out, explained to her the significance of the invented names and post office box numbers, then led her into the garage and pulled from the corner an ice bucket with a bottle of champagne, and a cardboard box filled almost to the top with dollar bills, rubber-banded together in 583 stacks of one hundred, and 1 stack of twenty six.

Eudora quit her job that afternoon, and spent the next two weeks trading in the stacks of one hundred at different banks—20 stacks per bank—in and around Atlanta, explaining, when the tellers looked suspiciously at the rubber-banded packets of one dollar bills, that she was a waitress who had, for ten years, been saving all her dollar tips for her son's college education. It gave her incentive, she told them, to watch the pile grow instead of putting it in the bank. The tellers shook their heads, lectured her on squandered interest, then cashed in her dollar bills for certified checks. At the end of those two weeks, when their total had topped 66,000 dollars, and their daily mail income had dwindled to less than 100 dollars a day, Mort and Eudora bought a four-year-old white Cross Country Rambler Wagon, and, while waiting for nightfall—waiting so that they could pack up and leave furtively—tried to explain to their eight year-old son (who was sullen and bewildered by the news that he would be leaving his home, his school, and his friends, without even the opportunity to say good-bye) that he was about to receive his greatest Christmas present ever. They finished with their packing before midnight, and, leaving no forwarding address, drove straight to Coconut Beach, where first thing in the morning they checked into the Sand and Surf Hotel.

Because they wished to avoid the trouble entailed in going through a bank for a mortgage (they knew they would never get a loan when the bank officer learned that in Atlanta Mort had been a homemaker, and Eudora a waitress and piano teacher, and that they were, at present, unemployed), they simply looked for a house they could buy outright, and on the third day found a three bedroom home, half a block from the Atlantic Ocean and half a block from Manatee Lake, with a good-sized, modern kitchen, a spacious living room with a cathedral ceiling, and a nice back yard bounded by three grapefruit trees, an orange tree, and an avocado tree (Mort knew they would never go hungry here), all for 61,500 dollars, a reasonable price for a Coconut Beach Home, even in 1969. And offering cash, they were easily able to talk the owner (a contract lawyer who was selling the home himself rather than through a realtor) into lowering the price by 3,500 dollars. After buying the home, and paying title, fire, and flood insurance, they had a little over 2,000 dollars left.

Eudora, who was determined that she would never again pick up an order pad or don a waitress apron, applied for jobs with half a dozen Coconut Beach and West Coconut Beach law and business firms needing secretaries. She also responded to an ad in the newspaper for A.S.C., the American Soap Corporation. "We want teachers and motivators," the ad read. "Not salesmen." She was interviewed by a skinny young man with a yo-yoing Adam's Apple and an impressive Cuban accent, who hired her on the spot after eloquently explaining that, depending upon her sales abilities, Eudora could make a fair to decent living selling ASC's superior line of soaps and cleansers, or, depending upon her motivating abilities, an excellent to phenomenal living persuading others to sell the product *for* her; earning a share of what *they* sold, as well as a share of what they earned persuading *others* to sell the product. Of course she would always be paying a percentage of what *she* earned to this smooth-talking young man who seemed so anxious to hire her. However, she knew that the only thing that would count, as far as her own income was concerned, would be the pyramid of sellers she was able to erect beneath her. To Eudora, this sounded not unlike Mort's scheme for exponential money-making, and she knew how successful *he* had been.

As it turned out, ASC was a brand new corporation (Eudora was not terribly far removed from the top of the pyramid; in fact, Alvaro—"Al"—Gutierrez, the young man who hired her, was the nephew of Manolo Gutierrez, an exiled Cuban who'd founded ASC only three years earlier, and who would later become infamous for designing impossible and unpopular golf courses throughout the Southeast), destined for a future of rapid growth. And Eudora quickly proved herself to be not only an excellent motivator, but a shrewd saleswoman as well. By the beginning of the summer she had, in addition to persuading forty people to sell ASC's products (and successfully encouraging them to earn more for themselves—and so for her—by finding others to sell the soaps, and encouraging them to find *others* to sell the soaps), convinced nearly every Coconut Beach Hotel manager of the superiority of her soaps and cleansers, and was earning over 3,000 dollars a month, a figure which would double over the next five years, and nearly quadruple by the time her son began to work at ARC House.

The Seizing of the Day

When I pull up to the curb in front of ARC House late Thursday afternoon in my father's newly painted—fire engine red—'65 Cross Country Classic Rambler Wagon, most of the residents appear to be waiting for me on the front porch. Before I can switch off the ignition, Lucius Moon hops up from the wooden swing to bend over and heat up his thightops, Billy, Elisha, and Amar wave and scream greetings, Moby takes a last long drag on his cigarette—Lythia bobbing beside him, tracing mysterious doodles in the air with her hand as she stares at the curling cigarette smoke, unaware that I've arrived, the commotion around her not yet registered—and Emmy bounces down the front steps, different parts of her bouncing in different directions, then stands there, her left arm pressed snugly to her belly, just beneath and supporting her breasts, and her right elbow resting in her upturned left palm, while she chews the tip of her thumb as if it were a cigar. When I step out of the car she slaps her hip, happily shakes her head and wails, "Come *on* now, *you*. Come *on* there."

"*You* come on, Miss Emilia," I kid her, as I stare over the car roof, scanning the porch for Nadia. "*All* of you guys. First come, first served."

They stampede down the steps, Amar spitting over the stairway railing, and Lythia finally looking up to see me as legs brush past her shoulders. Billy, Lucius, and Emmy pile in first, fighting for the seat next to me, Billy winning out, his long arm whacking into place, staking a claim for the rest of his body. Lucius sits beside him and Emmy backs out—not enough room for the three of them—slaps her hip, and slides, muttering and grumbling, into the back seat beside Amar and Elisha. Moby and Lythia settle for the far back cargo area, and are soon joined by Emmy, who apparently was unsatisfied with the seat next to Amar, probably because she doesn't want him leaning over her to spit out the window.

"Hi ya Benny," Billy says to me through my open door. "How are ya, Buddy? How are ya? We're having barbecue tonight, we are. A big barbecue. With ribs and chicken and steak. Chicken and steak. Chicken and a T-Bone steak."

"Whoa there, Billy." I bend down to look at him, my hands still on the car roof. "Where did you hear all that?"

"We're having a barbecue with you, Benny. With you, Old Buddy. Having a big barbecue feast with you."

"Uh, yeah, right. I'll tell you more about that in a minute. Now let's see . . ." I look back at everyone else. "Any of you guys know where Nadia is?"

They all—except Lythia and Lucius—answer in unison, pointing to the house, telling me she's in there with Angela. Lucius grins at his hands as they rub across his thightops, while Lythia stares, open-mouthed, at everyone's pointing fingers.

"Okay," I say, trying not to panic, hoping that Emmy didn't decide to squawk to Angela about Nadia and me visiting on the back porch so late, Saturday night. "I guess I'd better let her know we're all ready to leave. You guys just sit tight for a minute."

Inside, Angela is talking to Nadia at the kitchen table. But as soon as Nadia sees me she immediately hops up from her stool to beam at me with those overlapped teeth and black coffee eyes. "Mr. Barbecue Ben," she says. "Mr. Chef Boy-Ar-Dee." She's wearing baggy blue jean painter's pants and an untucked yellow golf shirt with a small rip in the shoulder.

"What do you need to do when someone is talking to you, Nadia?" It's Angela's calm but firm, hard-loving tone of voice. Nadia's teeth disappear into her mouth as she sits, and her face swings back toward Angela. "Thank you, Nadia," Angela says. "Now can you remember what it was we were talking about?"

Nadia thinks for a few seconds, then guesses, "About how I should do my hair right, without no clay or knots or nothing?"

"Good Nadia. And what did I say we'd have to think about doing if you didn't start to care for your hair the way we expect you to? The way we expect *any* adult to care for his hair?"

Nadia stares at her hands in her lap. "You said about cutting it. You know. Cutting it short so how I won't have to get no more clay in it, and knots and stuff."

"Good Nadia." Angela tilts and lowers her head to get eye contact with Nadia. "You listen well. And that makes me feel as though you're going to try hard so we won't *need* to cut your hair. You think you *will* try hard?"

Nadia bites her lip and nods, while Angela turns to me, smiling, her hard-loving tone of voice changing only slightly as she greets me and thanks me for waiting.

"No problem," I say, though my stomach seems to be clenching like a fist.

"Nadia was going to leave without brushing her hair," Angela explains. "She's very excited about the cookout. But she needs to learn," she's lowering her head again to get eye contact with Nadia, "that even when adults are excited they have to remember to care for themselves. Right, Nadia?"

"Yes," Nadia says, fidgeting with her hands. "I got to remember 'bout my hair 'cause of how an adult person would remember."

"Great, Nadia. You hair looks beautiful right now, and I'm sure Benny's parents will appreciate that. We want them to know we're all adults here at ARC House, and capable of caring for ourselves."

Angela glances at her watch. "Well, you'd better get going, I didn't mean to hold you up."

As we're about to leave the kitchen she tells me that Ty

will be expecting us back by 9:30, or any time earlier, then reminds me to mark down program time for the cookout when we return. "Have fun," she says cheerfully.

When we get to the car I scoot into the driver's seat, while Nadia slides into the back seat, directly behind me, and right beside Amar.

"We're going to Benny's house," Billy says as I start the car, shift it into drive, and ease down on the accelerator. "Going to Benny's house, we are. To Benny's house. Going to Benny's very own private house."

"To my parents' house," I correct him.

"Yeah," Elisha says. "To his parents' house."

"That's okay, Benny," Billy says, apparently forgiving me for not having my very own private house. "That's okay, Buddy, That's okay."

"I'll try to say this," Amar says. "He tries to be able to love his parents, and on top of that he cares for them very much. Because blood's redder than water, and a man's got to be able to fight for his mother and father just the way he'd try to be able to love them if they was his own son. And I'll try to say this—"

"What are we barbecuing, Benny?" Billy suddenly interrupts, as if Amar's voice was no more than background noise. "What are we barbecuing, Old Buddy? What are we barbecuing?" He's slumped so far forward in the car seat that he's not even blocking the rearview mirror, and I can see Amar grinning stealthily back and forth from Nadia to Elisha, having apparently already forgotten that he was just interrupted in the middle of a major speech.

"Well," I say, answering Billy loudly enough for everyone to hear. "The barbecue plans have changed slightly. I decided it might be easier for my parents if we just picked up a barrel of Kentucky Fried Chicken and ate it at the beach. Did you guys know I live just half a block from the beach?"

"Oh *do* you?" Emmy says. "*Hmmm* then with that *chick*en. O*kay* then about that *chick*en."

"Oooh wow," Lucius says, then, like a happy dog, thrusts his head out the window and into the wind.

Everyone seems to agree that eating fried chicken at the

beach will be fun, so I continue on toward Kentucky Fried, taking a right on Gardenia Street, then a left onto Dixie Highway. When we get there I park in front of the tall white pole with the giant barrel of chicken at the top. The barrel used to rotate to attract the attention of passing motorists, but it stopped working a few years ago and hasn't rotated since. As I shift into park, the car doors are already swinging open and everyone is piling out.

"Okay," I say, stepping out myself, now. "Just remember your manners, you guys. "You're representing ARC House. Right?"

We all—except Moby, who remains outside to smoke a cigarette, and Lythia, who bobs beside him, watching—file quietly through the front door, into the thick smell of frying chicken, which is always fifty times better than the taste. The girl behind the counter must be in her late twenties, but wears braces on her teeth, and is stick-figure thin. (If I worked around all this oil and grease long enough I'd probably turn anorexic, too.) She eyes us cautiously, hollers back our order—a 21 piece barrel—then, after taking my money, hands me a receipt with a number. I step back beside Nadia, letting the upper part of my arm brush, then settle, against hers.

"Mr. Warm," she says, the words coming out oozy and smooth as caramel.

"You too," I whisper, giving her back a quick rub. It's probably our first body contact in public.

A few feet away Amar has started speaking to a young Black man who's waiting for his chicken order. The guy is my age—maybe a year or two younger—wearing an untucked white t-shirt, torn at the shoulder, gray pants that are nearly half a foot too short, and black, high-top tennis shoes over black socks. A long-handled black comb is jammed into his afro like a mounted gun.

"You trying to be able to get some fried chicken?" Amar asks him, stepping close, pushing his nose right up to the nose of the Black guy, who nods once, poker-faced, then looks around as if to make sure he's not being cornered.

"Well I'll try to say this," Amar says loudly, his face not retreating an inch. "*I* try to be able to like fried chicken, too. And not only that, but pork and pig's knuckles and also watermelon." I shut my eyes here, while my heart does an arhythmic jig. "And just like my mother told me, she told me there ain't nothing wrong with trying to be a colored fella because we all got to be able to try to share this world with each other, whether or not whatever we are."

"Oh *do* we?" Emmy, who's waiting beside Amar, slaps her hip sharply. The Black guy and I both jump at the sound of the slap. "Hmmm then with *him*." She points, jabbing her finger toward him, her breasts bouncing. "O*kay* then about *him*."

Lucius grins and bends over to heat up his thighs, Elisha smiles hopefully up at Amar's new friend, and Billy stares out the window, bored, his body curved like the neck of a swan.

I'm feeling the need to intervene somehow, before Amar says anything else, but the Black guy's biceps are lumpy with veins, and his skin is looking violently taut. So I stand there holding my breath, hoping Amar doesn't decide to ask the guy if he's been hiding out in any woodpiles lately, then maybe follow up his question with a rousing chorus of "He Ain't Heavy, He's My Brother." Fortunately, the thin lady behind the counter shouts out the Black guy's number, and pushes his box of chicken across the countertop as he moves slowly away from Amar, still poker-faced, probably trying to decide if he should be ignoring him, or pulling his long-handled comb from its bushy holster and raking it across Amar's shit-grinning white face. When he picks up the box and heads for the door, Amar gives a big wave and, still grinning, says, "You try to take it easy now, hear? Don't try to be able to do nothing I wouldn't do. All right? Hah. Heh-heh." Turning to the rest of us. "See there?"

Back in the car Billy holds the chicken barrel on his lap and hunches over it. I ask everyone to roll up the windows so that the chicken smell can saturate the Rambler. Then, between deep breaths, I try to explain to Amar why his attempted conversation with the Black guy was so inappropriate. But Amar doesn't believe it.

"Try to be able to be nice around here and look what happens," he growls. "They all try to jump all over you."

"Am I jumping all over you, Hot Dog? I sure don't think I am. And I know you were *trying* to be nice. But you just don't walk up to a total stranger who happens to be Black, and tell him that you like pig's knuckles and watermelon. He probably thought you were making fun of him."

In the rearview mirror I watch Amar scowl. "I was *not* trying to be able to make no fun of him."

"Well I know you weren't *trying* to make fun of him, Hot Dog. But whether you were trying or not, that's exactly what you were doing. At least in *his* eyes. And I'm sure he was insulted when you called him a 'colored' person." We're stopped at a traffic light now, behind two high-schoolers in a mufflerless Chevy with rear tires so over-sized that the car's taillights are aimed well above our windshield. "A Black person prefers to be called 'Black,' not 'colored.'"

"Try to call a spade a spade?" he asks.

"No! I'm saying you call a Black person 'Black.' Not 'colored.' And certainly not 'spade.' 'Spade' is even worse than 'colored.'"

"Yeah," Elisha says. "Worser to be a spade than a colored."

"Oh *is* it?" Emmy says. "*Hmmm* then about that *spade*."

"No!" I practically scream, accidentally honking the horn with my elbow. In front of us the high school hot-rodders respond to my honk by sticking their arms out their windows and flipping me the finger. Billy sees what they're doing and flips one back, cackling happily.

"*Stop* it with that, *you*." Emmy slaps her hip.

"Ooh wow," Lucius says, working on his thightops.

"Listen you guys." I'm talking to all of them now, though in the confusion I've forgotten the original point I was trying to make. "All I'm really saying is that it's no better or worse to be Black or White."

"Hah! That's just exactly what I was trying to be able to tell you," Amar snaps. "And there ain't nothing wrong about it. So there. The stew is in the pudding."

"Take it easy, Hot Dog." The light has turned green and

we're rolling again, slowly though, so that the billowing black exhaust from the Chevy doesn't asphyxiate us. "I know you were just trying to be friendly when you told him it was okay he was Black and that whatever we are we've still got to live together. And I think you're absolutely right about that. But listen to me for a second. How would *you* feel if someone you'd never met walked up to you with a bunch of his friends around, and told you he thought it was all right that you were retarded because we've all got to share the world. See? It's the same thing."

Amar leans forward to grab the back of my seat and shake it. "I didn't try to call nobody no damn retard, and I'll try to say this." In the rearview mirror I can see him gritting his teeth. "I just wished I never had no pneumonia when I was a baby, and I wished I'd just gone ahead and died when I did!"

"Aw, shut your stupid trap, you stupid Hot Dog," Billy screams, turning halfway around to face him. "Shut your stupid trap. Your goddamned stupid trap."

"Make him *stop* it with those words," Emmy shrieks. "*Him.* Oh *him.*"

"Oooh. I hate the way he say about die," Lucius says, then rolls down his window and thrusts his head into the wind, an idea which suddenly has great appeal.

And so, while Amar and Billy are exchanging death threats, Elisha is clinging to Amar's arm, shouting for him to calm down, and Emmy is protesting with hip-slaps and loud screeches, I roll down *my* window and lean out. A rush of air blasts warmly over my face, stinging my eyes, filling my ears with a roaring which drowns out all the voices. The exhaust from the Chevy, far ahead now, has almost dissipated. Overhead, cumulus clouds piled thick as cotton candy crowd the sky like a great, silent, westward floating caravan. Along the lakefront the Coconut Palms are leaning over the lake wall—leaning at almost the same angle Lucius is leaning out his window—their fronds swaying and rustling in the wind like crisp green headdresses.

As we're approaching the Manatee Lake Bridge I pull back in, feeling numb-cheeked and energized. Everyone's quiet, and with the windows open the fried chicken smell has been blown away. In a corner of the rearview mirror I see half of Nadia's face—one of her dark, gypsy eyes, and one side of her wind-tangled black hair—then adjust the mirror until I've got her almost perfectly framed. When she glances up and sees me smiling at her, she laughs, her overlapped teeth flashing. "Mr. Brown Eyes Mirror Eyes."

Along the bridge sidewalk the old Black fishermen are out in full force, most of them sitting on overturned buckets, or leaning against the bridge railing and staring out over the lake, their fishing poles propped beside them like skinny companions.

"Catch anything?" It's Amar, leaning past Elisha to holler out the window. A fisherman throws up a hand in response, and Amar slaps the seatback behind my neck, laughing. "Hah! See there?"

Three miles north of the bridge I turn east off of Lake Way Avenue onto Gumbo Limbo Lane, and drive slowly, pointing out my house—my parents' house—halfway down the block, on the left.

"Not bad, Benny. Not bad, Old Buddy. Not bad a-tall. Not a-tall."

"I'll try to say this. He tries to be able to be proud of it and take care of it on account of how he has to for the property values. And on top of that he tries to have it to where he could be able to cut it with an electric lawn motor and spread it with fertilizer to try to keep it green."

"That a Avocado Tree?" Nadia leans forward to ask.

"That's right. And that small one to the left is a Papaya Tree. My father planted it after he found out Papayas are supposed to be good for your digestion."

"So's peanut butter very good for digesting," Amar says. "As well as for the kidneys and stomach lining. And I'll try to say this. If you got boils on your feet you can try to be able to soak them off in vinegar."

Not bothering to question or correct the good Doctor Hot Dog—I'm still trying to recover from our last debate—I continue to the east end of the street, past a row of tall Norfolk Pines, then park beneath a stunted Traveler's

Palm, its trunk gouged and blackened years ago by a bolt of lightning. When we've all piled from the car I point out the blind curve in the road, a block to the south, and ask everyone to stick together while we cross the street. But Lythia tilts forward, then fearlessly starts her free-falling run without bothering to check for cars, or even wait for the rest of us. We all shout for her to come back, but it's no use. Our shouts aren't going to register in time, and even if they do, they'll have no effect on her momentum. Fortunately, no cars come whizzing around the curve, so she makes it to the sidewalk, where she promptly trips on the curb and falls to her hands and knees.

"Oh *her!*" Emmy slaps her hip and gives a violent shake of her head, while Amar, Billy and I hurry over to help Lythia to her feet. She's smiling. Her knees are red and white with scrape marks, but she's not worried about it. It seems that her only concern is getting to the beach. Probably because she doesn't get here as often as the other residents since it's too long a walk for her.

With Amar and me escorting Lythia by the elbows, and Billy carrying the bucket of chicken, we all walk around the Gumbo Limbo Lane private cabana, a small blue, cinder-block building with a blue and white striped awning flapping in the wind. Inside the cabana there's a dressing and storage room, a shower, and a tiny bathroom with no windows. I point out the bathroom so everyone will know where it is if they need to use it, then lead everyone past the white plastic lounge chairs set up under the awning, and up to the beach wall, where we lean against the railing to stare down at the sand and ocean. It must be 4:30 by now, but the day is still hot. Probably close to 85 degrees with 99% humidity. Below us, half a dozen copper-toned girls, the last of the day's sunbathers, are scattered along the beach on their towels. Above us a flock of sea gulls floats slowly by, suspended like a mobile, seemingly connected by invisible strings, dipping and hopping with the wind currents.

"You guys want to have our picnic up here? Or down on the beach?"

"The beach," Amar says, kicking off his shoes and heading eagerly for the wooden steps that lead to the sand and bikinis.

"Yeah," Elisha says, staring after him. "At the beach."

We all pull off our shoes, drop them into a pile, and follow Amar down the steps. I didn't bring any towels for the residents to sit on, but they seem content to sit in the shaded sand in front of the wall, and eat over their laps. I sprawl between Nadia and Lucius and, when the barrel is passed to me, find and grab a couple of thighs. Most people prefer the breasts, but I've always thought thighs were twice as juicy. Twice as good. Back before my father turned vegetarian he used to buy 8-packs of thighs—two each for him and my mother, and four for me—and bake them in beer, teriyaki, lime juice, paprika, and maybe half a dozen cloves of freshly-pressed garlic. All he cooks now are vegetarian quiches, crepes, omelettes, stews, and casseroles. It's all very nutritious, sometimes even delicious, and, I've got to admit, morally superior to meat in every way. But it sure as hell can't get my mouth watering the way his garlic-lime thighs used to.

As I'm sucking my first thigh bone clean, Lythia suddenly stands, drops a half-eaten wing in the sand, and lurches off toward the stairway.

"Hey Lythia," I shout. "Where are you going?" A few seconds later, after she's pulled herself up the first step, she stops, then turns back toward me, grunting the words out slowly. She has to go to the bathroom. I ask if she remembers where the bathroom is and she nods, then smiles and, with both hands on the wooden guard rail, begins hoisting herself up again.

All around me, now, everyone's ripping away at his chicken, and every lip and cheek is covered with grease. Except Moby's. He grips his drumstick at the knobby end, between his thumb and forefinger, pulls off the deep fried skin with his other thumb and forefinger, then drops it cleanly into his mouth, looking just like a baby bird who turns up its head or beak to accept a worm from its mother. After swallowing the skin he leans forward, over the sand, and takes small, careful bites from the skinless drumstick.

I lean into Nadia, nudge her with my shoulder, and ask her how she's doing. She smiles and nudges me back with *her* shoulder. Her hair, clean and brushed an hour ago, is windblown from the car ride, salty and sandy from the beach, and greasy from the chicken because she keeps brushing it back from her face with her fingers. Fortunately, Angela will be long gone by the time we return to ARC House, so I'm not particularly worried about the condition of Nadia's hair, and feel no inclination to cue her to tie it back.

Billy tosses his second chicken bone into the empty Kentucky Fried barrel, then pushes himself to his feet. Moving quickly toward me, he rubs his fingers on his pants legs, then bends over me to whisper, three times, that he has to go to the bathroom. I tell him it's okay, he doesn't need to whisper, then remind him that Lythia is using the bathroom and that he'll need to wait until she's finished.

"But I can't wait," he continues to whisper. "I can't wait, Benny. I got to go right now, I do. Got to go right now."

"Well what can you do about that, Billy?"

"I don't know, Benny. I don't know, Old Buddy. I just don't know."

He sounds as though he's on the verge of tears, so I suggest that he run on up to the cabana and knock on the bathroom door. "Just let her know you're waiting. If it's an emergency then *tell* her it's an emergency. Maybe she'll hurry for you." I lower my voice to a whisper. "If she's not out in a minute, you can pee in the shower. Just be sure to run the water for a minute when you're finished, and it'll be all right."

"Oh *will* it?" It's Emmy of course. Old Antenna Ears. "*Hmmm* then with the *show*er. All *right* then about that *show*er."

"It's none of your stupid business, Emmy Oberst. None of your goddamned stupid business, so keep your stupid nose out of it. Keep it out. Keep your goddamned stupid nose out."

"Ohhh!" Emmy shrieks. "Make him *stop* it with those words. *Him!*"

"One more word out of *either* of you and we all go

home," I say, trying to sound authoritative as hell while Lucius rubs his thightops and grins at me. "Billy. You've got to go, so go! It's no big deal."

"Yeah," Elisha says. "It's not no big deal."

"Okay, Benny. Okay, Old Buddy. I'll go for you, I will. Go for you. Go just for you."

"Great Billy. You do that." I don't mean to be so sarcastic with him, but I'm anxious for us to finish with the chicken and bathroom business so I can take everyone down to meet my parents and tour my father's garden. Then, whoever wants to stay and visit with my parents can do *that*, and whoever wants to walk the beach can do that. And hopefully, Nadia and I will get at least an hour or two of privacy; a chance to be alone together, away from ARC House. We can hide out in the driftwood and beachgrass and maybe watch the moonrise. Snuggle up together as though we were on a date, testing the feel of it; the feel of us being together in an intimate way. I'm about to explain my plan to everyone—minus the part about me and Nadia disappearing into the driftwood and beachgrass—when Lucius suddenly says to me, "Friday be my birthday. July 10. Be fifty-six year old."

"Well damn. Happy Birthday, Lucius. That's great . . . God, fifty-six!"

"Yuh," he grunts.

"I'll be thirty-four the day before Halloween," Elisha says.

"I'll try to say this. I'll be thirty-one the next time around and still trying to be able to catch up with her." Amar's shoulders lift and fall, and his eyes squint, as he wheezes out a laugh at his own joke.

"How about you?" Nadia says to me. "You know. How old are you?"

"Me? I'm an old man," I tell her. "I'll be twenty-two in October."

"Come *on* now," Emmy says, slapping a hand to her cheek and shaking her head. "Come *on* with the twenty-two."

"Mr. Young Bunny," Nadia says. "Young Cheeks Young Bunny."

Up at the cabana I can suddenly hear Billy pounding on the bathroom door, swearing. I just hope none of my Gumbo Limbo Lane neighbors are coming up for a late afternoon dip.

"Pree soon be Christmas," Lucius says. "Then be my birthday. Next year, July 10, be fifty-seven year old."

This is without a doubt the most Lucius has ever said to me. It's not much, really, but at least I know now that he has concerns which extend beyond the heat of his thightops. With enthusiasm I tell him he's absolutely right; that if he's fifty-six this July 10, he'll be fifty-seven *next* July 10. Then I ask him what he's hoping to get for his birthday.

"Need too'paste," he says. "Too bad time go fast. Pree soon I be too old."

"Aw Lucius." So *that's* what he's getting at. I'd never have guessed. Not that it's such an unreasonable concern; Christ, I'm thirty-five years younger than he is and I *already* put a lot of energy into worrying about time going by too fast. But I sure as hell can't tell *him* that. "Listen," I say. "You're still a young guy. I mean my father's almost your age and he's healthier than *I* am." Across from me Moby stands and taps a cigarette from his pack, looking up to the cabana. "And you . . . Jesus, Lucius. You've got more energy than most twenty year-olds I know."

"Oh *does* he. Well *hmmm* then."

"That's right," Amar says. "You're every bit as young as you try to be able to feel."

"Yuh," Lucius grunts. But he sounds unconvinced. "Pree soon I be too old. Be dead."

"*Hey* with that." Emmy slaps her hands over her ears, shuts her eyes, and gives a violent shake of her head. "*Stop it with that.*"

"Well, I wouldn't worry about it," I lie. "I mean, sure, it happens to all of us. But you've still got a long way to go, Lucius."

"What happen be dead? Go heaven?"

"Geez, I don't know." Christ. Everyone except Emmy is leaning forward, waiting to hear my answer.

"I'll try to say this," Amar answers for me. "You can either be able to go to heaven, or if not, then the other place. And it's all according to whether or not you try to be able to help yourself or anybody else without trying to step on no toes."

"Well that's what some people believe," I say, not bothering to tighten up or expand upon his vague explanation. "But other people believe when you die it's just blackness. Like going to sleep and not having any dreams or ever waking up."

"Ooh," Lucius says, hugging himself. "Make me shake you say that. 'Bout die black."

"Well don't worry about it, Lucius. I'm just saying that no one really knows for sure what happens when you die. Some people even believe that after you die your soul leaves your body and finds another body to go into, so it can be born into another life. And they believe that happens over and over again; that everyone lives lots of different lives."

"Pre-corination," Amar says.

"Reincarnation," I correct him. "That's right, Hot Dog."

"Ooh wow," Lucius says, bending to rub his thightops. "That what I beeve."

"Ah. So you think after you die you're going to come back as someone else?"

He nods, grinning, his eyes beginning to bug out. "Be smart. Drive car."

God, so that's why he likes the idea of reincarnation. I don't want to encourage him along these lines—who knows, maybe he's thinking about jumping into the ocean and drowning himself so that he can be reincarnated as a smart person—so I again tell him that nobody really knows. "Maybe it's just blackness when you die. Or maybe you go to heaven. Or maybe, *if* you're reincarnated, you'll come back as a fish. Or a housefly."

"Nuh," Lucius says, looking nervous as hell again. I'm doing a great job, here, of pushing him from misery to ecstasy and back. He'll be a manic-depressive before I'm finished with him.

"How about the trees?" Nadia suddenly asks.

"The trees?" I say, not bothering to hide my bewilderment. It's incredible. *Everything* is trees with her.

"Do they do the re-narnated?"

"You mean, are trees reincarnated?"

She nods.

"I don't know, Nadia. Yeah, sure. Maybe. Hah! Maybe you were a tree last life, and that's why you like them so much *this* life."

"Maybe I can get to be one next time," she says. "You know. Get to be a big old Banyan. And do the whooshing and reaching. How they all the time do the whooshing and reaching."

"Too bad I be old, no read," Lucius says. "No drive car."

"Well damn, Lucius. How about if I let you drive *my* car. It'll be my birthday present to you. You can drive it from the end of the street down to my house." My father would instantly pass out if he knew I was encouraging a mentally retarded fifty-six year-old to drive his car. He thinks 95% of all *existing* drivers should have their cars impounded and licenses revoked. (Probably because he knows that if he ever gets in a car accident all his organic gardening, jogging, and other religiously observed health habits will have been in vain. Which is why he drives more slowly and cautiously than the average ninety year-old; never faster than five miles per hour *below* the speed limit. Then, when drivers are forced to gun their engines to speed angrily past him, he swears because they're all breaking the speed limit. And tailgaters he hates more than speedsters. If someone's following too closely he slows way down so that if he has to unexpectedly jam on his brakes for a dog or a cat, or a kid chasing after a football, the tailgater won't smash into him at too deadly a speed. Of course the more slowly he drives, the closer and more aggressively he's tailed; and the closer and more aggressively he's tailed, the more slowly he drives. It's a vicious cycle, a negative feedback loop, and after five minutes of it the poor tailgating driver behind him is usually ready to challenge a Mack Truck head-on if he thinks he's got half a chance to get past my father. He brings out the craziness in other drivers, then points to that craziness as indisputable evidence of the correctness of his own viewpoint. It's a good thing he rarely uses his car more than once a week. And it's a good thing he doesn't know Lucius is about to take his first driving lesson in a '65 Cross Country Classic Rambler Wagon, recently—*always* recently—painted fire engine red so that it will be more visible at night, or in the rain and fog; though he seldom, if ever, risks driving at night, or in the rain and fog.)

I'm about to suggest to everyone that we finish up the chicken so Lucius can drive us down the block to visit with my parents, when Billy leans over the railing above us and peers down. "The shower don't want to work Old Buddy," he says apologetically. "Don't want to work a-tall. Not a-tall."

I explain to him that there's a central valve which controls the flow of water to the cabana, and that it probably needs to be opened. "Hold on," I tell him, standing. "I'll show you how it works. You guys clean up here. Put all the bones in the bucket and I'll be back in a minute. Then maybe we can go visit with my parents. All right?" I touch the top of Nadia's head, then hustle up the steps to the cabana.

Billy is still pissed off at Lythia for not letting him use the toilet. "I asked her," he says, shaking his head. "But no, she won't even answer. Won't answer. Won't even give me an answer."

"Well, you know sometimes it takes awhile for Lythia to get her words out. Right? You just need to be extra patient and wait a minute for her answer."

"But I couldn't wait, Benny. Couldn't wait, Old Buddy. I couldn't wait."

I pat his back and tell him not to worry about it. "We'll get it all taken care of, Billy."

"Here, Benny," he says, making a beeline for the shower. "Right in here. Right in here." He seems anxious to prove to me that the shower really isn't working, so I follow him into the shower room and let him show me.

"Okay Billy." He's proved his point. The shower won't turn on, and the entire room smells like piss. "Now let me show *you* where that main valve is."

"Okay Old Buddy. Okay."

I lead Billy from the shower room, then, as we're passing the bathroom door, decide to ask Lythia how she's doing. I wait almost half a minute, but she doesn't answer. So I ask more loudly, then, after another half minute of silence, bang on the door three or four times.

"It's no use Old Buddy," Billy says. "She won't answer. Won't answer. Just won't answer."

"Hey Lythia!" I'm suddenly feeling a surge of panic. If she's had a seizure in there I don't know how the hell I'll get in. There are no windows to break through, and the door is one of those old solid oak jobs. I pound on it again, then shout to Lythia that if she doesn't answer I'm coming in.

No response.

"Okay Lythia, I'm coming in now." I turn the knob and push. Incredibly, it's unlocked. Lythia must be so habituated to the "no-locking" rule of ARC House that she's carried it over to public restrooms. "I'm pushing the door open now, Lythia. Okay?"

Billy bends to whisper in my ear. "She won't answer, Buddy. Won't answer a-tall. Not a-tall."

The door swings open a few inches then stops. I push harder but it's jammed tight against something and won't budge. It's while Billy's helping me push that the smell hits me. Not the ordinary bathroom smell of shit, but something much stronger. When we've got the door opened wide enough I force my way through, turning my head sideways, and scraping an ear. As soon as I've squeezed past the door edge, I see that the bottom of the door is jammed against Lythia's head. She's fallen forward off the toilet, onto her stomach, face to one side. Her eyes are closed, and her neck and jaw muscles are working, straining, as if she's grinding her teeth together. Her cheek is in a pool of puke. Shit is smeared on her ass and thighbacks, and all over her yellow shorts and underpants, which are accordioned around her ankles. Her bare feet straddle the base of the toilet. I lean against the concrete wall, feeling nauseous from the sight and smell, breathing only through my mouth. Billy asks what's going on, so I tell him to wait just a minute, then shut my eyes and try to clear my head. After a few seconds it occurs to me that I should be checking to see if she's breathing, or if she injured her head when she fell. From where I'm standing I can see, almost as soon as I open my eyes, that her back is lifting and falling. I squat, pull off my "Save the Manatees" t-shirt, and wipe the puke away from the area in front of her mouth to make sure she doesn't suck any of it into her lungs. I'm going to have to lift her—maybe set her on the toilet—to examine her head. I flip down the toilet seat cover, then straddling her, squat again and grip her firmly under the arm pits. I try to lift, but it's no good. She's like dead weight. A sack of half-dried cement. I'm obviously going to need help, so I drag her back by the hips a few inches, swing the door farther open and wave Billy in. He gawks at her while I tell him that she's going to need a change of clothes, and that when I get through cleaning her off, his shirt should be big enough to cover her like a robe.

After he pulls off his shirt and hangs it from the corner of the door, I instruct him to help me lift Lythia from the floor. He's thin as an amphetamine freak, and weak-looking, but those spaghetti-noodle arms of his are stronger than I would have guessed, and it's not long before we've got her onto the toilet seat cover, her back propped against the tank.

Our hands and bare feet are literally dripping with her puke and shit. I feel it caked between my fingers and toes. We're going to need to clean ourselves as much as her, so I ask Billy to go collect the shirts from Lucius, Moby, and Amar, but to keep quiet about Lythia's seizure so that we don't attract a crowd. While he's gone I check Lythia's head for injuries, then finding none, race around to the back of the cabana to turn the main water valve. On the way back to the bathroom I hear Billy down on the beach, swearing at Amar, telling him we've *got* to have his goddamned stupid shirt because Lythia had a goddamned stupid seizure. It's going to be mobbed up here in a minute, but I guess it's just as well. I'll need them all close by so we can make a quick get-away.

In the bathroom sink I rinse my hands and t-shirt, then wipe the puke from Lythia's lips, cheek, ear, neck, and hair. I wrestle her shirt off, then slide her shorts and underwear down her ankles and over her feet, so that she's completely naked except for her bra. Her body is pale and asymetrical, her right side slightly withered, and seemingly pulled tighter, so that there's a slight sideways curve to her. She's got a smooth, almost shiny scar hooking across the lower right side of her stomach. Her pubic hair is light brown, sparse, and shriveled, like a patch of herbicided grass.

Outside, a pack of voices closes in. Billy pushes his head through the doorway with Amar right behind.

"Get out of here, Hot Dog!" I shout almost viciously, snatching the three shirts from Billy. "Thanks Billy. Now tell Nadia and Elisha to get in here. And you can hand me *your* shirt now."

"Okay Benny. Okay Old Buddy." He pulls it off the door corner. "Here it is for you. For you, Old Buddy. Just for you."

Soon as the ladies step in with me I ask them to shut the door. I don't want this turning into a peep show for Amar. For some reason I'm feeling agonizingly protective of Lythia, maybe because her pubic hair is so pathetically sparse. It makes me want to cry to look at it. So I stop looking and explain to Elisha and Nadia what we need to do. Then, stooping in front of Lythia, I pull her forward, allowing her to slump over my shoulder while Nadia and Elisha clean her off, first with dry shirts, then with rinsed-off, wet shirts. It's a miserable job, but they work diligently and without complaint. In fact without a word of any kind. When they're through with her ass and legbacks they clean off the toilet, and I finally push her back up on the seat, against the tank. It's a load off my shoulders, and especially my knees. I feel as though I've just set down a ninety pound backpack after a long, uphill hike. Soon as I've stretched my legs, bent and unbent my knees a few times, I help Elisha and Nadia maneuver Lythia's arms through Billy's shirt. Her jaw is relaxed now, and with her body covered up and cleaned off she no longer looks so pathetic or deathly.

I thank Nadia and Elisha, tell them—sincerely as I *ever*

have—that they're great, then suggest they rinse their legs and feet in the shower. After pushing the door shut behind them, I do a haphazard clean-up of the floor (I don't have the time or equipment to get it half as clean as I'd like, but at least I clear a path wide enough for us to get to the door without having to do much sloshing), then, with my rinsed-off shirt, wipe Lythia's feet. Finally, I rinse my own hands and feet in the sink, then pull open the door and announce that I'm going to need help carrying Lythia to the car. Billy and Amar rush forward to volunteer. Billy's shirt decently covers Lythia all the way to her knees, and I feel guilty for having shouted at Amar earlier, so I explain to Billy that it's Amar's turn to help. Then I give Moby, Elisha, Lucius, and Emmy one dirty shirt each—including my own—and, hoping the salt water will help kill or at least partially cover up the odor, ask them to quickly go soak the shirts in the shallow part of the ocean.

The four of them hurry off with the shirts—Moby looking reluctant—while I grasp Lythia under her arms and instruct Amar to hold her tightly by the ankles. (I hate to have him in a position where he can look up under that oversized shirt, but if he has trouble with his grip I'd rather see him drop her ankles on the street than her shoulders and head.) Billy pulls open the cabana gate for us, and when we've made it through I tell Amar we're going to set Lythia down gently. Soon as we've lowered her to the ground I explain to Nadia and Billy that Amar and I will need their help when we cross the street; that it would be great if they would run on along the road twenty or thirty yards and wave down any cars that are zipping around that curve too fast. They hustle off, Billy leading the way, and when they've positioned themselves at the end of the curve I give a wave. I only hope my strategy doesn't backfire; that a driver coming around the corner won't decide to hit the gas instead of his brakes, when he sees those incredible arms of Billy's waving at him. "All right," I say to Amar. "Let's go," and we lift her and step into the street. It's slow going, but Amar is concentrating so intently, gripping her ankles so tightly, that my only concern is with her circulation. We've almost made it safely across the street, not a car in sight or earshot, when a windgust catches Billy's shirt and lifts it past Lythia's crotch. Instantly, Amar grabs for the shirt to pull it back down, and in so doing drops one ankle, which falls limply, the heel smashing onto the black tar and crushed-shell street. "It's okay, Hot Dog," I say, as he lunges for her ankle now. "Let's just get her across the street."

As we near the Rambler, Nadia and Billy come trotting up. Billy, eager to be helpful, practically knocks us out of the way in his effort to get past us and pull open the door.

"Here you go, Old Buddy. I got it open for you, I do. Got it open for you. All the way open for you."

"Great Billy. But she's not going to fit in the front seat, so how about if you get the back door for us."

"Oops. Sorry about that, Benny. Sorry about that, Old Buddy. I'm not all here, today, I'm not. I'm just not all here today. Just not all here."

Soon as he pulls open the door we slide Lythia across the back seat so that she's stretched out completely, face up, the top of her head practically flush with the left door, and her feet almost to the right edge of the seat. She's breathing deeply now, and her eyelids are bulging with movement, like soft-shelled eggs ready to hatch. By the time I've looked her over, readjusted her arms and legs so that she at least *appears* to be more comfortable, and carefully shut the door, Moby, Emmy, Lucius, and Elisha have returned with the ocean-soaked shirts.

With Lythia occupying an entire seat herself, the rest of us are going to have to squeeze in, four in the front and four in the cargo area. Right away there's an argument over who gets to sit up front. To settle it quickly I announce that the four men will sit in the cargo area and the three ladies in the front seat, a neat, easy, sensible division. But Billy grumbles that he's too tall for the cargo area. "I won't fit, Buddy. Won't fit a-tall. Not a-tall." He's probably right. But I could argue just as reasonably that he's too tall to fit in the front seat—too tall to fit in *any* car seat—so I ignore his complaining, roll down the back window, and pull open the hatch. It's a tight squeeze for them all right—Billy with his length and Moby with his girth, together take up maybe ⅔ of the cargo space—but there's not much else I can do.

The front seat, with Elisha's wide hips and Emmy's wide torso, is no picnic either. Nadia is wedged snugly between Emmy and me, her left leg pressing firmly against my right leg. Under different circumstances I'm sure I'd enjoy the secret excitement of touching legs with her. But under *these* circumstances our leg contact is nothing but a pain, literally, because in order for me to keep my foot on the gas pedal I have to steadily resist the pressure from her leg, and am finding that in the effort I'm straining some obscure thigh muscle which probably atrophied years ago from disuse.

By the time we're halfway down the street, Lucius is reminding me that *he* was supposed to be driving, everyone else is complaining about being cramped—shouting at one another, swinging elbows and flinging insults—the car is reeking of shit, puke, and salt-watered shirts, and my obscure thigh muscle is aching more than I can stand. As we're passing my house I suddenly swerve to the side of the road, tires onto the lawn edge, and shift into park, leaving the engine running. "All right," I announce. "We're going to have to do some quick shifting. I can't drive with four in the front."

I open my door and slide out, waving for the ladies to do the same. By the time they've hit the street I've got it figured out. Skipping around to the rear of the car, I pull open the hatch and ask Amar to climb out, which leaves Billy, Lucius, and Moby with a bit more breathing room.

"Okay Hot Dog," I say. "How strong is your lap?"

"I'll try to say this," he begins, but before he can go on to try to say *anything,* I grab him by the elbow and pull him toward the front passenger door, in no mood to wait out his wild circumlocutions.

"Okay Nadia. You can slide back in where you were. There. Good. Now you, Hot Dog. Great. No. Not too far. Okay. Perfect. Now Elisha. Right on your boyfriend's lap there." She climbs aboard and slowly settles herself, grinning, while Amar grimaces at her weight, and tries to figure out what to do with his hands.

"Don't forget *me,* you," Emmy screeches, slapping her hip.

"Emmy, how could I?" I say, pulling open the back door, gently lifting Lythia's legs, and telling Emmy to slide on in.

"O*kay* then," she says, nodding once, business-like, then sitting at the edge of the carseat and sliding over a few inches.

I set Lythia's legs across Emmy's thightops, explaining to her, to Emmy, that she'll need to keep extra still.

"I gotta go, Benny." It's Nadia, staring back at me over the top of the front seat. "You know. Gotta go to the bathroom."

"Uh, Benny." Moby is waving a hand at me, but I ignore him, asking Nadia if she can hold it until we get back. Emphatically, she shakes her head.

"Just pee?" I ask, hopeful.

Again she shakes her head.

"Oh *her*," Emmy screeches, slapping high up on her hip to avoid Lythia's legs. "She's got to do *that. Her.*"

"Knock it off, Emmy," I bark, pushing my face close to hers to show her I mean business.

"Yea," Elisha says. "Knock it off."

"Make her *stop* it with *that*," Emmy screeches again, giving her head a violent shake.

"Oh, shut your goddamned stupid trap, you stupid Emmy Oberst. Shut your goddamned stupid trap. Your stupid trap."

"Oooh wow," says Lucius, rubbing his thightops, delighted with the situation.

"Uh, Benny." Moby is still waving his hand.

"I swear," Amar says. "You all trying to be able to act like a bunch of chickens trying to run around with your legs cut off."

"Yeah," Elisha repeats. "Running like chickens without no legs cut off."

I'm about to shut them all up with a scream, when it hits me that this *could* be the chance I've been waiting for. In fact it's perfect. Almost too good to be true. "Okay Nadia. Come on. I'll be back in half a minute, you guys."

"All *right* then, with that half a *mi*nute. O*kay* then."

"Uh, Benny."

"Jesus, Moby. What do you want?"

He grimly stops waving his hand, and lets it drop to his side. "I would like to sit with Lythia. My girl."

It's about the only thing he's ever asked of me, and he asks it so gamely, with such quiet determination, that I can't refuse. "Fine," I tell him. "You and Emmy can switch around. Just be careful with Lythia."

"I don't *want* to switch!" Emmy screeches.

"Well I don't have time to argue." I back away, leaving Emmy's door open. "You and Moby figure it out."

Nadia's waiting for me, so I take her hand and race with her across the front lawn. We push through the front door, hurrying past the twin potted Colomandin trees and across the terrazzo floor to the maghogany baby grand piano, where my mother is playing the adagio of the Waldstein Sonata, rocking forward and back. (She's always liked to play for my father while he's cooking dinner because she knows that a well played Beethoven Sonata, or even a few Bagatelles, almost ensures a perfectly cooked meal; a guaranteed difference of two or three points on a culinary scale of one to ten.) When she looks up and sees us, I tell her to keep playing. Immediately she stops, hands dropping into her lap.

"I thought you were visiting with your patients," she says, then smiles at Nadia. "You didn't tell us you had a date. I'd have let you take the Mercedes."

"They're not *patients*—"

"Hey. What's going on, Dorie?" It's my father, shouting to her from the kitchen, upset that she stopped in the middle of the adagio. It's a good thing she wasn't yet into the rondo. He'd have probably burned the hell out of her dinner as a way of showing his displeasure.

"It's your son," she shouts to him, offering her hand to Nadia, then shaking. "With a very pretty young friend."

My father walks through the door, frowning, wooden spoon in hand, dripping a whiteish mornay or maybe hollandaise sauce, which he catches in a cupped palm. I introduce them to Nadia, then, quickly as I can, explain what happened at the beach, while my mother stares, astonished, at Nadia, a "patient;" and my father, hearing of Lythia's seizure, turns white as his sauce, then hurries to the front window for a look. (It's hard for me to imagine that he worked in a hospital for four years, and that at one time he even planned, so my mother tells me, to become a *doctor!*) He wants to call an ambulance or paramedic squad, or even old Dr. Schudwiller down the street. But I assure him the worst part is over; Lythia is breathing well now and there's nothing more we can do for her other than quickly getting her home and into bed. At least that's what I'm hoping.

Nadia is shifting from leg to leg now, impatient to get into the bathroom, so I point her in the right direction, then, as she's heading through the kitchen, explain her plight to my parents, and assure them I'll be back to pick her up as soon as I've dropped off Lythia and the rest of the residents. "Maybe I'll get a chance to bring a few of them by for a visit next week," I say. "They're all really anxious to meet you." Holding up both my hands for a double wave, I back away, pretending not to notice the anger in my mother's eyes, and the panic in my father's, then turn and head for the front door.

Eudora

It's crazy. A poor girl goes into a fit of epileptic convulsions and all of a sudden he's full of vim and vigour, pep and purpose, looking happier, more energetic and more alive than I've seen him look in months. It's as if he is somehow nourished to the core by all the things in this world that should rightfully depress him, and depressed by all the things that should rightfully uplift and elate him. I'd be willing to bet my life's savings that the day the scientists announce they've discovered how to eliminate the causes of mental retardation, he'll only mourn the passing of an era, instead of celebrating the new step up the ladder of human progress.

Of course none of this surprises me. What does surprise me is that he's genuinely, sincerely, eager for Mort and me to meet and spend time with all of his patients. As if an evening with them, a friendly get together with a group of brain-damaged young men and women, is going to somehow lift our spirits.

Not very damned likely.

I'll never forget that Saturday morning in Peach Tree Park (it has to be, what, fifteen years ago, yet it's all as clear in my mind as if it had happened yesterday); I was watching Benny and a group of other kids climbing the monkey bars, sliding down the huge, silver spiral slide, swinging, see-sawing, merry-go-rounding, chasing, wrestling, and doing all those other things that healthy five, six, and seven year-olds enjoy doing, when another young boy with a cowlick like a golden fountain, came teetering up—knock-kneed, mouth stupidly agape, one shoulder lower than the other—holding hands with his father, swinging a bagful of breadcrumbs with his free hand. The two of them walked right past me, and just beyond the playground to the duckpond, where the father sat on a bench, watching while his son followed after the ducks, haphazardly tossing bits of bread to them. Each step the boy took seemed to require a prodigious effort. Without his father's hand to steady him he looked like a drunkard attempting to walk a straight line, swaying first one way, then the other, sometimes flailing desperately to regain his balance, the bread bag doing loop-de-loops, crumbs spilling at his feet. Several times he swayed dangerously close to the pond edge, but his father, watching attentively from the bench, never interfered. The boy even fell once, struggling slowly back to his feet, then stooping to pick up his dropped bread bag, only with the most agonized of efforts. Again, the father watched closely, but without offering anything more than quiet encouragement. Occasionally he, the father, would glance over to the playground and watch all the normal kids running, climbing, sliding, swinging, and playing. Then, after a few moments, he would look back to his own child. And he would smile. Smile as if he was genuinely content. As if, in fact, he felt blessed. It was the bravest, saddest thing I've ever seen, and I don't think I have ever—before or since—felt such compassion for another human being.

I try to imagine—but cannot—the love and strength it must have taken that man to face each day. I try to imagine—but cannot—how *I* would cope, how I would endure, if I was in his place. My God, twenty minutes of it—vicariously—that afternoon was enough to last me a lifetime. And the thought of spending even a few hours with eight grown-up versions of that little boy is enough to overwhelm me.

Now this poor girl he dropped off (who couldn't even wait to get home to relieve herself), *may* be physically healthy—attractive even, in her own peculiar way—but to me, her physical well-being only makes her mental scars, her damaged brain, that much sadder, that much crueler.

Of course if my son can somehow find joy in all this, I can only presume it's a good thing. If he can truly find happiness in working with brain-damaged people, reading doomsday prophecies, and self-righteously sweating half to death in an un-air-conditioned bedroom to prove some awful point, I won't protest. I only hope he's still sane enough not to expect *me* to feel the same way.

Benny

When we pull up to the sidewalk and pile from the Rambler, Amar and Billy—like me, still shirtless—stand by the open back door, arguing over who's going to help me carry Lythia, while everyone else—except Moby, who stands to one side, lighting up a cigarette, an eye on Lythia—rushes in to tell Ty what's happening.

I cue Amar, asking him if he remembers whose turn it is to help with the carrying.

"Try to be able to do what you can," he grumbles, "and they try to take away your rights so they can be able to throw you to the wolves and take away the keys. Won't even let a man try to be a man and do what he has to be able to do in order to keep things going for himself."

"Oh, shut your stupid trap, Amar Beldoni. Shut your trap. Your goddamned stupid trap."

I instruct Billy to take Lythia's ankles, and we slowly work her out of the car. She's moving her head back and forth, working her jaw and lips as if preparing to talk; but her eyes are still shut tight. We've carried her only a few steps—Amar needlessly directing us down the walk, like an airport flagger directing a jet down the runway—when Ty comes racing down the front stairs and taps Billy on the shoulder. "I'll take it from here, Billy."

"Serves him right," Amar mumbles.

"That's okay Old Buddy," Billy says to Ty. "I got her real good by the ankles, I do. Got her right around the ankles. Right around the ankles."

"What do you need to do, Billy?" Ty cues him, then,

when Billy still refuses to let go, smoothly drops to directive verbal cue. "You need to let me take over, Billy. If you want you can hold open the door for us." He steps in front of Billy, grasps Lythia just below her calves—just above where Billy is hanging onto her—then says, "Go on now, Billy. You can help us out by holding open the door."

Billy jerks his hands from Lythia's ankles, backs away, and shouts at Ty that he won't help him at all because he's nothing but a goddamned stupid asshole, anyway. Then he walks off across the lawn, upper body tilted forward like a leaning coconut palm. Apparently he's headed downtown again to drown his sorrows.

"Hey Billy," I yell. "Come on back." But once he gets going that way he's like a salmon heading home to spawn. You'd practically have to shoot him to stop him.

"Don't worry about it," Ty says. "Let him go."

"Yeah, but he's already had two warnings," I point out, as I'm stepping backward up the porch stairway, my back muscles beginning to strain. "One more and he's gone."

But Ty just grins. "Oh yeah? How's he going to get drunk? You think anyone's going to let him into a bar or a store without a shirt?" Behind me, Amar is holding open the screen door. "And how much money has he got with him, anyway? Shee-it, I guarantee he'll be back in fifteen minutes."

"I guess you're right," I admit, as we carry Lythia past Amar, through the doorway, and into the living room where we carefully lower her onto the couch.

Ty brushes back her hair to examine her head for bruises, then, finding none, tells me it's a shame I had to bring everyone back so early just because Lythia had a seizure. "If she didn't smell so bad," he whispers, wrinkling his nose, "you could've just stretched her out on a bed at your home, and kept the party going."

I quickly assure him that even if Lythia—and the rest of us—had smelled like roses I'd have rushed her back to ARC House, because this is the first seizure I've ever dealt with and I didn't want to take any chances. Then I explain to him that Nadia had to stay behind to use the toilet, and that I'll be bringing her back as soon as she's finished visiting with my parents. Maybe an hour or two, depending on how well they're enjoying one another's company.

"No rush," he says, letting Lythia's hair fall back over her ears now. "Just so she's back by ten."

"Sounds good," I tell him trying to sound nonchalant. "I'll see you by ten o'clock."

Nadia

I pull up my panties and pants, and when I look I still see it there, how it's floating, big and strong, so I wait 'til the hissing stops, then do the flushing again. But it's still big and strong, and how it's too big and strong to do down the pipes, and when the hissing stops I flush again, and here comes the water and the poop, floating how a log floats, how it's floating up closer, then doing down in a circle, sucking down. But it won't go again how it's too big and strong and not-breaking, and looks like it don't want to break and do down to the pipes. And I can hear the hissing again, and hear him in the kitchen, cooking and doing around with the pots, and he can hear me how I'm doing the flushing, and how I've already done a bunch of the flushing a bunch of times already, and if I do it again he'll hear it and he might not like it how I keep doing the flushing. But I got to get rid of it so he don't think I'm bad how I don't flush it clean, and be mad I'm not no smarty britches how I don't flush it clean, and Benny will be mad, too, mad at me, how it's his father. But it's too big and strong and don't want to do down with the flushing, so I reach down the blue cloth from over shower and use it how if it was a glove to pick up the poop from the water and put it in the can with the kleenex and stuff, and put some kleenex on top of the cloth to cover it how he won't find it. But he will find it, how he'll smell it there in the can, and find it there in the can with the kleenex and the blue cloth, and be mad at me how I put it in there with the blue cloth and didn't flush it to the pipes, so I take it back out with the blue cloth and go quiet out the door with it in the blue cloth, and quiet out the other door, and out where it's the yard, past the big garden and the gratefruit trees with all the gratefruits, and throw it all over the wall how he won't find it there, and won't know it didn't do down to the pipes with all the flushing, how all the others do down to the pipes.

Mort and Nadia

With the fourth flush, Mort, trying not to panic, but convinced that the poor girl might be hemorrhaging into the bowl—too ignorant or afraid to do anything more than sit there flushing away her life by the pint full—asks Eudora if they should check to make sure she's okay. But Eudora simply shrugs, lifts her Miami Herald from where it's spread across the piano keyboard, folds it and tucks it under an arm, then disappears into the bedroom, as if to inform him that the girl is *his* responsibility, not hers; not even *theirs*.

And yet he's not as angry with his wife as he is with his son. He could kill Benny for this. No warning. No preparation. No information or advice. Insouciant, he just leaves her with them and expects that they'll know exactly what to do; exactly how to behave, how to speak.

A minute passes, then another minute, and he hears nothing. It's as if she'd at last, mercifully, flushed herself away. But he can't relax, and finally, working up the nerve to step into the bedroom, he calls out, "Hey. You all right in there?" When she doesn't answer he crosses the room, hesitant, and knocks at the door, which he sees now is cracked open. His knocking widens the crack, and though he's scared to look, he feels he has no choice. Tentatively, he eases his head past the door, preparing himself to find her sprawled on the white-tiled floor in a bloody heap.

But when, after his first peek around, he doesn't see her, he slowly pushes the door all the way back, then steps in decisively and glances about. He even sweeps back the shower curtains with a bold rattling of plastic hooks. But the bathroom is definitely empty, and it's only after he's turned away from the shower that he notices a movement out of the corner of his eye, and, peering through the open bathroom jalousies, sees her standing beyond the raised cucumber beds, beside the grapefruit tree, staring up at it. Rushing from the bathroom, he pushes through the back door and nearly stumbles down the two concrete steps. "Uh . . ." He's already forgotten her name. "You okay there?"

"Yes," she calmly tells him. "I like your garden with all the hills and vegetables and stuff."

"Oh, yes?" he says, trying for a natural smile.

"Yes, and the gratefruit trees with all the gratefruits. 'Cause of how they whoosh up out of the ground with the tree. You know. How they whoosh up through the tree," she flings her arms above her head, "and then poof . . . there's the gratefruits."

He laughs uneasily and asks if she's hungry.

At the dinner table, while the three of them are, in near silence, eating their Mornay Casserole—Nadia's already had two pieces of fried chicken, so only takes a small serving—Mort decides that she is retarded in an interesting, even curiously pleasant way, which surprises him, because he's always assumed retarded people were all retarded in the same way; that there was a specific and basic retarded personality. She's quiet, he thinks, but not necessarily because she is incapable of carrying on a conversation, or even because she is particularly shy or intimidated (as he and Eudora obviously still are). Mostly it seems to him that she is simply somewhere else; lost in the flowerettes of broccoli she forks up, in the workings of her hands and fingers, or in the Palm Tree design of the table cloth.

When Mort speaks she smiles at unexpected and unpredictable—Angela would call them "inappropriate"—moments. He could almost swear that instead of listening she is watching the actual shapes of his words as they emerge from between his lips and float before his mouth like bubbles; and that it is the shapes of those floating words she is smiling at, rather than the content, the meaning, of the sound.

After dinner Eudora starts in on her nightly business phone calls, and Mort washes dishes while telling Nadia—who stands beside him helping with the drying as she watches his words—all about the small farm he intends to buy, but which he's decided he *won't* buy, if after tomorrow's big visit his wife remains unimpressed.

"Do you got any Banyans there?" Nadia wants to know. "You know. Any Banyans out there where you got your little farm place."

He hands her the casserole dish and starts in on the silverware. "Well, aside from all the orange trees I was telling you about, I know that one side of the property—the side adjacent to the canal—is lined with Melaleucas, and another side—the south side, I guess it would be—is bounded by some big old Ficus trees. But I can't remember if there are any Banyans." He smiles at her now. "So I suppose you'll just have to come visit us and see for yourself."

"That would be okay," she says, setting the dried casserole rightside-up in the dishdrain. "I'd like to visit on your farm. Visit you and Benny and see all those Orange trees, and Melucas, and how if you got any Banyans."

When the dishes are finally all washed, dried, and put away, he takes her out for a tour of his garden and is touched by the way she kneels to handle the plants, stroking gently upward on the undersides of their leaves, caressing them as if they were kittens or puppies (or even, he only fleetingly allows himself to think, lovers).

Up The Tree

After waving to my mother, phone wedged between her shoulder and ear, I head to my bedroom to slip on a t-shirt and jeans, then find them out in the garden—where else?—crouched over the cucumber plants, Nadia munching a cucumber, watching my father as he turns over the plant leaves. Lifting his head when he sees me, he smiles, then glances back to the plant and pulls something—probably one of those little (but voracious) yellow cucumber beetles—off a leaf. "Just showing her some basic organic pest control," he says in a W. C. Fields tone of voice, then drops the beetle onto the soil and grounds it under his heel.

But Nadia's on her feet now, looking excited to see me. She tells me my father has invited her to help with the garden whenever she wants, and to visit him on his new farm, and look for Banyan Trees.

My father winks at me, his knees popping as he rises from his crouch, then asks if the girl who had the seizure is all right.

After assuring him that Lythia is fine, I tell them that much as I hate to break up the fun, I *have* to, because it's time for me to drive Nadia back to ARC House.

Nadia and my father shake hands. She thanks him for dinner, and he tells her she's welcome any time.

"If they're all this nice," he says, loud enough for her to hear, as the three of us are walking to the car, Nadia stuffing a final bite of cucumber into her mouth, "You must have a very easy job."

It's a patronizing, if well-intentioned, remark, but I'm not about to complain. They seem to have really hit it off—instant friendship due to a mutual interest in things that grow out of the soil—which is exactly what I was hoping and suspecting might happen.

As soon as I've assured my father that I'll drive carefully, I pull out of the driveway, then announce to Nadia that we're heading for California.

"Okay," she says. "I'll go with you to California." And I have to hastily explain to her that I was only kidding; that California is on the other side of the country and it would take us a week of almost non-stop driving to get there.

"Mr. Teasebox," she says, sliding across the car seat to squeeze-pinch my leg, hard, just above my knee. "Who likes to be a meanhead and a teasebox."

We're driving along the ocean now. The light is quickly draining from the sky, and a few stars are already beginning to glitter through the darkening blue. "So, did you like my father?"

"Yes," she says. "I like him how he's a strong nose; the same as how you're a strong nose, with the same strong nose." She beams up at my nose.

"How about that garden? Not bad, huh?"

"Not bad," she agrees enthusiastically. "How the vegetables come whooshing up through the plants, and poof . . . There's the vegetables. And you can eat them from the plants. How they taste alive and dirty and loud from the plants."

I nod, though I'm not sure exactly what she means. "And even more important than the good taste, he doesn't use any chemicals or pesticides or anything, so you can pick anything out of his garden and eat it raw without having to worry that you might be poisoning yourself."

"Mr Worry Head Worry Wart." She shakes her head and snuggles closer, smiling joyfully. "Mr. Silly Billy."

And God, she's right. I am a worry wart, no way around it. I worry about everything—the food I eat, the water I drink, the air I breathe, the energy I consume, the stockpiles of crazy killer weapons I try to forget about—though knowing what I know, with all the information I have access to, I'd be a damned fool *not* to worry.

Across the bridge I swing left onto Lakeview Drive, then right onto Hibiscus Street, and find a parking space half a block from the library.

"Mr. Surprise Package," Nadia says, beaming up at me. "Who likes to surprise me with good surprises."

I'm surprised myself. I can't believe I'm actually going to go through with this. We both slide out on the driver's side, and she immediately takes my hand and begins pulling me across the street. It's while wondering, as the Banyan looms larger and nearer, if I'm actually going to climb with her, that I suddenly remember the old Catalpa Tree I used to climb in the corner of our back yard while I was growing up in Atlanta. I'd stay up in the highest branches for hours at a time, hugging and sniffing the bark, plucking off those long cigar pods, spying on the neighbors, or hanging from the limbs by my fingers, or upside-down by the crooks of my knees. I broke my right arm twice, both clavicles, dislocated my left ring finger so that it was bent at a 45 degree angle across my other fingers, and had the wind knocked out of me at least a dozen times, falling from that tree. But all those falls never kept me from climbing. (Although it drove my parents nuts. My mother complained about the medical bills, and my father worried that I'd end up paralyzed.) I'm not sure exactly when or what it was that *did* make me stop. But by the time we left Atlanta I was too old to climb trees. I never even said good-bye to the old Catalpa, and haven't really thought about it since.

By the time we get to the Banyan I'm all psyched to haul myself up that massive trunk, and scramble with Nadia to the tip of the highest limb, the highest branch. But as I'm reaching for a handhold to get started, she drops her fingers on my shoulder and says, "Wait. Mr. Eager Beaver." Leaving her hand on my shoulder she shuts her eyes, then, after a few seconds, smiles. "Hear it? The sound? The rizzzzzzzzz?"

I listen, but hear nothing except the rustling leaves and the sound of traffic roaring up and down U.S. 1, four blocks to the west. "I don't know," I admit. "What am I supposed to be hearing?"

"Look." She opens her eyes, her fingers dropping from my shoulder. "You see it? How it whooshes from way underneath up to the sky? Like whoooshhhhh." As she says the word, "whoosh," she stretches her arms the way she did last Saturday night when I saw her way up in the Banyan, straddling that limb and stretching. She lets her arms slowly fall, then stares at me, suddenly disappointed. "You don't see no whooshing? How it whooshes?"

"I'm not sure," I tell her, hesitant, not wanting to upset her and ruin our rare opportunity to be alone, before it even gets started. "I don't exactly know what you mean by 'the whooshing.'"

"Shhh." She waves for me to be silent, then again shuts her eyes. In seconds a smile is spreading across her face. "There," she says, triumphant. "The sound." Then she opens her eyes and points to where the sidewalk is cracking under pressure from the toes of the Banyan roots. "See? See?" She points, excited, her finger following the thick root along the ground, toward the trunk. "See?" Like a conductor signalling to her orchestra that she wants more volume, Nadia suddenly lifts both arms, then spreads them. "Whooooshhhh," she says, dropping her arms, then sweeping them upward again. "Whooooooshhhhhhhh."

When her arms fall to her sides and she looks at me expectantly, I ask, "Where did you learn about the trees whooshing? And the sound? I mean, is there some kind of connection there? Between the sound and the whooshing?"

"Don't know nothing about no connecting," she says, impatient as hell. "Listen. Like a whole bunch of crickets everywhere in your head and all around in your head and ears and eyes, and everywhere all around."

"Oh. You mean you're talking about the crickets!" I laugh, relieved. "Yeah, sure, I can hear the crickets."

"No." She shakes her head sharply, obviously frustrated with me, and covers her ears as if she doesn't want to listen to me anymore. She's starting to remind me of Emmy. In fact I'm half afraid she's going to stamp her foot next, or slap at her hip. But instead, she pulls her fingers from her ears, pauses, then again covers them. "See," she says a moment later, her hands dropping. "It's not no crickets. How it's in my head. You know. How it's in my head when I do my ears shut."

"Oh yeah? Hmm." What the hell am I supposed to say? "So when did you first hear this sound?"

"I don't know. I always heard it. Just the same how with the night fuzzies. How they always been there to see. How when the dark stuff comes."

"The night fuzzies?"

"Yes. How you always see 'em at night with the dark stuff, how when the dark stuff comes. You know. How it always comes at night, how when it's dark and all fuzzy with the night fuzzies, and you hear the rizzing that's the same like the night fuzzies, and how it's everywhere all around."

I have no idea if she's speaking now of dreams or fantasies, or maybe even hallucinations. Christ, if she's hallucinating it's probably not such a great idea for her to be climbing this monster Banyan.

"Come on," she suddenly says, as if reading my fear. "Let's do up the tree."

"Okay," I say. "But how about if we take it nice and slow? All right?" I'm still groping for a good hand hold when I look up and see that she's already climbed the main part of the trunk and is scrambling upward along a thick limb, her hands following a branch above her head. I want to catch up with her to be close by in case she starts to grab hold of or step onto some hallucinated limb, but for every two or three feet I climb, *she* climbs ten.

"Wait up, Nadia. Jesus!" The bark is smooth as an asphalt-worn basketball, and I've got no faith in my grip, particularly with these incredible limbs as thick as they are. I'm relying more on my tennis shoes to keep me tree-born than my fingers. As an eight year-old, the thought of falling from a treetop hardly phased me. Long as I had a decent grip with a foot or a hand, I was never concerned. But now, barely halfway up the base of this damned trunk, my head's already filling with visions of me toppling backward through the darkness, my skull cracking open on the roots, my spine snapping in half, my legs buckling beneath me, bending backward at the joints, compound fractures poking through my skin like toothpicks through a club sandwich.

Nadia waits for me and when I've finally, carefully, caught up with her we sit in the dip of an elbow-shaped limb, Nadia's back to my front, as if we're riding double on a flying horse. After a few minutes of sitting that way I'm not only bored, but my tailbone is nearly numb; and I'm starting to feel panicked about being so high up—at least twenty or twenty-five feet—with no place to anchor or even rest the soles of my tennis shoes, my one sure contact point with safety.

I finally ask Nadia if she'd mind climbing with me to a place where I'd feel more at ease, a place where we can talk without me having to worry that my next word might be my last.

"Silly Billy," she says fondly, beaming back at me over her shoulder. "Mr. Worry Head. Who worries about the bad things'll happen."

"Sticks and stones and ninety foot drops may break my bones," I start out, not bothering to finish because I'm sure she's already heard Amar recite the rest of the jingle half a dozen times, anyway.

Standing, grabbing and hanging onto the branch above her, she swings one leg, then her crotch, then another leg past me, and steps to a lower limb. I spit on my hands, rub them together, then grabbing the overhead branch, stand and slowly follow. A minute later we reach a spot I like; the hub or nucleus of the trunk, where the limbs start branching upward and outward. We're maybe eight or ten feet off the ground here. Definitely more my style. We can stand on a relatively level surface, while leaning against any one of a number of thick, sturdy limbs. There's room to move, yet it's as if we're caged together in the darkness, a feeling I like.

"So," I say, feeling cockily comfortable enough in my

new surroundings to continue our discussion. "You ever think about building a tree house up here?"

"No," she says. "Listen. How you got to listen close all around 'til you hear it, how it rizzes. Like rzzzzzzzz!"

God, she's a fanatic about this rizzing shit. "You mean the sound is so soft I've got to strain my ears to hear it?"

"No," she says. "You don't got to do no straining 'cause of how it's always there, loud. But the hardest is how you got to find it to hear it, and sometimes how it's so loud you can't hear nothing else when you find it and hear it, and everywhere you look you hear it." She takes a step toward me and whispers, "Listen! How you got to listen all around 'til you find it."

I start to tell her that if she can hear the rizzing with her hands over her ears, then it seems likely that her sound is simply something inside *her* head, and no one else's. (I have, after all, heard of "ringing in the ears," though it's generally a condition people complain about and try desperately to have cured.) But before I can tell her of my suspicions, she puts a finger to her lips, then leans into me, hugging me gently. The soft flesh of her bowed-out belly presses warmly against me as I let my hands slide down the perfect curve of her spine.

"Listen!" she commands, giving a sharp squeeze.

But it's hard to listen because she feels so good pressed against me, and I want to press back, lock her to me with my arms to make sure she doesn't suddenly slip free and fly into the sky, riding her sound, her inaudible rizzing, out to the stars. I press into her, rolling my hips slightly, my hands rubbing down to her ass. I'm ready now. Really ready. No doubt about it. And I know she can feel it, too, which somehow gives me confidence. I only wish we could climb down to the grass, but it's not quite dark enough and there's no place to go.

I hear the sound and feel his flooding and how he's wanting to give me his flooding and whoosh with his flooding, and the sound is all around and loud in my head and all around, and he must hear it how loud it is, and when I tell him to listen, to listen for the sound, it's so loud and all around and I can't hardly hear me how I tell him, how when I tell him to listen for it, and he pulls my bottom to where he's flooding, and he's not-listening and I'm not-flooding, how the sound is so loud and the fuzzies are loud in my eyes, how I see them through my eyes, and through my ears hear them how loud they are with the fuzzies and rizzzing, and I can talk to him some how I can't talk to the other smarty britches or to no one about it, 'cause how he asks and wants to know about it, know about the sound, but how with his flooding he's a Mr. Excited, and too much of a Mr. Excited with his hands on my bottom to know how I'm not-flooding, and how I can't with my flooding cause how it's not-flooding, not now, how the sound is so loud and the night fuzzies so loud in my eyes and all around and how I want him to find it, find the sound, and stop with the flooding, 'cause how I'm not-flooding. And with the sound all around and so loud how he MUST hear it if he could listen to find it how it's so loud with everything in the sound, with him in it, and his flooding wanting to whoosh with it. And I wish he could know how I'm not-flooding and stop 'cause how he knows how I'm not-flooding, wanting him to listen for it, for the rizzing, how loud it is, and everywhere all around. And he does down my pants and feels for my flooding, but does it scared, how he's still scared about it, how he wants to feel it and make me whoosh with it and whoosh with his flooding, and he's doing the pants down for both of us and feeling for my flooding that's not-flooding, and pulling me to his flooding, leaning back, holding on the Banyan with one hand and pulling me close to his flooding with the other hand, and leaning back and making mmmmm sounds how he's wanting to whoosh with his flooding, whoosh up in me with his flooding, and I wish he could know how I'm not-flooding and stop cause how he knows it. And then he says like a "ugh" and swings out his arm that was holding the Banyan and screams loud, and everything, the flooding and rizzing and whooshing stop, and everything stops but his screaming and jumping and hitting at his arm and in the dark I see the big ants moving on his arm how he must've found where they live in the Banyan where he was holding on, and I scream and help him hit at his arm, but how the hitting and screaming is funny how it stopped his flooding how I wanted, and I laugh out loud with my screaming how he's such a funny bunny with his hand that found where the ants live and stopped the flooding how I wanted.

And he's pulling up at his pants and hitting at the ants and climbing down, and then climbing too fast down, and falling, and saying ow and shit how he must have fell on something that hurt. And I do up my pants and climb down slow, laughing hard how he's such a funny with the ants that he found and stopped the flooding, and he says shit and walks off fast with a hurt leg, walking funny, how people do the walking when they hurt their leg, and I'm running after him and he's running funny and fast and still fast with his hurt run, and I'm laughing like a laugh head 'cause how he stopped how I wanted, how he made it happen with his worrying and holding on how he was a worry head, and then with the ants how he was holding on. And he's running across all the big grass, front of the library, past where the big gold fishes swim in the pool, and running his hurt run and not-looking when I shout at him to stop, and even with his hurt running how he's running faster than I can catch him, and I shout at him to stop and how he stops now, and turns around now and looks at me mad, how he's a funny head mad head.

Here she comes, still laughing her miserable head off, spraying her laugh through her lips, without even the decency to let me live with my failure, *another failure*, alone. (It's a failure all right, plain and simple. I can't blame the ants. Because even *before* they started swarming over my arm I could feel myself starting to soften and shrivel. Same as always.) My ankle is throbbing slightly now that I'm standing still, but for some reason I'm relishing the pain, wishing it was even worse.

Nadia has stopped maybe fifteen feet from me. Her arms are folded and she shakes her head, still laughing. And Christ, no wonder. Who *wouldn't* be laughing? There I was trying to keep it up while standing in the mouth of a giant goddamned tree, my ass scraping Banyan bark, and ants chewing the flesh off my arm, when I can't even keep it up in an antless bed on solid ground. And she was certainly no help, leaving me to do all the work, lifting her up to me as if I was Marlon Brando or something, and trying to guide myself into her while she leaned her head back, shut her eyes and waited, obviously more interested in her crazy whooshing or rizzing, or whatever the hell it is, than in my ludicrous tree-born advances. God, what a joke it was. Too much, really. I take a deep breath, attempt a half-assed smile, and step toward her.

"Mr. Funny Runner," she says, backing away. "Mr. Ants In Your Pants."

I limp three steps closer and she backs three steps away. "Whatcha scared of there, Miss Gigglepuss?" I'm once again talking the way *she* talks, but without even thinking about it, now. I walk toward her faster and she backs away faster. "Even though I've got a severely broken ankle you *know* I can easily outrun you."

"It's not no severely broke ankle," she says, then turns and runs, howling, and I run after her.

My ankle is still hurting, but not badly, and I'm enjoying the chase too much to even consider stopping. We race across the lawn, then around the fish pond three times before I finally stop, and she stops directly across from me. It's a small pond, maybe eight by twelve, but just large enough to keep me from catching her. Soon as I start to move one way, she moves the other. Even if my ankle wasn't twisted it would be tough for me to catch her. She grins at me, crouched across the water.

"All right," I say. "I'm in no rush." I yawn here, loudly, with an exaggerated stretching of arms. "*I* can wait all night if I have to. But guess who has to be back at ten!"

"I'll be back," she says. "Don't worry 'bout me. Mr. Meanhead."

"All right, then," I say. "I'm afraid you leave me no choice." I roll my jeans to my knees, watching to see if she'll panic and run.

"Hah!" she says. "No way."

"You don't think I'd do it?"

"No way."

"You sure about that?"

Laughing, "No way. Mr. Teasebox."

I squat, pushing an arm through the water until I can feel the bottom. Not bad. The pond's no more than a foot and a half deep. Just past my elbow. As I pull my arm from the pond I splash water toward her, but she just laughs and splashes me back. Slowly, I lower a foot into the pond. Her eyes grow wide. She knows now I'm willing to wet my shoes. "Here I come," I sing-whisper, then launch myself into the pond, splashing through like a madman—Godzilla vs. the Goldfish—while she screams loud and runs, circling past me around the corner of the pond, just beyond the reach of my outstretched arms, then making a beeline for—where else?—the Banyan. If she gets there first she's home free. She can climb circles around me. I hurdle over the pond edge, leaving the goldfish to battle tidal waves. "The ants!" I scream, a warning to deter her as I squish across the grass in pursuit. But she doesn't stop or even break stride, and hell, why should she? She probably knows each ant by name since they live in her Banyan. Probably gave the order for them to attack my arm.

I gain on her, but slowly. She's not fast—Christ, to see her run you'd think she'd never have the coordination to climb a tree, much less roar up one as if she had suction cups for hands and feet—but my ankle is sore enough, and my shoes squishy enough, to slow me by half.

I lunge for her maybe fifteen feet before she can reach the trunk, grabbing the back of her yellow golf shirt. She screams again, swinging back an arm, her old shirt stretching to its limit as I continue to hang on, until I've slowed her to where I can wrap my arms around her waist and stomach, and lift her, kicking, off her feet. "Gotcha." I say.

"Mr. Fast Runner Funny Runner!" she blurts out, twisting in my arms until she's facing me. "With the wet feet and strong nose." She rubs her nose against mine, panting, out of breath, then with three fingers touches the ridge of my cheek, grinning. "Mr. Runner Who Runs Away From Me Then Runs To Catch Me." Again pausing to catch her breath. "Mr. Gentlepuss. With the gentlepuss cheeks and eyes. That I love."

She has the most wonderful voice. A voice that oozes with—saturates each word with—everything that she's feeling; saturates it inside and out. And her beaming, love-saturated smile is hardly even human. *Isn't* human. Or even female. Her face, when she smiles out her love, is like the face of a fantastic new species of animal; a face which could transform the world in half a second. And it makes me sad to think that *everyone* can't see her grin-wrinkled, beaming, loving face the way I'm seeing it now; sad that it's changing only me, and *not* all the world.

I smile and press my cheek to hers, hugging her firmly, allowing the warmth to wash everything else away. She's like a furnace the way she gives off warmth. Like a woodstove dressed in jeans and a golf shirt. Hug her and you absorb a bit of her fire.

When he pulls back he looks at my eyes with his eyes, and keeps looking, and says how he DOES love me and how he is sure he knows he loves me, and when he tells it to me, looking at me with his kind eyes brown eyes that want to find a place to come inside, it makes me smile bigger and hurt in my throat, how if something was hurting in my throat, how it's too big and happy and hurting so the tears almost come, and we're both smiling close so the tears almost come, and I tell him to listen for the sound 'cause of its loud loud LOUD now, and how he could hear it if he listens to hear it, hear how it's all around, and everywhere all around, but he shakes his head no and says how no he can't hear it, but how I can hear it for both of us how I got special ears and eyes like some portant famous people who got special ears and eyes, and sees and hears things how other people don't-see and don't-hear. And he tells me he hopes it's catching, how a cold is catching, but a good cold you WANT to catch, and I call him a rosey nosey 'cause of his red nose that's red and wet a little bit with the tears, and how I do feel the flooding now, and how it's strong now, and we kiss and hard with our tongues soft, and then how we're flooding together, and both feeling the flooding how it's flooding, 'cause now we know we are going to whoosh with the flooding, and with the sound loud, whoosh with the flooding.

Still kissing, we slowly drop to the grass, to our knees. I help pull her golf shirt over her head, watching as her tangled hair falls in front of her shoulders, partially veiling her small breasts as she reaches behind to unhook her bra, then set it beside her in the grass. Her stomach is bowed out and perfectly smooth, except for her bellybutton, which looks like a knot at the neck of a balloon. She unzips her painter's jeans, revealing a narrow V of light green underwear, a slice of Key Lime pie. I strip off my shirt now, while she pulls down her jeans and underpants, then takes my hand, places it at the upper edge of her frizzy black jungle of curlicues, and moves it slowly down to where she's all softness and goo. Inhaling sharply, she shuts her eyes and lets her head fall back. I slide my left arm behind her, pulling her to me so that our bare chests are touching warmly and our cheeks are pressing together while my fingers follow the goo and softness inward and upward, and she rolls her hips and slides her face back across mine so that our cheeks continue to touch until our lips brush together, and then our tongues. And as I work my fingers I can feel her softness opening up farther, turning outward, like a blooming, blossoming flower.

Then suddenly, looking as if she swallowed something that hurt going down, she stops kissing and, bowing her head, pushes harder against my fingers and hand, and continues to open and turn outward in increments, by degree, two degrees out and one back in, so that it feels as though a part of her is wanting to turn out—turn completely inside-out, like a sock or a shirt sleeve—and part of her wants to pull everything, all the world, back in. And now she unzips my pants, pulls them down, and slowly cups me with her cool palm while still rolling herself around my finger, pushing against my hand, more and more of her opening up and turning out, until I'm half afraid maybe she *will* turn completely inside-out like a sock—a secret world, a universe, exploding out of her, out of her center, out of nowhere—and she will be gone forever, completely and utterly transformed. And she pushes and pushes against my hand, against the **hard heel of my** palm, my finger working like some automatic radius, straining to trace circles as large as it can, pushing against and stretching out her inner walls. And now she's gasping as she pushes and pulls and pushes, and it's as if she's trying to give birth; trying to give birth to that secret universe inside her. And she gasps and pushes, turning two more degrees out and one degree back while I push against her and she rubs me harder, then lying back, pulls me onto her and helps me slip in. And we're suddenly both exploding and exploding, contracting back, then exploding. And my eyes are shut tightly and filled with exploding stars as I heave and contract, heaving out a universe, while she heaves out her universe, and we explode and contract and explode, heaving and gushing and laughing, exploding the night, *exploding like the Big Bang of Creation.*

Until at last I'm empty.

And after heaving soft and empty, then not at all, we hug. And there's that peculiar-familiar silence in the space between our voice-sounds; that palpable, intense, snowfall silence.

"Mr. Silly Billy," she says with sincere delight, squeezing my hips with her thighs, the shape of the squeeze merging with her face and her voice, while she shakes her head and beams at me, as if a Silly Billy was the most wonderful thing in the world to be.

I don't now what to say, so I just keep staring at her beaming, grin-wrinkled face as I hug and rock softly, feeling as if I've just held the Miracle of Creation at my fingertips. Literally so. The secrets of the universe opening and exploding outward at my fingertips. And every breath feels holy now. With every breath there's an explosion of miracles, while deep inside I can feel an ocean still receding to its secret center.

After whooshing with all the flooding, and how all the flooding is finished flooding, we stay in the grass, and wet and warm in the grass, how we hug warm in the grass, and with our arms and our legs, and look at the moon how it comes there over the library roof, and all big and yellow there over the library roof. And he hugs me with his strong arms warm arms and does his strong nose against my nose and says how he is going to tell Angela about it, about how we want to be more time together and do more time together all the time, and how she will want to fire him but it's okay how he can do another job not at ARC House, and visit all the time at ARC House, not-doing no programs but visiting at ARC House, and with me all the time, and how it will be better with the visiting all the time and how he won't have to do no worrying all the time about my hair how it gets dirty with the clay 'cause he don't mind, how it's me, and good how it's me, and it don't all the time matter about the clay. And we get up and do the clothes back on, laughing and helping do the clothes back on, and he says how it's all miracles everywhere he looks, and how 'cause of me it's all miracles, and everywhere miracles.

Knowing and Knowing

He drops Nadia in front of ARC House five minutes before her bedtime (not even thinking to follow her in and check to see how Lythia's doing, or if Billy ever returned), and promises her that he will try to listen for the rizzing after he turns off his bedroom light and crawls into bed.

But when, fifteen minutes later, he pulls the Rambler into his driveway and steps out onto the moonlit pebbles, he's in no mood for bed so turns toward the ocean and walks giddily down Gumbo Limbo Lane, the air around him thick with the sounds of Palm Fronds, crickets, and crashing waves, and the scents of citrus and ocean. And when he sees and hears the Palm Trees now, looming out of the darkness from either side of the street, fronds swaying and rustling, he's seeing and hearing the same Palm Trees he's seen and heard a thousand times, *ten* thousand times, before. And always before, he's known that these same Palm Trees are, of course, alive. And busy creating more life. *Always,* he's known this. But not as he *knows* it now. And it's not just the Palm Trees. It's everything. Everywhere. From the soil to the stars. All alive. All filled with the same driving, Big-Banging Miracle energy.

So many times he remembers (ever since he was old enough to realize that his father might not be right about everything) staring hard, staring aggressively, at the sky, waiting, hoping, even expecting, to see some vision or miracle, to hear a voice, or to experience some mystical, supernatural, providential "something." When he was younger he would try to move things with his mind; to will them into existence or non-existence. By the time he left home to go to college he'd have even, with freshmanically eager banality, settled for a glimpse of a flying saucer. But when he continued to see and hear nothing out of the ordinary—not even during the months he was devotedly practicing transcendental meditation (which he'd hoped might serve as some sort of cosmic taxi cab to the world of the metaphysical)—he would shrug and forget about his vision-wish for another month or two, and sometimes, particularly as he grew older, a year or two. And the more he let loose of that vision-wish, the more frightened he became. As if without the hope of some sphere beyond the material—beyond his mother's money-making and future-building, and his father's fanatical efforts to prolong health and life—he would be left with nothing.

But now . . . now there's literally nowhere he can aim his eyes and *not* see a Miracle. Right here! (In the very "material" he was so desperately attempting to see beyond.) All around, a million fabulous microcosms of The Creation. Grapefruits, Hibiscus, and Coconuts out of nowhere, out of that same secret, inside-out, Big-Banging universe he's just discovered with Nadia.

Walking along the beach he kicks up sand and watches boatlights bobbing on the water like floating stars, while his cheeks turn damp and salty. The roar of the ocean sounds to him like a million hands applauding wildly, and he imagines it is the sound of The Creation giving itself a thunderous ovation. Eagerly he joins in, clapping enthusiastically, adding a two-pinkied whistle as he turns his face to the stars and three-quarter moon.

Back at his house, tired but exhilarated from his beach walk, he stops to admire his father's vegetable garden in the moonlight. Two-toned Marigolds, caramel and blood-rust, border each of the garden's raised beds. At the north end of the garden, just in front of the Grapefruit Trees (where, during the winter, half a dozen rows of corn run perpendicular to the raised beds, towering over the rest of the garden like a tropical mini-jungle), long vines of cucumbers criss-cross the ground in a crowded, swirling network, some of the vines climbing the winter snow pea trellises, the huge cucumbers dangling like green torpedoes. At the east end, in front of the Banana Tree, Sweet Potato Plants are spread beneath the winter Pole Bean tee-pees. At the west end, Okra grows beside the beds of ripening Cantaloupe and Musk Melon. And at the south end Benny is now standing among a dozen or so small hills of Zucchini and Yellow Squash; mini-volcanoes of erupted vegetables. At the corners of the yard, and along the walls, grow bushes of Hibiscus, all in full bloom, their incredible colors—red, white, yellow, pink, and orange—roaring up miraculously from the earth, from the dirt, trumpeting out through the stalks and stems. As he stares slowly around, the soil in the garden seems so fertile and fecund he can almost swear he senses it—feels it and sees it, even—pulsating and rumbling beneath his feet, undulating before his eyes. Drop a seed in that soil, and like a tiny egg in a womb it will soon bang open, pushing and driving its way into the world. "Same as me," Benny thinks, shaking his head and at last heading for the back door, marvelling at the grass as it swishes beneath his tennis shoes, flattening, then rising behind his heels. "All alive. And all of it a fucking Miracle." And as he reaches for his bedroom doorknob, then turns for a final peek at the yard and garden, it hits him quite clearly that Nadia, retarded Nadia, is his sure link to this Miracle, his connection to all that matters; that it is retarded Nadia who somehow holds the key to the greatest and most debilitating of his fears.

A Half-Remembered Dream

Oddly, he wakes in the middle of the night, laughing aloud, almost deleriously; laughing not at a remembered dream or a funny thought, but laughing because he is—without even thinking about it—so utterly delighted, of all things, to be alive and occupying his body. The ecstatic gratitude he feels is so absolute, yet so simple and effortless, so thoughtless, that he literally cannot imagine he has not *always* been able to feel this ecstasy, this gratitude, in precisely this way.

But no more than a few seconds after his laughter subsides, his eyes fall shut while he turns to his other side, and falls instantly, deeply asleep. And when he wakes early the next morning, all that's left of the experience is the ghost of some peculiar, half-remembered dream.

The Miracles Lost

It's not yet nine o'clock, but the temperature must already be close to 90 degrees, and the humidity 100%, and, though I took a cold shower before leaving and pedaled here at a leisurely pace, by the time I wheel my ten-speed up the ARC House walkway and chain it to the railing of the front steps, my shirt is wet at the armpits, and clinging to my back in half a dozen merging spots. To go along with this miserably muggy weather, I'm feeling utterly depressed, and dreading my meeting with Angela.

Inside, as outside, ARC House is eerily quiet because the residents are all gone for the day, working at the rehabilitation center. I look around, but no one is in the living room or kitchen, so I skip down the basement stairs until, as I near the bottom, I hear Angela's liquid voice, apparently coming from her office. A few seconds after I knock on the door, she pulls it open, still talking, then seeing me, smiles and covers the mouthpiece to the phone. "I'll be through in two minutes," she says. "Can you wait?"

"No problem," I tell her, startled to see that she's wearing a black dress—I didn't think she *owned* any dresses—with hundreds of tiny, multi-colored flowers. "Take your time."

Still smiling, she nudges shut the door with the toe of her thick-heeled wooden sandal, and I cross the basement to wait on the couch, my eyes burning when I shut and rub them.

Ever since I dragged myself from bed this morning at five, unable to sleep and exhausted after a restless and fitful night, I've been staring about in search of the Miracles. But, simple as it was for me to see them, to be dazzled and awed by them, last night—anywhere and everywhere—today it is impossible. I can stare at the grass and trees, I can strain, literally, like some poor constipated crapper—the way I used to strain through the starlit darkness, searching, always unsuccessfully, for some inexplicable flash or movement—but it's no use. The grass and trees are nice, as always, but they are only grass and trees.

And my inability to see the Miracles is, at this point, the least of my worries. Because when I haven't been busy straining, in vain, to see the Miracles, I've been attempting during the last three hours, to prepare for this terrible meeting by piecing together in my head a compelling explanation of my relationship with Nadia, which Angela would find both understandable and acceptable. But every approach, every explanation, no matter how I arrange the puzzle of words, seems equally absurd; equally implausible and unacceptable. *Even to me.*

It's obvious that no matter *what* I tell Angela—no matter how carefully and cogently I present my case—she will believe I'm taking advantage of Nadia. (I know my case better than anyone, and *I'm* not even convinced that I'm not, by the very nature of our relationship, taking advantage of her.) And even if, impossibly, she doesn't suspect or believe that I'm taking advantage of Nadia, she will without a doubt be horrified by the "appearances" of such a relationship, and the damage to public/community relations that could easily result from these appearances. And how could I blame her for worrying? After all, what parents would be willing to send their daughter to a group home where they suspect she might be in danger of getting screwed, literally, by the people who are supposed to be training and caring for her.

And so, in order to abort a potential scandal which could ruin the credibility of ARC House, and to avoid the hassles of getting fired, as soon as Angela gets off the telephone I'll explain to her that I'm quitting my job.

It's maybe ten minutes after she asked me to wait for two minutes, that she pulls open her door, smiles and invites me in. As I move through her office doorway she gestures to the orange, vinyl-cushioned chair beside her desk, and I sit, thanking her. Jesus Christ! I'm *always* thanking her. If she fires me before I quit I'll probably thank her.

Her office isn't air-conditioned, but it must be 10 degrees cooler in here than in the rest of the house. Sitting, she swivels her desk chair until she's almost—but not quite—facing me. Her legs, which I'm seeing bare—from the knees, down—for the first time ever, are well-tanned, muscular, and fuzzy with small arcs of golden-brown hair. It surprises me, somehow, to find that she doesn't shave her legs cleanly and precisely up to her crotch.

"You look nice," I tell her, shifting my legs, my sweating thigh-bottoms peeling from the vinyl cushion like scotch tape. "That's a nice dress you're wearing."

"Thank you," she smiles, surprising the hell out of me by blushing, then admitting that she doesn't often wear skirts or dresses because she's self-conscious about her "swimmer's legs." "Too much muscle," she says, looking me steadily in the eye so that it's impossible for me to sneak another peek at her muscular swimmer's legs. Then she goes on to tell me that she joined every swim team from third grade through high school, and filled her bedroom with swimming trophies; even a few surfing trophies. During her summers she always found jobs as a lifeguard. And it was while lifeguarding at the Seminole Springs Public Pool (which is, she tells me, just seven miles west of Palmview), the summer after her freshman year at Florida State University, that she first became involved with the mentally handicapped. Every day at one o'clock a busload of residents from Palmview were dropped off at the pool where Angela was, she tells me, so accustomed to dealing with obnoxious eleven year-old boys racing around the poolside, wrestling on the diving board, plunging in and cannonballing great splashes of water from the pool, soaking everyone, then flipping her the finger when she blew her whistle at them, that working with the handicapped residents of Palmview (who, though goofy and often bizarre, were almost always respectful and cooperative, and, after she got to know them better, even appreciative and loving) was a pleasure. "Believe me. They were a breath of fresh air," she says, "after those shit-kicking eleven year-olds."

This is the first time she's ever spoken so informally to me. The first time she's ever spoken about anything other than business. And now that I know her pants fit tightly only because she's a swimmer with muscular thighs and calves, I feel embarrassed and silly for having surrounded her with that diabolical mystique of tightness, which has, perhaps until this moment, kept me from feeling more at ease around her. It makes me sad, in fact, to have to tell her now that I'm going to quit; though *now,* while I'm feeling so comfortable with her, is undoubtedly the best time. And so, almost as soon as she finishes her story, while we're still looking at each other and smiling, I tell her that the reason I came in to see her this morning was to give her my two week notice.

"Really?" she says, pushing her head a few inches nearer to me, and sounding genuinely surprised and concerned. "I'm sorry to hear that, Benny."

"Well," I tell her. "I'm sorry to *say* it."

She smooths the lap of her dress and asks, "What is it? Did you decide to go back to school?"

"Yes," I tell her without hesitating. "For the fall semester . . . Maybe."

"Maybe?"

"Well, that's the plan. At least for now."

"Ah," she says. "That sounds good. But do you mind if I ask what made you change your mind about going back to school so soon? Because when I interviewed you for the job last month, you seemed to be sure that you wouldn't return to school for at least a year."

"Well, I *was* sure," I tell her. "But I feel different now. I mean, I feel *ready* to go back . . . I think."

"You think?"

"Well, I'm pretty sure."

For maybe half a minute we say nothing, then Angela smiles, shrugging, and thanks me for giving her a two week warning.

"No problem," I tell her, waving away her thanks.

We sit in silence for a few more awkward seconds before she finally tilts her head and says, "Well. Is that all?"

"I guess so," I say. "Except that I was wondering if, after I quit, it would be all right to come back and visit some of the residents."

"Of course," she says. "Anytime."

"Great," I tell her. "And how would it be if I took some of them out sometimes?"

"Just so long as you call ahead, and they plan for it appropriately."

"Okay," I nod. "Great." I'm tempted to leave it at that. But I can't. "And how would it be if I took just *one* resident out with me?"

"One resident?"

"Right," I say. "One."

"You mean a particular resident?"

I nod.

"Do you mind if I ask who?"

I swallow, then look away. "Nadia."

"Nadia?"

I nod again. I can feel her staring hard at me.

"Why Nadia?"

I squirm in my seat, my thigh bottoms clinging to, but not quite peeling from, the vinyl. I feel the same way I felt the first time I creeped out to the edge of a high dive and looked down. Except that I'm already beyond the point of no return. My weight has shifted and I'm teetering at the edge, my destiny in the hands of gravity. "I want to spend more time with her," I finally say, gripping the chair arms. "Alone."

"Alone?"

"Yes," I say. "Alone. Just Nadia and me."

"Why?"

Why?! Jesus Fucking Christ. I thought I'd already jumped, but I'm right back where I started. Teetering at the edge of the dive, looking down and about to shit in my pants. I grip the chair arms harder, knowing there's no way to explain about Nadia and the Miracles; no way to explain my feelings for her. "Because I think she's great. So I want to spend more time with her. And that's *really* why I'm quitting. Because I know how awful this must sound to you."

Angela swivels to face her desk and pick up a pen. "God, Benny." She shakes her head grimly. "My father is always telling me that I'm the only 'shockproof' woman he's ever known. But if he could see me now . . ." Rolling back her chair and swiveling away from me, she pulls open the middle drawer of her metal filing cabinet and flips through the individual files, finally snatching one out and swiveling back to spread it open on her desk top. "Let me show you her file, Benny. You've seen it, I know—you've seen them all—but I want you to look again." When I make no move to look, she reads it to me. "There," she points. "On the Weschsler Adult Intelligence Scale she tests consistently at a 12½ year-old level adaptively, and a 13 year-old level intellectually. Corresponding IQ's of 68 and 71."

"Those are numbers," I glumly tell her, knowing I'll never convince her. "They don't tell the whole story. I mean even the scientists are beginning to find out that if you break something into pieces, then try to study one of those pieces, all you're *really* going to learn is maybe a little bit about what one of those broken pieces is like while you're studying it. Because it's been broken. It's already lost its integrity. And it's the same with Nadia. Those numbers aren't Nadia. They're numbers. They're a broken-off piece of her."

"But that's exactly my point." She's slapping at the file with the tip of her pen, seeming more angry now than shocked. "Those numbers basically *are* Nadia. Every time she's tested they are. It's quite accurate. Quite predictable." She waits for me to respond, but I don't. I can't. I'm still hanging tight to the chair arms, waiting for the splash. Waiting for this to be over. "Well there's no sense in belaboring the point," she finally says, folding shut the file. "The figures are there for you to see, and if you can't—or won't—see them there's nothing I can do about it."

"Right!" I blurt out, startling both of us. "That's exactly right. And that's why I'm quitting. So you won't *have* to do anything about it."

She picks up Nadia's file, leans back to drop it in place,

and slides shut the drawer. "I'm afraid it's not that simple," she says, swiveling to face me once again, carefully crossing a leg, her hands interlocking at the front of her top knee. "The problems aren't going to just disappear when you quit. For instance, whether you quit or not it's likely that because of your relationship with Nadia—and I'm assuming you haven't been keeping it a secret from her—it is going to be far more difficult for her to accept the implications of her handicap in terms of potential partners. And, again, whether you quit or not, if we allowed you to continue to see Nadia it wouldn't just be *her* we'd have to worry about. Think of how your relationship would affect the expectations of *all* the residents here. Female *and* male. They'd all have their sights set on a non-handicapped partner. On their favorite staff person. And if we tried to explain that their expectations were unrealistic, they'd simply point to you and—"

"What do you mean, if you *allowed* me to continue to see Nadia?" I finally interrupt. "Now that I've quit you don't have a whole lot of say-so over who I see or don't see." I'm starting to feel self-righteous as hell. I even let go of the chair arm here. "I mean, what could you do to stop me from seeing Nadia? Short of breaking my legs?"

"What we could do," she answers without pausing, "is insist that she leave ARC House if her relationship with you continues."

"Kick her out?"

"Yes. Kick her out."

"You could do that? Legally?"

She rocks back in her chair and folds her hands calmly in her lap. "If Nadia is refusing to follow—or if anyone or anything is interfering with—her official habilitation plan, then yes, she can be legally discharged from ARC House; same as Billy and Lucius with their alcohol abuse. Of course, legalities aside, discharge is always a last resort, particularly in a case like Lucius's, or like Billy's, where the problem can be fairly easily controlled by use of appropriate reinforcers. However, in extraordinary circumstances, if I felt strongly that discharge was, as it is in *this* instance, for the best, I can assure you that I would not hesitate."

"Okay," I say. "If you really believe kicking her out is for the best, then go ahead and kick her out. She can live with me." Of course I'm talking like a madman now. My mother would obviously never stand for such an arrangement in her home. But crazy as my bluff might be, I'm ready to stand by it. If I had to I could find a cheap apartment for Nadia and me. I've still got some savings left, and I could always find *some* kind of work to support us.

Angela leans forward, as if to more closely scrutinize me. "You know, Benny, what worries me most at this point is your attitude toward Nadia. You've shown no interest whatsoever in my comments on her future welfare. And now you're talking about her moving in with you—challenging me, even, to kick her out—without ever giving a thought to the possible consequences."

"Well God Damn," I say, hopping to my feet, furious with her miserable calmness. "You're backing me into a corner. What the hell do you *want* me to say?" Feeling foolish I sit again and stare at my tennis shoes.

"I don't doubt for a minute, Benny, that you are genuinely attracted to Nadia. Emotionally perhaps, as well as physically. So I don't mean to be cruel or unsympathetic, or to imply that your motives are in any way impure. And it is not my intention to back you into a corner." She's speaking even more calmly now, almost serenely, backing me into a *deeper* corner. It's the same way she speaks to the residents when she knows she's in complete control. "I want you to make your *own* decision on this," she goes on. "I only wish you'd show a bit more interest, for example, in what I have to say about the possible consequences of Nadia leaving ARC House and moving in with you."

"Fine," I say. "I'm listening."

"And I'm not even going to get *into* the problem of intellectual incompatibility."

"Go on then," I plead, "with whatever it is that you *are* going to get into."

"All right. Good. I can see you're going to listen. Now I want you to think about this, Benny. I want you to think about what happens if, say, Nadia moves in with you, and after two weeks you realize you've made a mistake, and that you can't or don't want to continue to live with her."

"That won't happen. Not after two weeks."

"All right." She shrugs, as if my denial is beside the point. "Let's say two months then. Or, if we really want to stretch our imaginations, two years. You *would* agree it is at least a remote possibility that you might decide to split up after two years?"

It's not meant to be a real question, so I don't bother answering.

"Okay. So what would happen to Nadia then, Benny? Where would she go? She obviously, at least at this point, doesn't have the skills necessary to live on her own."

"You know I'm not so sure about that," I say. "I mean, maybe she's not great about making her bed, or keeping her hair brushed. But neither are half the people I went to college with. And she's got something most of my college friends *didn't* have. She's an artist. She's really got talent. In fact, with a little guidance I'll bet she could make a *living* selling her trees. Hell, to tell you the truth I think she *ought* to be earning a living with her art *now*, instead of working in that goddamned awful"—Christ, I'm starting to sound like Billy—"assembly line job."

"Oh come on, Benny. Use your head, not your emotions. Not your fantasies. If she lived alone she'd do nothing *but* build her trees. You know that as well as I do. And where would she buy the clay? How would she get her trees bisqued or fired? Where would she sell them? And when I'm talking about independent living skills I'm not necessarily talking about hair-brushing or bed-making. I'm talking about shopping, cooking, budgeting, bill-paying; I'm talking about calling the doctor when she's sick, or the dentist when her teeth are aching. It's a hard world out there, Benny. There are people *without* handicaps—and I don't have to tell you how many of them are artists and craftspeople, far more talented than Nadia—who aren't making it. Nadia wouldn't have a chance. Not without at least another two or three years of the kind of formal training she'd get at ARC House, and then a follow-up program in a satellite apartment with a Community Skill Trainer."

"Okay," I say. I've already lost the debate with her, I know, so at this point I'm really just trying to convince myself. "Maybe she wouldn't make it on her own right now. But if we were living together I could help her learn budgeting and cooking skills, and all that. I mean, I *have* been trained to help her do those things, haven't I?"

"Yes, of course, Benny. And let's even assume, for argument's sake, that you've become an *expert* skills trainer in the month you've worked here. Now even if that were true, it wouldn't be much help to Nadia; not if you stayed together for only a few weeks. Or months. Just try to entertain that possibility for a moment."

I shrug. "So what if you're right? If we *do* split up before she's ready to make it on her own, she could always get into another halfway house and pick up her training where she left off."

"Ah, she could try," Angela says eagerly, as if playing her trump card. "But you know there's a big push going on in this state to de-institutionalize. They want to pare the Palmview population down to the severely retarded. So there's a long waiting list for every residential training facility in Florida. Of course it's possible that she might be able to find an opening in foster care; though I can assure you there are too few decent care facilities in the area. But even if she *could* get into a care facility she would receive no formal training. She would learn no skills. And so she'd have a home, she'd be fed and cared for. But, because of your gamble, she'd have no opportunity to improve herself; to move into the community and become an independent person." She looks at me, on the verge of smiling. She's obviously enjoying herself now. "On the other hand, Benny, if you truly had *her* best interests at heart, I think you would encourage her to stay at ARC House and learn those skills she'll need for independent living. Then, when she completes the program here—and she will complete it, I believe, within three years—then she can get into our semi-independent living program, and move to one of our satellite apartments downtown, where she'll continue to get help from a Community Skills Trainer. Once a week. Shopping, budgeting, menu-planning. All the necessities. And of course if you want, you can spend time with her then. I might still object. In fact I can assure you that I *would* object. But at that point no one would have any real control over whom she chooses to see."

I rub my chin and stare back at my tennis shoes, pretending to be thinking about what she's said; weighing out my options. But I have no options. She's taken the fight right out of me. It's one thing, after all, to be risking my own time and emotions. But it's quite another to ask and encourage Nadia to do the same thing, when she's the one most likely to suffer the consequences of our risk-taking; when she's the one who would have the most difficult time recovering from those consequences. I push myself to my feet, the vinyl cushion clinging to my thigh-bottoms for the first few inches before ripping loose and falling back into place. Then, backing toward the door, I feel for the knob, and, finding it, squeeze tight. "Okay," I say, more relieved at this point than anything else. "You win. I'll talk to her when I come on shift tomorrow morning."

"Well I'd really rather not drag this out for two weeks, Benny. So what I'm going to try to do, I think, is find a substitute for you this weekend. And of course I'll be willing to compensate you in part for not giving you your two week notice."

"Well," I say. "I really don't give a shit about your compensation, Angela. So you can keep it. I'll just drop by this afternoon when Nadia gets back from work, and talk with her then."

"Ah, well, I'm sorry Benny. But I don't think that's a good idea, either. Because you see, it will be difficult, if not impossible, for us to work with Nadia if she believes we're preventing her from seeing you."

My hand falls from the doorknob. I can't believe what she's telling me. "But I wouldn't have to tell her you're keeping me from . . . I mean, I just want—"

She's shaking her head, "no," so emphatically that I stop

in the middle of my sentence. "I'm sure you understand, Benny. An explanation might help *you* feel better. But right now we've got to think about what's best for Nadia."

"Oh, right," I say, nodding. "Fine." She's uncanny. She has an answer to each of my objections. A strong counterpoint for every point. I want to at least get in a good last lick—a real kicker—but nothing comes. It's as if my brain circuits are all jammed. Overloaded. So I simply shake my head miserably and walk out, not even bothering to slam the door behind me. Never in my life have I felt more impotent.

The Sound Of The Dream Of The Great Equalizer

Outside, he unchains his ten-speed and pedals off, hard, across the bridge, past the old fishermen with their poles and buckets and sweat-stained white undershirts, and directly up to the public beach, where he leans his bike against the beach wall and impatiently strips off his shirt—ripping a seam at the underarm when the shirt, *even the shirt now,* resists him—and flings it at the rear wheel of his bike. Then, sitting on the wall, he faces the sun, allowing it to beat on his chest and shoulders.

It's not yet 10:30, but up and down the beach the serious sunbathing queens are already out in full force, lying about on their towels in scattered clusters, faces down, bright bikini'd asses bubbling up like batches of multicolored Easter eggs. They could all, he thinks, be right out of a fucking Pepsi commercial, so perfect are they with their tans and long smooth legs. And he would never, he is certain, catch *one* of them wearing green tennis shoes; much less green tennis shoes with a white bathrobe. And if any of their teeth were *ever* overlapped, he would be willing to bet that they were long ago braced perfectly back into place until uniform and symmetrical as a suburban housing development.

Over the water he watches while a trio of pelicans swoop across the glassy face of a wave swell, so low they're practically skimming the surface, like winged barbers shaving the face of the ocean. Down the beach, to his right, an army of sandpipers advance and retreat before the gliding tongue of each wave, their toothpick legs whirring in a comical fast-motion frenzy, Keystone Cops-style. Behind him he hears the palm fronds rustling. Above him seagulls float, tilt wings, dive and squawk. And it's all, he thinks, very nice. All very tropical. But there are no Miracles. And it occurs to him now that he might never know if last night's Miracles were even real; if they weren't simply the result of some momentary or temporary anomaly in the workings of his mind, catalyzed by God knows what synergetic combination of freaky phenomena; maybe starlight and the loss of his virginity, or Bull Ant bites and the rising moon.

Hopping from the wall he snatches up his t-shirt, stretches it across his handlebars, and pedals off along the oceanfront, the sunlight strobing through the slatted palm fronds across his bare back and shoulders. Fifteen minutes later he's coasting down Gumbo-Limbo Lane, then turning into his pebbled driveway, startled to see not only his father's Rambler wagon, but his mother's Mercedes. (She's usually out until at least 3:00 in the afternoon, distributing her products among the Coconut Beach Hotels, or giving inspirational speeches on "The Building of Futures" to her new recruits or struggling old veterans.) He's not even ready to break the news of his quitting to his father, much less to his mother.

Soon as he pulls open the kitchen door he knows something out of the ordinary is going on, because the second movement of Beethoven's Ninth Symphony is thundering over the living room speakers, and his father always reserves the Ninth for special occasions. Peeking into the living room he sees his father dusting the window sills in rhythm with the scherzo, his head dipping and rising like the tip of a baton. "Hey Dad," he says loudly, his voice battling the kettle drums. "What's up?"

Mort turns, grins, then calls out, "Dorie! He's home. Come to the table."

"I have ears," she yells from the bedroom. "I know he's here."

Benny looks to the table and sees the champagne bottle

chilling in the icebucket. "Again?" he says, feeling suddenly exhausted.

"Come." Mort takes him by the elbow, leads him to and sits him at the table, then turns down the stereo. "It's a *real* celebration this time," he explains.

Eudora steps out of the bedroom. She's wearing blue jeans and a red-checkered cowboy shirt. It's an outfit she dresses up in maybe once every year or two; usually for the Jayceyettes Chili Feed or the State Fair ASC exhibit.

"What is this?" Benny wants to know.

And while Mort untwists the safety wire and pulls on the cork, Eudora explains to Benny that she just returned from her tour of the farm. "It's a dream house," she says.

"I told you she'd like it," Mort winks at his son, then pops off the cork and fills the glasses.

"So we're really going to move?" Benny asks.

"We figure we'll start this weekend. There's no realtor involved, so no closing date to wait for. And he moved out over a month ago." Eudora holds up the glass, and the three of them clink, then drink.

"He was anxious to sell," Mort says. "So we're buying it for a song."

"The only thing is," Eudora wipes champagne suds from her lips with a checkered sleeve, "I've told your father I'm not ready to sell *this* house. Because there's a chance I'll find that I miss Coconut Beach too much. You know it's easy to get spoiled by quiet streets, and an ocean at the end of your block." Benny can't remember the last time his mother walked the half block to the ocean—she's fair-skinned, burns easily, and hates hot sand, and the feeling of salt water drying on her skin—but he says nothing, watching while she nods, smiling, at her husband. "So we've both agreed it makes sense to hang onto this old house."

"So what will you do?" Benny wants to know. "Rent it out?"

"That, my boy, is where *you* fit in," Mort says, clinking glasses with Benny, then taking another swill.

"Me?"

"Why not?" Eudora switches her glass to her left hand so

that she can wipe her right hand across the hip of her jeans. "You know we bought this house outright, and never made a monthly payment. So all *you've* got to do is come up with 130 dollars a month—what's that, a third of your monthly salary?—and we'll break even on the property taxes. Or, if you want, you can find a friend to *share* the house with you, and that way your payments would only be 65 dollars a month. And you *never* use air conditioning, so your electricity payments should be next to nothing."

"And if you keep up the garden," Mort adds hopefully, "you'll have free vegetables. Not to mention grapefruits, bananas, papayas, and avocadoes, and, after I buy a cow and goat, and some chickens, free milk, cheese, and eggs. I'll send them over with your mother."

"Right," Eudora says. "I've got so much business in Coconut Beach I figure it will be nice to use the house as a base of operations. But don't worry. It would only be for a few hours a day."

Mort is pouring another round for himself, and then for Eudora. "Come on, son. You're way behind." He refills Benny's glass even though he's taken only one sip. "Of course this might be just a temporary arrangement. Depending upon how we feel about living outside of Coconut Beach. But even if it is temporary, it's still quite a set up for you, huh?"

"And for us, too! I get a convenient base of operations to work from, and your father gets a renter he trusts to take care of the house. *And* the garden. And if we miss Coconut Beach too much, or if for any other reason the farm doesn't work out, I'll feel good knowing we can move back whenever we want."

"It's better than an insurance policy," Mort says, then holds his glass high, tilts it back, and drains it.

Benny, meanwhile, is astounded that they've had time to figure this all out. He often forgets how clever his parents are. How clever *all* human beings are. And, reluctant as he is to burst their expanding bubble of excitement, he figures it's now or never, and trusts that they will be clever enough to work out another appealing scheme. "You know, that all sounds great," he tells them. "And I hate to ruin your plans or anything, but see, I quit my job this morning and I figure I'll be going back to Duke next month." He shrugs. "But I could house sit for you *until* then."

"You quit?" Mort practically whispers, lowering his empty champagne glass, his smile gone. "Why? I thought you were happy with your job."

"Yeah, well I thought so, too. But lately I've been feeling as if I was never really cut out for that kind of work."

Eudora admits that, while surprised, she's delighted to hear he'll be returning to school so soon. And they both assure him that he hasn't "ruined" their plans at all; that in fact it makes far more sense for them, financially, to rent the house for the going rate.

"And you *know*, Benny, as far as I'm concerned your education is always number one."

"I know, Mom. And I appreciate it." And he *does* appreciate it. They are both, he thinks, being terrifically supportive. And right when he most *needs* their support.

Mort holds up his glass. "To our son's education."

"Here here," Eudora says. "To his first degree." And they all smile and clink. A happy family. Except that after sipping to his education and first degree, Benny hastily excuses himself with the explanation that it's been a rough twenty-four hours—what with Lythia's seizure last night, his job-quitting announcement to his boss this morning, the excitement of the new farm, and his impending return to school—and that he needs a bit of rest; and hurrying down the hallway, through his bedroom and into the bathroom, sticks out his tongue, examining it in the mirror above the sink, then bends over the toilet to barf up his half ounce of champagne.

In the shower he brushes his teeth and tongue for twenty minutes while the hot water pounds upon his back. After turning off the water, Benny drapes a towel across his shoulders and steps from the tub. He stops drying himself for a moment to stare hopefully through the bathroom jalousies, but all he sees is a nice backyard scene of grass, vegetables, and trees. Instead of mourning, he shrugs, then finishes drying himself and heads back to his desk to read and take notes. It is clear to him now, that his time will be more wisely spent searching not for Miracles, but for logical, workable solutions to the world's myriad horrible problems. Perhaps he'll go on to graduate school—pleasing his mother with a second, maybe even a third, degree—emerging after three or four years to find a job in some government think tank. And if he wakes up one morning to find that forty years have slipped past like a dream, at least he won't be caught by surprise.

A few hours after dinner, he heads back to his bedroom to shut his books, turn out his light, and crawl, naked, into bed. For a long time he restlessly kicks off sheets, then pulls them back up; turns from side to side, and from back to front. Exhausted, he finally begins to take slower, deeper breaths, and sink into his mattress.

Outside there are angry voices. I crawl from the couch, move to the screen door, and gaze out, my nose and fingers pressing against the cold wire mesh. Billy and Amar are standing beside my father's Rambler, arguing over who's going to carry Lythia inside. Shaking my head and chuckling, I push open the screen door and hurry down the front steps to cue Billy, asking him whose turn it is to help carry Lythia, and what he needs to do.

Billy tells me he doesn't give a goddamn stupid fuck what he needs to do, then calls Amar a goddamned stupid asshole, and stomps off, crossing the street without bothering to look. Across the street he hops onto the lake wall and flips a finger to the sky as he slouches along, apparently headed for a downtown bar.

"Hey Billy!" I shout after him. "You've already had two warnings. One more and you'll be kicked out. Remember?"

But he's ignoring me, so I wait for two cars to pass, then jog into and across the street. "Hey Billy," I sing now, sounding devious as I can. "I'm going to get you, Old Buddy."

Hearing my joking threat, he turns, and seeing that he's being chased, laughs, and says, "Whuh-oh!" He takes two or three long-legged running steps, head still turned back so that I can see his laugh, then stumbles, teetering for an awful moment at the edge of the wall before falling silently back, out of sight.

Fast as I can, I race to the wall and lean over. Billy is maybe six feet below, thrashing about like a netted pompano, sending great splashes into the air as he flails, windmill-style, hands slapping from the smooth concrete wall to the water. He obviously can't swim a stroke. The only thing keeping him above water is sheer adrenalin energy.

I glance around, hoping to spot a long palm frond, or anything else I might be able to extend to him. (If the bridge was just a few blocks closer I could borrow one of the old fisherman's poles, cast a line to Billy and reel him in.) But there's nothing.

I rip off my shirt and dive in. All around my head are explosions of bubbles where Billy's arms are thrashing. The bubbles confuse me. Disorient me. There's nothing I can do to help him unless I get a breath of fresh air, but I don't even know which way is up. I kick like a frog and feel myself rising through the water, until my fingers—then the rest of my arms, up to my elbows—break the surface. I'm about to replenish my lungs when one of Billy's arms comes out of nowhere to slap across my shoulder like a giant tentacle, and drag me under. I struggle to push him away, gagging on a mouthful of water, but now his other arm has looped round my waist and his hug has tightened. I flail and kick, but those incredible arms of his are everywhere, wrapping around and around me like long vines of seaweed. The harder I struggle, the tighter he seems to grip me. I feel like a fly caught in a web. I'm starting to sink deeper, and Billy is sinking with me.

My lungs are begging to suck in on something, anything—air or water, it doesn't matter to them—and I'm starting to feel crazy with anger. Here I am, five fucking times as smart as he is, and it doesn't count for shit now. I jerk an arm free and punch at his face, two, three, four times, hard as I can. But with the water between us my punch travels in terrible slow motion, and impacts without power or effect.

We continue to sink, and it is clear now that we are both going to drown. Even if he lets go I'll never make it to the surface in time. We've sunk too far. It's finally come down to the basics. We're two bodies with the same fill of life. Same fill of energy. Perfectly equal here at the threshhold of death.

I grab him now, afraid, and we squeeze each other tighter, still sinking, knowing that in this squeeze we are feeling life for the last time. At last my lungs give in, and as I gulp water, I see Billy's mouth opening wide, his chest heaving and his eyes rolling back. I'm expecting the water to fill me with a painful heaviness. With a darkness and a deadweight. But as I drown my lungs in a great *gulp, I'm all at once filled with an incredible lightness. A drunken dizziness. And instead of sinking, I'm suspended, weightless, and then floating upward! And Nadia—not Billy—is floating, ascending, with me. I can't see her, but I know it is her that I'm hugging. I can tell by feel; by the sense of her presence. We're ascending together, hugging, a warm, relaxed hug. And there's an energy, a force, flooding through us both. Sounding through us. Loud enough to hear. Rizzing up my spine, and into and around my ears and head, surrounding and filling it like the chirpings of ten million crickets.*

As they continue to ascend he begins to understand that the surface he is rising toward is the edge of a dream. And when at last he breaks that edge, that surface, and blinks open his eyes, the rizzing still fills his head. Only for a moment. But long enough for him to be sure; long enough for him to subliminally wonder why it is that the sound which surrounds and fills him is so pleasantly, painfully, familiar; why it pulls his mind inward and downward to a time of cool sheets, freshly settled upon his small chest and groin, feeling perfectly, sensually weighted, as he stares out from under them at nights clogged with shimmering motes of color, suspended thickly between his eyes and all that he sees, blurring the distinction between him and the world in a dancing mosaic of connective energy.

The memory fades quickly with the sound. He sits bolt upright, straining his ears, barely breathing. But all he hears now is the wind, singing through the leaves and fronds, and, in the distance, the soft roar of the ocean, constant as a waterfall. Then a digital minute clicks into place and he breathes again, turning his head to stare through the dark at the luminescent numbers. 12:35. It's Friday night, he thinks (though it is technically Saturday morning), but he's suddenly as certain as he's ever been of *anything*, that she is there. If she climbs and dances every Saturday night, why not every Friday night as well? He has to see her and tell her. And it doesn't matter anymore if Angela knows or not.

He swings his legs over the mattress edge. The shaggy rug feels pleasant on the soles of his bare feet, and he takes half a minute to swirl them across it. As he's dressing he notices that none of his clothes—socks, tennis shoes, jeans, and t-shirt—seems to feel or fit quite right. Yet that somehow doesn't surprise him. He steps quietly into the back yard, and everything is movement, scent, and sound. Everything is alive and seething, writhing, with energy. It's a fantastic magic show. Right out his back door. A circus out of the soil. Out of the sky. Out of nowhere. He smiles his way past the vegetables and trees, past the Hibiscus bushes, and around the side of the house, where he wheels his ten-speed into the street. His right leg swings up and over the center bar and he pedals off, hard, the world roaring past him, faster and faster, until his lungs are burning and his heart pounding so furiously that he has to stop pedaling and coast.

The half moon—humpside down—is ten degrees up from the Atlantic horizon and still huge. The ocean is thundering, sending up a fine, drifting mist of spray and salt. The Coconut Palms lean over the seawall, into the wind, fronds sweeping in arcs and circles, coconuts dangling in the moonlight like egg-clusters, like a Big-Banging Miracle hatchery.

He begins to pedal again, pumping harder and faster, shifting into ninth gear, then tenth. The rolling rubber screams across the asphalt, the pitch rising steadily with the speed. His legs lift and fall like pistons as he gulps air, mouth opened wide, eyes squinted, his breathing even louder inside his ears than the self-created bicycle wind he blasts through. He pedals across the bridge so fast that he half-suspects the old fishermen can't see him.

By the time he reaches the Banyan, sweat is flowing down his arms in long-tailed droplets, and his t-shirt is clinging to his back. But he feels terrific. As alive as the wind and the trees. As alive as the moment he occupies, fecund with possibility. He strips off his shirt and straddles the bike, allowing the breeze to cool his skin while he catches his breath.

Then he drops his t-shirt on the lawn, sets his bike on its side, the rear wheel still spinning, and walks toward the tree, stepping over and between the long, twisting root system, and looking up into the limbs and branches, where he *knows* she is; where he *feels*—as he did in the dream—her presence.

He's scanned every limb and branch three times before he's convinced she's not there. For a moment he feels betrayed—though he's not sure by whom—and utterly alone. But the feeling quickly passes as the wind swirls and whispers through the great shroud of leaves, building to a crescendo before diminishing, then starting back up again. Standing beside the tree trunk he can sense its upward thrust, its lifting energy, starting below the ground and pushing up, reaching, stretching, pointing through the limbs and branches to the sky, a constant flowing. A nonstop celebration. He climbs with the flow, following it upward and outward along a thick limb. He's not even scared because it seems impossible for him to fall.

Finally, he stops climbing and sits where he can see through a gap in the branches and leaves. He's a good thirty feet above the library lawn, his legs dangling freely, his arm draped lightly over a branch, beside and just above him. The wind blows and a leaf snaps off and falls past him, spinning haphazardly to the ground and landing among the twisted roots where he can see that it will eventually sink into the soil to become a part of the upward flowing and stretching again.

As he stares through the gap in the leaves, onto and over the rooftops of the dilapidated downtown buildings, the limbs creak about him like the masts of a ship. And he suddenly feels as if he *is* riding a ship, a great, powerful, living ship, growing right out of the heart of this dying downtown, lifting him above the death and decay, even the roots splitting open the tombstone sidewalks, sucking up the death, converting it back to life.

"Mr. Surprise Package."

He glances down, startled, and spots her standing on a limb ten feet below him, her face turned up.

"Mr. High Climber." Her lips slide back from her teeth, and all at once he feels melodramatically silly. As if those unpretentious, overlapped teeth have caught him up here on his fantasy ship, sailing in a wild sea of pretensions. But it's okay and he smiles back.

"You feel the whooshing?" she says.

"Yes, I think so," he tells her, hanging onto his branch as he swivels, easily, to face her.

"Mr. Smarty Britches." She climbs closer, stepping up a crisscrossed ladderway of branches, then sitting and shimmying toward him along the limb. "They told me we wouldn't be seeing you no more."

"Well, I won't be working at ARC House anymore, so I guess you *won't* be seeing me *there*."

"Oh," she says, then shakes back her dark curtain of hair. They're sitting face to face now, their knees practically touching. "I finished the Banyan tonight. You know. Finished it with the clay."

"Great," he says, nodding, though he's a bit taken aback by her sudden, insouciant switch of topics. And by the fact that the earlier news of his permanent departure did not, apparently, send her reeling into a deep depression. At least not deep enough to keep her from sitting down to an evening of her usual tree building. But then it hits him that her attitude is the perfect answer to his own hesitations. *Her* sense of self is even stronger than his own. She will survive and remain "Nadia," with or without him. And with or without ARC House.

"You still interested in selling your Banyan?" he asks. "I mean, now that you've finished it."

"I'll sell it." She kicks lightly at the toe of one of his tennis shoes, and her lips pull back farther, the smile in her eyes deepening proportionately. "Long as you promise to be nice to me. And not no Mr. Meanhead."

"I promise," he says, and she reaches out, beaming, to touch his nose.

Epilogue

I been a long time here with Benny and Mort and Billy and Lue Ellen, and how we all been a long time here, except Lue Ellen, and working on the farm with the orange trees and vegetables to make money, and now with the toe food to make money, except how I don't work as much how they work on the farm, and with the oranges and toe food, how I'm working all the time on my trees, how Benny helped so I could work on them all the time how I wanted, and sell them at the galley in Coconut Beach where they sell them, sell my trees, and send me the check in the mail, and treat me nice and portant when Benny takes me in to bring them more trees to sell at their galley.

I came with him here after he quit ARC House, and came back from that school, and his father had the farm, but how his mother didn't like it and wanted to leave the farm to do back to Coconut Beach, and Benny went here to the farm with his father (except how his father on weekends spends the weekends with Benny's mother in Coconut Beach, how he still loves her, and don't want no divorce 'cause of how he don't want to do back to Coconut Beach, and leaves Friday, and don't come back till Monday every weekend to be with her), and did it into a foster home with his father so he could have me back, and have back the others of the handicapped people, how he could make money doing the foster care, and with his father, money doing the farm, but not in no group home with no programs all the time to run. And Billy came the same as when I came, how his mother and father always was on a farm, and saw Benny's farm and how Billy could work on it with the oranges and vegetables, doing the picking and the planting, and going in the truck with him, with Benny, to take them to the ones who wants to pay for the oranges, and how he could make his money with the oranges, and not in no Rehab, and make more money with the oranges, and eat them here from the tree, how we eat them here when they come whooshing up through the tree, and poof, there's the oranges, and how sweet it is when you bite them in your mouth and the sweet stuff whooshes everywhere in your mouth.

And then after Billy and me, Lucius came, how he's older, and too old to live in a apartment and on his own in a apartment, and not no good working at the Rehab how they wanted to have him not-work there no more at the Rehab how he's too old and not no good. But he worked good here, and with the oranges, until when he died, how he died on the swing when he was doing the swinging in the swing, same as how he did the swinging at ARC House, how he would all the time swing, and with a Silly Billy smile, how he was smiling and swinging like a Silly when he died on the swing, and still smiling when the swing stopped swinging with the swinging, and we saw how he was dead and smiling, like a Silly Billy but dead, and not-whooshing. And when he died, Lu Ellen came from Bell Grade where on the farms there in Bell Grade they do the sugar all the time, how Benny's father don't like no sugar in nothing how he's a Silly Billy Worry Head about the sugar, and she's nice and black, and with long black arms and a long black face, and wears a helmet how all the time she has the seizures, and she's nice and all the time smiles with a smile white and round like a white flower.

And every Sunday Benny and I do the picnic up the Banyan back of the orange trees, and sometimes he feels the whooshing, and he listens for the sound, but mostly don't-hear no sound, how he can't hear it when he tries to hear it, how he says you can't see none of the real little stars how when you try to see the real little stars, but only see them from the side, from the side of your eye and when you are not-looking, and how it's like that with him when sometimes he does hear it, hears the sound, and he hears it before he knows he hears it, and then how he can listen and hear it, but only sometimes.

And he's not such of a worry head no more, how he says he knows now what he wants to do, and is doing now what he wants to do, working here on the farm, and doing the foster care with me and Billy and Lu Ellen, and he says he don't all the time worry, how he used to all the time worry about how it does by too fast with the time, because how he can stop it now from doing by too fast, how he stops it with the Miracles, and how he says he knows now everywhere it's Miracles, and all the time it's Miracles, and he's trying how to learn to find them and preciate them everywhere and all the time, but how it's hard, and he don't know why it's so hard, and too hard to find when he can't find them, and so easy to find when he finds them, and he don't know why, how they're everywhere and all the time and should be easy to find and preciate everywhere and all the time. And he says how when he finds and preciates them, finds and preciates the Miracles, it right away stops doing by too fast with the time, and how it still does by too fast sometimes, but he don't worry so much when it does by too fast, how he knows he will stop it when he finds and preciates the Miracles, and stops it even when he don't-find the Miracles when he tries hard to find them. And that's why he says we every Sunday do the picnic up the Banyan, back of the Orange Trees, how even if he forgets to try to all the time find and preciate them, and don't know how he can forget to all the time try when they are everywhere and all the time, on Sunday he remembers to try to find and preciate them, how that's why we do it, do the picnic up the Banyan, and even if he don't-find them, and don't understand why he don't-find them, it will stop doing by too fast with the time, because how he tried to find them, tried to find and preciate the Miracles.

And yesterday up the Banyan, when he was doing the picnic up the Banyan, he told me how I am doing better with my trees, and making much more money with my trees, and how it is doing better some on the farm with the oranges, and making money now on the farm with the oranges and vegetables, how they are special oranges and vegetables without none of the bad stuff, how they are worry heads about the bad stuff, and want to buy the toe food his father started doing from the soy beans, and doing into the bags to sell, how it's so healthy. And how making some money with the foster care, and money on the farm now with the special oranges and vegetables, and the new toe food, how he's sure now he wants to keep doing this with the foster care and me and on the farm, how we might as well be married to each other, how we been knowing each other for five years anyway, and I told him all right I'd be married with him, and he right away brought everybody to the Banyan, and stood with me there under the Banyan, and holding *my hand with his warm hand soft hand, and told them how he wanted to marry me, and how we both wanted to marry each other, and was going to marry each other.*

And he's a smarty britches, but I'll marry him how he's not too much of a smarty britches to listen about the sound and feel the whooshing and climb the Banyan every Sunday to do the picnic so he can feel the whooshing and try to find and preciate them, find and preciate the Miracles how he says are all the time and everywhere, and stop it from doing by too fast with the time so how he don't have to all the time worry about it when he remembers to worry. And I'll do my trees and he will help me with my trees, and do the oranges and vegetables, and with his father the toe food, and with me and Billy and Lu Ellen the foster home, and we will have each other, and be married with each other, and I'll have him with his brown eyes kind eyes, and strong nose that I love, and how I'll be together with him in the sound, and always together with him, with everything, in the sound.